W9-DAX-144

MAY - - 2013

Hawkwood

JAMES McGEE

Hawkwood

A Regency Crime Thriller

PEGASUS CRIME
NEW YORK

HAWKWOOD

Pegasus Books LLC
80 Broad Street, 5th Floor
New York, NY 10004

Copyright © James McGee 2006

First Pegasus Books cloth edition 2012

Library of Congress Cataloging-in-Publication Data is available.

ISBN: 978-1-60598-368-4

10 9 8 7 6 5 4 3 2 1

Printed in the United States of America
Distributed by W.W. Norton & Company, Inc.
www.pegasusbooks.us

PROLOGUE

The prey was running late.

The horseman checked his pistol and returned the weapon to the leather holster concealed beneath his riding cloak. Bending low over the mare's neck, he stroked the smooth, glistening flesh. At the touch, the animal whickered softly and stomped a forefoot into the soggy, waterlogged ground.

A large drop of rain fell from the branch above the rider's head and splattered on to his sleeve. He cursed savagely. The rain had stopped thirty minutes before, but remnants of the storm still lingered. In the distance, a jagged flash of lightning sprang across the night sky and thunder rumbled ominously. Beneath him, the horse trembled.

The rain had turned the ground into a quagmire but the air smelled clean and fresh. Pale shafts of moonlight filtered through the spreading branches of the oak tree, illuminating the faces of the highwayman and his accomplice waiting in the shadows beneath.

1

The horses heard it first. Nervously, they began to paw the ground.

Then the highwayman picked up the sound. "Here she comes," he whispered.

He pulled his scarf up over his nose and tugged down the brim of his hat until only his eyes were visible. His companion did the same.

The coachman was pushing the horses hard. Progress had been slow due to the foul weather and he was anxious to make up for lost time. The storm had made the track almost impassable in places, necessitating a number of unavoidable detours. They should have left the heath by ten o'clock. It was now close to midnight. The coachman and his mate, huddled beside him in a sodden black riding cape, were wet, tired, and irritable, and looking forward to a hot rum and a warm bed.

The coach had reached the bottom of the hill. Mud clung heavily to the wheel rims and axles and the horses, suffering from the extra weight, had slowed considerably. The driver swore and raised his whip once more.

By the time the coach crested the brow of the hill, the horses were moving at close to walking pace. Which was fortunate because it gave the driver time to spot the tree lying across the road. Hauling back on the reins, the driver drew the coach to a creaking standstill. Applying the brake, he climbed down to the ground and walked forward to investigate. A lightning bolt, he presumed, had been the cause of the obstruction. Another time-consuming detour looked a distinct possibility. The driver growled an obscenity.

It was the driver's mate, perched atop the coach, who

shouted the warning. Hearing the sudden cry, the driver turned, and started in horror as the two riders, their features shrouded, erupted from the trees. In the darkness, the horses looked monstrous.

"Stand where you are!" The rider's voice bellowed out of the night. Moonlight reflected off the twin barrels of the pistol he pointed at the driver's head. The driver remained stock-still, mouth ajar, terror etched on to his thin face.

The driver's mate was not so obedient. With a muffled oath, he reached down for the blunderbuss that lay between his feet and swung the weapon up. His heavy rain-slicked cape, however, hampered his movements.

The highwayman's accomplice reacted with remarkable speed. The night was split with the flash of powder and the crack of a pistol. The driver's mate threw up his arms as the ball took him in the chest. The blunderbuss slipped from his weakened grasp and dropped over the side of the coach, glancing off a wheel before it struck the ground. The guard's body fell back across the driving seat.

The first highwayman pointed his pistol at the terrified coachman. "You move, you die." To his accomplice, he said, "Watch him while I take care of the rest."

As his companion guarded the driver, the highwayman trotted his horse towards the coach. As he did so a large, pale face appeared at the window.

"Coachman! What's happening?" The voice was male and, judging by the tone, belonged to someone used to wielding authority. "What's going on out there?"

The passenger's features materialized into those of a middle-aged man of lumpish countenance. His jaw went slack as his eyes took in the anonymous, threatening figure towering above him and the weapon aimed at the bridge of his nose.

The highwayman leaned out of his saddle. "All right, everybody out." He motioned with the pistol, whereupon the gargoyle head withdrew sharply and the door of the coach opened.

The highwayman caught the cowering driver's eye and jerked his head. "An' you can join 'em, culley. Move yourself!"

The driver, herded by the highwayman's accomplice, backed timidly towards the coach, hands held high.

The passengers began to emerge. There were four of them.

A stout man in a dark tail coat, now identifiable as the individual who had stuck his head out of the window, was the first to descend, tiptoeing gingerly to avoid fouling his fine buckled shoes. Next was a woman, her face obscured by the hood of her cloak. She held out a hand and the stout man helped her down. She reached up and withdrew the hood, revealing a haughty, heavily powdered face. The highwayman clicked his tongue as the man pulled her to him and placed his arm protectively around her thin shoulders. Husband and wife, the highwayman guessed. She was too old and too damned plain to be his mistress.

The third person to step down from the coach was a slightly built man dressed in the uniform of a naval officer; dark blue cloak over matching jacket and white breeches. The face beneath the pointed brim of his fore and aft cocked hat showed him to be younger than his fellow passengers, though he appeared to alight from the coach with some difficulty, like an old man suffering from ague. He winced as his boot landed in the mud. His brow furrowed as he took in the two riders. Glancing up towards the driver's seat, his expression hardened when he saw the still, lifeless body of the guard.

The last occupant to step down caused the highwayman to smirk behind his scarf. The man was elderly and cadaverous in appearance. He was clad entirely in black, the wispy white hair that poked from beneath his hat an almost perfect match for the white splayed collar that encircled his scrawny neck.

"All right, you know what to do." As he spoke, the highwayman lifted a leather satchel from the pommel of his saddle and tossed it to the driver. "Hold on to that. The rest of you drop your stuff in the bag. Quickly now. We ain't got all bleedin' night!" The pistol barrels moved menacingly from passenger to passenger. "And that includes the bauble around your neck, Vicar."

Instinctively, the parson's hand moved to the cross that hung from his neck on a silver chain. "You'd dare steal from a man of the cloth?"

The highwayman gave a dry laugh. "I'd take Gabriel's horn if I could get a good price for it. Now, 'and the bloody thing over!"

Obediently, the parson lifted the chain over his head and lowered it carefully into the satchel. The driver's hands shook as he received the offering.

"By God! This is an outrage!"

The protestation came from the passenger in the tail coat, who, with some difficulty, was attempting to remove a watch

5

chain from his waistcoat pocket. Beside him, the woman shivered, wide-eyed, as she fingered the gold wedding band on her left hand.

"Come on, you old goat!" the highwayman snapped. "The ring! Sharply, now, else I'll climb down and take it off myself. Maybe grab a quick kiss, too. Though I dare say you'd like that, wouldn't you?"

Horrified, the woman shrank back, twisted the ring off her finger and dropped it into the bag. A flicker of anger moved across the naval officer's face as he lifted a small bag of coin from an inner pocket and tossed it into the satchel. Drawing his cloak around him, he stepped away.

"Whoa! Not so fast, pretty boy. Ain't we forgetting something?"

The air seemed suddenly still as the highwayman gestured with his chin. "What's that you've got hidden under your cloak? Hoping I wouldn't notice, maybe?"

The officer's jaw tightened. "It's nothing you'd be interested in."

"Maybe it is, maybe it ain't." The highwayman lifted his pistol. "Let's take a look, though, shall we?" Wordlessly, after a moment's hesitation, the passenger lifted the edge of his cloak to reveal his right hand, holding what appeared to be a leather dispatch pouch, but unlike any the highwayman had seen before. What made it different were the flat bands of metal encircling the pouch and the fact that the bag was secured to the passenger's wrist by a bracelet and chain.

The highwayman threw his accomplice a brief glance. His eyes glinted. "Well, now," he murmured, "and what've we got here?"

6

"Papers," the man in the cloak said, "that's all."

The highwayman's eyes narrowed. "In that case, you won't mind me takin' a look, will you?" The highwayman handed the reins of his horse to his companion, and dismounted.

Walking forward, the highwayman waggled his pistol to indicate that the young man should move apart from the other passengers. With his free hand, he snapped his fingers impatiently. "Key!"

The officer shook his head. "I don't have a key. Besides, I told you, it holds nothing of value."

"I won't ask you again," the highwayman said. He raised the pistol and pointed the twin muzzles at the officer's forehead.

"Are you deaf, man? I don't have a damned key!"

The highwayman snorted derisively. "You expect me to believe that? Of course you've got a bloody key!"

The officer shook his head again and sighed in exasperation. "Listen, you witless oaf, only two people possess a key: the person who placed the papers in the pouch and locked it, and the person I'm delivering them to. You can search me if you like." The young man's eyes glittered with anger. "But you'd have to kill me first," he added. The challenge was unmistakable. Kill a naval officer and suffer the consequences.

It was a lie, of course. The key to the bracelet and pouch was concealed in a cavity in his boot heel.

The highwayman stared at the passenger for several seconds before he shrugged in apparent resignation. "All right, Lieutenant. If you insist."

7

The pistol roared. The look of utter astonishment remained etched on the young man's face as the ball took him in the right eye. The woman screamed and collapsed into her husband's arms in a dead swoon as the officer, brain shattered by the impact, toppled backwards into the mud. He was dead before his corpse hit the ground.

Holstering the still smoking pistol, the highwayman sprang forward and began to rifle the dead man's pockets. Several articles were brought to light: a handkerchief, a silver cheroot case, a pocket watch, a clasp-knife and, to the highwayman's obvious amusement, a slim-barrelled pistol. The highwayman stuffed the cheroot case, knife and watch inside his coat. The pistol, he shoved into his belt.

"By Christ, I'll see you both hanged for this!" The outburst came from the tail-coated passenger, who was still cradling his stricken wife. Beside him, the parson, grey-faced, had dropped to his knees in the mire. Whether at the shock of hearing the Lord's name being taken in vain or in order to be sick, it was not immediately apparent.

The threat was ignored by the highwayman, who continued to ransack the corpse, his actions becoming more frantic as each pocket was inspected and pronounced empty. Finally, he threw his silent accomplice a wide-eyed look. "He was right, God rot him! There ain't no bleedin' key!"

In desperation, he turned his attention to the dispatch pouch. His hands traced the metal straps and the padlock that secured them.

Finding access to the pouch beyond his means, the highwayman examined the chain and bracelet. They were as solid and as unyielding as a convict's manacle. He rattled

8

the links violently. The dead man's arm rose and flopped with each frenzied tug.

"Christ on a cross!" The highwayman threw the chain aside and rose to his feet. In a brutal display of anger, he lifted his foot and scythed a kick at the dead man's head. The sound of boot crunching against bone was sickeningly loud. "Bastard!"

He stepped away, breathing heavily, and regarded the body for several seconds.

It was then that he felt the vibrations through the soles of his boots.

Hoofbeats. Horsemen, approaching at the gallop.

"Jesus!" The highwayman spun, panic in his voice. "It's the Redbreasts! It's a bloody patrol!" He stared at his companion. An unspoken message passed between them. The highwayman turned back and stood over the sprawled body. He reached inside his riding coat.

In a move that was surprisingly swift, he drew the sword from the scabbard at his waist. Raising it above his head, he slashed downwards. It was a heavy sword, short and straight-bladed. The blade bit into the pale wrist with the force of an axe cleaving into a sapling. He tugged the weapon free and swung it again, severing the hand from the forearm. Sheathing the sword, the highwayman bent down and drew the bracelet over the bloody stump. He turned and held the dispatch pouch aloft, the glow of triumph in his eyes.

As if it were an omen, the sky was suddenly lit by a streak of lightning and an ear-splitting crack of thunder shattered the night. The storm had turned. It was moving back towards them.

Meanwhile, from the direction of the lower road, beyond the trees, the sound of riders could be heard, approaching fast.

The highwayman tossed the dispatch pouch to his accomplice, who caught it deftly. Then, stuffing his pistol into its holster and snatching the satchel containing the night's takings from the startled coachman, he sprinted for his horse. Such was his haste that his foot slipped in the stirrup and he almost fell. With a snarl of vexation, the highwayman hauled himself awkwardly into the saddle and his accomplice passed him the reins.

Rain began to patter down, striking leaves and puddles with increasing force as the highwayman and his still mute companion turned their horses around. The sound of hooves was clearly audible now, heralding the imminent arrival of the patrol; perhaps a dozen horsemen or more.

The two riders needed no further urging. Wheeling their horses about, digging spurred heels into muscled flanks, they were gone. Within seconds, or so it seemed to the bewildered occupants of the coach, swallowed up by the night, the sound of their hoof-beats fading into the darkness beyond the moving curtain of rain.

1

It had quickly become clear to the crowd gathered in the stable yard behind the Blind Fiddler tavern that the Cornishman, Reuben Benbow, the younger of the two fighters, was far more accomplished than his opponent. The local man, Jack Figg, was heavier built and by that reckoning, a good deal stronger, but there was little doubt among those watching that Figg did not have anything to match his opponent's agility.

The Cornishman was tall, six feet of honed muscle, with features still relatively unscathed. Having served his apprenticeship in fairground booths the length and breadth of his home county, he had been taken under the protective wing of Jethro Ward, the West Country's finest pugilist. Under Ward's diligent tutelage, Benbow was fast gaining a reputation as a doughty, if not ruthless, fighter.

Jack Figg, on the other hand, was square built with a face that betrayed the legacy of half a lifetime in the bare-knuckle game. A stockman by trade, it was said that in his youth Figg could stun a bullock senseless with one blow of his mighty fist, and that he had once sparred with the great Tom Cribb. But now Figg was past his prime. His body bore the scars of more than seventy bouts.

The opening seconds of the new round were an indication that Figg was continuing with the close-quarter approach; a technique to be expected. Only too aware that he was slower and less nimble than his opponent, he was attempting to exploit his size and strength by grappling his man into submission. The rules of the fight game were simple and few: no hitting an adversary below the waist. Any other tactics that might be employed were considered perfectly acceptable, even if it meant breaking your opponent's back across your knee.

Benbow, however, had been well coached and was wise to the older man's game. He knew if he could keep out of Figg's reach he would eventually tire out his opponent. There was no knowing how long a fight could last – forty, fifty, perhaps as many as sixty rounds – which meant the fitter man would inevitably prevail. The majority of bouts were decided not by knockout but by the loser's exhaustion. Besides, full blows often led to shattered knuckles and dislocated forearms and as the hands became swollen so they began to lose their cutting power. Much better to wear away your opponent's defences with short jabs. In any case, a quick finish would certainly displease the crowd.

The afternoon bout had attracted several hundred spectators. Workers from the timber yards rubbed shoulders with Smithfield porters, while Shoe Lane apprentices jostled for space with ostlers from the nearby public houses. The latter formed the rowdiest contingent, heckling the Cornishman mercilessly, protesting vigorously whenever Figg received what was perceived to be a foul blow, and cheering wildly on the occasions their hero managed to retaliate.

There were other, more respectably dressed onlookers: square-riggers, toffs and dandies who'd forsaken their own haunts among the fashionable clubs of Pall Mall and St James in order to savour the delights offered by the less salubrious parts of the capital. Enticed by the flash houses with their cheap whores who were only too eager to accept a coin in exchange for a quick fumble in a dark alleyway or in some rat-infested lodging house, a prizefight and the lure of a wager were added attractions. Dotted around were several men in uniform, a smattering of army officers and a raucous group of blue-jackets on shore leave from the Pool.

Hawkers and pedlars moved among the crowd, while at the edge of the throng, beneath the cloisters, mothers suckled infants, and snot-nosed children crawled on hands and knees between the legs of the adults, oblivious to the filth that coated the cobblestones. A tribe of limbless beggars masquerading as wounded veterans appealed for alms, while beside them drunks sprawled comatose in the gutter. In one corner of the yard a mullet-faced individual with the staring gaze of the fanatic teetered on a wooden box and railed vexedly against the sins of the flesh and the evils of gambling.

Prizefighting was unlawful. So around the perimeter of the yard lookouts patrolled the entrances and alleyways, ready to warn the fighters and spectators of the arrival of the constables. Were a warning to be given, the ring would be dismantled within minutes, leaving the fighters and their promoters to melt into the crowd.

There were other parties in attendance, too, interested in neither prizefight nor preacher. These were creatures of a different kind, opportunists drawn by the whiff of rich pickings, thieves of the street.

The pickpocket was nine years old. Stick thin, small for his age, known to his associates as Tooler on account of his skill at winkling his way into a crowd to relieve a mark of wallet and watch in less time than it took to draw breath. A graduate of the Refuge and Bridewell, and a thief since the age of four, by now he was an old hand at the game.

Tooler had had his eye on the mark for a while. The crowd was dense and there were plenty of distractions on hand to mask the approach and snatch. Tooler scanned the boundary of the mob, checking his escape route. Jem Whistler, Tooler's stickman and his senior by a year and two months, wiped a crumb of stolen mutton pie from his lips and nodded slyly. The two barefooted urchins threaded their way towards their intended victim.

To the crowd's delight Figg had begun to stage a comeback. A number of his blows were landing, admittedly more by luck than judgement, but the Cornishman's upper body was at last beginning to show signs of wear and tear.

Spurred on by his supporters, Figg aimed a roundhouse blow at his opponent and the crowd roared. If the punch had connected, the fight would have been over there and then, but Benbow parried the uppercut with his shoulder and scythed a counterstrike towards Figg's heart. Figg, wrong-footed with fatigue, shuddered under the impact. Pain lanced across his bruised and battered face. Blood dribbled from his nostrils. His shaven scalp was streaked with sweat.

Tooler's mark was a red-haired, florid-faced individual dressed in the scarlet jacket and white breeches of an army major. He was standing with his companion, also in uniform, beneath one of the stable arches. Head down, with Jem dogging his heels, Tooler made his approach from the major's right side.

In the ring, Figg launched a massive blow to the Cornishman's ribcage and the crowd sucked in its collective breath as Benbow took the punch over his kidneys. The mob clamoured for more.

Amid the excitement, Tooler seized his opportunity. His light fingers brushed the major's sash, unhooking the watch chain in one swift movement. In the blink of an eye, the watch was passed underarm to Jem Whistler's outstretched hand. Turning immediately, Tooler and his stickman separated and within seconds the two boys had dissolved into the crowd, with neither the major nor his companion aware that the theft had taken place.

Behind them, Benbow was responding hard. Figg wilted under the Cornishman's two-fisted attack. Blood and mucus flowed from his split nose as the mob shouted itself hoarse. There was no finesse in the way the two fighters traded blows. The bout had degenerated into a ferocious brawl. So fierce was the battle that the spectators closest to the ringside were splattered with gore.

Ignoring the growing excitement, the two pickpockets weaved their way through the mass of bodies. At the rear of the yard lay the entrance to a narrow alley. The boys ducked into it, unheeded by the lookouts, who were more interested in the outcome of the fight and scanning the area for uniformed law officers than the passing of two grubby children. In no time Tooler and his stickman had left the babble of the stable yard and entered the maze of lanes that lay behind the inn.

As they picked their way through dark, damp passages lined by walls the colour of peat, the boys paid little attention to their surroundings. They were on familiar ground in this netherworld of densely packed tenements and grim lodging houses; buildings so old and decrepit it hardly seemed possible they were still standing. An open cess trench ran down the middle of each alley. Rats skittered in the shadows. The waterlogged carcass of what could have been either animal or human floated in the effluent. Vague, sinister shapes haunted dark doorways or hovered in silhouette behind candlelit windows. Only the occasional voice raised in anger indicated that the slum was inhabited by humankind. With the late afternoon sun sinking slowly below the cluttered rooftops, the boys hurried deeper into the warren.

Mother Gant's lodging house was nestled into the side of a small courtyard at the end of a hip-wide passage. With its overhanging eaves, narrow doorway and dirt-encrusted windows, it was typical of the many doss houses that infested the area. A tumbledown sty occupied one corner of the yard. Two raw-boned pigs rooted greedily in an empty trough. They looked up, snouts thrusting, grunting with curiosity as the boys ran past.

The hovel was low roofed, dim lit and smoky. The soot-blackened walls were of bare brick, the floor unboarded. A hearth ran along one wall. An oaken table took up the middle of the room. Seated around it were a dozen children of both sexes. Pale, unwashed, dressed in threadbare clothing, they ranged in age from six to sixteen. An old woman, garbed in black with a tattered shawl around her shoulders, stood at the hearth, ladling the contents of a large cooking pot. She looked up as the boys entered. In the flickering glow from the coals, her rheumy eyes glittered.

No one knew Mother Gant's age, only that she had run the lodging house for as long as anyone in the neighbourhood could remember. It was well known that she had outlived three husbands; two had succumbed to disease, the third had disappeared one dark night never to be seen again. Rumour had it that the latter had been dropped into the river, his throat slit from ear to ear, after a tavern brawl. A drunkard and a wastrel, he had not been missed, certainly not by the Widow Gant.

The children seated around the table were not Mother Gant's blood kin. The old lady had been named not for the size of her own brood but due to her habit of taking in waifs and strays. This display of generosity was not born of a sense of charity. It was greed that made Mother Gant open her doors to the orphans of the borough. She expected her young tenants to pay for the roof over their heads and the food in their bellies. And the rent she exacted was not coin of the realm – though that would not have been refused – it was contraband.

Mother Gant was a receiver of stolen property. She took in her orphans, she fed them and she housed them. Then she trained them and sent them out into the streets to steal for their supper. And woe betide anyone who returned empty-handed.

Fortunately for Tooler and Jem, their afternoon's activity had yielded a good haul: three watches, two breast pins, a silver snuffbox, and no less than four pocketbooks. As the proceeds were deposited on the table, Mother Gant left the cooking pot and cooed softly to herself as she sifted through the valuables.

"You've done well, boys," she simpered. "Mother's very pleased."

The old woman picked up the silver snuffbox and turned it over in her hands. Lifting the lid, she placed a pinch of snuff delicately on to the back of her hand, lowered her head and snorted the powder up each nostril in turn. Snapping shut the lid, she wiped her nose on her sleeve, grinned ferally, and slipped the box into her pocket.

"Extra helpings tonight, my lovelies," she whispered, hobbling back towards the hearth. "Them as works the 'ardest deserves their reward. Ain't that right?"

At which point a long shadow fell across the open doorway.

"Hello, Mother – got room for one more?"

Mother Gant's eyes blazed with alarm as the visitor stepped into the room.

The man was tall and dressed in a midnight-blue, calf-length riding coat, unbuttoned to reveal a sharp-cut black waistcoat, grey breeches and black knee-length boots. He was bareheaded. The face was saturnine, the hair black, streaked with grey above the temple. What was unusual, given the fashion of the time, was his hair, which was worn long and tied at the nape of the neck with a length of black ribbon. Below the man's left eye, a small ragged scar was visible along the upper curve of his cheekbone.

If Matthew Hawkwood had expected an extreme reaction to his entrance, he was not disappointed. Even as his gaze fell upon the pile of stolen artefacts, the room erupted.

Stools and benches were overturned as the children scattered like rabbits before a stoat. In a move that was remarkably sprightly, the old woman twisted and hurled the soup ladle towards the new arrival, at the same time letting loose a high-pitched screech. Whereupon the massive figure seated in the corner of the room who had, up until that moment, remained still and silent, rose to its feet.

All told, Mother Gant had given birth to three sons and one daughter. Her first-born son had been smitten by the pox, the manner by which her first and second husbands had met their demise. Her second son had also been taken from her, but not by illness. Press-ganged at the age of sixteen, consigned to a watery grave at the age of eighteen, his innards turned to gruel by a ball fired from a French frigate during an engagement off the coast of Morocco. As for the daughter, no one knew her exact whereabouts. Last heard of, she was earning a precarious living as a whore, working the streets and arcades of Covent Garden and the Haymarket. Which left Mother Gant's youngest son, Eli, as the only child not to have flown the coop. Though, if the truth were told, it was doubtful if the youth could have survived the separation.

At the age of twenty, Eli had the neck and shoulders of a wrestler, forearms the size of oak saplings, and the hands of a blacksmith. But though he possessed the body of a man, he had the brain of an infant. Unable to fend for himself or perform anything beyond the most menial tasks, he had become little more than a chattel to his widowed mother, who used him as she might have done a dray horse: as a beast of burden. On the occasions that she conducted the more nefarious of her enterprises, however, she used his size and strength for intimidation and protection. Eli's sole purpose in life was to serve his mother, a duty he carried out unconditionally.

As Tooler and Jem and the other children ran for the door, the lumbering, moon-faced figure of Eli Gant emerged from the gloom. Hearing Mother's cry, Eli was reacting solely on instinct. The shrill note in the old woman's voice told him that there was trouble and that she needed his help. That was all he needed to know. When he rose to his feet, the cudgel that had been propped against the arm of the chair was in his hand.

Hawkwood avoided the thrown soup ladle with ease. As the utensil clattered against the wall a flicker of amusement passed over his face. Then he caught sight of the apparition looming towards him and his expression changed. He turned to confront the new threat.

"Stop him, Eli! He's here to hurt Mother!" The old woman's voice pierced the room.

The attack, when it came, was sudden. For a man of his huge bulk, Eli Gant moved with surprising speed.

But Hawkwood was quicker. Even as the cudgel was raised, he swung his foot and kicked Gant hard between the legs. Eli's jaw went slack. Dropping the club, he doubled over. A baton appeared in Hawkwood's hand. Without losing momentum, he sidestepped and drove the short club viciously against the side of Gant's head. The ground shook as Gant's body hit the earthen floor. Staring down at the wheezing, prostrate form, Hawkwood shook his head wearily. He'd seen it all before.

When he looked up, Mother Gant had disappeared.

Hawkwood cursed and turned. "Rafferty!"

A bulky figure materialized behind him. Red-faced and coarse-featured, wearing the uniform of a conductor of the watch: black felt hat, double-breasted blue jacket and matching waistcoat. His eyebrows rose as he took in the man on the ground.

His eyes widened further as Hawkwood leapt over the stricken Gant, crossed the room and ripped away the ragged curtain that hung on a rail on the opposite wall. Concealed behind the curtain was an open doorway. Pausing on the threshold, Hawkwood peered into the darkness that lay beyond. A cold draught caressed his face and a vague shuffling noise sounded from somewhere ahead, then his eyes caught the feeble glow of a lantern and a hunched, dark-clothed figure scurrying away. Mother Gant, having abandoned her idiot son to guard her back, was on the run.

Hawkwood knew he had to act quickly. There was no telling how far the tunnel stretched or where it emerged. Given the nature of the area, it was likely the shaft led into a honey-comb of passages, trap doors, hidden stairwells and twisting alleyways running above and below ground level. And the old woman, of course, would know the place like the back of her crabby hand.

There was no time to find a lantern of his own. He'd

have to rely on the faint light ahead of him as a guide. He turned and nodded past the constable's legs to where the hapless Eli Gant was still curled foetally on the floor. "Watch him." Clasping the baton firmly, he plunged into the hole.

The smell was dreadful. It was the stench of damp and decay, pungent enough to clog the nostrils and make the eyes water. The floor of the tunnel was firm underfoot, but here and there the ground squelched alarmingly, sucking at his heels. More than once, his ears picked up the faint squeak of rodents and he felt the soft touch of their tiny paws as they ran across the toe of his boot.

It was hard to tell what the walls were made of. Sometimes his fingers brushed brick, sometimes wood, often so rotten it flaked off in his hand. Similarly, it was impossible to determine if it was sky over his head or stone. As his eyes grew accustomed to the dimness, he began to make out openings in the tunnel walls: junctions leading to even more escape routes. Occasionally, through a chink in a wall, he caught a glimmer of light, the flicker of a candle flame, a sign that somewhere within this strange subterranean world there existed vermin of a higher intellect than rats and mice. And always the fluttering lantern carried by the Widow Gant drew him further into the maze.

Abruptly, the glow ahead of him died. He paused, listening. He moved forward cautiously, senses alert for the slightest movement. He wondered how far he had come. It seemed like a mile, but in the darkness, distance was deceptive. It was probably no more than a hundred paces, if that.

He could just make out a pale crescent of light ahead. It

appeared to be low down, perhaps an indication that there was a dip in the tunnel or a stairway. And then he saw there was a bend in the passage. He continued slowly, the baton held tightly in his fist.

He turned the corner and saw that the lantern had been placed on the ground next to what looked to be the old woman's shawl. He bent to examine it.

It was then that the wizened, bat-like creature detached itself from the wall to his right, accompanied by a scream of such intensity it was almost impossible to imagine the source could be human.

Even as he turned, dropping the shawl, the glow from the lantern caught the glint of the knife blade as it curved towards his throat. Hawkwood hurled his body aside. The sliver of steel whipped past his face and he heard the grunt as the old woman realized she had missed her target. Christ, but she was fast! Faster than he would have thought possible, and hate had given her added impetus. Already she was turning again, driving the weapon towards his heart.

He felt the cloth tear on his upper arm as the razor-sharp blade sliced through his coat sleeve, the material parting like grape skin. Transferring the baton to his left palm, he struck upwards to turn the strike away, at the same time reaching for her wrist with his other hand. Her arm was no thicker than a child's, but the power in the reed-thin body was astonishing. His fingers encircled her wrist, deflecting the blade's cutting edge. At the same time, he struck down with the baton and heard the brittle snap of breaking bone. The knife dropped to the floor and her squeal of pain reverberated off the walls.

But, incredibly, she wasn't finished. In the next second, her left hand was reaching towards his face as she launched herself at him, spitting and swearing as if possessed by devils, clawing for his eyes with nails as sharp as talons. So ferocious was the force of her attack, he was slammed against the wall of the tunnel. Air exploded from his lungs.

One-handed she clung to him, kicking and gouging. Flecks of spittle landed on his face. He felt, too, her hot breath on his cheek, as rancid as a midden, and knew that somehow he had to finish it. He hooked the end of the baton into her stomach, felt the grip on his collar loosen, used his full body weight to drive his fist under her ribcage and punch her away.

There was a flat thud as the back of her head hit the wall, the screech dying on her lips as her frail body slid to the ground. She landed awkwardly, winded, legs akimbo, dress around her knees, thin breasts rising and falling as she gasped for air.

Hawkwood straightened and wiped the smear of phlegm from his jaw.

"Bitch."

The crumpled figure at his feet let out a low moan.

Slipping the ebony baton inside his coat, he bent to retrieve the discarded shawl. He used the shawl to bind her wrists, making no allowances for the broken arm. In the vapid glow from the lantern, he could see that her eyes were glazed with pain. Her resistance was clearly spent.

When he had finished trussing her arms, he picked up the lantern. Holding it aloft, he lifted the old woman by the collar of her dress and began to retrace his steps down the tunnel, dragging her limp, unprotesting body behind him.

24

2

In the kitchen of the house, Constable Edmund Rafferty scratched his ample belly and gazed at the display of valuables on the table. He cast a wary eye on the figure of Eli Gant who, having recovered from the baton blow, was seated on the floor, his back to the wall, rocking slowly from side to side, while staring mournfully down at the handcuffs that had been fastened around his wrists. In his present predicament, he looked as harmless as a puppy.

Rafferty stole another surreptitious glance at the table and started as a voice behind him said, "We caught four of the little beggars, Irish. What should we do with 'em?"

The speaker was a thin, ferret-featured individual dressed similarly to Rafferty, save for the colour of his waistcoat, which was scarlet instead of blue. His right hand was clamped around the collar of a small boy. He was holding the boy in such a way that the tips of the child's toes only just touched the cobbles. The child was trying to pull away.

His attempt to escape, however, was instantly curtailed when his captor cuffed him violently round the back of the head.

Rafferty eyed the figure at the door with scorn. "You hold on to 'em, Constable Warbeck, until I tells you otherwise. Now, take him outside, there's a good lad."

The constable touched his cap and moved away, and Rafferty breathed a sigh of relief. It was Rafferty's considered opinion that Constable Warbeck hadn't the brains he'd been born with, and his habit of addressing Rafferty as "Irish" was also beginning to irk considerably. Unfortunately, Warbeck was married to Rafferty's younger sister, Alice, who had persuaded her brother to sponsor Warbeck's entry into the police force; an act of charity about which he was beginning to have severe misgivings. Not least, regarding the said constable's apparent inability to look the other way at opportune moments. Clearly, the man had much to learn. Still, Rafferty concluded, it *was* early days.

Moving to the table, Rafferty eyed the small array of pocketbooks and jewellery with increasing interest. Looking over his shoulder to ensure he was not being observed, he investigated the contents of the pocketbooks. Several of them, to his delight, held banknotes. He extracted one crisp note from each and replaced the pocketbooks on the table. Then his eyes alighted on the watch.

It was a very fine watch; gold-cased, with matching chain. Undoubtedly the property of a gentleman. Rafferty held the timepiece up to his ear. The ticking was like a tiny heartbeat. He inserted the end of a blunt fingernail under the clasp and was about to flick open the cover when his ears detected footsteps and a curious scraping sound. Quickly, Rafferty dropped the watch into the deep pocket of his coat. Just in time. He grinned expansively as Hawkwood emerged from behind the curtain, dragging the body of Mother Gant into the room.

"Well now, Captain, there I was wondering where you'd got to. Thought we might have to send out a search party, so I did." Rafferty's glance dropped to the body of the Widow Gant, who had regained consciousness and was staring up at Hawkwood with a degree of malevolence that was chilling in its intensity.

"See you caught the old crone, then?" Rafferty studied the rent in Hawkwood's sleeve and frowned. "Gave you a bit of trouble, did she?"

Hawkwood hauled the old woman across the floor and dropped her next to her son. When he looked up his eyes were as dark as the grave.

"How many?"

Rafferty sighed. "Four. The rest scarpered. My lads've got 'em outside." Rafferty found himself wavering under the other man's gaze. There was something in that hard stare that made Constable Rafferty's blood run cold. To his relief, Hawkwood merely nodded in acceptance.

"Probably as many as we deserved. All right, you know what to do. Take them away."

Rafferty nodded. "Right you are." The constable aimed a kick at Eli Gant's shin. "On your feet! You, too, Mother, else you'll get my boot up your skinny arse!"

Hawkwood turned away as Rafferty bundled his charges out of the house.

27

"Wait!"

The command cut through the air. Rafferty paused on the doorstep. A cold wind touched his spine. When he turned around he found that Hawkwood was looking at him, and his breath caught in his throat.

The bastard knew!

Hawkwood held out his hand. "I'll take the watch, Rafferty."

"Eh?" Instinctively, in voicing that one word of feigned innocence, Rafferty knew he'd betrayed his guilt. Conceit and fear, however, dictated that he make at least a half-hearted attempt to extricate himself from the mire.

"Watch? And what watch would that be, then? Sure, and I don't know what you mean."

Hawkwood's expression was as hard as stone. "I'll ask you once more, Constable. You've already made one mistake. Don't compound the error. Hand it over."

Even as he blustered, Rafferty knew the game had been played to its conclusion. His only recourse was to try and retire with as much bravado as he could muster. He frowned, as if searching his memory, and then allowed a broad smile to steal across his face.

"Och, sweet Mary! Why, of course! What was I thinking? Sure and didn't I just slip it into my pocket for safekeeping and then forget all about it? Memory'll be the death of me, so it will. Here it is, now! I'm glad you reminded me, for it's likely I'd have walked off with it, so I would."

And with a grin that would have charmed Medusa, Constable Rafferty reached into the pocket of his coat and brought forth the watch with the dexterity of an illusionist producing a rabbit from a hat.

"There you go, Captain." Rafferty handed the watch over. "And a very fine timepiece it is, too, even if I does say so myself. Cost a pretty penny, I shouldn't wonder." A mischievous wink caused the right side of the constable's face to droop alarmingly. "Take a bit of a liking to it yourself, did you? And who'd blame you, is what I'd say. Why, I –"

Hawkwood turned the watch over in his hands and looked up. His expression was enough to erase the grin from the constable's face.

"You can dispense with the bejesus and the blarney, Rafferty. It might fool the ladies and the scum you drink with, but it doesn't impress me."

Rafferty's skin reddened even further and he shifted uncomfortably, but Hawkwood hadn't finished.

"A warning, Rafferty. You ever work with me again, you'd best keep your thieving hands to yourself. Otherwise, I'll cut them off. Is that clear?"

The constable opened his mouth as if to protest, but the words failed him. He nodded miserably.

"Good, then we understand each other. The watch stays with me. Take the rest of the loot to Bow Street. It can be stored there as evidence. And mark this, Rafferty. I'm holding you responsible for its safe arrival. You never know, the owners may actually turn up to claim it. Now, get the hell out of my sight."

Hawkwood waited until Rafferty and his constables had left with their prisoners, before flicking open the watch cover and reading the inscription etched into the casing. Then, closing the watch, he dropped it into his pocket and let himself out of the house.

In the stable yard behind the Blind Fiddler, the fight was nearing the end. It was the forty-seventh round. By the standards of the day, and by common consent, it had been an enjoyable contest.

Both fighters had taken severe punishment. Benbow, his face a mask of blood and nursing two broken ribs, waited for his opponent to come within range.

Figg, rendered almost deaf and blind by the injuries he had received, his wrists and hands swollen to twice normal size, wits scrambled by a barrage of punches to the face and leaking sweat from every pore, spat out a gobbet of blood, and circled unsteadily.

Both men could barely stand.

The end, when it came, proved to be something of an anti-climax. Benbow, swaying precariously, hooked a punch towards his opponent's belly. The blow landed hard. Figg collapsed. Blood gushed from his mouth, and the crowd groaned. It was a certain indication that Figg's lungs had been damaged. The sight was sufficient cause for the referee, in a rare display of compassion, to end the contest and award the bout to the Cornishman.

So suddenly was the decision announced that a hush fell over the spectators. But then, like ripples spreading across a pond, an excited chatter began to spread through the assembled gathering. Benbow sat down on a low stool, probed his mouth with a finger, spat out a tooth, took a swig from a proffered brandy bottle, and looked on without pity as the defeated Figg was helped away by his seconds.

Beneath the stable arch, the red-haired major clapped his companion on the back and shook his head in admiration. "By God, Fitz, that was as fine a contest as I've witnessed, and I'm ten guineas better off than I was before the bout, thanks to the Cornishman. Damn me, if winning hasn't given me a raging thirst. What say we wet our whistles before we meet the ladies? I do believe we've an hour or two to kill before we're expected."

The major reached into his sash and his face froze with concern. "Hell's teeth, Fitz! My watch and chain! Gone! I've been robbed!"

The two men looked about them. A futile gesture, as both were fully aware. Whoever the thief was, he or she was long gone, swallowed up by the rapidly dispersing crowd.

"Damn and blast the thieving buggers!" The major swore vehemently and gritted his teeth in anger and frustration.

It was the sense of someone at their shoulder that caused them both to turn. The red-haired officer's first impression was that the stranger was a man of the cloth. The dark apparel hinted as much, but as the major took in the expression in the smoke-grey eyes he knew that the man was certainly no priest. It was then the major saw the object held in the stranger's open hand.

"I'll be damned, Fitz! Will you look at this! The fellow has my watch! May I enquire how the devil you came by it, sir?"

Hawkwood held the watch out. "Sorry to disappoint you,

31

Major, but sorcery had nothing to do with it. I spotted the boy making the snatch. As for the rest, let's just say that I persuaded him to see the error of his ways."

Reunited with his property, the major could not disguise his joy. Clasping the watch in his fist, he smiled gratefully. "Well, I'm obliged to you, sir, I truly am. It's fortunate for me you've good eyesight. But here, I'm forgetting my manners. Permit me to introduce myself. The name's Lawrence, 1st Battalion, 40th Light Infantry. My companion, Lieutenant Duncan Fitzhugh."

The younger officer gave a ready smile and touched the peak of his shako. "Honoured, sir."

Hawkwood did not reciprocate. Instead, to the surprise of the two officers, he merely gave a curt nod of acknowledgement and turned away.

The major was first to protest. "Why, no! Stand fast, sir! You'll allow me the opportunity to express my gratitude. The watch means a great deal to me. The lieutenant and I were about to partake of a small libation. You'll join us, of course?"

"Thank you, no." Hawkwood's reply was abrupt.

"But, sir!" the major remonstrated. "I insist –"

Skilfully interpreting the expression on Hawkwood's face, the lieutenant took his companion's arm. "You'd best let him go, sir. You're embarrassing the poor fellow."

The major made as if to argue, but then changed his mind and shrugged in acceptance. "Oh, very well, but it don't alter the fact that I'm indebted to you. If I can repay the favour in any way . . ." The major's voice trailed off. Putting his head on one side, he frowned. "Forgive me, sir, this may seem an odd question, but have we met before?"

Hawkwood shook his head. "Not to my knowledge, Major."

"You're certain? Your face seems familiar." The major narrowed his eyes.

"Quite certain." Hawkwood inclined his head. "Good day, Major . . . Lieutenant." Then he turned on his heel and strode away without a backward glance.

"Damned odd," the major murmured. He paused, looked around quickly, caught the eye of a hovering street vendor and crooked a finger. The hawker, scenting custom, touched his cap. The wooden tray suspended from a cord around his neck offered a variety of sweetmeats. Several bloated flies arose lazily from the tray. Fitzhugh wrinkled his nose in disgust.

The hawker grinned, showing blackened teeth. "Yes, your honour, what's your pleasure?"

The major dismissed the proffered titbits with an impatient wave of his hand. Instead, he nodded across the yard. "The severely dressed fellow with the long dark hair, disappearing yonder. Do you know him?"

The man peered in the direction the major indicated. To the officers' surprise, the hawker's face appeared to lose colour. He eyed them suspiciously. "What's it to you?"

Lawrence smiled easily and retrieved a coin from his pocket. "Curiosity, my friend, nothing more. His face looked familiar to me, that's all."

The hawker eyed the coin furtively, but only for a second before his thin fingers closed around it. Biting into the coin, he muttered darkly, "If I was you, your honour, where that one's concerned, you'd best turn and walk the other way."

Lawrence and Fitzhugh exchanged startled glances. "How so?"

"Because he's the law, that's why."

Lawrence's eyebrows rose. "The *law*?"

"Works out of Bow Street, don't he. One of them special constables. Runners, we calls 'em. Mean bastards every one."

The two officers stared across the yard. The hawker spat on to the cobbles. "You take heed, friend. You ever find yourself in trouble, you'd best pray they don't put *him* on your trail."

"Well, I'm damned," Lawrence said, adding, "but his name, man! Do you know his name?"

The pieman's expression hardened. "Name? Oh, yes, I know his name, right enough. It's Hawkwood, may God rot him. Now . . ." the hawker lifted his tray pointedly ". . . if you gentlemen 'ave no intention of buyin' . . ."

But the major wasn't listening. He was staring off in the direction the dark-haired man had taken. He looked like a man in shock. It was Fitzhugh who finally dismissed the waiting pieman. Muttering under his breath, the vendor limped away.

Fitzhugh regarded his companion with concern. "Are you all right, sir? You look as though you've seen a ghost."

Lawrence remained motionless and said softly, "Maybe I have." He turned and favoured the lieutenant with a rueful smile. "By God, Fitz, memory's a fickle mistress!"

"You do know him, then? You've met before?"

"We have indeed," Lawrence said softly, adding almost abstractedly, "and both of us a damned long way from home."

Fitzhugh waited for the major to elaborate, but on this occasion Lawrence did not oblige. Instead, the major nodded towards the door of the tavern. "I think I'm in need of a stiff brandy, young Fitz. What say you and I adjourn to yon hostelry and I'll treat you to a wee dram out of my winnings." Lawrence clapped his companion on the shoulder. "Who knows? I may even have an interesting tale to tell along with it."

From the shadow of an archway, Hawkwood watched the major and his companion enter the inn. It had been a strange sensation seeing Lawrence again. In Hawkwood's case, recognition had been immediate, confirmed by the engraving on the watch casing:

Lieutenant D.C. Lawrence, 40th Regiment.
A gallant officer.
With grateful thanks, Auchmuty.
February 1807

An inscription which could not be ignored. The watch was not merely an instrument for keeping time but a reward for services rendered; an act of outstanding bravery. The words alone indicated, to the recipient at least, that it was worth far more than gold. Hawkwood had seen the anguish on the major's face when he'd discovered the loss.

It would have been an even greater crime had the watch

remained in Constable Rafferty's thieving clutches. Despite his warning to Rafferty, Hawkwood wondered just how many of the other stolen items would find their way back to their rightful owners. Precious few, he suspected. Sadly, men like Rafferty, guardians of the public trust with a tendency to pilfer on the side, were only too common.

Hawkwood's thoughts returned to the major. His intention to return the watch had been instinctive. Call it duty, a debt of honour to a former comrade in arms, albeit one whose companionship had been fleeting in the extreme. There had been little hesitation on his part.

So, why deny recognition? The answer to that question was easy. Old wounds ran deep. Reopening them served no useful purpose. He shook his head at the thought of it. A chance encounter and it was as if the years had been rolled away. But sour memories were apt to leave a bitter after-taste. What was done was done. He'd performed a service for which thanks had been given; a public servant performing a civic duty. That's all it had been. Now it was over. Finished.

Hawkwood was about to step away when a discreet cough sounded at his elbow.

Shaken out of his reverie, he looked down and found himself confronted by a small, bow-legged, sharp-nosed man dressed in funereal black coat and breeches. An unfashionable powdered wig peeked from below the brim of an equally outmoded three-cornered black hat. Eyes blinked owlishly behind a pair of half-moon spectacles.

Hawkwood gave a wintry smile. "Well, well, Mr Twigg. And to what do we owe this unexpected pleasure?" *As if he didn't know.*

The little man deflected the sarcasm with an exaggerated sigh of sufferance. "A message for you. Magistrate Read sends his compliments and requests that you attend him directly."

Hawkwood's eyebrows rose. "'Requests', Mr Twigg? I doubt that. And where am I to attend him, *directly?*"

"Bow Street. In his chambers."

As he spoke, Ezra Twigg allowed his gaze to roam the stable yard. By now the crowd had all but disappeared. The God-botherer, sermon concluded, had dismantled his home-made pulpit and was steering a course for the tavern door. A handful of pedlars remained, ever hopeful of attracting late custom. Close by the ringside, a small knot of people had gathered. In their midst, Reuben Benbow, nursing cracked ribs, joked with his seconds and celebrated his hard-fought victory.

The bewigged clerk's eyes took on a calculated glint. Removing his spectacles, he breathed on the lenses and polished them vigorously on the sleeve of his coat.

Hawkwood grinned. "You were right, Ezra. The Cornishman *was* the better man."

Ezra Twigg replaced his spectacles, looked up at Hawkwood and blinked myopically. His gaze turned towards the open door of the tavern and the corner of his mouth twitched.

Hawkwood patted the little man's shoulder. "It's all right, Ezra. I'll see you back at the Shop."

Without waiting for a response, Hawkwood turned and walked away. He did not look back. Had he done so, he would have seen the bowed figure of Ezra Twigg hurrying briskly towards the tavern door, the spring in the clerk's step matched only by the broad smile on his lips and the twinkle in his eye.

Shadows were lengthening as Hawkwood picked his way through the chain of courts and alleyways.

The few street lamps that did exist were barely adequate, and small deterrent to footpads who continued to stalk the darkened thoroughfares with impunity. Even in broad daylight, it was almost impossible to walk the streets without being propositioned or relieved of one's belongings. For the unwary pedestrian, dusk only brought added risk. A few gas lamps had been installed in the West End but they were the exception, not the rule. For the most part, night-time London was a world of near impenetrable darkness, fraught with hidden dangers, where even police foot patrols and watchmen feared to tread.

Hawkwood, however, walked with confidence. His presence was acknowledged, but there were no attempts to impede his progress. There was something about the way he carried himself that caused other men to step aside. The scar on his face only added to the aura of menace that emanated from his purposeful stride.

Not that Hawkwood was immune to his surroundings. It was merely that he was hardened to it. He could not afford to be otherwise. London was a fertile breeding ground for every vice known to man. As a Bow Street Runner, Hawkwood had seen more of the city's dark underbelly than he cared to recall. The shadowy, refuse-strewn byways held precious few surprises, but nevertheless he remained alert as he continued on towards his appointment.

3

"So," Fitzhugh said, "our Samaritan – who was he?"

The two officers were seated in a candlelit alcove in the Blind Fiddler. The fight had attracted a lot of extra custom and the tavern was doing brisk business. Both men were drinking Spanish brandy.

Lawrence pursed his lips. "Well, the pedlar was right, Fitz. Our friend Hawkwood's certainly not a man to be trifled with."

Lawrence gazed into his drink, remembering. "Four years ago, it'd be . . . The Americas. We were part of Sam Auchmuty's expedition, sent to reinforce Beresford." Lawrence smiled grimly. "We were fighting the damned Spaniards then. Now they're our allies. Who'd have thought it?"

It had been before Fitzhugh's time. A misconceived and ill-fated attempt to liberate South American colonies from Spanish rule. The first wave of troops under the command of Brigadier-General William Carr Beresford had achieved some initial success by taking Buenos Aires, at which point disaster had struck.

Lawrence winced at the memory. "Turned out we weren't reinforcing Beresford, we were rescuing the silly sod! By the time we got there, the Spanish had regrouped and recaptured the city, and Beresford along with it!"

Lawrence leaned forward, warming to his story. "Now, old Sam knew that if we were to stand any chance of getting to Beresford we'd have to take Montevideo first, as a bargaining tool. Which we did, but by God they gave us a fight! The bastards were waiting for us on the beach. We forced 'em back, of course. Then found they'd fortified the bloody place, so we had to lay siege. Bombarded them with the ships' twenty-four-pounders. Took us four days before we finally secured the breach."

Lawrence's voice trailed off. Fitzhugh realized that the major was holding the watch. The cover was open and Lawrence was fondling it abstractedly, running his thumb across the engraved surface. He looked up, recovered himself, slipped the timepiece back into his sash and continued. "Lost a lot of good men before they surrendered. Took a host of prisoners, too, including the governor, Don Pasquil. But there was one fellow, a general he was, in command of the citadel. Can't remember his blasted name. Refused to give himself up. Auchmuty sent a flag of truce promising safe passage, but he declined the offer. So Sam ordered in the sharpshooters."

Fitzhugh's eyed widened. "Sharpshooters?"

"We had a detachment of the 95th with us. A brace of their

40

riflemen were ordered to a nearby tower with orders to pick this general out and shoot him dead. I was directed to assist. Our friend was one of the riflemen. A lieutenant he was. Didn't know his name then, though I recall thinking it strange that they should have sent an officer to do the job."

Fitzhugh frowned. "How can you be sure it was the same fellow?"

"Because of what I witnessed that day. It's not something I'm likely to forget. We were atop the tower, the riflemen, myself and a couple of privates, waiting for the general to put in an appearance. Sure enough, out he came, up at his ramparts, strutting around in his frills and finery, proud as a turkey cock."

The major reached inside his jacket and extracted a short-stemmed clay pipe and a leather tobacco pouch. With what seemed to Fitzhugh like maddening deliberation, Lawrence packed the pipe and returned the pouch to his jacket. Fitzhugh watched in frustrated silence as Lawrence lit a taper from the candle on the table and held the flame to the pipe bowl. When the tobacco was glowing to his satisfaction, Lawrence extinguished the taper with his thumb and forefinger and returned it to the container by his elbow. At first Fitzhugh suspected the major was toying with him, prolonging the agony. Then he realized that Lawrence was using the opportunity to collect his thoughts.

The major sucked noisily on the pipe stem. "Never saw anything like it, Fitz. Our friend stands there, looking out over the rooftops towards the general's position. Doesn't say a word, just stares. Then, calm as you like, he takes up his rifle, loads it, rests it on the parapet, and takes aim.

41

"One shot, Fitz, that's all it took. I was watching the general through my glass. The bullet took the bugger in the head. Blew his brains out."

"What was the range?"

"Two hundred and twenty yards, if it was an inch."

"Good God!" Fitzhugh's jaw dropped.

"Best damned shooting I've ever seen."

"I can believe it," Fitzhugh said, marvelling.

"Did the trick, of course. Spaniards surrendered almost immediately."

"And the rifleman?"

"Returned to his unit. Never saw him again. Never forgot that shooting, though. Quite outstanding." Lawrence fell silent, lost in a quiet moment of reflection. He drew on his pipe, then lifted his mug and drained the contents.

"Another?" Fitzhugh asked.

Lawrence stared down at his mug, as if noticing for the first time that he had emptied it. "Why not?"

Fitzhugh raised his hand and beckoned to one of the serving girls. At the summons of a handsome young man in uniform, she approached the table with a ready grin. Rounded breasts strained against her low-cut bodice as she bent forward and retrieved the empty mugs. Fitzhugh gave his order and the girl pulled away, her left breast pressing heavily against his arm, reminding the lieutenant of his and Lawrence's plans for the evening: a visit to a small and very discreet establishment off Covent Garden, in which hand-picked young ladies of beauty and charm provided entertainment of a kind not found in the Officers' Mess.

Fitzhugh watched the girl depart, following her passage

through the gauntlet of roving hands and lewd enticements. A thought occurred to him and he turned back to Lawrence.

"Why do you think he denied having met you before?"

Lawrence shrugged. "Hard to say, though he has less cause to remember me than I do him."

Not strictly true. The major was being modest. Fitzhugh knew for a fact that Lawrence's contribution to the taking of Montevideo had been considerable. The watch that the major prized so highly was testament to the fact. It was a part of regimental lore handed down to junior officers.

The British had laid siege to the city's Spanish fortifications using tried and tested means, albeit medieval in conception. They had constructed batteries and breastworks, gabions and fascines to protect the guns brought up from the men-of-war that had transported them from Rio de Janeiro.

The walls of the city were six feet thick. As Lawrence had said, it had indeed taken four days for the cannon to knock down the gates. The British troops had attacked in the early morning, under cover of darkness. The forlorn hope, the forward troops charged with leading the frontal assault, had been led by a Captain Renny. When Renny had been felled by a Spanish musket ball, it had been the young Lieutenant Lawrence who had, quite literally, stepped into the breach and pressed home the attack, leading his men across the wall and on into the town.

Sir Samuel Auchmuty had presented Lawrence with the watch, his own timepiece, as a measure of his regard for his junior officer's bravery. As further reward, Lawrence had also received his captaincy, courtesy of the late, lamented Renny.

The girl returned bearing their drinks. Another smile for Fitzhugh and she was gone, with perhaps just a slight exaggeration in the sway of her broad hips.

"Damned curious change of career," Fitzhugh mused, taking a sip from his freshly filled mug. "Rifleman to Runner."

"And a damned efficient one would be my guess," Lawrence responded, adding ruminatively, "though I doubt it's gained him too many friends."

Before the lieutenant could query that observation, the major rose to his feet and drained his mug. Tapping his pipe bowl against the table leg, Lawrence grinned at his lieutenant's expression. "Come now, young Fitz, drink up. It's time you and I took a stroll. The way that serving girl's been giving you the glad eye reminds me we've to keep our appointment at Mistress Flanaghan's. Seeing the dumplings on that young wench has done wonders for my appetite!" Without waiting for a response, the major stowed his pipe, reached for his shako and started for the tavern door.

Realizing he was about to get left behind, Fitzhugh gulped down his brandy and followed suit.

As the two officers emerged on to the darkening street, Lawrence's thoughts returned to the encounter in the tavern yard. There was certainly more he could have told Fitzhugh about the taciturn ex-rifleman; a lot more, as the lieutenant probably suspected, following their hasty departure. But there had been something in Hawkwood's eye that had caused Lawrence to stay his hand. It had been clear, from their exchange, that there was a reluctance on Hawkwood's part to revisit the past. Absently, the major's hand reached for his watch chain. Reassuring himself that the timepiece was intact and in place, the major breathed an inner sigh of relief. And a man's past was his own affair. Hawkwood could disappear back into the obscurity he obviously preferred. As for young Fitzhugh, well, the lieutenant would have to remain in blissful ignorance.

Lawrence traced the watch casing with his thumb. I owe Hawkwood at least that much, he thought.

The early evening crowds were beginning to gather as Hawkwood made his way along Bow Street. Theatre-goers mingled beneath the wide portico of Rich's Theatre, while others wended their way towards the Lyceum and the Aldwych. The coffee shops, gin parlours, brothels and taverns that were housed within and around Covent Garden were already full to overflowing, and the bloods, pimps and molls who frequented the area were out in force. The jangle of horse-drawn carriages added to the general noise and bustle. From somewhere within the mêlée arose the grinding strains of a barrel organ.

Number 4 Bow Street was a narrow, five-storeyed town house with a plain façade. Save for the extra floor, there was little to distinguish the building from the adjoining architecture. It was the room at the rear of the ground floor, however, that gave the place its name. To those who toiled within its confines, it was referred to as "The Shop". To the rest of the city's inhabitants it was known as the Public Office.

Hawkwood pushed his way through the handful of loiterers camped on the front step and entered the open doorway. A narrow passage ran towards the back of the building. Hawkwood's boots echoed hollowly on the wooden floor.

The offices were not yet closed for the day. Studious, whey-faced clerks laden with paperwork, scuttled along candlelit corridors. In the Public Office itself, a late court was in session. The room was crowded. Seated at the bench, the presiding magistrate gazed out over the proceedings with a look of resigned boredom on his puritanical face.

Hawkwood removed his riding coat and ascended the stairs to the first floor and the Chief Magistrate's private chambers. Hawkwood laid his coat across the back of a chair, walked across to the door and knocked once.

"Come!" The order was given brusquely.

The room was square and oak panelled. Several portraits lined the walls. They showed dour, waxen-faced men in sombre dress; previous occupants of the office. A desk filled the space in front of the high, curtained windows. A large fireplace, flanked by a matching pair of high-backed, heavily upholstered chairs, stood against the wall to Hawkwood's left. Logs were burning brightly in the grate. A long-cased clock stood guard in the corner. Its hypnotic ticking added to the air of solemnity.

The silver-haired man seated at the desk did not acknowledge Hawkwood's entrance but continued writing, the scratch of nib on paper tortuous in the still, quiet room.

Hawkwood waited.

Eventually, the man at the desk looked up. He placed the pen in the inkstand, straightened his papers and gazed at Hawkwood for several moments. "The operation against the Gant woman went well, I trust?"

46

"Better than I'd expected," Hawkwood said.

The news was received with a frown.

"I didn't think we'd get close enough to catch her, but she hadn't bothered to post lookouts. She must be getting careless in her old age."

The silver-haired man pondered the significance of the statement. "She's in custody?"

"She and her lackwit son. They're in the cells across the road."

Curiously, the Bow Street Public Office did not possess facilities for detaining felons. A long-standing arrangement was in force by which the landlord of the Brown Bear pub on the opposite side of the street was paid a nominal sum to provide special strong-rooms that could be used as holding cells.

The silver-haired man nodded in quiet satisfaction. "Excellent. They'll be dealt with in the morning. They gave you no trouble?"

Hawkwood thought about the knife tear in his coat. "Nothing I couldn't handle."

"And the children?"

"I gave the constable instructions to send them to Bridewell."

"From where, no doubt, they will abscond with ease."

The silver-haired man sighed, placed his palms on the desk and pushed himself upright. His movements were unhurried and precise.

James Read had held the office of Chief Magistrate for five years. He was of late middle age, with an aquiline face, accentuated by the swept-back hair. A conservative dresser, as

47

befitted his station, his fastidious appearance was deceptive, for there were often occasions when he displayed a quite dry, if not mordant, sense of humour. Read was the latest in a long line of dedicated men. One factor, however, set him apart from those who had gone before. Unlike his illustrious predecessors, and whether as a measure of his indifference or as a throwback to a lowly Methodist upbringing, James Read had refused the knighthood which the post of Chief Magistrate traditionally carried.

Read walked across the room, stood in front of the fire, his back to the flames, and lifted his coat-tails. "This damned house is like a barn. Nearly midsummer and I'm frozen to the bone."

He studied Hawkwood without speaking, taking in the unfashionable long hair, and the strong, almost arrogant features. Shadows thrown by the flickering firelight moved across Hawkwood's scarred face. A cruel face, Read thought, with those dark, brooding eyes, and yet one which women probably found compellingly attractive.

"I have another assignment for you," Read said, his face suddenly serious. He adjusted his dress and stepped away from the fire. "Last evening there was an attack on a coach. Two people were killed: the guard and one of the passengers."

"Where?"

"North of Camberwell. The Kent Road."

Hawkwood knew the area. Wooded heath and meadowland, and a well-known haunt of highwaymen. Of late, attacks had been few and far between; a result of the reintroduced horse patrols, bands of heavily armed riders, mostly ex-cavalry men, who guarded the major routes in and out of the capital.

"What was the haul?"

"Money and valuables; perhaps fifty guineas' worth. They were very thorough."

Hawkwood looked up. *"They?"*

"A man and a boy, judging from the accounts of the witnesses." Read gave a short, bitter laugh. "Master and apprentice."

The magistrate reached into his pocket and extracted a small, oval snuffbox. With practised dexterity, he flicked open the mother-of-pearl lid and placed a pinch of snuff on the juncture between the thumb and forefinger of his left hand. He inhaled the fine powder through his left nostril. Repeating the procedure with his right, he closed the box and tucked it away.

"Any descriptions?" Hawkwood knew the answer to that question. A shake of the Chief Magistrate's head confirmed his suspicion.

The Magistrate wrinkled his nose. As he did so, he removed a silk handkerchief from his sleeve.

"Both were masked. It was the older man who did all the talking. It's possible the boy was a mute. They are, however, both murderers. 'Twas the older man who killed the courier. The –"

"Courier?" Hawkwood interjected.

"An admiralty courier. He joined the coach at Dover. The guard was shot by the accomplice. This is a pair of callous rogues, Hawkwood, make no mistake."

"Anything else?"

Hawkwood winced as the Chief Magistrate let go a loud sneeze. It took a moment for Read to recover. Pausing to wipe his nose with the handkerchief, the Chief Magistrate shook his head once more. "Nothing substantial. Though there was one rather curious observation. The surviving passengers had got the impression that the older man was not much of a horseman."

"How's that?"

"In the course of the robbery, they were surprised by a mounted patrol. In his haste to make an escape, the fellow very nearly took a tumble. Managed to hang on to his nag more by luck than judgement, apparently."

"A highwayman with no horse sense," Hawkwood mused. "There's an interesting combination."

"Quite so," Read sniffed. "Though I don't suppose it means anything. Still, it was a pity. Had Officer Lomax and his patrol arrived a few minutes earlier they might well have caught them. As it was, the villains got clean away. It was a foul night. The rain covered their tracks."

"A man and boy," Hawkwood reflected. "Not much to go on."

Read stuffed the handkerchief back up his sleeve. "I agree. Which is why I've sent for you. We'll leave Lomax to deal with the passengers. I suggest you concentrate on the items that were stolen. Tracing their whereabouts could be the only way to find the culprits. You have unique contacts. Put them to good use. Murder and mutilation on the king's highway – I'll not have it! Especially when it involves an official messenger! And I understand the coachman, poor fellow, leaves a widow and four children. By God, I want these men caught, Hawkwood. I want them apprehended and punished. I –" The Chief Magistrate caught the look on Hawkwood's face.

"Mutilation?" Hawkwood said.

The Chief Magistrate looked down at his shoes. Hawkwood followed his gaze. James Read, he noticed, not for the first time, had very small feet; delicate, dancer's feet.

"The courier's arm was severed."

A knot formed itself slowly in Hawkwood's stomach.

"They *cut off his arm?*"

"He was carrying a dispatch pouch. The robbers were obviously of the opinion that it held something of value. When the courier refused to give it up, he was shot and the pouch was taken. The other passengers said he refused to hand over the key. The horse patrol was almost upon them. The robbers panicked."

"And *did* the pouch contain anything of value?"

The Chief Magistrate waved his hand dismissively. "Certainly nothing that would interest a pair of common thieves. They probably tossed it away at their first halt. It was the money and jewels they were after. Easily disposable, and the means by which we may precipitate their downfall."

"I'll need a description of the stolen goods."

"See Mr Twigg, he has the details." The Chief Magistrate returned to his desk and sat down. His expression was severe. "I want these people found, Hawkwood. I want them run to ground!"

Hawkwood frowned. The Chief Magistrate's vehemence was uncharacteristic. If he hadn't known any better, he might have suspected that James Read had been one of

51

the passengers held up and robbed. It was unusual for the magistrate to take what sounded like a personal interest in such matters.

Read reached for his pen. "That is all. You may go."

Hawkwood was on the point of letting himself out of the room when Read's voice halted him in his tracks. "There is one more thing."

Hawkwood turned.

The Chief Magistrate was perusing a document. He appeared to be deep in thought and did not bother to look up. "I am not unaware, Hawkwood, that in the pursuit of the criminal element it is sometimes necessary to turn a blind eye to certain other . . . lesser transgressions. Let the minnow go free in order to catch the pike, and so forth. In this case, I am referring to this afternoon's bare-knuckle contest at the Blind Fiddler public house, where it was deemed prudent to allow the fight to continue in order to lull the Widow Gant and her brood into a false sense of security.

"However, this does not give leave for my staff to profit from such leniency. Suffice it to say that I deem it singularly inappropriate for a member of these chambers to wage a proportion of his salary on the outcome of what is still, may I remind you, an unlawful activity."

For the first time, the Chief Magistrate lifted his eyes. He regarded Hawkwood with a mild, almost weary expression. "And spare me the innocent look, Hawkwood. While you may profess your ignorance of such matters, my clerk's involvement has already been established, though I doubt he would confess it in so many words.

"And should you be wondering how this came to my

attention, it was through deductive reasoning; in short, from the observance of Mr Twigg when I sent him to rendezvous with you at the Blind Fiddler. The alacrity with which he departed my office was a sight to behold, not to mention the gleam in his eye. The very fact that he was not present to show you into my office suggests to me that he did not accompany you here. I therefore suspect that when next I see him there will be the distinctive reek of brandy on his breath, the consequence of a celebratory rather than medicinal infusion."

Hawkwood tried, unsuccessfully, to stifle a grin.

"Ah," Read said wryly, "I see I have struck a chord. Very well, I'll say no more upon the matter, save that in future I'd be obliged if the two of you were a deal more circumspect. You take my meaning? As officers of the law, we are, after all, expected to set something of an example."

"Yes, sir." Hawkwood managed to keep his face straight. "Will that be all?"

The Chief Magistrate nodded. "For the time being. Keep me informed."

James Read waited for Hawkwood to close the door before placing his pen on the desk and sitting back in his chair. He made a steeple of his fingers and placed them under his chin. His expression was pensive.

Read had not told Hawkwood the full facts of the case and, to his consternation, that bothered him more than he had expected. Hawkwood had only been at Bow Street for a short period. Nevertheless, in that time he had proved himself to be the best Runner in the team. The man was intelligent, resourceful and, when it proved necessary, quite ruthless. He probably deserved to be told more, but the assignment was a delicate one and, as such, Hawkwood's involvement was on a strict need-to-know basis. Read himself was operating under specific instructions. Like a chess player, all he could do for the moment was place Hawkwood on the board and pray that he made the right moves.

Meanwhile, in the ante-room, Hawkwood was trying to hide his astonishment at being confronted by Ezra Twigg, seated at his desk, sober, and holding a list of the stolen items in his hands. Surprisingly, the clerk didn't even appear to be out of breath, despite what must have been a very hasty return from the Blind Fiddler tavern. Hawkwood took a surreptitious sniff. The smell of brandy was barely noticeable. He stared at the clerk, but Twigg's face, as he handed over the list, was a picture of innocence.

Ezra Twigg may have looked like some downtrodden scribe, with his rounded shoulders, ill-fitting hat and ink-stained cuffs, but those with an intimate knowledge knew that behind that mild-mannered façade there lurked a wily brain capable of shrewd cunning and tenacious investigation.

Twigg, clerk to Bow Street's Chief Magistrate, had held his current position for a great many years. Chief Magistrates might come and go, but Ezra Twigg endured. He'd served James Read during his entire tenure and had been a loyal retainer to both of Read's predecessors, Richard Ford and William Addington. It was hinted that Ezra Twigg's contacts rivalled those of any intelligence service. The role of Chief Magistrate was a high-profile one, but it was the servants of the court, men like Twigg, who were the lynchpins of the police and judiciary. Without them, the edifice would crumble.

The list of stolen items was short and not particularly impressive. Three rings, a snuffbox, a bracelet and a silver cross. There was a brief description of each piece. James Read had placed their combined value at around fifty guineas. The highwaymen, in fencing the goods, would be lucky to make ten pounds between them. Not a huge profit, but quite respectable for one night's work.

It was likely that an attempt had already been made to convert the valuables into cash. The city's back streets were home to a multitude of receivers, willing to fence anything from silk handkerchiefs to lead from a church roof. A few preferred to specialize, like Ma Jennings of Red Lion Market who handled hats and gowns, or Joshua Roberts, a pigeon-fancier from Duck Lane, who dealt only in livestock. Others, like the ex-cracksman Edward Memmery, traded mainly in foodstuffs. For everything there was always a price and somebody willing to pay.

And deep within the more notorious rookeries there existed the half-dozen or so receivers who dealt only with goods of the very highest quality. Men like Jacob Low in Field Lane and Isaiah Trask of the Caribee, or Sarah Logan in Rosemary Lane, known to her associates as the Widow. Any one of them had the means to fence the items on the list. Hawkwood knew that James Read had set him a task equivalent to searching a very large beach for a particular grain of sand.

He was going to need assistance.

There were several informers he could call upon. Hawkwood employed a dozen or so to keep him informed of criminal activity. Tradesmen, whores, hawkers, street urchins, many of them criminals in their own right. Hawkwood used a good deal of subterfuge to keep their identities secret. Snouts with an intimate knowledge of the streets were invaluable. Without them, Hawkwood and his colleagues would not have been able to operate effectively. They functioned as the Runners' eyes and ears to the underworld.

On this occasion, however, there was only one person he could approach. And to speak with that individual he would have to enter a dangerous place; a world into which no officer of the law would dare venture if he valued his life. But first, certain arrangements would have to be made.

Blind Billy Mipps was at his usual pitch: the pavement outside the Black Lion Chop House on Little Russell Street.

Blind Billy was as thin as a whip. His hair was long and matted with filth. His threadbare, lice-infested clothes hung loosely upon his weedy body. The tray from which he sold his tapers and tallow candles hung from his neck by a frayed cord. Also around his neck was suspended a card upon which was scrawled in barely legible script: *Old soldier. Wife and three children to support.* The description was at least two-thirds inaccurate. Blind Billy had never been a soldier, neither did he have a wife. As to the number of children he might have fathered, even Billy Mipps would have conceded that three was probably a mite conservative.

A yellowing, blood-encrusted strip of bandage was tied around Billy's head, covering his eyes. A white stick hung from his wrist by a leather thong. Even among the other beggars and hawkers who plied their meagre wares on the capital's crowded streets, the candle seller cut a pathetic figure.

Like every other mendicant of note, Blind Billy had

established his own particular routine. Whenever he sensed the passing of a potential customer, Billy would tap his stick, rattle his tin mug and whine beseechingly, "Buy a candle, yer honour. Penny candles. Spare a copper for an old soldier!" or variations thereof.

Business so far this evening had been poor. Even the theatre crowds, traditionally a prominent source of income, had failed to display their usual generosity. Blind Billy's tin mug did contain a few coins, but mixed in with the money was a substantial number of buttons and nails. Perhaps it was time to move on and find another stand.

Then Billy's sharp ears picked up an approach and he went into action. "Spare a penny, sir, for the sake of the children. Buy a candl—"

"You can spare me the speech, Billy," a harsh voice said. "I've heard it before."

Billy immediately feigned deafness. He put his head on one side and rattled his tin mug in pitiful anticipation. "What's that y'say? Spare a pen—"

Billy's whine was cut short by the hand that gripped his wrist and the voice that murmured in his ear.

"You're not listening, Billy. Pay attention."

The pressure on Billy's wrist increased. For a second or two he thought his bones might snap.

"I want you to take a message for me. To Jago. Tell him the Captain wants a meeting."

"Jago?" Billy wheezed hoarsely. "I don't know no Jago. I –"

Another plaintive wail as pain shot through Billy's arm from wrist to shoulder.

"Don't argue, Billy. You haven't the wit for it. Just do as you're told. Deliver the message. Understood?"

Blind Billy nodded vigorously, whereupon the hold on his wrist slackened and the pain in his arm subsided to a dull throb.

"Good. That wasn't so difficult, was it?"

The question was followed by the tinkle of coinage dropping into the tin mug. Footsteps retreated into the distance.

Blind Billy waited a full twenty seconds before lifting the edge of the eye bandage and glancing nervously up and down the street. There were plenty of people around, but either no one had seen the threat or else they had chosen to ignore it. Billy lifted the mug and peered into it. He tipped the contents into his palm. Several donations had been made since he had last inspected the profits. Discarding the nails and the broken belt buckle, Billy transferred the coins to the pouch beneath his tattered waistcoat. He followed this by removing the placard from around his neck. Then, showing a remarkable fleetness of foot for a blind man, he proceeded along the street at a shuffling run.

Seated at a window table inside the Black Lion Chop House, Hawkwood watched the pedlar's departure with a grim smile. All he had to do now was wait.

4

Whitehall echoed to the uneven clatter of hooves and the rattle of wheels as James Read stepped down from his carriage. He stared up at the imposing entrance of the Admiralty building before turning to the driver.

"You may wait, Caleb. My business should not take long."

The driver touched his hat. "Very good, your honour."

Read swung his cane and made his way under the archway into the main forecourt. The driver watched the trim, black-coated figure disappear from view before retrieving the nosebag from the carriage's rear compartment and looping it over the mare's head. As the mare dipped her nose and began to feed, the driver regained his seat, removed a pipe from his pocket and began to fill it with tobacco. His movements were leisurely. The Chief Magistrate was a regular customer and, while his interpretation of a short time did not always correspond to everyone else's, he did have a tendency to tip generously so it was often worth the wait.

Read strode briskly up the steps between the tall white columns and into the main building. Despite the early hour, the place was already humming with activity. Blue-uniformed naval personnel seemed to fill the hallways. They gathered in corridors and lingered on the stairs, all in the hope of catching the eye of an admiralty clerk who might speed their passage to whatever audience they hoped to arrange with the high and mighty.

Read, however, was not required to wait. The lugubrious lieutenant who escorted him through the building under the curious stare of onlookers did so in silence. Only after he had passed Read into the care of the admiral's clerk at the entrance to the Board Room did he salute and bid the Chief Magistrate a formal "good day" before walking quickly away.

Entering the room, Read was struck, not for the first time, by the confines of the Admiralty Office. Considering it was the nerve centre of Britain's naval administration, exerting influence that spanned every continent, it was unexpectedly modest in size.

The walls were hung with maps and roll-down charts. At one end of the room a huge globe was framed by tall, narrow, glass-fronted bookshelves. Mounted on the wall above the globe was a large dial scored with the points of the compass. This indicator, linked to the weather vane on the roof, gave an instant reading of the wind direction. The reading showed the wind was from the north east, which probably explained, Read thought, why he felt so damned cold.

A heavy, rectangular oaken table bracketed by eight chairs dominated the room. At each end, suspended from the ornate ceiling, was a tasselled bell-pull. Books and manuals formed a ridge down the middle of the table.

Three men were in attendance. Two were seated, the third stood gazing out of the window. Middle-aged, dressed in a well-fitting, double-breasted tail coat, he turned abruptly.

"Ah, Read! There you are! About time! Well, what progress?"

Charles Yorke, First Lord of the Admiralty and Fellow of the Royal Society, was a barrister by profession and a former Member of Parliament.

Read ignored the imperious greeting. Elegant and composed, he approached the table. "Good morning, gentlemen."

The two seated men, their expressions solemn, nodded in quiet reply.

"Well, sir?" The First Sea Lord could barely conceal his impatience. His brow creased into a scowl while his pendulous lower lip trembled defiantly. "Do you have anything to report, or not?"

Read turned and answered calmly: "Only that the investigation is in hand and that I have assigned my best man to the task."

"And how much have you told him?"

"The minimum. Sufficient for him to initiate enquiries."

"You're aware time *is* of the essence?"

"Naturally," Read said, refusing to be intimidated by the First Sea Lord's arrogant manner. A flash of annoyance showed on Yorke's face as he watched Read place his cane on the table and remove his gloves. The First Sea Lord obviously regarded Read as something of a fop. Had he chosen to examine the cane more closely, however, he might well have revised his opinion. Concealed within the slim shaft was a twenty-four-inch, perfectly balanced blade crafted from the finest Toledo steel. Made specially for him by William Parker of Holborn, it was a weapon with which James Read was extremely adept.

Over the years he had held office, Read had received numerous threats from criminals he'd sent down or from their associates who'd sworn revenge for seeing their kith and kin hanged, imprisoned or transported. Most of the threats, issued in the heat of the moment, would never be carried out. The will to exact vengeance usually faded with the passage of time, but Read was of the opinion that it paid to be cautious. Twice he had been forced to defend himself. The first assailant had managed to limp away with only a superficial leg wound. The second had died from a pierced lung. On both occasions, Read had emerged unscathed.

"He's trustworthy, this officer of yours?" the First Sea Lord enquired bluntly.

There was a pause. "*All* my officers are trustworthy," Read said. The Runners at any rate, he thought to himself. Constables and watchmen were a different matter.

"Er – quite so, quite so," the First Sea Lord said, suddenly and surprisingly contrite. "No offence meant." He wafted a placatory hand.

"May we be permitted to know the fellow's name?"

The question came from one of the seated men; a sandy-haired, austere-looking individual in naval dress. The three stripes on his sleeve denoted his rank.

It was not uncommon for the post of First Sea Lord to be held by a politician rather than a navy man. In such circumstances, the senior naval officer on the Admiralty Board was employed by the First Sea Lord in an advisory capacity. In this instance, Charles Yorke's advisor was Admiral Bartholomew Dalryde.

From midshipman to admiral, Dalryde had served his country with distinction. His first command, the frigate *Audacious*, had been gained at the age of twenty-four. Since then, he had fought in the American War of Independence, served under Hood in the Mediterranean and with Nelson at Cape St Vincent and Trafalgar.

"His name is Hawkwood."

"Hawkwood?" The chin of the second man seated at the broad table came up sharply.

The First Sea Lord fixed the speaker with a stern eye. "You *know* him, Blomefield?"

Thomas Blomefield, Inspector General of Artillery and Head of the Ordnance Board, frowned. In his late sixties, he was the oldest man present. In many respects his career mirrored that of the Admiral. Blomefield had begun his service as a cadet at Woolwich Military Academy. He, too, had fought in the American War, suffering wounds at Saratoga. It had been Blomefield who'd commanded the artillery during the Copenhagen expedition. His speciality was armaments. The Ordnance Board controlled the supply of guns and ammunition to both the army and the navy. As well as controlling the distribution of the guns, Blomefield also designed them. Many of his designs had become the standard pattern used on board ships of the line.

"There's something about the name," Blomefield's brow

63

furrowed. He looked at Read. "How long has he been with you?"

A sixth sense warned Read that he might be straying into potentially dangerous waters, but it was too late to retract. The truth would out anyway, given time. "Not long. A little over a year."

"And before then?"

"He saw service in the military."

Blomefield stiffened. Read could tell that somewhere in the dark recesses of the Inspector General's brain a light had suddenly dawned.

"Hawkwood?" Blomefield repeated the name and sat up suddenly. "Of the 95th?"

Read said nothing.

"I'll be damned!" Blomefield said.

An expression of displeasure flitted across the Admiral's face. Dalryde was a strict church-goer who disapproved of strong language, especially when it involved taking the Lord's name in vain. At sea, his reputation as a disciplinarian had been founded upon an unhealthy appetite for flogging any luckless seaman he overheard blaspheme. It was said that his appointment to the Admiralty Board had been met with considerable relief by the officers and men serving under his direct command.

"Would the Inspector General care to share his knowledge?" The First Sea Lord turned flinty eyes towards his fellow Board member.

Blomefield looked towards Read as if seeking his approval to continue, but the Chief Magistrate's face remained neutral.

"I was merely thinking, if it is the same man, he has rather an interesting past."

"Explain."

Blomefield, obviously wishing he'd held his tongue, hesitated fractionally before replying. "There was an incident during his army service, I seem to recall. An affair of honour. He, er . . . killed a fellow officer."

As Blomefield shifted uneasily in his seat, the First Sea Lord turned to James Read in bewilderment. "Is this true?"

The Chief Magistrate nodded. "The Inspector General is quite correct."

"And you were aware of his past *before* you recruited him?"

"Naturally. I vet all my officers with the utmost care."

The First Sea Lord stared aghast. "Good God, man! I'm due to report to the Prime Minister and the Home Secretary later this morning. How the devil do you expect me to tell them that the officer we've assigned to the investigation was a common soldier who once killed a man in a duel? Answer me that!"

"A *common* soldier?" Read responded quickly. "Hawkwood was an uncommonly fine officer, and I hardly need remind you, my lord, that the Rifle Company's reputation is second to none."

"I am quite familiar with their reputation," the First Sea Lord replied tartly. "And I'm equally aware that certain accounts of their activities have been less than favourable."

The Chief Magistrate pursed his lips. "I concede their tactics lean towards the unorthodox. Nevertheless —"

"Unorthodox?" Yorke rasped. "Unorthodox is naught but

a highfalutin' term for undisciplined. Why, I understand the officers even drill alongside the men!"

"But they achieve results," Read countered. "Hawkwood's an excellent officer, a shade unconventional in his methods, perhaps, but it has long been my experience in dealing with lawbreakers that the end quite often justifies the means."

The First Sea Lord stared at the Chief Magistrate aghast. His mouth opened and closed soundlessly. He appeared lost for words.

"You've got to admit," Blomefield broke in, "there is a kind of justice to it. Set a killer to track down a brace of murderers. Why, I'd say the fellow's ideally suited to the task. Mind you, I confess I'm curious to know how you came by him."

There was a half-smile on the Inspector General's face. Read realized that Blomefield was offering him an opening.

"He was recommended," Read said.

The Inspector General raised a quizzical eyebrow.

"By Colquhoun Grant."

The Inspector General gave a sharp intake of breath. Blomefield had a right to be impressed. Colquhoun Grant was one of Wellington's most experienced exploring officers. Exploring officers operated behind enemy lines, observing the enemy's strength and troop movements. Revered by Wellington, Grant was the chief liaison between the *guerilleros* and the Duke's intelligence service and, despite the clandestine nature of his work, or possibly because of it, was well known in military circles.

"I'll be damned," Blomefield murmured. "So, the rumours *were* true. Your man *did* take to the hills." The Inspector

General turned to the First Sea Lord and smiled. "Well, it'd take a braver man than me to argue with Captain Grant, my lord. What say you?"

The remark was rewarded with a glare from Charles Yorke. The Inspector General grinned.

Significantly, none of the Board ventured to enquire of James Read how he came to be acquainted with Wellington's senior intelligence officer. They probably knew better than to ask, for it had long been rumoured that Chief Magistrate Read's responsibilities extended beyond those of a purely domestic nature. There had been whispers of links between Bow Street and a number of government departments, not all of them available to public scrutiny. The word *Spymaster* hovered on some lips, but such was the nature of the murky world of espionage, that the truth of these rumours could never be confirmed. But then, more pointedly, they had never been denied either.

"As a matter of interest, this duel you mentioned, may one enquire as to the identity of the man he killed? You didn't say." The question was posed by Dalryde.

A nerve flickered along James Read's cheek. "His name was Delancey. A nephew to the Duke of Rutland."

"And not greatly missed, as I recall," Blomefield murmured.

Dalryde raised an eyebrow. "Rather a harsh judgement."

The First Sea Lord fixed the Inspector General with a baleful stare. "Indeed. The family is, by all accounts, an honourable one. And what was that about the man taking to the hills? I'd say the Admiral and I were due some sort of explanation, wouldn't you, Blomefield? Chief Magistrate? *Anybody?*"

Blomefield looked towards James Read, as if seeking guidance. There was a pause, then the Chief Magistrate nodded imperceptibly.

Thomas Blomefield collected his thoughts. "It was Talavera," he said eventually.

The First Sea Lord frowned. "The 95th were with Crauford, weren't they? I thought the column missed the fight; didn't arrive until the next day."

Blomefield nodded. "That's true, but Hawkwood wasn't with the main column. Seems that Wellington had asked for a handful of riflemen to accompany the advance guard. Old Nosey wanted to see if their reputation was justified. Hawkwood was one of the chosen few." Blomefield smiled. "He has the irritating habit, it appears, of being in the right place at the right time."

"Evidently," the First Sea Lord muttered, clearly not sharing Blomefield's sense of humour. "So, what happened?"

The Inspector General hesitated, then said, "It was following the Frog assault by Lapisse and Sabastiani, when they were repulsed by Sherbrook's division. You recall how the Guards and the Germans over-ran themselves? Crossed the river in pursuit?"

The First Sea Lord nodded wordlessly. The circumstances of the battle had been covered in the newspapers and were well known, except, apparently, for Hawkwood's contribution. Which was probably just as well.

"It was Captain Hawkwood who advised the Guards' major commanding the flank to hold his ground. Told him it would be unwise to follow. If they crossed the river, they'd run the risk of being cut off. Turned out the major was a

68

fellow called Delancey, nephew to . . . well, you know who. Hawkwood might just as well have shown a red rag to a bull. No way was a captain going to tell a major, let alone a future peer of the realm, what he should or shouldn't do. Delancey ignored the warning. And it happened just the way Hawkwood said it would. No sooner were the guards across the river than the Frogs counterattacked.

"It was a bloody disaster, of course. Not only did they open up a hole in our line, but the guards lost more than a quarter of their men. If it hadn't been for Wellington sending in Mackenzie's brigade to fill the gap, we'd have been done for."

Blomefield shook his head. "Mackenzie died, of course, along with Lapisse, which I suppose was a kind of justice, but it was a close-run thing and no mistake.

"Anyway, the way I heard, at the end of the day, our Captain Hawkwood sought out Delancey and confronted him. Accused him of reckless behaviour and complete disregard for the lives of his men. In short, told him he was a bloody idiot and a disgrace to the uniform, and it would have been a blessing all round if he'd been among the poor bastards who hadn't made it home. Bad enough man to man, of course, except this was in full view of Delancey's friends. Only one thing to do and that was to call Hawkwood out."

The First Sea Lord looked as if he was about to speak, but Blomefield beat him to it. "Oh, I know, regulations. Duelling strictly forbidden and all that, but for Delancey this was an affair of honour. Insult to the family name and so forth."

"And Hawkwood killed him," the First Sea Lord said bluntly.

"Aye. Shot him dead. Straight through the heart. Not only is our man undoubtedly a crack shot with a rifle, he can use a pistol as well."

"And no one tried to stop it?"

Blomefield shook his head. "Delancey's friends probably thought the affair was a foregone conclusion, thought Delancey would best the upstart. Turns out they were wrong. Only one outcome of course: court martial. I understand there were those who wanted Hawkwood sent back to Horseguards in chains and tried for murder, but nothing came of it." Blomefield dropped his voice low. "I did hear it was Wellington himself who intervened."

"How so?" Dalryde asked.

Blomefield shrugged. "No one knows for certain. When Hawkwood was cashiered it was generally assumed he'd be shipped back to England, but that didn't happen." Blomefield cast a sideways glance at the Chief Magistrate.

"So what became of him?"

Blomefield pursed his lips. "There was a rumour he'd upped and joined the *guerrilleros*."

"The Spanish?" The First Sea Lord's eyes widened.

"Went to fight with them in the mountains. He could speak the lingo, you see. French, too, it was said." Another look towards James Read. "Whether it was with Wellington's blessing, I wouldn't know. I believe it was hinted that a man of Hawkwood's experience would be better employed fighting the French than returning to England. It could be Wellington was planning to use him in some liaison capacity

– that's where your man Grant comes in, I'm thinking." The Inspector General frowned. "I did hear another rumour that a number of his company deserted the ranks to join him. A sergeant and a brace of chosen men. Whatever the circumstances, the word was that Captain Hawkwood disappeared off the face of the earth. Until now, that is."

There was a long silence during which the Admiral regarded James Read gravely. "That's quite a story," he said, finally. "And yet you're telling us you have faith in this Hawkwood fellow? I would remind you this is more than a mere criminal matter. We are concerned with nothing less than the defence of the realm."

"I have the utmost confidence in *Officer* Hawkwood," Read said firmly. "He's my best thief-taker. His contacts within the criminal fraternity are considerable. If anyone can track the villains to their lair, it is he."

There followed several moments of reflection while the First Sea Lord exchanged exasperated glances with Blomefield and Dalryde. Finally, he sighed heavily. "Very well, Read. It seems we've little choice but to accept your recommendation. Let's see what the fellow can do. However, I'll require you to keep the Board informed on a daily basis. Is that understood?"

Read inclined his head. "As you wish."

Whereupon the First Sea Lord pointed a blunt finger towards James Read's chest. "But you had better be right, sir. Because God help you if your man lets us down. In fact," he added with emphasis, "God help us all."

*   *   *

The girl couldn't have been more than twelve or thirteen, but the look in her eyes was as old as time. She had gazed up at him, a sly expression on her grubby face, before running her tongue suggestively between parted lips. Then she'd said simply, "Jago sent me."

She walked beside Hawkwood, a barefoot waif in a threadbare dress. Hawkwood was conscious of the looks the pair of them were attracting, the knowing grins, the nudges and winks. The girl was aware of them, too. She'd have to be blind not to be. But she seemed unconcerned. It was, no doubt, something she'd grown used to.

Along Great Earl Street, through the squalor of Seven Dials, towards the church of St Giles; she was leading him on a merry dance through the back alleyways. Hawkwood presumed this was in case they were being followed. It was a precaution he'd expected.

At the corner of the street, in the shadow of the church tower, she had taken hold of his sleeve and in a thin voice had said, "Stay close."

It had been a warning, not an invitation.

Nearly a full day had passed before he had been contacted. He had been prepared for that and had used the intervening time to track down the officer commanding the horse patrol that had interrupted the coach robbery and put the two highwaymen to flight.

Lomax, the officer in charge of the patrol, was an ex-major of dragoons. Meeting the man for the first time, Hawkwood had been unprepared for the sight that met his gaze. He knew that revulsion must have shown momentarily on his face but, having received no prior warning, there was nothing he could have done to prevent it.

Almost the entire right side of Lomax's face, from brow to throat, was a mass of scar tissue. It was as if half of the major's face had been turned inside out. The eye had gone. The socket was a crater of ragged flesh while the lower jaw, from cheek to jowl, was as fissured and pitted as if it had been scourged with a branding fork.

Hawkwood, trying hard not to avert his eyes, had steeled himself and listened to the major's description of events.

It had been luck rather than judgement that had found the horse patrol on the heath at the same time that the robbery was taking place. If the mail coach hadn't been delayed by the storm, Lomax and his riders might have missed the incident altogether. Lomax explained how he had directed two men to remain with the coach while he and the rest of his patrol had given chase. They had managed to track the robbers for a mile or so before conceding defeat. They hadn't been able to compete with the driving rain, which had, to all intents and purposes, rendered the fleeing highwaymen completely invisible.

About the only information Lomax had been able to reveal was that their quarry was last seen in the Bermondsey area, heading north towards the city. Which meant they could have taken any one of a dozen routes. Suppressing his disappointment, Hawkwood had thanked Lomax for his time. In truth it was as much as he had expected.

It had been at the moment of parting when Lomax had said, hesitantly, "There's something I'd like you to know. I was at Talavera with the 23rd, under Anson. I . . . that is . . .

we . . ." Lomax took a deep breath. "What I mean is . . . the Delancey boy was a poor officer, not much liked by all accounts, and it was a damned fool thing he did; a waste of too many brave men. You said what had to be said and you did what had to be done. There were those of us who thought you deserved better." The words had come out in a rush. Lomax had shrugged awkwardly. "Anyway, I just wanted you to know."

At which point the ex-dragoon had fallen silent, his good eye cast down at the ground, as if embarrassed by his own frankness.

So, that was how he had come by the dreadful disfigurement, Hawkwood realized, remembering the dreadful aftermath of the battle.

Many soldiers had died at Talavera, on both sides, not all of them by feat of arms. Another enemy had been present that day, an enemy common to both sides, a pitiless enemy that had attacked without mercy, laying waste all that stood before it.

Fire.

Perhaps it had been a stray spark from a musket or the heat from a cannonball that had ignited the tinder-dry grass, no man knew for certain. Whatever the cause, the result had been terrible to behold. The flames, fanned by the midsummer breeze, had spread with extraordinary speed and fury, consuming all in their path. Men had been engulfed where they lay, the wounded as well as the dead. The screams of the burning men had been clearly heard over the crackle of the flames. The sights and sounds and the smell of roasting flesh had lived with Hawkwood for months afterwards.

Lomax must have been one of those trapped on the field. By some miracle he had survived, but at an appalling cost.

"I was wounded and trapped under my horse," Lomax said, as if reading Hawkwood's thoughts. "Couldn't move, y'see." The major's good eye glistened as he remembered. "Damnedest thing, but it was a Frog officer who pulled me free. Heard me yelling. My horse was charcoal by the time he dragged me out. Which is what I would have been if he hadn't got to me in time." Lomax shook his head at the memory. "A bloody Frenchie! Who'd have thought it?"

As the major recounted the story, Hawkwood looked down and saw for the first time the full extent of Lomax's injuries. He tried to imagine the man's pain, what he must have gone through.

"Couldn't carry on, of course," Lomax said. "Could still ride a horse, but a cavalryman ain't much use if he can't swing a weapon at the same time." He held up his right hand, which didn't resemble a hand so much as a blackened claw. "Can just about pick my bloody nose, if I put my mind to it." Lomax's ruined mouth split into a travesty of a smile.

It must have taken a great deal of effort, Hawkwood knew, for the man to say what he had. Even before the fire, the 23rd Light Dragoons had faced their own demons during the battle. Through mistake and misfortune, less than half the regiment had returned from the fight.

But for all Lomax's well-intentioned words, the past could not be rewritten. Hawkwood had left that life behind. Now he marched to a different drum. On this occasion, it was leading him along a path he did not relish taking. A pilgrimage to a place whose very name was a mockery. A crawling cesspit known as the Holy Land.

The St Giles Rookery was a world within a world. Bounded by Great Russell Street to the north, Oxford Street in the west and Broad Street to the south, and occupying nearly ten acres, it was a festering sore deep in the heart of the city.

Built on a foundation of poverty and vice, its impregnability lay in the sheer congestion of its dilapidated buildings, narrow alleyways, yards and sewers. The wretched tenements with their soot-blackened tiles made the Widow Gant's miserable lodging house appear a palace in comparison. Between them ran dark passages, some so low and narrow it was impossible for two people to walk abreast. Entry into this rat-run could be gained from a hundred directions by way of the dives and alleys around Leicester Square and the Haymarket and from the dank tunnels leading off Regent Street. To the east lay a timber yard, beneath which, it was rumoured, there existed a passage that ran all the way to High Holborn.

It had been christened the Holy Land by its inhabitants: Irish Catholic immigrants for the most part, though over the years outcasts of a different kind had found sanctuary within its stinking slums. Murderers, deserters, beggars and whores, along with the poor and the hungry, had all sought to establish some kind of haven for themselves away from the prying eyes and unwelcome attention of the Parish Officers and the police. Free from the constraints of conventional society, the inhabitants of the Holy Land had set up their own kingdom, their own laws, their own courts, their own form of justice and punishment. Any representatives of officialdom who chose to venture into the St Giles Rookery did so at their peril.

The girl's name was Jenny. She had no mother or father, at least not that she could remember. She was just one of the thousands of children who lived on the streets and who scratched a living by their wits or, as in Jenny's case, by selling their bodies.

Hawkwood could feel the eyes on him as he and the girl picked their way along the overflowing gutter that was the entry point into the rookery. The watchers hovered in worm-eaten doorways and hid behind windows draped with rags, their lifeless faces as grey as brick dust, eyes dark with distrust. Everywhere there were signs of deprivation; mounds of rotting waste, human and animal; dampness and decay.

Somewhere, a woman screamed, the sound rising in a wavering note of terror from a bleak alley, before ending abruptly. Another voice, male, bawled an obscenity. There followed a crash and a squeal. The girl clutched Hawkwood's sleeve. As the scream was cut off, Hawkwood felt the girl's grip tighten. For all her brashness, she was still a child, susceptible to fear and dread.

A figure slouched in an open doorway, eyeing their approach. It was only as they drew closer that Hawkwood saw the apparition was female. As they passed, the woman pulled aside her shawl and lifted her tattered skirt to reveal her nakedness. Her breasts and legs were the colour of fish scales and covered in welts. She threw back her head and laughed loudly. "Come on, darlin'! Let the nipper go an' Molly'll show yer what a real woman can do!"

As they walked on, the girl pressed against Hawkwood's side, the whore's raucous laughter following them up the alley.

By now, they were deep inside the rookery and Hawkwood was well and truly lost. The girl had made certain of that by leading him in all directions, sometimes recrossing their path or by doubling back the way they had come. Hawkwood was beginning to doubt he'd ever find his way back to civilization, or at least what passed for it.

The houses were becoming even more closely packed, the streets narrower, the smell much worse. And it was getting darker. He noted there didn't seem to be too many people around. It was as if they had been swallowed up by the encroaching shadows. He wondered how much this was due to his own presence.

Without warning, the girl tugged him sideways. He found himself ducking under a low archway. A flight of stone steps led downwards. A heavy wooden door barred their way. Beyond the door, Hawkwood could hear voices. There were other noises, too, guttural and indistinct, and what sounded like the rasping strains of a fiddle. As the girl knocked on the door, Hawkwood felt the short hairs on the back of his neck begin to prickle. The door opened. The girl pulled him through and Hawkwood was plunged into darkness.

5

It took several seconds for Hawkwood's eyes to adjust, finally allowing him to take stock of his surroundings. The cellar was huge with dung-coloured walls, flagstone floor, low arched roof. At the far end of the room, just discernible through the press of bodies and a swirling fog of pungent tobacco fumes, a short flight of wooden stairs led up to a second level, separated from the rest of the cellar by a wooden rail. A crude counter constructed from empty barrels and bare boards stood along one wall.

The drinkers lounged around rough wooden tables or stood at the counter, bottles and mugs in their hands. The women were as rough-complexioned as the men. Without exception, all were poorly clothed, faces gaunt with hunger or ravaged by drink. A fiddle player was seated in the corner. Several male customers were singing in bawdy chorus, coarse voices slurred with drink.

The rest of the clientele, a score or more, were gathered around the dog pit.

There were at least half a dozen dogs in evidence. Bull terriers, squat, broad, powerful beasts, weighing in at a good forty pounds apiece, bodies crisscrossed with scars, and ear flaps removed to make it more difficult for an opponent to get a grip. A couple of the animals, Hawkwood saw, were taste dogs upon which the fighting dogs served their apprenticeship. They'd had the more vulnerable parts of their anatomy shaved so that the trainee dogs learned to attack specific areas of flesh. At the side of the pit stood barrels of flour, used to separate the dogs during fights. It blocked the nasal passages, forcing the animals to relax their grip in order to breathe, allowing their owners to prise them apart.

The place reeked of tobacco smoke, sawdust, spilt liquor, stale bodies, vomit, and piss.

At Hawkwood's entrance, conversation petered out. The silence, when it came, was so acute it was as if every person in the place was holding his or her breath. Hawkwood felt his skin crawl.

The girl released her grip on his coat. A scrape of a boot from behind made Hawkwood turn. Two men moved to the door, blocking his exit. Each man carried a thick wooden stave. Their gaze was malevolent. Several of the dogs, sensing a stranger and tension in the air, growled menacingly.

"Well now, and what have we got here? Reckon you've taken the wrong turning, squire."

Hawkwood stood perfectly still.

"Christ!" A second voice broke the spell. "I knows 'im. 'E's a bleedin' Runner!"

Several of the men sprang up quickly, chairs scraping. A dog barked, a woman yelped. Candlelight glinted off a knife blade. Hawkwood sensed the girl starting to back away. His first thought was that she had played her part well. A trap had been set and he had walked right into it. He cursed his stupidity. He should have changed his clothes before accompanying the girl. He was too well dressed to be anything but an outsider.

Someone in the gauntlet hawked noisily and spat. A ribbon of mucus struck the floor an inch from Hawkwood's boot. It was as if a signal had been given. Knives and razors were drawn as the men began to close in. Hawkwood could feel the strength of their hatred. He reached for his baton.

"LEAVE 'IM BE!"

The voice came from the top of the stairs. What the speaker lacked in height he made up for in girth, but it was solid muscle, not fat, that gave him his wrestler's build. The face was square and rough-hewn, framed by close-cropped hair the colour of pewter. He would not have been out of place gracing the canvas against the likes of Figg or Reuben Benbow. One hand rested on the rail, the other gripped a heavy blackthorn cudgel. He gazed down at Hawkwood, holding the pose for several seconds without speaking. Then, unexpectedly, his mouth split into a wide, leathery grin and he threw out his arms in a broad expansive sweep.

"Ev'ning, Cap'n! Welcome to Noah's Ark!"

In the eerie glow of the tallow candles, the scar beneath Hawkwood's eye shone white as he breathed a sigh of relief. He waited as the interloper descended the stairs. Hawkwood saw how the other men moved apart to give the man room.

He sensed a subtle change in the mood of the cellar's occupants, watched as expressions shifted from malice and suspicion to surprise and curiosity. The eyes of the dogs gleamed jewel bright.

"Hello, Nathaniel," Hawkwood said. "How are you?"

Still grinning hugely, ex-sergeant Nathaniel Jago, late of His Britannic Majesty's 95th Rifles, held out his hand. "Fit as a fiddle, sir, and you ain't looking so bad yourself, considering."

Hawkwood returned the smile and the grip. Jago's hand was calloused and as hard as knotted rope.

"By God, sir, it's grand to see you, and that's no word of a lie!"

Out of the corner of his eye, Hawkwood noticed that the girl had reappeared at his side. She was staring up at them both.

Jago looked down. "Well done, Jen. Here you are, my love, and don't go spendin' it all at once."

The girl's eyes widened as the coins were pressed into her hand. Then, with an impish grin, she darted away.

"She'll spend it on rotgut, as like as not," Jago said. There was genuine sadness in his voice. He watched the girl go with knowing eyes. "Come on, Cap'n, let's you and me find a bottle and a quiet corner. What'll it be? Gin? Rum? Or how about something special? A drop o' brandy perhaps?" Jago winked conspiratorially. "French, not Spanish. Took a delivery only this morning. Word is it's from Boney's own cellars."

"*French* brandy, Sergeant?" Hawkwood said drily. "I'll pretend I didn't hear that. Anyway, I thought there was a war on?"

82

Jago grinned. "Never let political differences get in the way of business. First rule o' commerce."

Sticking the cudgel in his belt and taking a bottle and two tankards from beneath the counter, Jago led Hawkwood up the stairs to a table at the back of the room. Hawkwood could feel the eyes of every person in the cellar following their progress.

"Ignore 'em," Jago advised. The big man laid his cudgel on the table, then took the bottle and poured a liberal measure of brandy into each tankard. "Novelty'll wear off soon enough."

Hawkwood doubted that. Nevertheless, by the time they had taken their seats the conversation in the rest of the room had resumed. But Hawkwood could still feel eyes burning into his shoulder blades.

Jago raised his mug. "To old times."

Hawkwood returned the toast. The brandy was smooth and warming at the back of his throat. Hawkwood wondered if it really had come from the cellars of the Emperor. And, if so, by what tortuous route had it ended up on this table, in a drinking den in London's most notorious rookery?

There was a silence, then Jago said softly, "I hear you've been busy." The big man took a sip of brandy and sat back. "Been makin' a name for yourself." He put his head on one side and fixed Hawkwood with a leery eye. "I heard tell it was you who closed down the Widow Gant." Jago's expression was all innocence as he added, "An' not before time, too, if you ask me. The way the old bitch used to corrupt young minds and such." He tut-tutted and shook his head at the sheer injustice of it all.

Hawkwood wondered about that. Putting the Widow Gant out of business had probably done all the other criminals in the district a substantial favour. Jago and his confederates would undoubtedly profit from the decrease in competition. Which, come to think of it, might well have accounted for the reason why nobody had bothered to warn the widow about the presence of law officers in the vicinity of her clearing house. Quite obviously, the old adage about there being honour among thieves didn't apply to the denizens of the St Giles Rookery.

Observing his former sergeant, Hawkwood thought that Jago didn't appear to have changed much in the months since he'd last seen him, except for having shed a little more hair and gained a few pounds. In fact, the ex-sergeant appeared to have taken to the civilian life like the proverbial duck to water; the mark of a born survivor.

The son of a farm labourer, raised in an isolated village on the Kent marshes, orphaned after his parents had fallen victim to the cholera, Nathaniel Jago, during his formative years, had turned his hand to many things, not all of them legal – blacksmith, drover, poacher and smuggler – with varying degrees of success, until a chance meeting with a recruiting party at a Maidstone fair had changed his life for ever.

The promise of a fine uniform, a roof over his head, and three square meals a day, not to mention the two guineas he'd receive for signing on, had seemed like a dream come true for a young man, homeless and hungry and only one step ahead of the Revenue. And so it was on a warm afternoon in early summer that Nathaniel Jago had accepted the King's bounty and gone to war. From the lowlands of Flanders to the jungles of the West Indies and the dusty plains of India, Jago had marched and fought his way across the world. From private to sergeant, he'd served his country well.

He'd served Hawkwood well, too.

They'd faced the enemy together under Nelson at Copenhagen, marched with Black Bob Crauford in the Americas and with Moore in Spain and Portugal. Jago had stood with Hawkwood on the ramparts at Montevideo. He'd guarded his back at Rolica and Vimeiro and at Talavera they'd both watched in horror as the Coldstreams and the King's German Legion had fallen victim to the French counterattack.

It was a friendship forged on the squares at Blatchington and Shorncliffe. Since then, Jago had stood by him through ten years of war and skirmish; a staunch ally, sharing canteens on the march across the searing heat of the Spanish plains and shivering under the same blanket in the bone-chilling cold of the mountains. It had been Jago's loyalty to Hawkwood that had caused the sergeant to become a fugitive from justice.

When Hawkwood had taken to the mountains to join the *guerrilleros*, Jago had deserted from the ranks to be with him, an offence for which there could be no reprieve. At the time Hawkwood had been appalled. He had tried to persuade the sergeant to return, but to no avail. Jago had just laughed in his face.

"Too late now, sir," he'd said. "In any case, what would I go back to? The army don't take kindly to deserters, even them that 'as second thoughts. Why, if I was to go back now, they'd either flog me or 'ang me. Seen men flogged and I've seen men 'anged. Not a pretty sight. No, reckon I'll take my chances with you, sir, if it's all the same. Besides, you'll need somebody to watch your back."

"You're a bloody fool, Sergeant," Hawkwood had told him. "The chances are we'll both die in these mountains. Is it worth it?"

"'Tis if we take a few Frenchies along with us," Jago had responded, and then he'd favoured the exasperated Hawkwood with an irrepressible grin. "The army can get along fine without Jago. You, on the other hand . . . well, admit it, Cap'n, you'd miss me if I was gone."

Words uttered in jest, but they had added up to one indisputable fact. For all Hawkwood's attempts to dissuade Jago from following through with his reckless decision, he knew that not having the sergeant by his side would have been tantamount to losing his rifle or his sword. It was inconceivable that Hawkwood should continue his personal war against the French without Jago's support. So Hawkwood had admitted defeat and they had spoken no more of the matter.

Until Hawkwood had made his decision to return to England.

It had been late September. The first snows of winter had begun to settle on the high peaks. Wrapped in blankets around a flickering campfire, Hawkwood had revealed his intentions, and what had surprised him had been the lack of surprise shown by his sergeant. Jago had asked only one question: "When do we leave?"

They'd secured passage on a merchantman bound for

Tilbury. They had been passing the Kent coast, close to the mouth of the Medway, when Jago had jumped ship in the early hours of a chilly dawn. Officially, Jago was still listed as a deserter and it was not unheard of for ships to be met by provost sergeants on the lookout for such individuals. By leaving the vessel before it docked, Jago had pre-empted that possibility. Hawkwood, watching Jago tread water as he made his way ashore, had felt the loss hard but, in retrospect, the sergeant's actions had been understandable.

Given the sergeant's background, Hawkwood had assumed Jago would head for familiar territory, the Kent marshes, there to rekindle his skills in smuggling and other diverse activities. He'd had no fear that Jago would suffer arrest. The sergeant was too cunning for that. By the same token he had not taken it for granted that Jago would try and seek him out. He knew that if Jago felt the need to do so he would.

And that's how it had been. Hawkwood had heard nothing of Nathaniel Jago until, during his first few months as a Runner, he had begun to pick up vague rumours which suggested that Sergeant Jago might well have left the safety of the salt marshes behind him and embarked upon more urban pursuits.

The capital's criminal fraternity was close knit. When Hawkwood's informers began to let slip snippets of information pertaining to the exploits and growing reputation of an ex-soldier who, deep in the rookery, ran a small band of ruffians with what amounted to military precision, he began to pay very close attention.

Not that he should have been that surprised. Jago's child-hood, in the company of tinkers and horse thieves, had served as a fine apprenticeship for his life in the army, where he had gained a name for himself, not only as a first-class soldier but as a scavenger and protector to the men under his command. Twenty years in the military had only served to sharpen those skills. So it was hardly unexpected that he should have continued to utilize the same degree of artistry in his current, albeit dubious, means of employment.

In fact, as Hawkwood had subsequently discovered, Jago had infiltrated the London underworld with considerable success. It was hinted that the sergeant had his fingers in several pies, most of them lucrative; from protection and pilfery to piracy and prostitution, though how much was fact and how much fiction, Hawkwood had been unable to determine. Where rumour led, a grain of truth was gener-ally not far behind. What was certain was that in the short time since his arrival in the rookery Jago had won himself a position of some influence. Whether through the use of brain or brawn, one could only surmise. Knowing Jago as he did, Hawkwood presumed it was a combination of the two. Either way, it placed the ex-soldier in the position of being able to provide Hawkwood with the kind of information he sometimes sought.

There had been occasional meetings over the intervening months, always on Jago's home territory. Nothing personal, Jago had told Hawkwood. Only you could never tell when the provosts were likely to walk round the bloody corner. As Jago had chided softly, "Don't want to be caught with my breeches down, do I, sir?"

And so the partnership had endured, albeit in a somewhat circumspect capacity. A snippet of criminal information here, in exchange for a warning of impending interference from the authorities there. So far, both parties to the agreement had profited.

Jago placed his tankard on the table and leaned forward. "Right, Cap'n, now don't get me wrong. It's not that I ain't pleased to see you, but these old bones tell me this ain't no social visit. I doubt you're here to chat about old times. Strikes me there's something on your mind. You care to tell old Nathaniel what that might be?" The candle flame flickered in a draught. Jago's shadow, cast on the wall behind him, ebbed and flowed, one moment nothing more than a vague shapeless blob, the next a crook-backed goblin about to spring out of the corner of the room.

There was a sudden commotion on the lower floor. The dog fight had resumed. Two animals had been dropped into the straw-littered pit. Snarling and yelping, their smooth-pelted bodies erupted into a frenzy of snapping teeth and gouging claws. Hawkwood turned his head away. "Information."

Jago raised a quizzical eyebrow. "You buyin', or sellin'?"

Hawkwood did not waste time in preamble. "Two nights ago, a coach was held up and robbed on the Kent Road. Two men were killed: the driver's mate and a passenger."

Jago frowned. "And you thought I might have had something to do with it?"

Hawkwood looked at his former sergeant long and hard. "No, but I'm guessing the incident might not have gone unnoticed. Am I right?"

Jago tipped his head to one side. "Could be I did hear something."

"Like what?"

Jago fixed Hawkwood with a steadfast gaze. "You aimin' to bring 'em to justice, Cap'n?"

"Them?" Hawkwood said quickly.

Jago took a sip of brandy and wiped his lips. Hawkwood knew the sergeant was giving himself time to think, weighing his options.

"Two men. Old 'un and young 'un, so I 'eard."

"What else did you hear?"

Jago sighed. "Not much. Only that they ran foul of the Redbreasts and got away with naught but a few trinkets." Jago shook his head. "Hardly worth the bleedin' effort! Bloody amateurs!"

"The passenger was an admiralty courier," Hawkwood said.

"Was he now?" Jago replied, eyes narrowing. "I was wondering why you was so interested. Tell me, what if it had only been the driver's mate that was shot, would you and me be 'avin' this conversation?"

"Murder's a serious business," Hawkwood said. "Doesn't matter if the victim's a prince or pauper. It's not the same as stealing a loaf of bread."

"Try tellin' that to the magistrate," Jago grunted. "It's an 'anging offence, either way."

Hawkwood shook his head. "I'd not begrudge any man who'd steal a loaf to feed his family."

"In that case," Jago murmured, "I'd say you was definitely in the minority." He stared at Hawkwood. "Y'know,

90

Cap'n, strikes me, this is becoming too much of a bleedin' 'abit."

"What is?"

"You comin' and askin' me for favours, Just because you an' me were former comrades in arms don't mean I can be taken for granted."

"I thought you said it was always a pleasure to see me?" Hawkwood grinned.

Jago stared back at him. "Christ, I'll say one thing, you sure ain't lost your sense of humour."

Hawkwood smiled. "I'll not deny that you and me knowing each other makes it easier to ask for favours. You have to use what you've got."

"And right now," Jago said, "all you got is me."

Hawkwood smiled again.

Jago listened as Hawkwood explained how Lomax and his patrol had failed to pick up the highwaymen's trail.

"Bleedin' cavalry!" Jago retorted. "What did you expect? Couldn't find their own arses if they were sitting on 'em!"

An image came to Hawkwood: the face of Lomax, the ex-major of dragoons, mutilated almost beyond recognition. Had Jago seen those ruined features, Hawkwood knew the sergeant would not have been so ready with the slander.

"I'm no informer, Cap'n," Jago said.

"I know that," Hawkwood replied softly.

"So, what we're talking about is our usual arrangement. I scratch your back an' you scratch mine."

There was a moment's pause, followed by a theatrical sigh from Jago. "All right, I'll bite. What do you want me to do?"

91

"Just keep your eyes and ears open. Let me know if anyone tries to fence the goods."

"That's all?" Jago asked doubtfully.

"That's all."

"You do realize it'll play 'avoc with my reputation? Me consortin' with an officer of the law."

"I'm sure you'll survive," Hawkwood said.

A blood-curdling howl rose suddenly from the pit below, followed by a collective groan from the spectators. Jago curled his lip in disgust. "Bloodthirsty sods." He looked on as the defeated dog was hauled out of the pit by its disappointed owner. The dog's flanks were heaving. Blood streamed from more than a dozen bite wounds.

Hawkwood was watching Jago's face so he noticed the shift in eye direction and change in expression. Jago's gaze was centred on the occupants of a nearby table. One man in particular caught his attention. Heavy set, shaven-headed with a dark scowl on a face pitted with smallpox scars, he was staring back with undisguised hostility. A brindle dog lay across his feet; a huge, savage-looking beast, heavy at the shoulder, with a broad muzzle. It appeared to be dozing but, as if sensing the mood in the air, it opened its eyes and raised its massive head. Razor-sharp teeth gleamed brightly.

"You got something to say, Tom Scully?" Jago enquired. "'Cause if you do, best not to keep it bottled up. Best to spit it out, so's it's over and done with."

The big man stiffened. Judging from the uneasy looks he was getting from his companions, he had elected himself spokesman for the group. "'Pears to us you're keepin' bad company, Jago."

"Is that a fact?" Jago responded. "An' what makes you think I give a toss?"

The man's face clouded. He jerked his chin towards Hawkwood. "All of us 'eard Dick Brewer say how he recognized your man. He's the law. A bloody Ratcatcher! So we were curious to know how come you and him are sharing a bottle. Looks from where I'm sitting as if you two are just a mite too close for comfort."

Jago's jaw tightened. "Who I drinks with is my affair, Scully, not yours – nor that of any other man in this room."

" 'Tis if'n he brings the law down on our 'eads."

"That ain't going to happen."

"Who says?"

"I do."

"You?"

"That's right, Scully. Me. You doubting my word?"

Scully, realizing he had backed himself into a corner, looked to his cronies for support. When he discovered none was forthcoming, he turned back and ran a nervous tongue along bloodless lips.

"All I'm sayin' is that it ain't right."

Jago rolled his eyes. "Ain't right? Jesus, Scully! There's lots of things ain't right. Ain't right there's people dying in the streets, ain't right that I 'as to listen to you witter on like a bloody fishwife! Now, less'n you got something constructive to say, I suggest you shut your trap, otherwise you an' me'll be continuing this conversation in that bloody dog pit. You hear what I'm saying?"

There was a tense silence.

"I'm waiting," Jago said.

Scully's jaw twitched. A spark of anger flared in his eyes. "I hear you," he said softly.

"Good," Jago said. "Now, anyone else got anything to say?" He glared at Scully's companions. "No? Well, that's a relief." He turned back to Hawkwood, muttering darkly. "Stupid buggers! Now, where was I?" He raised his mug.

"Who's he?" Hawkwood asked.

"Scully?" Jago spat out the name with contempt and lowered his drink. "He's naught but a lower-deck lawyer. You don't want to pay him no heed."

"Seaman?"

"Aye, and he's a fine one to talk. When it comes to keeping bad company, Scully could write a bleedin' book. That's if the bastard could write in the first place, mind," Jago added with grim humour.

"What's his story?"

Jago stared into his mug before looking up and shrugging dismissively. "Ex-navy. Claims he was a gun captain on the old *Inflexible*." Jago smiled thinly. "One of Parker's bully boys."

"Parker?"

"Aye, you remember. Delegates of the Whole Fleet at the Nore, they called themselves. A right bloody mouthful. Though I knows a better word for 'em."

It came to Hawkwood then. "Mutineer?"

Jago nodded. "One of the ringleaders, so it's said."

It may have seemed ironic that Jago, a deserter, should have cast a mutineer in such a dark light, but Hawkwood knew that in Jago's eyes there was a world of difference between the two.

"So, how come *he* slipped through the net?" Hawkwood asked.

"Ah, now there's a tale, right enough," Jago said. "You recall how I said he was a gunner on the *Inflexible*?"

Hawkwood nodded.

"Well, it were the *Inflexible*'s crew who was last to surrender, all except a dozen or so, Scully included, who wanted to fight on. The rest of the crew, though, had had enough and they locked Scully and his diehards down below. It was while the rest of 'em were waitin' to surrender that Scully and his men climbed out of a gunport and made off in a couple of longboats."

Hawkwood listened as Jago told him how the escapees had made it as far as Faversham, where they had stolen a sloop and set sail for Calais, in the hope of joining the French.

"Reckoned they'd be welcomed with open arms," Jago continued, sitting back in his chair. "Stupid bastards! Soon as they landed, the Frenchies threw them in prison. Probably planned to exchange them for prisoners of war we was holding."

"Is that what happened?"

"Nah, they were freed after a time. Most of 'em were allowed to sign on with Frog privateers."

"Including Scully?"

"That's the way he tells it. Served for eight years before he made a run for it. Jumped ship off Martinique, made his way back 'ome and took up the smuggling game. He's from my neck of the woods – Sheerness. Knows the coast like the back of his hand, the best places for offloading and lying up to avoid the Revenue. Mind you, you got to admire the bugger's application. Can't be too many who've gone over the side from two navies!" Jago snorted with contempt.

"He's a fair way from home," Hawkwood said.

"Ain't we all," Jago murmured. His eyes roamed the cellar, missing nothing. "Fact is, Spiker's one o' the best light horsemen on the river."

There were two kinds of horsemen. Heavy horsemen was the name given to thieves who operated during daylight hours. Light horsemen plied their trade under cover of darkness: professionals who worked in gangs, usually with the aid of copemen, who received and distributed the stolen goods. Their hunting ground was the river and the vessels that sailed upon it. Their knowledge of the moon and tides enabled them to prey on the barges and lighters. Their method was to cut the chosen vessel adrift, allowing it to drift downstream to a chosen spot where they would run it aground and strip it of its cargo. It was a good living for those with nerve and the right connections.

"Why 'Spiker'?" Hawkwood asked.

Jago gave a grim little smile. "We call 'im that on account of he's got an interestin' way of dealing with people who cross him. What you might call 'is trademark . . ."

Hawkwood waited.

"Most men'll use their fists to settle an argument, or a blade, like as not." Jago indicated the table over Hawkwood's shoulder. "Your man Scully uses a marline-spike. Fearsome weapon in the wrong 'ands," Jago commented reflectively.

Not that the disclosure needed embellishment, certainly

not as far as Hawkwood was concerned. He had ceased to be surprised at the variety of means by which the more murderously inclined members of society were prepared to perform grievous bodily harm upon their fellow men – or women and children, come to that. The ex-seaman, Scully, was just another piece of human jetsam to have drifted in with the tide. The capital's rookeries were full of men like Scully. Rootless, violent types, willing to use any means of intimidation to further their own ends.

"As an abidin' 'atred of authority, does our Spiker," Jago went on, warming to his subject. "Wanted to string the *Inflexible*'s officers from the nearest yardarm, so I 'eard. Funnily enough, it was Parker who stopped him. Though I did 'ear he killed an officer before he went over the side o' that Frog ship he was on. Stove his 'ead in, poor bugger, an' speared his 'ands to the deck."

A cackle of laughter erupted from the table behind and Jago's face darkened. He drained his mug. "You want toppin' up?"

Hawkwood shook his head. "Time I was going. My guess is I've overstayed my welcome."

"Then you'll need someone to guide you back," Jago advised. "It's getting dark out. We don't want you roamin' the streets and getting into trouble, not with this lot around. You never know who you're likely to run into. Why, I'd never live with myself if you was robbed on your way home." The ex-sergeant winked broadly.

Jago beckoned with his finger. A small figure detached itself from the cluster of bodies around the dog pit and scampered up to the table. Hawkwood assumed the girl,

Jenny, had been pressed into service once more, but he was mistaken. The small, tousle-haired, stick-thin figure who answered Jago's summons was male and instantly familiar. It was the boy he had last seen fleeing Mother Gant's lodging house, the one who had so deftly relieved Major Lawrence of his watch and chain. Somehow, somewhere between the Widow Gant's and the Bridewell House of Correction, young Tooler the pickpocket had managed to do a runner.

Tooler favoured Hawkwood with a cheeky grin and a mock salute and looked to Jago for orders, while Hawkwood promised himself a serious talk with Constable Rafferty.

Jago placed a hand on the boy's shoulder. "You're to see him safely home, Tooler. And that means all the way, mind. I don't want you runnin' off and leavin' him at the mercy of footpads and ne'er-do-wells. You got that?"

Tooler nodded obligingly.

"And I want you to come straight here afterwards. No dilly-dallying along the way. No puttin' your sticky fingers where they don't belong, like in other people's pockets, f'r instance. Understood?"

Hawkwood could see that Jago was enjoying himself, but he had to concede that had he been in Jago's position he'd probably have milked the situation for all it was worth too.

Jago held out his hand. "Mind how you go, Cap'n."

"You, too, Nathaniel."

The pressure in Jago's grip confirmed to Hawkwood the bond between them. Translated, it meant that if Jago received any information about the coach robbery, he would pass it on.

Jago watched Hawkwood and the boy make their way down the stairs, sensed the relaxation of tension in the cellar as the tall Runner departed.

At the next table two men rose to their feet.

Jago's voice was a growl of warning. "You hold it right there, Asa Hawkins. You, too, Will Sparrow. I've a feeling you gentlemen are bent on mischief. Am I right, Spiker? Your boys weren't plannin' an ambush, by any chance?"

"We was only goin' to take a piss, Jago. That's all," the man called Hawkins whined.

"An' I suppose Sparrow was goin' to hold it for you and give it a wee shake afterwards, right? Sit down, both of you. You can hang on a while longer. What about you, Spiker? You got any plans to answer the call o' nature?"

"You think you're so bleedin' clever, Jago, don't you?" Scully fixed Jago with a fierce glare. "That bastard's a Runner. He's got no right comin' in 'ere. Do you know how many of our lot he's taken down?"

"Can't say as I do, offhand," Jago said. "But then, anyone who's stupid enough to get themselves caught probably deserves it. And is that why you were sending these idiots out after 'im? To teach 'im a lesson? Not prepared to do your own dirty work? You 'ave to employ others to do it for you? Maybe I should have let 'em go. They'd have been taught a pretty lesson."

"We could have taken him," Sparrow, the slighter of the two men, said truculently. "No trouble."

Jago threw Sparrow a pitying look. "Don't make me laugh. You wouldn't 'ave stood a chance. Believe me, I did you a favour."

"He's only one man," Scully grated.

Jago stiffened. "That he is, but let me tell you about that one man, Spiker. That man was a soldier, an officer in the 95th Rifles. You've heard of them, I take it? Hardest regiment in the bloody army. He's killed more men than you've supped pints of ale, and he's the best officer I ever served under. You saw that scar below his eye? He got that pullin' me out of the way of a Frog Hussar. Took a cut from a sabre that was meant for me. That makes him more of a man than you'll ever be, Spiker. So while he's under this roof, he's under my protection. You got that? And anyone here who thinks different'll 'ave me to answer to." Jago's right hand curled around the blackthorn staff. "*Is that clear?*"

The men around the table shifted uneasily. All except Scully, whose eyes grew as black and as hard as stone. Scully stood up. His bald head and pockmarked face gave him a forbidding appearance. The chair on which he had been sitting fell backwards with a clatter. The sudden movement and noise brought the brindle dog to its feet. Scully unfastened the leather strap that anchored the dog to the table. The beast growled in anticipation, a low rumble at the back of its throat.

"One day, Jago, you and me are going to have a serious talk, and then we'll really see who's king o' the castle." Scully jerked hard on the leash and turned away.

Jago watched Scully lead the animal towards the pit on the ground floor. "Any time, Spiker," he murmured quietly to himself. "Any bloody time."

6

"I'm sending you, Hawkwood, because there's no one else available. Besides," James Read said wearily, looking up from his desk, "I'd have thought you would welcome the diversion."

Hawkwood gazed disconsolately down at the Chief Magistrate, knowing from the latter's expression that this was an argument he was unlikely to win.

The diversion, as Read had called it, was a grand ball. It was often the case that Runners were assigned to attend such entertainments to guard against thieves and other miscreants who might view the event as an opportunity to indulge themselves in both petty and grand larceny.

On this occasion, the ball was being held at the London home of Lord Mandrake. Lord Mandrake, who held estates in Cheshire and the Americas, had made his fortune through trade and banking and was a well-entrenched member of the establishment. He was a confidant of several members of

101

parliament, including the Foreign Secretary. There was a rumour, Read told Hawkwood, that the Prince Regent might well put in an appearance.

On hearing this, Hawkwood groaned inwardly, He had attended similar functions and detested them with a vengeance. He would rather have faced a frontal assault from a detachment of French lancers.

"What about Redfern?"

This time Read did not bother to look up. "Redfern's in Manchester. A forgery case. He's unlikely to return in the immediate future."

"Lightfoot, then?"

"Protection duty at the Bank of England, overseeing the transportation of a bullion consignment."

With studied deliberation, James Read laid down his pen and sighed audibly. "Hawkwood, you are perfectly aware how many special constables I have at my disposal. Precious few. Seven, to be precise, including yourself. Now, whilst I'm not obliged to furnish you with details of their individual assignments, I will do so, if it will help to ease your troubled mind.

"Redfern and Lightfoot, we've already mentioned. George Ruthven is in Dublin, attempting to serve a warrant on the embezzler, Patrick Doherty. McNiece is investigating a double murder in York. Lacey is recovering from wounds sustained in the arrest of the Taplin brothers –"

"And Warlock?" Hawkwood enquired desperately, sensing as he did so that it was a futile exercise.

"Also unavailable. The Woodburn case."

"Woodburn?" Hawkwood queried, mystified; though

there was no reason why the name should have meant anything. Given the demands of the job, each Runner was usually too concerned with his own workload to take note of a fellow officer's assignments.

"The missing clockmaker."

Hawkwood feared he had misheard. "You've sent Warlock off to look for a *clockmaker?*"

"Not just any clockmaker," Read responded sharply, with just a hint of rebuke. "Josiah Woodburn is a master craftsman. A clockmaker to the nobility. Examples of his work grace half the salons in London, not to mention the grandest houses in the country."

"And he's disappeared?" Hawkwood said hollowly.

"It would appear he failed to return home from his workshop last evening."

"Probably spent the night tumbling some Haymarket doxy and lost track of the time."

There was a pause. A small nerve tremor dimpled the flesh on the magistrate's left cheek.

"Hardly," Read said. "The man is sixty-eight years old and a strict Presbyterian."

The Chief Magistrate frowned suddenly, drew a watch from his pocket and compared the hour with that shown by the tall clock in the corner of the room. "Though perhaps it's Officer Warlock's timekeeping that has gone astray. He was supposed to call in and make his report but he has not yet done so. Most curious. It's not like him to be tardy." The frown disappeared, to be replaced by a beatific smile. "So, as you can see, Hawkwood, there's no choice in the matter. You *shall* go to the ball."

The expression on Hawkwood's face spoke volumes.

"Frankly," Read said, putting his watch away, "I would have thought you'd be flattered."

"I should? Why?"

"You were requested by name. Upon the recommendation, I understand, of Sir John Belvedere. It seems Sir John was most impressed by the way you conducted yourself at his wife's recent birthday celebrations."

Hawkwood recalled the evening a month previously: a well-attended but dull affair in Chelsea, enlivened only by an ill-fated attempt to remove, by stealth, Sir John's birthday gift to his wife; an ornate and expensive necklace, reputedly once owned by the wife of the first Duke of Marlborough.

Hawkwood had run the thief to ground, ruining a good pair of breeches in the process. In retrospect, though, he had to admit that the night had not been without its reward. Sir John had been effusive with his thanks and generous in his compensation, to the extent that it had almost restored Hawkwood's faith in human nature. But he still loathed the pomp and ceremony.

"What about the coach robbery?" Hawkwood said, grasping at one final straw.

"I think it most unlikely that a breakthrough will be forthcoming between now and breakfast," Read said. "Don't you?"

The Chief Magistrate pursed his lips and sat back. "Your lack of enthusiasm confounds me, Hawkwood. Had any of the others been available for duty, they would probably be fighting to attend."

Read was pointing out, none too subtly, a long accepted understanding. A Runner's salary verged on the pitiful; just over a guinea a week, supplemented by equally meagre expenses should the assignment entail travel to a distant part of the country. A Runner also received a share of the parliamentary awards given for the seizure and conviction of criminals, but by the time the awards were split among the arresting officers the final sum usually amounted to little more than small change. Most Runners made their money through private enterprise; as bodyguards to royalty and politicians, or by hiring themselves out to institutions and wealthy private citizens for investigative and security work.

"Now," Read continued, ignoring Hawkwood's pained expression, "while I'm sure you have your reasons for not wishing to attend, they are in this instance irrelevant for, had the others been here, I would still have assigned you, seeing as you're the only one of my officers who speaks French."

It was Hawkwood's turn to frown.

The Chief Magistrate sat back in his chair. "As you may or may not be aware, Lord Mandrake has gained something of a reputation as a benefactor to the less fortunate members of our society: orphans, widows of the parish, war veterans and so forth. Meritorious causes, one and all. And his good works have not been limited to these shores. His patronage has also extended beyond our nation's boundaries."

Hawkwood's attempt to appear interested was only marginally successful.

"Émigrés, Hawkwood. One of his most ardent suitors is the Comte d'Artois."

Hawkwood knew all about the Comte d'Artois, brother

to Louis XVIII. In the early months of the Terror, the Comte had fled to England to escape the guillotine and set himself up as leader of the French in exile. Determined to see the monarchy restored, d'Artois and his compatriots, using funds donated by British sympathizers, had been running military training camps at Romsey, on the south coast, in preparation for the eventual overthrow of Emperor Bonaparte.

"I'm told it's Lord Mandrake's desire that tonight's ball will help forge even stronger links between Britain and the legitimate Bourbon government. It's expected that several of the Comte's inner circle will be attending the festivities. Hence the request for a French speaker. I need not remind you," Read continued sternly, "that you are expected to conduct yourself in a manner befitting an officer of the law."

The Chief Magistrate scribbled on a card. "Here's the address. You are to present yourself without delay."

Mandrake House was situated on the corner of St James's Place and, although the long shadows of evening were still some way off, the mansion was already lit as brightly as a chandelier. Hawkwood, having presented his credentials to Lord Mandrake's secretary, was watching the scurry of the servants with some amusement. He knew it wouldn't be long before the first guests began to arrive. The string of carriages would probably stretch around the corner to Pall Mall and beyond. It was imperative, therefore, that Mandrake House was at its most resplendent. So the mirrored walls gleamed, the lights twinkled like stars in the firmament, the gold and silver columns glowed, and the servants ran hither and thither like frightened mice in a granary.

The secretary returned. "His lordship will receive you in the library."

Hawkwood had never met Lord Mandrake, but of the two men who were present in the comfortable book-lined room, it was not difficult to pick out his employer for the evening. Tall and rotund, with a hooked nose and red-veined cheeks, Lord Mandrake exuded authority and bonhomie in equal measure. He greeted Hawkwood with bluff cordiality.

"Ah, you'll be Read's man. Hawkwood, isn't it?"

Hawkwood confirmed his identity and looked beyond Lord Mandrake's shoulder towards the room's other occupant, a thickset man with short, gunmetal grey hair, handsomely attired in formal evening wear, standing by the fireplace, leafing idly, with the help of a conveniently placed candelabra, through the pages of a small leather-bound volume of de Montaigne's essays. The choice of reading matter suggested to Hawkwood that this was probably one of his lordship's Bourbon associates.

"Excellent!" Mandrake said. "Now, Magistrate Read's explained what's required of you?"

"Yes, sir."

"Splendid, splendid! I must say, Hawkwood, my friend Belvedere was fulsome in his praise. Tells me you're a damned fine officer. Most reassuring. Not that we're expecting a similar occurrence, of course." Lord Mandrake chuckled before turning to indicate the man by the fireplace, still engrossed in his book. "Oh, by the by, this gentleman is a house guest of mine; the Comte de Rochefort. The Comte's

107

newly arrived from the Continent. Indeed, we're most fortunate in having several of his countrymen and their ladies here with us this evening." Lord Mandrake drew close and spoke in a quiet aside. "I'm afraid the Comte's command of English is lamentably poor, though he assures me he understands it better than he speaks." Lord Mandrake raised his eyebrows questioningly. "You speak French, I believe?"

Again Hawkwood replied in the affirmative.

"Capital!" Lord Mandrake beamed with pleasure. He turned to the man by the fire and spoke in French. His accent was execrable. "Our man here's a special constable, come to make sure no one runs off with the knives and spoons, ha! ha! ha!"

Hawkwood glanced towards the Frenchman. While Lord Mandrake chortled loudly at his own wit, the Comte, sensing he was being addressed, looked up from his book. A pair of pale blue eyes passed over Hawkwood with what looked to be complete indifference, before resuming their study of the printed page.

"So, Officer Hawkwood," Lord Mandrake spoke jovially, "any questions? No? Excellent." Lord Mandrake smiled and indicated his aide who was waiting patiently, framed in the open doorway. "My secretary, Carrington, will see to all your requirements. Anything you need, he will arrange it."

And Hawkwood found himself dismissed. It had been smoothly done.

Lord Mandrake watched Hawkwood's departure with a cool eye before turning to his guest. As the door closed, he addressed the Comte in English. "Well now, there's an interesting fellow."

The Comte closed the book, placed it on top of the mantelpiece, and replied fluently in the same language. "He certainly looks capable enough."

His lordship smiled. "Oh, I'd say he's a deal more than capable. I'm reliably informed he's Read's best man. I'm also told our Captain Hawkwood's a former army officer – the Rifle Corps, no less – with a very impressive record. Brave, intelligent and resourceful."

"A formidable combination," the Comte mused.

"Indeed." Lord Mandrake nodded. He gazed thoughtfully at his guest for several seconds, as if expecting the other to speak, but the Comte had taken up the book of essays once more. Caught at a loss by the Comte's marked lack of response, Lord Mandrake fumbled for his pocket watch and feigned surprise at the time on the dial. "Bless my soul, is that the hour? Here we are, engaging in idle chatter, when I have urgent duties to attend." Lord Mandrake closed the watch lid with a sharp snap. "You'll forgive me, my friend, if I leave you for a time, but I fear there are retainers to harry and guests to welcome. I'm sure you understand."

The Comte de Rochefort waited until Mandrake had departed the room before laying his book down once more. Reaching inside his coat, the Comte removed a thin Moroccan leather case. He took a cheroot from the case and placed it between his lips, then returned the case to his coat pocket. Lighting the cheroot from one of the nearby candles, the Comte inhaled deeply, letting the smoke fill his lungs. He picked a shred of tobacco leaf from his lip and stared into the candle flame. Then, taking the book of essays, he moved to a nearby chair, lowered himself into the soft leather, took a second draw on his cheroot and began to read.

Hawkwood, dressed in black, felt as conspicuous as a crow in a flock of parakeets. The ball was in full spate, with every room in the Mandrake mansion a vibrant swirl of light and colour.

The women's dresses caught the eye at every turn. The current fashion for a high waist and low bodice tended to suit the more slender form and for those ladies who were blessed with attractive figures, the effect was exquisite. Several of the women, confident in their looks and with only a passing attempt at modesty, had elected to wear creations of such finely woven material they were almost transparent. Even though he was forced to admire them from the sidelines, Hawkwood thought it small wonder the men were perspiring like dray horses. The underlying odour of sweat mingled uneasily with the sweeter scents of perfume and eau de cologne.

A jewel thief, Hawkwood reflected, might well have thought he'd died and entered paradise. Diamonds, pearls, rubies and sapphires sparkled in the bright candlelight, their brilliance reflected back a thousand-fold in the huge chandeliers.

The male guests were as glitteringly attired as the women. A substantial number wore uniform, bedecked with all manner of sashes, ribbons, medals and stars. By his own reckoning, Hawkwood estimated that upwards of two score regiments and a scattering of naval personnel were represented. Between them, there was enough gaudy plumage to stock an aviary.

Even the servants were not to be outshone. The liveried, bewigged footmen, who at first glance appeared to outnumber the guests by at least five to one, were adorned with so much gold braid they could well have been mistaken for generals. And generals there were aplenty; along with admirals and luminaries from every tier of nobility.

From his discreet observations, Hawkwood could see that the ball was a great success. It was hard to believe that, less than a mile away, in the pitch-black, rat-infested city slums, entire families were dying of disease and starvation. As to the war with France, despite the presence of so many military personnel, it might just as well have been raging on the moon for all the relevance it appeared to have to the immediate festivities.

While Lord Mandrake's guests disported themselves beneath the bright lights and dined at tables groaning under the weight of enough sumptuous food to feed a small army, British soldiers were dying in Spain. It wasn't the wealth of the rich that Hawkwood detested. It was their indifference.

By the late evening, with most of the guests wined and dined to repletion, the atmosphere had relaxed considerably. In the library, declared a masculine domain for the duration, several games of hazard were in progress. Cigar fumes roiled like cannon smoke, while in the drawing rooms the women had gathered in discreet groups to discuss the eligibility of the younger and more handsome male guests. The strains of a minuet drifted from the ballroom, where the more energetic guests continued to take their turn across the dance floor.

Hawkwood, fortified by a plate of cold roast beef and a

glass of claret, courtesy of Lord Mandrake's well-stocked cellar and an over-friendly and well-endowed kitchen maid, made his way along one of the many long corridors in search of trespassers.

He was turning into one hallway when a young couple suddenly appeared around a corner, hand in hand, giggling in unison, faces flushed with excitement. The man paid Hawkwood no heed but the girl caught the Runner's gaze as she skipped by. She was very pretty, the white feather in her hair bobbing as she ran. It was possible they had taken a wrong turn, but more than likely they were looking for a discreet alcove where they could enjoy each other's company, away from the prying eyes of the girl's chaperone. There had been a precocious glint in the girl's eye that made Hawkwood suspect this was probably not the first time the young lady had managed to slip the leash. Hawkwood grinned inwardly at the thought and left them to their clandestine rendezvous, envying their youth and audacity.

Several women had attracted Hawkwood's attention during his patrols. Some of them, although only glimpsing him in passing, had been astonishingly forward in their appraisal, raising their fans on the occasions he caught their admiring glances, often just slowly enough for him to read the invitation in their eyes and on their lips before anonymity was re-established. Given the quality of the barely concealed charms on display, it was difficult to remain immune. But the job, Hawkwood reminded himself, always came first. Well, nearly always.

Twice during the evening he had spotted the Comte de Rochefort. The first time, the Comte had been on the other side of the room, Hawkwood having espied him through a gap in the crowd, talking to a portly individual dressed in a general's uniform. The second time, he had found himself staring into de Rochefort's calm blue eyes, an experience which he had found faintly disturbing. He didn't know why. The Comte had not openly acknowledged Hawkwood's glance but had held the look for a few seconds before turning his attention to another point in the room. It had been as unsettling as it had been curious.

It was warm inside the house, oppressively so, and the narrow servants' corridors added to the feeling of claustrophobia. In search of a clear head, Hawkwood made his way down a passage towards the rear of the house and let himself on to the first-floor terrace.

The terrace overlooked Green Park. An ivy-covered wall separated the house and gardens from the wide green expanse, but so cleverly was it concealed by trees and shrubbery, it looked as if the grounds extended far beyond their true borders, thus giving the property the feel and appearance of a vast country estate.

The Mandrake family had always been able to afford the best, be it architecture or landscaping, and a great deal of thought had been employed in the layout of the gardens. Thus there was much to please the eye. There were lawns, flower beds, rose-covered terraces, all linked and bisected by gravel pathways bordered by high hedges. Hidden behind the hedges were secluded groves and leafy arbours. There were several fountains and in one corner of the garden there was even a small, intricately patterned maze.

Anticipating that many of his guests would at some point

feel the desire to take the evening air, Lord Mandrake had arranged for the grounds to be illuminated by braziers lining the main pathways. In addition, gaily coloured Chinese lanterns hung from the branches of the trees.

Making his way down the steps from the terrace and along the side of the house, Hawkwood checked the time. It was just past midnight. So far, the assignment had proved singularly undemanding, and for that Hawkwood was exceedingly grateful. The past few days had not been without incident and he was looking forward to the comfort of his own bed. He recalled the laughing eyes of the girl in the corridor and smiled to himself.

It was the sound of hurrying footsteps that broke the spell. By the light of a brazier, Hawkwood saw that it was one of the footmen, not quite running, but clearly agitated nonetheless. Seeing Hawkwood, the footman checked suddenly. "Officer Hawkwood?" The footman's hands fluttered as he spoke. "I fear there's trouble brewing. Some of Lord Mandrake's young gentlemen friends . . ." An expression of anguish moved across the footman's face. "They've been drinking. There's a young lady . . . Please, come quickly . . ."

Hawkwood groaned inwardly. This was all he needed. "All right. Where are they?"

The footman looked behind him and pointed a wavering finger. "By the pavilion. I'm fearful for the lady's honour . . . I . . ."

Hawkwood sighed. "Show me."

They had not gone fifty paces when a movement among the trees to his right caught his eye; a dark, indistinct shadow which hovered briefly at the edge of his field of vision and then was gone. He paused, uncertain. Had he imagined it? Perhaps it had been nothing more than his eyes playing tricks. The night suddenly seemed unnaturally quiet. He took a step forward when a sixth sense made him turn. The footman had gone. Hawkwood looked around. He was alone.

The snap of a twig breaking underfoot made Hawkwood spin. There! Someone moving away behind a bank of tangled foliage. Man or woman, there wasn't enough light beneath the trees to tell the difference. Perhaps it was the footman. He was on the point of calling out when he heard a snort of laughter and what sounded like a cry of distress. He moved forward quickly.

A slatted trellis rose before him, some ten feet high and woven with honeysuckle. The scent of blossom hung heavy in the night air. Through gaps in the trellis he could make out what appeared to be a grassy clearing and the outline of a small wooden structure, painted white.

Rounding the trellis, the summer house came into view; octagonal in design with a gently sloping roof, ringed by a veranda. Several lanterns hung from hooks under the eaves. Hawkwood's appreciation of the architecture was fleeting. Hardly had he taken in the scene when he became aware of a slim figure flying out of the shadows towards him. He had a brief impression of a pair of dark eyes set in an oval face below a crown of raven hair, but by then it was too late. Even as he put out his arms to protect himself, the woman was upon him.

It occurred to Hawkwood that the last woman to have clasped him to her bosom had been the Widow Gant, a far from pleasant experience. The old harpy's foul breath still lingered in his memory. In contrast, the shapely form now struggling in his grip was as far removed from the Widow Gant as was humanly possible, a fact made obvious in the seconds before he relinquished his hold and regained his balance. As he did so he saw the reason for her fear.

He knew their type. He could tell simply by looking at them. Sons of the aristocracy; young, handsome, expensively dressed in their silk knee-breeches and buckled shoes. He had met their kind in the army. The officer corps was rife with them: vain, arrogant young men, commissions secured by virtue of the family name and the depth of their father's purse. They treated the army as a game and the lower ranks with contempt, convinced that advancement was a right rather then a privilege, and secure in the erroneous belief that the world owed them a living. In civilian life, they were no different.

Of the three, it was clear that the one on the right had been drinking. Even if the bottle hadn't been dangling from one hand, the lack of focus in the young man's eyes told its own story, as did the bleary grin on his face. His companions did not appear quite so tipsy, though from their demeanour Hawkwood had no doubt that they, too, had been enjoying Lord Mandrake's generous hospitality.

It was the one holding the bottle who broke the silence.

"I say, Ruthers, old man, looks like we've got company! A bloody servant, no less! Come for a peek, have you? Go on, bugger off! Or else you'll get my boot up your arse!" A shock of wavy hair fell over his eyes as he swayed forward, flagon raised.

Hawkwood said nothing, nor did he retreat. He was aware that the woman had moved to his side. Her gloved fingers grabbed his arm, as if seeking tactile confirmation that protection was at hand. Hawkwood found himself wondering why she was without an escort. He recalled the figure he thought he'd seen among the trees. Perhaps whoever it was had been frightened off or had gone to summon help. If that was the case, Hawkwood wondered what sort of man would leave a woman to the tender mercies of three drunken revellers.

"Don't think the fellow heard you, Giles!" the one on the left drawled. "Obviously deaf as well as stupid!" The speaker, chubby-faced and porcine in stature, cupped his hands around his mouth. "Didn't you hear, my friend? He told you to bugger off!" He laughed and looked to his companions for their approval.

Hawkwood ignored him and turned to the woman. "Are you hurt?"

Silently, she shook her head. She was quite beautiful, Hawkwood saw, with the most expressive dark eyes he had ever seen. A strand of pearls had been woven into her hair. They shimmered in the lantern glow. Her breasts rose and fell under the thin muslin of her gown. Reluctantly, Hawkwood dragged his gaze away.

An inner voice told him that the middle one of the three was the ringleader. He was in his early twenties, with sharp features and a thin, petulant mouth: a young man used to getting his own way. He stared back at Hawkwood, his expression one of acute irritation.

"Well?"

Hawkwood regarded the speaker levelly. "Well, what? Clearly the lady's grown tired of your company. I suggest you and your friends seek your entertainment elsewhere."

The air seemed suddenly still. From the direction of the mansion, muted by the barrier of trees, the sound of music and merriment could be faintly heard. Distant lights glimmered.

The young man's eyes narrowed. "*What* did you say?"

"I thought I was supposed to be the one who was hard of hearing," Hawkwood said.

The speaker raised an imperious eyebrow. "Do you know who I am?"

"No, and I can't say it interests me much, either," Hawkwood said.

The young man gasped, but to Hawkwood's surprise the man on the right, who appeared to have sobered slightly, laughed. "By God, Ruthers, I wonder where Mandrake found this one. He's a surly brute and no mistake." Still grinning, he said, "Perhaps we should enlighten him. Allow me to make the introductions. This, my impertinent friend, is John Rutherford, son of Sir Pierce Rutherford. The stout gentleman is James Neville. And I, for my sins, am Giles Campbell. My father is Sir Greville Campbell. And you are . . . ?"

"Someone who deserves a lesson in manners," Rutherford said archly. "And I've a mind to teach him myself."

Hawkwood sighed. "That would be a mistake."

Three heads lifted in unison.

"A mistake! D'you hear that, Ruthers?" Neville cried. "A mistake indeed! By God, you've got to hand it to the fellow. He's a game one! What say you?"

"I say he's an upstart who's about to feel the back of my hand," Rutherford snapped. "I'm damned if I'll be dictated to by a bloody servant!"

"Quite right, too!" Neville agreed solemnly. "Don't know what the world's coming to!"

"You'd best be on your way, friend," Campbell advised good-naturedly, his words only slightly slurred. "Back to the kitchen while you have the chance!"

His friend Neville grinned. "That's right, run along now. Only leave the doxy, there's a good fellow. Haven't quite finished makin' her acquaintance."

Hawkwood felt the woman stiffen. He looked at Neville. "I'd say you owed the lady an apology. And, for your information, you drunken sod, I'm no bloody servant!"

It was probably the look in Hawkwood's eyes as much as the words and tone of voice that stopped Neville in his tracks, warning him that he might indeed have made a grave error. His gaze moved slowly over Hawkwood and for the first time an expression of doubt flickered across his fleshy face.

Hawkwood watched Rutherford. He could see the youth's brain working as he considered the implications. If this man who had interrupted their evening's pleasure was not a servant, that made it likely he was a fellow guest. And yet one whose style of dress seemed oddly sober. Hawkwood could tell that Rutherford was intrigued by the possibilities.

"So, sir, who are you?" Campbell demanded. "Come on, out with it!"

"My name's Hawkwood."

"Well, *Mr* Hawkwood, if anyone deserves an apology, I'd say it was my friend Neville here. Rutherford, too, for that matter, seein' as it was he she was fixing with the glad eye, leading him on. Ain't that so, Ruthers? Why, she's no more than a calculating bit of skirt. It's a sorry world if a fellow can't so much as smile at a filly without her branding him a damned libertine! Apologize, indeed! The very thought! Go on, Ruthers, tell him!"

"Quite true," Rutherford said with disdain. "She's naught but a tease, plain and simple."

"*Ce n'est pas vrai!*"

The woman's eyes blazed. Hawkwood could feel the heat of her anger.

A flush spread across Rutherford's pale, haughty face. His jaw tightened. It was obvious he had understood what the woman had said; if not the words themselves perhaps, then certainly their meaning. Through compressed lips, he said, "The bitch called me a liar. You'd take her word against mine?"

Hawkwood returned Rutherford's direct gaze. "With the greatest of pleasure."

The insult stopped Rutherford in his tracks. Campbell sucked in his cheeks. Neville just looked confused.

"Why, you insolent –" Rutherford, strumming with rage, took a pace forward, fists clenched.

"Don't be a fool, boy," Hawkwood said. "Give it up. Walk away."

It was the final straw. Rutherford's face contorted, but even as he swung his arm, Hawkwood was ready. He assumed that Rutherford had intended it to be a slap across the face. The blow, however, never landed. Instead Rutherford found his right wrist held in a grip of iron.

"I warned you, boy," Hawkwood said. Contemptuously, he released Rutherford's arm. "Don't make me hurt you."

Rutherford, white with anger, rubbed the circulation back into his wrist. "How dare you! By God, I'll not be man-handled or spoken to like this." Rutherford's voice rose. "I demand satisfaction!"

Hawkwood blinked. "What? Are you mad? You're calling me out? I'm an officer of the law, for Christ's sake! Here to guard the crowns and cutlery! And you're challenging me to a duel. Do you want me to arrest you?"

A nerve pulsed along the side of Rutherford's forehead. "*Arrest* me? My father buys and sells scum like you! And constable or chief justice, I'll not have you slandering me in front of my friends. I demand an apology! Or else name your second and by God I'll teach you to guard your tongue!"

This was lunacy. Hawkwood couldn't believe what he was hearing. He was aware that the woman was looking at him. He tried to interpret the expression on her face. Bewilderment? Apprehension? Or something else? He couldn't tell. Her outburst had identified her as French though evidently she understood English and had had no trouble following the exchange. Was she now expecting him to withdraw his remarks and run away, tail between his legs?

It was Neville who attempted to restore a sense of order by laughing nervously. "Good lord, Ruthers, you can't call him out! Why the fellow ain't even a gentleman!"

121

At which Campbell nodded vigorously. "He's right, old man. Wouldn't do at all."

For a moment it appeared as if their words might be having a calming effect. One look at Rutherford's face, however, and the still clenched fists, told Hawkwood that the youth was strung as tight as a bow string.

Then, as he watched, Rutherford's expression changed. As quickly as it had appeared, the fire in Rutherford's eyes flickered and died, to be replaced by a cold and calculating gleam.

"Why, I do believe he's afraid. That's it! D'you see, Campbell? Neville? Go on, tell me if the fellow ain't scared witless!"

It was then that Hawkwood felt it; a swift and savage loathing and a desperate urge to wipe the supercilious smile from Rutherford's face.

"Well?" Rutherford smirked. "Hawkwood, did you say? What's it to be? Speak up! Are you man enough to face me, or are you going to hide behind your warrant and slink away to your sewer like the gutter rat you are?"

It had gone deathly quiet, as if time was standing still and nothing around them existed; not the gardens, the summer house, the distant music, the scent of the flowers, not even the woman. It was just the two of them, face to face.

From a great distance Hawkwood heard himself say, "I have no second."

The smile on Rutherford's face was that of a spider enticing a fly into its silken web. He bowed in mock deference. "In that case, may I offer you the services of my companion here? Neville, my dear fellow, perhaps you'd consider acting for our chivalrous friend?"

Neville, clearly stunned by the escalation of events, blinked dazedly. But before he could respond, a voice behind Hawkwood broke the tension.

"That will not be necessary. I'll gladly act as his second, if he so wishes."

Everyone turned. Emerging from under the trees was a stoutly built, ruddy-faced individual in full dress army uniform. Peering out from behind the officer's back was the missing footman. Something about the newcomer struck Hawkwood as immediately familiar. The officer took a step closer and in the lantern light his face became clear. Hawkwood found himself staring into the stern features of Major Lawrence of His Majesty's 40th Regiment of Foot.

Ignoring Hawkwood's astonishment, Lawrence's gaze moved over the small gathering, settled briefly on Rutherford, and continued on to the woman, whereupon he bowed formally. "Major Douglas Lawrence at your service, ma'am. You're safe, I trust? The servant here advised me of your predicament."

The woman inclined her head. "Quite safe, Major. Thank you." The words, spoken in English, carried a soft yet distinct accent. "Perhaps I should not have ventured out alone, but it did not occur to me that I might be in need of protection. Had this gallant gentleman not come to my assistance, I fear . . ." The woman's voice faltered and her hand went to her throat.

Hawkwood recalled the shadowy figure he thought he'd

seen beneath the trees. Yet the woman said she had been alone. It must have been his imagination, after all.

Lawrence, apparently oblivious to Hawkwood's stare, was sympathy personified. "Quite so. Most fortunate." The major nodded towards the footman. "However, may I now suggest you allow our man here to accompany you back to the house. My friend and I have private business to discuss with these . . . er . . . gentlemen."

The woman nodded. She looked directly at Hawkwood. "I'm in your debt, monsieur."

Hawkwood was struck by the depth of colour in her eyes. The irises were very dark. Touched by the lantern glow they seemed to burn with a feline intensity. Her full lips parted slightly as if she was about to speak further then, without a word, she turned and was gone, the footman in her wake. Hawkwood was left with a curious sense of loss, the hint of a message left unspoken, and the realization that he didn't even know her name.

Lawrence watched her depart. "Exquisite," he murmured. "Quite exquisite." He waited until she had disappeared behind the trees. Abruptly his mood changed. He turned to Rutherford. "You'll allow us a moment?" Without waiting for a reply, the major took Hawkwood's elbow and led him aside.

"Well now, Captain, I'll confess I'd not expected our paths to cross quite so soon." Lawrence's eyes bored into Hawkwood's own. In a low voice he said, "Oh yes, *Captain* Hawkwood, I know who you are. I knew you when we met at the Blind Fiddler. Truth is, I saw you earlier this evening, but after our last meeting I was hesitant about making myself known." Lawrence's grip tightened. "Tell me you don't really intend to go through with this?"

"The die's been cast, Major, though I appreciate your concern."

"But this is madness!"

"Quite possibly," Hawkwood admitted.

"Good God, man, you don't have to fight him. Arrest him, for Christ's sake!"

Hawkwood sighed. "Major, he has two witnesses who'll vouch for the fact that he helps old ladies across the street and gives alms to the poor. My threat to arrest him was an attempt to dissuade. There's little chance I could make the charge stick."

"But the risk! Have you forgotten the last time? And you're a police officer! You'd forfeit another career? What if he bests you? What then?"

Hawkwood smiled thinly. "In that case, it won't matter a damn, will it?"

Lawrence emitted a groan of despair.

"It's not too late to change your mind, Major," Hawkwood said.

But Lawrence shook his head. "No, I've said I'd stand with you and I'll not go back on my word." An unexpected wry grin transformed the major's face. "Fact is, I should probably thank you for enlivening an exceedingly dull evening. I'm a soldier, damn it. I've no time for these affairs. What do these fops know of campaigning? Closest most of 'em have ever come to a battle is attending one of those bloody pageants at Astley's. Frankly, I'm sick of the lot of them. Now that we've got Boney on the run, I can't wait to get back to my regiment. I leave for Spain in two days and, between you and me, it won't be a moment too soon." Lawrence looked suddenly contrite. "Forgive me. Didn't mean to stir up memories. My apologies."

"Forget it, Major. It was a long time ago."

Lawrence acknowledged the gesture. "Aye, well, I meant it all the same. But look here, let me speak with our hotheaded friend over yonder, see if I can't persuade him to withdraw. You'll not begrudge me that?"

Hawkwood looked on as Lawrence walked over to the three men. It was Campbell to whom Lawrence spoke. Hawkwood couldn't hear what was being said, but there was no hiding the surprise that blossomed on Campbell's face as he listened to the major. He watched as Campbell left Lawrence and hurried to confer with his principal. Suddenly, Campbell didn't look so tipsy.

Campbell and Rutherford exchanged words, Campbell looking agitated. Rutherford's head came up sharply and he stared at Hawkwood. Something moved in his eyes. Unease? Doubt? Campbell took hold of his friend's sleeve. Rutherford came out of his trance, jerked free and shook his head violently. It was an unhappy Campbell who walked back to Lawrence. The major listened as Campbell relayed Rutherford's response and gave what looked like a resigned shrug. In a gesture that told Campbell to wait, Lawrence came plodding back. His anger was apparent.

"The fool! The arrogant bloody fool!"

Hawkwood waited.

"I thought if I told them you weren't without experience in these affairs, they might reconsider. I was mistaken."

"You tried, Major. Can't blame yourself for that."

"Either too proud or too stupid to back down, the idiot! I'd hoped Campbell might persuade him to see sense but I fear my attempt to procure a peaceful resolution has fallen on deaf ears. The man will not listen to reason."

"You really didn't expect otherwise, did you?" Hawkwood said.

Lawrence shrugged. "Maybe I was being a trifle optimistic. Still, if that's his game, so be it. The boy's made his choice, 'tis he who must live with it." The major drew himself up. "Now, seeing as I can't dissuade either of you from continuing with this reckless adventure, there's the matter of venue and weapons to arrange." Lawrence fixed Hawkwood with a penetrating eye. "You were the one challenged, so the choice is yours. What should I tell them?"

And Hawkwood smiled.

7

The meeting place had been carefully chosen. Situated adjacent to the southern boundary of Hyde Park, close to the bank of the Serpentine, the grassy clearing, hidden inside a small stand of trees, was known locally as the Dell.

The location was one of several similar venues, dotted around the city, that had, over the years, become synonymous with the settling of personal scores. To the north, the stretch of pathway known as the Ring Road was also a favoured spot, as were Lincoln's Inn Fields and Bloomsbury Square.

It was an hour past sunrise. A watery sun hung low above the city's smoky rooftops, bathing the scene in a hazy orange glow. With the grass still damp and silvery from the morning dew, the park was at its most peaceful. To the uninitiated it might have seemed an incongruous choice for trial by combat, but the remoteness of the place and the early hour lessened the risk of uninvited spectators or discovery by the authorities.

Accompanied by the major, Hawkwood had arrived to find his adversary already in place. Their welcome was in the form of a curt nod from both Neville and Campbell. It could have been Hawkwood's imagination, but he had the impression that Rutherford was somewhat surprised to see him, as if he hadn't expected the Runner to turn up. It was with some satisfaction that Hawkwood marked the possibility that he may have caught his opponent temporarily off guard, and any advantage, no matter how slight, was always welcome. In any case, failing to meet with Rutherford had not been an option.

Rutherford scowled darkly and turned his back. Standing to one side in sickly isolation, a frail-looking figure wrapped in a dark cloak sniffled into a sodden handkerchief.

"Jesus," Lawrence muttered. "Bloody surgeon looks to be on his last legs. I wonder which grog shop they dragged *him* from."

Hawkwood refrained from comment. It wasn't the surgeon's duty to be hale and hearty, merely discreet. Both principals were required to contribute to his fee. This covered not only his services but, more importantly, his silence. The surgeon would be the only one guaranteed to profit from the morning's activity.

Forsaking preamble, Neville stepped forward, his manner brisk and officious. "Good morning, gentlemen. If neither of you has any objection, I shall be conducting the proceedings. No? In that case, to business. First, I must ask – now that both parties have had some hours to reflect upon the matter – if either of you has reconsidered."

Campbell, acting for Rutherford, looked pensive and

shook his head. Lawrence, after throwing Hawkwood a wistful look of appeal, followed suit.

Neville accepted each man's response with a grim nod. "So be it. This way, then, if you please."

Neville led the way to the edge of the clearing, where a small folding table had been erected under the trees. Upon the table lay a fold of black velvet. As they drew closer it was clear from the contours of the cloth that something lay concealed beneath the material.

Neville moved to the table and lifted away the edge of the cloth to reveal a flat mahogany case. Wordlessly, Neville opened the lid of the case and stepped away. He addressed Hawkwood. "I trust they meet with your approval?"

Hawkwood looked down and nodded.

"Very well, if the seconds would care to make their examinations?"

The pistols were identical Mortimers, with sixteen-inch octagonal barrels; in their simplicity, supreme examples of the gun maker's art. Hawkwood and Rutherford stood to one side while their respective seconds examined the pistols. Mutual satisfaction expressed, Neville gestured towards the case. "So, gentlemen, if you'd each be so kind as to choose your weapon."

Hawkwood removed his coat and handed it to Lawrence. He lifted out the pistol nearest to him. He had no qualms over his choice. He knew Lawrence would have ensured that each weapon contained exactly the same-sized ball and an equal charge of powder.

Neville cleared his throat. "You will stand back to back. On my count you will each walk away for a distance of twelve paces, at which point, upon my signal, you will turn and fire. Is that understood?"

Both men nodded. Hawkwood found that his throat was as dry as sand. As he took up his position, he wondered if his opponent was experiencing the same degree of discomfort and stomach-gnawing apprehension. He could feel Rutherford's shoulder blades chafing against his own.

It had been like this when he had fought Delancey; the same coldness running down his spine, the prickle of wetness under the arms, the gut-wrenching fear that in less than a minute he might be dead. Or worse, severely wounded, with no future other than to roam the streets with all the other cripples, begging for scraps and shelter. All things considered, he thought death was probably the better option.

But at least he wouldn't die in ignorance.

Her name, he had discovered, was Catherine de Varesne.

She had vanished by the time Hawkwood and Lawrence had returned to the house – no doubt having made her departure in order to avoid further confrontation with Rutherford and his associates – so the major had taken it upon himself to make discreet enquiries.

Not French, as Hawkwood had first supposed, but half French and half Portuguese, on her mother's side. Her father had been the Marquis de Varesne, a minister under Louis XVI, and one of the hundreds of aristos sent to the guillotine. More relevant was the fact that he had been a close associate of the Comte d'Artois, currently in exile in England, and friend to Lord Mandrake, which explained her presence at the ball.

"I'll say one thing, my friend," the major had commented,

"you've excellent taste in women, but by God your method of making their acquaintance leaves a lot to be desired."

The sound of Neville's voice brought Hawkwood out of his reverie.

"On my mark, gentlemen." There was a pause. "Begin!"

Glancing to his right, Hawkwood saw that Lawrence was talking to himself. He realized with a jolt that the major was counting off the paces in accompaniment to Neville's metronomic drone.

"Two . . . three . . . four . . ."

Their footsteps fell soft and silent on the damp grass. Rutherford was facing north, Hawkwood south. The direction was deliberate. It meant neither man had the advantage of the sun at his back.

"Five . . . six . . . seven . . ."

Hawkwood adjusted his grip on the pistol butt and felt warm beads of perspiration slide beneath the hairs at the back of his neck.

"Eight . . . nine . . . ten . . ."

Something nagged at Hawkwood. He couldn't think what it was. Then he realized. There was no birdsong. Not a chirrup, not a whistle, not a single note broke the silence. He laid his thumb across the hammer of the pistol, curled his finger round the trigger, felt the cold curve of the barrel touch his right cheek.

"Eleven . . ." Followed by a pause that seemed to last for ever.

"Twelve . . . Gentlemen, you may turn and fire."

Hawkwood spun quickly, sucked in his stomach muscles. A bright flash as the powder in Rutherford's pistol ignited.

The crack of the report was surprisingly loud in the crisp morning air. The sound echoed around the glade.

Hawkwood felt the strike on his left side, a moment of acute pain and a fierce burning sensation as the ball parted the cloth of his shirt and the flesh beneath, searing across his exposed ribcage with the ferocity of a white-hot poker.

The powder smoke dispersed slowly, revealing Rutherford frozen in shock at the sight of his opponent, not only still standing but with pistol not yet discharged. A second passed. Two seconds stretched to three. Hawkwood watched the blood drain slowly from Rutherford's face. With great deliberation, Hawkwood extended his right arm, winced as the edge of his shirt rasped against his wound, took careful aim, and fired.

Rutherford spun around. The pistol dropped from his fingers, and he went down. White faced, left hand clamped around the wound in his right arm, he stared up at Hawkwood as if unable to comprehend the fact that he had been shot. Hawkwood, feet braced, looked down at him for several moments before slowly lowering his pistol. Absently, he ran his hand along his belly. When he pulled it away it was smeared red.

Lawrence was the first to recover. He ran up quickly, his face ashen. "Jesus! You're shot! Here, let me see!" The major expelled air and looked around. "Goddammit! Where the hell's that bloody sawbones?"

Hawkwood grunted as Lawrence's fingers probed his side. "It's all right, Major. Only a flesh wound. I'll live. The boy has greater need of him than I do."

Accompanied by a still fussing Lawrence, Hawkwood

walked over to where Rutherford lay, supported by his second. By the time they got there the sleeve of Rutherford's shirt had already been ripped away. It was steeped in blood. The surgeon's mottled hands shook as he examined the wound. Teeth gritted, Rutherford writhed at the touch. Hawkwood couldn't see if the ball had passed through the arm, but he suspected the bone was probably broken. He tossed the spent pistol on to the grass. "I believe that concludes our business."

Rutherford, blinking away tears, looked up. "You could have killed me," he whispered hoarsely. "Why didn't you?"

Hawkwood shrugged. "Take your pick. It's a beautiful morning. I've got better things to do. I've a criminal investigation to deal with; places to go, people to see. But you pay heed, boy. You ever get the urge to throw down the gauntlet again, you'd better be damned sure you can win."

Hawkwood retrieved his coat from Lawrence. "We're done here, Major. Time to go. I've no wish to try and explain my presence to a roving police patrol. I'm in enough bloody trouble as it is." He nodded to Neville and Campbell, who were looking back at him with something like awe on their faces. "Good day, gentlemen."

"You do know," Lawrence said, as they left the clearing, "if it had been you who'd shot first and missed, it's unlikely the boy would have been so merciful."

"You're probably right," Hawkwood admitted. "But then *I* wouldn't have missed."

Lawrence threw a look at the Runner, but there was no humour or arrogance in Hawkwood's expression. He had been stating a fact.

"My God, you wanted him to shoot first! You expected him to miss? Jesus, you took a chance."

Hawkwood shrugged. "It was a calculation. I doubt he's ever pointed a loaded pistol at anyone before. I had a feeling his nerves would get the better of him."

"Bloody hell," Lawrence said. "So that's why you spared him?"

They emerged from the other side of the trees. A swathe of broad green meadow stretched before them.

"There's a time and place, Major. This wasn't it. Call it a lesson in life."

Lawrence regarded Hawkwood with some doubt. "He'll bear you a considerable grudge."

Hawkwood shrugged. "A grudge I can live with. Better than having his death on my conscience."

Lawrence blinked. "You were a soldier. You've killed before. What about Delancey? You killed *him* in a duel."

Hawkwood stopped walking. "Delancey was a professional. He'd fought other men in duels, and won. I couldn't afford to give *that* bastard the edge. As I said before, Rutherford's a boy, a foolish, arrogant boy, who got carried away. And in case you've forgotten, Major, I'm a police officer. I'm supposed to prevent bloody duels, not take part in them!"

Lawrence fell silent. Then he grinned. "Has anyone ever told you, my friend, you've a tendency to sail mighty close to the wind?"

For the first time since he had met him, Lawrence watched a smile of genuine amusement break across Hawkwood's face. It was startling, he thought, how the Runner's expression softened. The scar beneath Hawkwood's eye all but disappeared.

Hawkwood laughed. "Frequently, Major." He thought it was probably wise not to tell the major about the ribbons of sweat that had been running down his back as he had listened to Neville counting out the steps.

They had reached the footpath that ran alongside the King's Road. Ahead of them lay the Hyde Park turnpike and the road leading to Piccadilly.

"Well, at least we can be thankful for one thing," Lawrence mused. "Rutherford's unlikely to announce his defeat, especially when it was at the hands of someone who's not even a gentleman!" The major grinned again then added seriously, "And I doubt Neville and Campbell will be anxious to spread gossip."

That was probably true, Hawkwood conceded. Duels were generally accepted to be private affairs. Although, over the years, there had been a few notable exceptions; usually when one or both of the principals possessed a high public profile. Fortunately, neither he nor Rutherford, despite the latter's own high opinion of himself, fell into that category, so it was conceivable the affair would remain undetected by the authorities. The major had already assured Hawkwood that Mandrake's servant had been taken care of. The jingle of sovereigns and the threat of reprisal had been sufficient to ensure that the footman's mouth would remain for ever closed. As for the other witness, the woman, Hawkwood reasoned she was unlikely to advertise the incident. More probably she would want to put the whole sordid business behind her.

Had he killed Rutherford, of course, it would have been a

different matter. The major had railed against Rutherford's arrant pig-headedness in not retracting his challenge. If the truth were told, Hawkwood asked himself, was he any different? In a moment of crass stupidity, aggravated by his own bitter prejudices, he'd allowed himself to be goaded into a senseless confrontation. The fact that he'd survived was due to nothing less than good fortune based on the inexperience and poor marksmanship of his opponent. In short, he had been lucky.

He thought about James Read. The Chief Magistrate was a stern taskmaster but a fair one. He worked his officers hard, but in doing so, mindful of the often adverse conditions in which they operated, he allowed them an extraordinary degree of latitude. In exchange, he demanded and expected total dedication and loyalty. It was a matter of trust. By rising to the bait and accepting Rutherford's challenge, Hawkwood was fully aware he'd betrayed that trust. And in doing so he had jeopardized everything; not only his career but his relationship with a man to whom he owed a great deal, a man he admired. Had he killed Rutherford, Hawkwood knew that his severest punishment would have been facing the look of disappointment on James Read's face.

Hawkwood flinched as pain from the wound flared across his belly. He should have let the physician examine him, he reflected, but then he remembered the man's palsied hand shake. Medical attention would have to wait.

They had reached the public road. Opposite was the path that cut through to Knightsbridge.

Earlier, when they'd first arrived at the park, the roads

had been empty. Now, however, the city was emerging from its slumbers and the streets had started to fill. The number of vehicles had increased considerably, as had the flow of pedestrians. Barrow men, flower sellers, knife grinders and chimney sweeps rubbed shoulders with candle makers, coal men and rag pickers; soon the trickle would become a flow and the flow would become a flood. It reminded Hawkwood of the rag-tag columns of camp followers that trailed in the wake of Wellington's armies as they marched across the Peninsula. A meandering river of pathetic pilgrims in search of a promised land.

They were on the point of crossing the road when the rattle of carriage springs caused them to pause. Hawkwood stepped back and waited for it to pass. Then he realized the carriage was slowing. As it drew abreast, the coachman hauled in the reins and the carriage stopped. The door opened.

"Captain Hawkwood?"

The breath caught in his throat. He recognized the voice immediately. He stared. She was alone in the carriage, a dark cloak drawn across her shoulders. She leaned forward, inclined her head, and acknowledged Lawrence's presence with a seductive smile.

"Good morning, Major."

"Indeed it is, ma'am," Lawrence agreed, doffing his shako. The major glanced at Hawkwood and a broad grin broke out across his face.

Transfixed by Lawrence's imbecilic expression, it occurred to Hawkwood that the major did not seem at all surprised by the woman's appearance. His suspicions were further heightened when Lawrence, in a woeful impersonation of spontaneous thought, pulled out his watch, gave it a cursory glance, held it to his ear, shook it, and announced, apologetically, "Ahem . . . well, now, if you'll both forgive me, I must be away. Regimental duties, you understand. Fact is I'm due to meet up with young Fitz in an hour. I packed the lad off to his family for a couple of days. Thought it best, as there's no knowing when we'll be home again. As it is, we've precious little time to lick our new recruits into shape before we ship 'em off to Spain."

Before Hawkwood could respond, the major stuck out his hand. "Goodbye, my dear fellow. It was a pleasure. I do hope we'll meet again." He glanced into the carriage and gave a short bow. "Your servant, ma'am."

Hawkwood had to admit it had been neatly done. One moment the major was there, as large as life, the next he was gone. If nothing else, one had to admire his nerve.

The rustle of a petticoat made him turn. She was gazing at him, her expression both mischievous and beguiling. "Well, Captain Hawkwood, won't you join me?"

Hawkwood looked up at the driver. The man's features were indecipherable, hidden as they were behind his collar and cap. His whip was poised.

The moment of indecision passed. Hawkwood climbed into the carriage. As if on a given signal, the driver flicked his whip and the vehicle moved off.

"You're surprised to see me?" Amusement illuminated her dark eyes.

Hawkwood stared at her, his senses racing.

"Then perhaps my appearance disappoints you?" she challenged.

Hawkwood found his voice. "How did you know I'd be here?"

The cloak slipped off her shoulder. She was wearing a high bodice, but even that could not disguise the curve of her breasts. She returned his stare and, with disarming frankness, said, "The major sent me word."

So, Hawkwood thought, Lawrence's guilt was proven. No wonder the bastard had been grinning like a lunatic.

She smiled bewitchingly. "Did you think we wouldn't meet again?"

He took in the smooth line of her throat, the soft swell beneath the bodice. "I thought it unlikely."

"But you hoped we might?" Her eyes searched his face.

He nodded. "Yes." He was amazed at himself for admitting it so readily. He recalled that she had addressed him by his former rank and wondered what other information the major might have given away.

"Did you kill him?" she asked suddenly, interrupting his thoughts.

Hawkwood collected himself. "Rutherford? No, he'll live. He might die from embarrassment, but that's all."

She considered his answer in silence. He couldn't tell if she was pleased or disappointed. He decided to match her directness. "So, why *did* you come?"

She looked across at him, the smile still hovering on her full lips. "You realize, Captain Hawkwood, we've yet to be formally introduced. My name is Catherine –"

"I know who you are," Hawkwood said, before he could stop himself.

Her eyes widened. "And how do you know that, Captain?"

140

Hawkwood grinned. "The major sent me word."

She laughed then, the light dancing in her eyes. *I could fall for this one*, Hawkwood thought, and wondered why, despite her obvious attractions, the possibility disturbed him.

"So," he repeated, "why did you come?"

Her reply and gaze was as direct as before.

"Why do you think?"

8

Hawkwood lay pressed back against the pillow, his arm around her waist. Her cheek rested on his chest. Her eyes were closed. She was breathing softly. The bed sheets lay in disarray around them. They were both naked.

The carriage had delivered them to a fashionable house on the corner of Portman Square. There were no servants in evidence, other than a maid who had opened the door and curtseyed low before disappearing, at her mistress's bidding, to her own quarters. Her services, she had been told, would not be required for the rest of the day. The girl had expressed no surprise at Hawkwood's presence.

Once inside, her first action had been to tend his wound.

She had become aware of his injury when the carriage wheels hit a pothole. The carriage bounced hard on its springs, jolting Hawkwood out of his seat. He had let out an involuntary grunt of pain and pressed his hand to his stomach. Her reaction had been immediate.

"You're hurt!"

"A scratch. It's nothing."

"Let me see." Before he could stop her, she had pulled his jacket away. "My God! There is blood! You're wounded!"

"It's not as bad as it looks."

"But you need attention! A doctor!"

"The hell I do! I'll not be prodded and poked by some damned apothecary. Bastards pass on more infections than they cure."

It occurred to Hawkwood that he should probably have been more mindful of his language, given that he was in the company of a lady and not in some dockside tavern. The amusement playing across her lips, however, hinted that his vocabulary was not her main concern.

"Then you will let me take care of you. No, not another word, Captain," she cautioned as Hawkwood opened his mouth to protest. "I insist upon it!"

The look in her eyes warned Hawkwood that it would be wiser not to resist.

She had shown him to a couch in the drawing room before removing her cloak and disappearing, returning with a bowl of hot water and bandages.

"Take off your shirt," she commanded.

Hawkwood hesitated.

"Must I do it for you?" Her eyes flashed. "If you are concerned about my being compromised, there's no need. My maid is discreet and gone to her room, and there's no one else to disturb us." She smiled. "Or is it that you are embarrassed? Surely not? Not my brave captain?"

Hawkwood sighed. "I'm not a captain. I'm not anything. Not any more."

"But you're still *my* hero," she murmured softly. "Now, take off your shirt."

She did not look away. Instead her gaze moved frankly over his body, taking in not only the blood-encrusted runnel below his ribs but the older scars that crisscrossed his torso. Her attention was drawn to a crescent of puckered skin etched into the flesh beneath his left arm. Caused by a heavy blade of some kind, she presumed. A circular, discoloured indentation high on his right shoulder suggested a bullet wound, while a thin weal an inch below his left nipple looked as if it might have been made by a knife. It was a body mauled by war and almost twenty years of soldiering.

As with most superficial wounds, the degree of blood was disproportionate to the damage sustained. Nevertheless, despite her gentle ministrations, he was forced to bite his lip more than once as she dabbed away the rind of congealed blood. Once the wound was cleansed, he knew the healing would be quick. As a result, the scarring was likely to be negligible, just another addition to the painful legacies of battle.

By the time she had finished, the water in the bowl had cooled to lukewarm and turned crimson. She reached for the bandages.

"Sit up," she instructed.

A frisson of pleasure moved through him as he caught the faint scent of her perfume; jasmine, he guessed, with perhaps a hint of wild lemon. He felt her breath, light as a feather on his neck, as she leaned in and wound the bandage

144

around him. For a moment, their eyes met. Her hands stopped moving, her breasts rose and fell invitingly before him.

"I think it's time," she whispered.

Hawkwood frowned. "For what?"

Her steady gaze transfixed him. "Your reward."

She looked down on him through a tangle of lustrous black hair. Her skin was the colour of cinnamon. The dark tips of her breasts brushed his skin. Wordlessly, reaching down between them, her fingers searched for him. Hawkwood felt himself respond. She bent her left knee, straddled him, and gave a small moan of pleasure. All the time her eyes remained open, watching him. Encircling him with her hand, she began to massage him gently.

"I want you," she breathed.

She released him, lowered her head and kissed his neck, her teeth nipping playfully at his skin. Her tongue flickered along the line of his jugular. Her lips were warm and moist. She moved down his body, nuzzling his chest, kissing his scars. Her hands traced his hips, caressed his thighs. Her head sank lower. Her lips enfolded him and Hawkwood surrendered to the moment.

When she sensed he could hold back no longer, she disengaged her mouth and tongue, raised herself on to her knees and lowered herself carefully. Head thrown back, eyes closed, she began to move urgently against him.

She cried out as she came, the shudders moving through her. Hawkwood held her tightly as she fell across him, trembling like a bird.

He had been unprepared for the aggressive way in which she had taken the initiative, undressing with tantalizing slowness until, clad only in silk stockings, she had opened her legs and spread herself before him. His skin still smarted where her nails had raked his shoulders as he had taken her.

A bright sheen of sweat covered their bodies. A light breeze rippled coolly through the open window, ruffling the drapes. Hawkwood pulled the sheet over them both.

Hawkwood stroked the smooth cleft of her buttocks. She sighed, pressed herself to him, rotated her hips, and kissed the underside of his jaw. "You realize," she murmured, "I don't even know what they call you."

He frowned. "Who?"

"Why, your friends, of course. Or do you expect me to address you as Captain Hawkwood all the time?" She looked up at him and smiled. Her fingers traced small circles on his chest.

A moment passed.

It occurred to Hawkwood that the number of people he might have regarded as friends was depressingly small. Over the years there had been acquaintances, men he had fought alongside; some brave, some foolish, a few cowardly. But true friends? Individuals he would willingly have given his life for away from the fever of battle? Precious few, when it came down to it. Probably no more than could be counted on the fingers of one hand, and most of them already dead. There was Jago, of course. All things considered, he supposed the ex-sergeant was as close to him as anyone, or at least had been before their return to England. These days, he wasn't so sure, given that Jago now ran with the hares while his own

146

allegiance lay with the hounds. And in any case, in all the years they had been together, Jago would never have had cause nor, for that matter, the inclination to address him by his first name. In the army, even where friendship was concerned, rank would always prevail. As for the present, there was a well-worn saying among his fellow officers: a Bow Street Runner never made friends, only informers.

"Matthew," Hawkwood said. "My name's Matthew."

"So, my Matthew," she said softly. "Tell me about the scars on your throat."

Not so much scars as an uneven necklace of faded bruising running from the hollow below his right jaw-line to the area of skin below his right ear. Hidden beneath his collar, the discoloration might have gone unnoticed, but in removing his shirt the marks had become visible.

Hawkwood reached up and covered her exploring hand. Sensing the change in him, she frowned. "You're afraid to tell me?" Then she gave a small intuitive gasp. "Wait, I understand. *C'est une . . .*" her brow furrowed as she searched for the words ". . . a mark of birth, yes?"

Hawkwood stroked her flank, marvelling at the satin texture. It was not the first time he had been asked about the marks on his throat, nor was it the first time he had avoided an explanation of their origin. They were not a birthmark, nor were they a souvenir of his soldiering or his career as a Runner. They belonged to a more distant past; a dark time of his life he had no desire to revisit, and a reminder of how, in the blink of an eye, a man's destiny could be changed for ever.

"Oh, my poor Matthew," she said, sensing his disquiet.

Resting her arms across his chest, fingers entwined, she looked up at him. "Tell me everything. I want to know it all." She eyed him speculatively. "Is it usual for an officer of the law to fight a duel? Over a woman?" Her kittenish expression mocked him.

"It would probably depend on the woman," Hawkwood said.

She feigned annoyance and gave his arm a playful slap then lowered her head and kissed the spot tenderly. She regarded him levelly and her expression grew serious. "So, tell me, my Captain, when you were a soldier, did you kill many men?"

"I never kept a tally."

She elevated herself on to one elbow, ran a fingertip along the muscle in his forearm. "But you did fight and kill?"

"Yes."

"Frenchmen? Bonaparte's soldiers?"

"Mostly." Hawkwood wondered where this was leading.

She sensed his hesitation. "You do not like to talk about it?"

"Not particularly."

She frowned. "It disturbed you? The killing?"

"Not at the time."

She stretched languorously. "So, you enjoyed it?" It sounded almost like a challenge. Once again Hawkwood was reminded of a cat sated after a saucer of cream.

"It was war. I was a soldier. They were the enemy. I didn't have a choice."

"Is that why you let Lord Rutherford live? You had the choice?"

"Let's just say I've grown tired of seeing men die needlessly."

She sat up quickly. "Had I been you, I would not have been so forgiving. I would have killed him!"

Her sudden vehemence startled him.

"You doubt me?" she asked. Her look dared him to contradict.

"Not for a moment," Hawkwood said truthfully. He went to sit up. As he did so, his hand brushed the underside of the pillow.

"Christ!"

The pain was so sudden and so intense he thought at first that he'd been stung by something. He jerked his hand away quickly and stared at the tiny dark red bubble of blood that had appeared as if by magic on the end of his finger. Certainly no wasp or bee sting.

Hawkwood lifted the pillow cautiously. The knife lay on the sheet. The blade was some six inches long, very thin, and needle sharp. The handle was of a similar length to the blade, black in colour and inlaid with an intricate gold filigree design. The workmanship, Hawkwood could see, was exquisite. It was a weapon as finely wrought as it was deadly.

Humour danced in her eyes. Her hand moved to her mouth as if to stifle laughter. She reached over him. The tips of her breasts dimpled his arm as she lifted the stiletto from its hiding place. "Oh, my love, forgive me! I'd quite forgotten it was there!" She laid the knife aside and took his hand in her own. "Here, let me see."

She bent her head, as if to examine the wound. Before he could stop her, she had closed her mouth around his

149

fingertip. He felt the warm curl of her tongue. Slowly, she slid her lips down the length of his finger. Hollowing her cheeks, she closed her eyes as she sucked the still warm blood from his flesh.

Releasing his finger from her mouth, she raised her head and smiled again. "Am I forgiven?"

Hawkwood stared down at the knife.

She followed his gaze. "We live in dangerous times, my love. A lady needs protection."

"From whom?"

"Why, Bonaparte's agents, of course. It is not unknown for the Emperor to send his people against us."

"Us?" Hawkwood said.

"Those of us who wish to see Bonaparte deposed."

"Royalists?"

"King Louis *is* the rightful heir. Did you know that this year alone the Emperor has twice sent agents to murder the Comte d'Artois? That means anyone who supports the Bourbon cause is at risk. We must be able to defend ourselves. Would you deny me that right?"

Hawkwood was about to suggest that her honour would probably be better protected by a brace of pistols, but he was silenced when she leaned over and plucked the weapon from the bed sheet. He watched, fascinated, as she raised the stiletto to her lips and kissed the blade. It was a mime as erotic as her scent and the feel of her lips sliding over his knuckle. Looking down, he thought he saw her nipples harden. For a fleeting second, it was as if she and the knife were one, bonded together like lovers and, despite the incongruity of the moment, Hawkwood felt the stirrings of arousal.

150

Her dark eyes flashed. "Had you not come to my rescue, I'd have used it on that pig Rutherford without a moment's regret."

She stood, placed the knife on the armoire, turned to him, and grinned.

"But enough of this! What must you think of me, speaking of such things?" She leaned over him, breasts swaying invitingly, and chuckled seductively. "When I can think of much more pleasurable ways of passing the time!"

It was mid morning by the time Hawkwood arrived at the Blackbird. The tavern occupied the corner of a quiet mews at the lower end of Water Lane, one of the many winding arteries leading from the south side of Fleet Street down towards the river. Hidden deep within a maze of secluded courtyards and passageways, less than a stone's throw from Kings Bench walk and the Inner Temple, it was inevitable that the majority of the tavern's patrons should be members of the legal profession. The tavern's proximity to Temple Church and St Dunstan's also ensured regular custom from those of an ecclesiastical persuasion. Writers, actors and politicians – callings that often went hand in hand – had also been known to duck through its low portals in search of a late supper and a soothing dram.

To Hawkwood, however, the Blackbird was more than a convenient watering hole. It was home. The two rooms he inhabited beneath the tavern's sloping roof were a quiet haven to which he could retreat from the bustling streets that were such an integral part of his life.

Several booths were occupied. One or two of the regulars

glanced up and nodded in silent recognition as he entered. Not everyone was eating. Some groups conversed over drinks. A few customers had paired off and were engaged in games of chess. Others played whist, while a number of individuals, at ease with their own company, were content merely to sip coffee, enjoy a quiet pipe, and peruse the morning papers.

"Well, now, if it isn't *Officer* Hawkwood! And I suppose you'll be wanting breakfast?"

The voice came from behind. Hawkwood turned and smiled.

"Morning, Maddie."

Maddie Teague was a woman who carried her beauty without a trace of vanity. Tall and slender, her most arresting features – a pair of emerald eyes framed by a halo of dark auburn hair – had been known to strike men dumb at over fifty paces. It was safe to say that those striking good looks were as responsible for attracting the many and varied customers into the comfortable dining room as the tavern's Epicurean delights. Maddie Teague ruled the place with an effective combination of grace and efficiency. Under her guiding hand, the Blackbird had become one of the area's most respected establishments.

Watching Maddie and her girls distribute an assortment of steaming platters among the diners reminded Hawkwood that it had been a while since he had last eaten. The aroma of the food wasn't helping matters either. A late breakfast, Hawkwood decided, wouldn't go amiss. He placed an order for eggs, ham and cheese.

"Coffee, too, Maddie, if it's no trouble."

Maddie wiped her hands on her apron, all efficient. "No

trouble at all, *Officer* Hawkwood. You just sit yourself down and I'll be with you in two shakes." She looked Hawkwood up and down and arched an eyebrow. "You look as though you could do with a decent meal inside you. Hard night was it?"

Hawkwood forced a grin. "You know what they say, Maddie. No rest for the wicked."

"Do they indeed?" Maddie responded wryly. "And that's why you'll be wanting me to send your shirt to the seamstress, I suppose?" She paused before aiming the killer punch. "That'll be after the blood's been washed out, no doubt?" Having delivered her parting salvo, Maddie straightened her shoulders, turned on her heel and headed back towards the kitchen.

God's teeth! Hawkwood thought. The woman was as sharp as a tack. Speechless, he could only stare in admiration at the landlady's shapely form as she made her departure.

An hour later, his meal over, Hawkwood sipped the dregs from his second mug of coffee and sat quietly. A copy of the *Chronicle* had been abandoned at the next table. He picked it up and skimmed the latest news. The war had been relegated to a couple of columns on the second page. There were two prominent articles on the front page. One was a description of a failed insurrection by French prisoners on a prison hulk anchored off the Woolwich shore. The other concerned an upcoming prizefight at Five Courts, the calibre of which was destined to be far higher than the brawl in the yard of the Blind Fiddler. One of the fighters belonged to the stable of Bill Richmond, the ex-slave turned pugilist who, the previous December, had taken on Tom Cribb. Cribb had won the fight, but rumour had it that Richmond had a new fighter under training who had the potential to beat Cribb and the Five Courts contest was to be the first taster of his protégé's abilities. Hawkwood read the articles with only half an eye. He was unable to concentrate. Oblivious to the murmured discourse going on around him, his thoughts returned to the morning's events.

By anyone's reckoning, it had been an extraordinary day. He doubted he could remember a stranger one. Not only had he participated in and survived a duel, he had just spent the last three hours with one of the most beautiful and enticing women he had ever met. Had it not been for the nagging pain from the wound on his stomach and the scratches on his back, he could well have thought he'd imagined the entire episode. Only the throbbing hurt along his ribcage and the dull yet not unpleasant ache that was permeating another, more intimate, part of his anatomy swiftly dispelled that notion.

And in the quiet aftermath of their lovemaking, he had learned more of Catherine de Varesne.

Seated cross-legged on the bed, a silk robe over her shoulders, she had relived her childhood.

"I was twelve years old when they sent my father to the guillotine."

Prior to his arrest, the Marquis de Varesne, aware of the fate that awaited him, had arranged for his wife and daughter's escape from France. The Marquis had remained behind in order to allay suspicion, fully intending to make his own way out of the country at a later date. The Committee for Public Safety, however, in carrying out its own sinister agenda, had apprehended the Marquis before he could put the final stage of his plan into operation.

"We were taken across the mountains into Spain and then on to Portugal and my mother's family estate." Fists clenched, she had blinked back the tears. "My mother never recovered from my father's death. She died less than a year later. They told me she died of a broken heart. Perhaps it's true. I know she adored my father. He was a sweet and gentle man who loved his country. I was brought up by my aunt. That was how I learned to speak English. I had cousins my own age. The family employed an English governess. I was very happy there."

Hawkwood had watched as a shadow stole over her face.

"But even then we were not safe."

Bonaparte's invasion of the peninsula had forced the family to break apart once more. At the first rattle of French musketry, Hawkwood recalled, the Portuguese king and queen had taken flight to Brazil, along with a good number of Portuguese aristocrats. It had been the beginning of a chain of events that had led, eventually, to Britain's involvement with the war in Spain.

And yet she had remained behind. At risk. Why?

She had given a wistful sigh. "Here, in England, I am close to France, among friends who feel as I do, who will never rest until Bonaparte is defeated and we can all return home."

Her eyes had flickered to the stiletto on the nightstand. It had been her father's, she told him, pressed upon her when he had engineered his family's escape from the guillotine. She had kept it with her at all times, during her flight across the mountains into Portugal, concealed within the folds of her dress by day and beneath her pillow at night. Because, she told him, those who opposed Bonaparte were never safe and the English Channel was no protection against determined agents whose sole agenda was to eradicate the Bourbon dynasty and all those who supported it.

"They took my father," she had told Hawkwood. "They will not take me!"

The chiming of the tavern clock brought Hawkwood back to the present with a reminder that a day and a half had passed since his meeting with Jago. He had hoped that the ex-sergeant might have come up with something by now, a clue that would lead to the identities of the two highwaymen. But he had heard nothing. Experience had taught Hawkwood that Chief Magistrate Read, a man not widely known for his patience, would be expecting, if not demanding, a progress report. And the Chief Magistrate was not a man who accepted disappointment lightly.

To be fair, Hawkwood, due to circumstances not entirely unpleasurable, had not made it easy for Jago to track him down. Which meant it was now his responsibility to search out his old comrade and see if the former sergeant had come up with anything. He did not relish making another pilgrimage into the Holy Land, but he had no choice. An unannounced journey into the rookery was asking for trouble, however. It looked as if he'd have to have another discreet word with Blind Billy Mipps.

As he set his empty coffee mug aside, Hawkwood wondered if and when he would see Catherine de Varesne again. He would need to gather his strength beforehand, he reflected wryly. He thought about those bewitching eyes, that smooth skin and the way her body had arched above his and, as the serving girl took away his empty plate, he couldn't help but smile to himself at the memory of it.

His attention was drawn again to the clock on the wall. The hours had sped by all too quickly. The day was nearly half over. It was time to pay that call on Blind Billy. Tossing payment for the meal on to the table, Hawkwood left the booth and exited the tavern.

His first thought as he felt the brush of the boy's hand against his sleeve was that of all the marks available, it was the young pickpocket's supreme ill luck to have chosen a Bow Street Runner as his target.

Hawkwood's arm shot out with the speed of a striking cobra. His fingers encircled a thin wrist.

"Not so fast, lad."

But instead of the expected cry of protest and whine of innocence, there was only the breathless, "Ease up, Hawkey! It's me, Davey!"

Hawkwood looked down. The face peering up at him was streaked with mud and set on a rail-thin body that would not have looked out of place on a sick sparrow. A fringe of ginger hair sprouted from beneath a filthy woollen cap.

Hawkwood released the wrist. "Christ, Davey! You should know better, sneaking up on a body like that . . . And don't call me Hawkey. I've told you before."

157

The boy pouted. "I weren't sneakin'! An' if I 'ad've been, you'd never 'ave spotted me! Never in a million bloody years!" The pout disappeared to be replaced by a disarming gap-toothed grin. "*Mr 'Awkwood.*"

Hawkwood couldn't help but grin back. For indeed, had he been a legitimate mark, he knew that young Davey would have made the snatch and been off and running without him being any the wiser.

Not that picking pockets was young Davey's sole source of income.

Davey was a mudlark, one of the many homeless children who prowled the Thames at low tide, wading through the stinking black mud and silt on the lookout for items that might have been washed ashore or had fallen or been tossed from a ship, boat or barge. Anything that could turn a profit. They operated alone and in packs, living by their wits, like rats in the darkness.

Young Davey had other talents, too. They lay in the use of his eyes and ears, for the boy was one of Hawkwood's most reliable informers. Despite the best efforts of watchmen patrols and the Wapping-based River Police, crime along the river was rife and the authorities relied on any help they could get.

Davey and his cohorts were certainly no angels, it had to be admitted, but in the general scheme of things, they were small fry. Hawkwood and his fellow law officers were prepared to overlook instances of petty pilfering in order to land the bigger fish, the organized gangs of thieves and traffickers who stole to order from ships and warehouses the length and breadth of the water front.

"So, what's up, Davey? What have you got?"

The boy glanced around. He looked apprehensive, as if afraid of being overheard. The cockiness of the previous few moments had evaporated. When he spoke his voice was low. "We've found a dead 'un, Mr 'Awkwood."

The first uncharitable thought that entered Hawkwood's mind was that if the boy had only seen one dead body so far that morning he obviously hadn't been trying hard enough.

Not that the streets of the capital were strewn with corpses, but they were not that uncommon, providing one knew where to look. Old age, disease and foul play all took their toll, particularly among the poor and destitute. Venture down any dark alley in one of the rookeries and you could guarantee a cadaver most days of the week. Which, given the sort of company that young Davey ran with, made it all the more curious that the lad should have thought the matter worthy of Hawkwood's attention. Hawkwood started to say as much when something in the boy's eyes stopped him cold.

"But, Mr 'Awkwood, this ain't no ordinary stiff. This 'un's different. 'E's one o' yours. 'E's a Runner!"

9

The body lay partially embedded in the mud, head on one side. One arm was outstretched as if reaching for something. The other was twisted beneath the corpse.

The smell coming off the river was foul even by the city's grim standards. A stew of gut-churning odours – tar, damp cordage, stagnant water, rotting vegetation and raw sewage – vied with a thousand other noxious, throat-searing smells from the tanning factories, timber yards, mills and dye houses that lined the river bank.

Cautiously, Hawkwood picked his way down the rough stone steps. Stepping off the bottom tier, he cursed as the stinking black ooze sucked at his boots. The boy, lighter on his feet, skipped across the treacherous surface with the agility of a sand crab. The broad span of Blackfriars Bridge loomed above them, blocking the sunlight.

Two children squatted at the bottom of the steps; members of Davey's gang. They stood up at Hawkwood's approach. At first sight he'd taken them for boys, but then he saw that one was a girl of about nine or ten. Both looked to be on the point of bolting for cover. A quietly spoken word from Davey, however, was enough to persuade them that Hawkwood's presence posed no threat, whereupon the girl picked up a stone and tossed it on to the mud. It was only when she began to hop and skip in between throws that Hawkwood realized she was playing some sort of game. A variation of hopscotch, he supposed. The girl's companion remained seated and, with equal disregard, began to pick his nose, wiping the findings on the side of his breeches. Their features, beneath the layer of grime, were close enough alike to suggest they might be brother and sister.

Hawkwood bent down. The sickly sweet smell of putrefaction and the sound of buzzing flies rose to meet him. He swallowed hard and tried not to retch.

His first attempt to turn the body over met with scant success. The thick black mud was reluctant to relinquish its glutinous hold and the water-sodden clothing didn't help. Hawkwood had to call on Davey to help. Together, after much tugging and with a sickening wrench, they managed to pull the corpse free. A series of long, liquid farts erupted from the various body orifices, as deep inside the intestinal tract disturbed stomach gases erupted. Hawkwood bit back on the sour taste of vomit as he wiped slime and weed from the dead man's cheeks. A stab of horror moved through him as his eyes took in the bloated yet still familiar features.

In life, Runner Henry Warlock had been a small man with a wiry physique. Neat in both manner and appearance, his somewhat timid looks had concealed a sharp mind and a terrier's talent for hunting villains. Something of a loner – as indeed, given the nature of the job, were all the Runners – he had been a highly skilled operative.

Death had not been kind to Runner Warlock. Immersion in the river had not only caused the body to swell, it had also transformed dead flesh into the colour and consistency of cheese curd.

And Warlock had died hard; that much was immediately evident. The area of damage behind his left ear was not extensive, but beneath the ragged mess of matted hair and riven tissue, it appeared as if the wound ran exceptionally deep. Hawkwood wondered what sort of weapon had been used to deliver the fatal blow. Some kind of hammer, perhaps.

"Looks like the rats have been at 'im," Davey observed matter-of-factly, nodding at the corpse's extended right hand. The boy seemed impervious to the smell and the deteriorating state of the corpse.

Hawkwood followed Davey's stare and saw the chewed and bitten flesh. Vermin, most likely, as the boy had suggested, or perhaps a hungry dog seeking an easy meal. Hawkwood wiped his hands on his coat hem. "How'd you know he was a Runner, Davey?"

The boy looked at Hawkwood with something like pity. "Do us a favour, Mr 'Awkwood. We can spot you lot a mile off. Besides, we knew this 'un on account of 'e caught Pen napping a clout a couple o' weeks back." The boy nodded towards the girl, then, squatting on his haunches, he ran his eyes down the body and sniffed. "He was all right. Not like the rest of 'em 'Orneys. Let 'er off wiv a warning. She'd've been sent to the 'ulks otherwise."

Hawkwood knew that Warlock's sympathy for the children of the street had been regarded as a failing by many of his colleagues, a weakness ripe for exploitation. Certainly, most law officers made little or no concession when it came to apprehending felons. Be they adult or child, it made no difference. With Warlock it had been different. Few of Warlock's fellow officers knew the reason for his soft-hearted – some had called it foolhardy – attitude. Those, like Hawkwood, who were in possession of the facts, did not allude to it openly. There had been a young wife, Hawkwood had learned, who'd died giving birth, and an infant – a son – who had succumbed to the fever less than a week later. Knowledge of such tragic events made it easier to understand why Warlock had not been the sort of man who'd have wanted the incarceration of a nine-year-old girl on his conscience. Eight years' imprisonment would not have been an unusual sentence for stealing a lace handkerchief. There would have been precious little room for hopscotch on the overcrowded deck of a prison barge, Hawkwood reflected gloomily.

He stood and looked around and wondered how many people had noticed the body. For, despite the squalid surroundings, the place was well frequented. The bridge was in constant use and there was a lot of water-borne traffic in the area. Large ships were unable to navigate beyond London Bridge, but lighters and small boats could pass through the arches of the bridge and travel upstream with comparative ease. Blackfriars was a convenient mooring place and an oft-used dropping-off point for the flotilla of bumboats ferrying passengers to and fro between shores.

It was just feasible, Hawkwood supposed, given that the body had been half submerged and lying in shadow, that it might have remained undiscovered for days. What was more likely, however, was that passers-by had seen the corpse and simply chosen to turn a blind eye, viewing it as just another victim of a drunken brawl. In other words, a death of no consequence.

Except that hadn't been the case. Henry Warlock had been a law officer and he had been murdered. Savagely.

Hawkwood had witnessed death in many forms. In war, he'd seen men hacked to pieces by sabres and blown to shreds by cannon shot. And in his relatively short career as a Runner, he'd dealt with enough murder and maiming to last a life-time. Viewing death was always hard. When it involved a stranger you could look upon it with a certain detachment, but when it came to one of your own, that was different. Hawkwood had experienced it on the battlefield with members of his own company. Staring down at Warlock's distended carcass, he felt it now; the feeling of personal loss, the senseless waste and, above all, the stirrings of intense anger.

Smothering his revulsion, Hawkwood began a search of the dead Runner's pockets. Not a pleasant task, but it had to be done. In the event, the search produced nothing. The dead man's pockets were empty. No pocketbook, no coins, no personal belongings of any kind.

Hawkwood gnawed the inside of his lower lip. In-conceivable though it seemed, the evidence appeared beyond doubt. Runner Warlock, for all his experience in dealing with assorted villainy, had apparently fallen victim to one of the commonest crimes in London. Murdered and robbed by the very breed of criminal he had been obligated to pursue. Hawkwood wondered if Warlock had died appreciating the irony. A thought occurred to him. He turned to the boy. "Have you been over him already, Davey?"

The boy looked startled, then indignant. "Not me, Mr 'Awkwood. No way."

Hawkwood clasped the boy's arm. "The truth, Davey. It's important."

The boy shook his head vehemently. "Swear to God, Mr 'Awkwood."

The boy's expression told Hawkwood he was telling the truth. He nodded, accepting the response. "And I don't suppose any of you saw anything?"

Davey shook his head. "Sorry, Mr 'Awkwood. We only just found 'im. It was Ned there who spotted 'im." Davey indicated his companion.

"You tell anyone else?"

"Nah, you're the only one we does business with."

Hawkwood frowned. "How did you know where I'd be?"

The boy shrugged. "Didn't. T'were only a guess. I sent Dandy to the Black Lion and Teaser to Bow Street. Reckoned you'd turn up sooner or later."

Sound reasoning, Hawkwood thought. Dandy and Teaser being, he assumed, the remainder of young Davey's band of ragamuffins. He fished in his pocket and handed over the coin. "You did the right thing, Davey. I'm grateful."

As the boy bit into the coin, Hawkwood stared down at the body. Despite his urgent need to contact Jago again, it

165

looked as if the ex-sergeant would have to wait a while longer for the pleasure of his company.

The Chief Magistrate regarded the stout man standing before him with expectation. "Well?"

The response was a declamatory spreading of the hands. "My dear sir, you must understand that determining the precise moment of death is hardly an exact science."

James Read sighed in exasperation. "Very well, Doctor. In that case, in your *learned* opinion . . ."

The stout man shrugged. "Half a day, perhaps. Not more than one at the most." He removed a silk handkerchief from his sleeve and wiped his brow.

The Chief Magistrate's mouth formed itself into a thin, grim line. "And the cause?"

The handkerchief was placed back inside the sleeve. "Ah, now, of that there can be no doubt. Fracture of the cranium. The occipital bone –"

Read waved his hand impatiently. "In plain English, Dr McGregor, if you please."

"He means," Hawkwood said, "that the poor bastard was beaten to death."

Beside him, the doctor winced. McGregor, the surgeon appointed by the coroner to examine the body of the murdered Runner, was overweight and round-faced and gave the impression that he was rather taken with his own importance and thus not used to being interrupted, whether by a Chief Magistrate or his subordinate. The web of red veins radiating across his nose and upper cheeks suggested that his high self-esteem was matched

166

only by his fondness for port. He fixed Hawkwood with a cold glare.

"Not strictly true. The indications are that the skull was pierced rather than battered."

"Either way, he died of it." Hawkwood did not feel in the mood for niceties.

"Well, yes," McGregor said, sniffing disdainfully. "Eventually."

The Chief Magistrate's head snapped back. "Explain."

The doctor drew himself up. "It's clear from the condition of the body and the deceased's clothing that he spent some considerable time in the water. Initial examination of the victim's lungs, however, has revealed that death was not due to drowning. Indicating, as I have said, that it was the blow to the head that killed him. The fact that the body was discovered above the high-water mark lends foundation to my own particular theory."

Read frowned. "Which is what, exactly?"

"I think he's telling us," Hawkwood said, "that in all probability, the blow wasn't immediately fatal. In other words, he was hit on the head and either fell or was pushed into the river, and it was the effort of dragging himself ashore that killed him."

Read stared at the physician. "That's your conclusion?"

McGregor, clearly annoyed that Hawkwood had stolen his thunder, scowled and nodded. "It is."

There was a long silence. "What about the weapon?" Hawkwood asked.

The surgeon, still rankled by Hawkwood's presence and lack of grace, pursed his lips. "The blow was driven with excessive force. I'd suggest an instrument both sharp and heavy, perhaps a pick or chisel of some kind. Beyond that, I cannot say with any certainty."

"Jesus!" Hawkwood snapped. "Is there anything you can be certain about? Besides your bloody fee!"

McGregor jerked back as if he had been struck. "How dare you, sir! I –"

"Enough!" The Chief Magistrate's voice cut through the air like a whip.

The doctor looked as if he was about to continue his bluster, but one look at James Read's face persuaded him otherwise. Hawkwood discovered that both his own fists were tightly clenched.

Read stood. "Thank you, Doctor. As ever, you have been most helpful. My clerk will see you out."

As if on cue, the door opened. Ezra Twigg stood framed in the opening. "This way, Doctor, if you please."

The Chief Magistrate waited for the door to close before fixing Hawkwood with a stern eye. "That was uncalled for."

"He's a pompous oaf."

James Read sighed. "Pompous he may be. He certainly has an unenviable capacity to irritate. But an oaf? He's an excellent surgeon, Hawkwood, and I would remind you that we require his services rather more than he requires ours."

"It doesn't mean I have to like him," Hawkwood said.

"True," Read agreed wearily. "Nevertheless, while I appreciate your feelings over the death of a colleague, I'd be obliged if you would refrain from insulting the man to his face, particularly in my presence."

The warning glint in the magistrate's eye was only too clear. Hawkwood gave way. "Yes, sir."

Read nodded. Honour had been satisfied. "So, to business. Warlock's murder – you've thoughts on the matter?"

Hawkwood shrugged. "Robbery or revenge. It has to be one of the two."

The Chief Magistrate looked thoughtful. "Well, the area's a notorious haunt for footpads. However . . ."

Hawkwood nodded. "I know. But the more I think about it, the less likely robbery seems. He was too fly to let himself be waylaid by a cutpurse. And the fact that his pockets were empty is no indication. Hell, another hour and he'd have been stripped naked. There's not many who'd pass up the chance of a coat and a free pair of boots. My guess is revenge. He was a good thief-taker. He must have sent down a fair number of villains in his time, made plenty of enemies along the way. That's a lot of people who'd like to see him dead."

Read looked glum. "If it was a revenge killing, the search for his murderer may prove to be a long one. It would be like looking for a needle in a haystack."

"Depends on the size of the needle," Hawkwood said. "Maybe we should begin by looking at his most recent assignments."

Hawkwood tried to recall the details of Warlock's current case. Something innocuous, if memory served. Certainly nothing to suggest there might be violence involved. What the hell had it been? His mind went back to the previous meeting with James Read, when the latter had listed each Runner's case load. Then it came to him.

The missing clockmaker. Hardly a problem to set the pulse racing, one would have thought.

Even the Chief Magistrate looked dubious.

"It's as good a place to start as any," Hawkwood offered.

James Read was silent for several moments. Finally, with some reluctance, he nodded. "Very well. It would appear we've little else to go on." A frown creased the magistrate's face. "You say the children saw nothing?"

"That's what they told me."

"You believed them?"

"Yes."

The Chief Magistrate looked sceptical. "I wish I shared your confidence. Still, I've no doubt you know your informants. I will, therefore, trust your judgement. Now, regarding the investigation, you're the only Runner immediately available to me, so I'm placing you in charge. I'd hoped to recall Lightfoot from his protection duties but the bank will require his services for at least another day. I've also had a word with Lacey's physician. He tells me Officer Lacey may be able to return to light duties, but again it won't be for a day or two. Until then, I'm afraid you're on your own. I've arranged for reward notices to be posted and I've ordered extra constables to begin enquiries in the area. Though, frankly, I've little expectation of them discovering anything of note. I can assign one of them to assist you directly, if you feel it necessary."

"I don't," Hawkwood said quickly. It had been Hawkwood's experience that, with very few exceptions, constables were about as much use as watchmen, which meant none at all. He refrained from voicing his opinion out loud and was relieved when the Chief Magistrate did not seem too surprised at his decision.

"As you wish." Read massaged his temples. "By the way, I take it from your lack of report that there has been no progress with regards to the coach murders?"

"Not so far."

"I see," the Chief Magistrate said pensively. "That is most regrettable."

"I'm going to need information on all Warlock's cases," Hawkwood prompted.

"What?" For a second, the magistrate's thoughts appeared to be centred elsewhere. "Ah, yes, of course. Well, see Mr Twigg. Use him to your best advantage." James Read grimaced. "At least we know now why Warlock failed to report the other evening."

Hawkwood moved towards the door.

"A moment, Hawkwood. There's another matter that concerns me."

Hawkwood tensed. The sudden coldness in the Chief Magistrate's tone was unmistakable. Hawkwood knew instinctively what was coming. Squaring his shoulders, he looked back to find that James Read had returned to the sanctuary of his desk.

The Chief Magistrate laid his palms flat. He looked to be composing himself. "Tell me, Hawkwood, did you give *any* thought as to what the consequences might have been had the Rutherford boy died?"

The clock in the corner sounded unnaturally loud. The seconds ticked away into minutes.

Hawkwood felt his stomach muscles contract. The skin around the wound in his belly tightened violently.

The Chief Magistrate shook his head in despair. "You astound me, Hawkwood, you really do. When I learned of this morning's incident I racked my brain to come up with a logical explanation, but I confess you have me at a complete loss. Perhaps you'd be so kind as to enlighten me. In short, sir, would you mind telling me what, in the name of God, you thought you were doing?" The magistrate's voice vibrated with anger.

Despite the question, Hawkwood had the distinct impression that it would be in his best interest to remain silent and let the Chief Magistrate vent his wrath. He fixed his concentration on a point six inches above James Read's head, and waited for the sky to fall.

James Read rose to his feet and spread his arms to encompass the room. "I'm intrigued. Were you somehow under the illusion that being part of this grants you some kind of immunity? Was that it? Well, I'm here to inform you, sir, that it does not!"

The Chief Magistrate paused. "You know, Hawkwood, after my implicit instruction to you about upholding the reputation of this office, I'm unsure which grieves me most. The fact that you allowed yourself to become embroiled in such a fiasco, or that you actually harboured the ludicrous belief that I wouldn't find out!"

The Chief Magistrate closed his eyes as if in pain and pinched the bridge of his nose. Ignoring Hawkwood, he moved to the window and stared out. Eventually, he spoke.

"By rights I should relieve you of your duties, pending

further investigation. However, current circumstances give me little choice in the matter." The Chief Magistrate turned to face the room. "The fact is, I need you."

There was a stony silence. But Hawkwood sensed that James Read had not finished. He was also wondering how the Chief Magistrate had found out. Lawrence had assured him that Rutherford and his seconds would remain silent, and the surgeon's and servant's palms had been well greased. The woman? Unlikely. Which left Lord Mandrake, who, as far as Hawkwood had been aware, had remained in ignorance of the event. Certainly Lord Mandrake had made no reference to the contretemps when Hawkwood had left the house. Hawkwood's mind turned to the figure he thought he'd seen in the undergrowth. Maybe there had been someone there, after all. But he knew further speculation was pointless. The cat was out of the bag and he was about to suffer the consequences.

Read's eyes bored into him. "Mark this, sir, and mark it well. While I'm not without influence in certain quarters, my position here is purely transitory. There will come a time when I'm no longer able to use my authority to protect you. You would do well to remember that.

"Your foolish actions have placed me in an invidious position, Hawkwood. That is not something I enjoy. Fortunately for you, I've discussed the matter with the boy's father and persuaded him that it would be in neither his nor his family's best interest to advertise or pursue the matter. He has agreed. Not unsurprisingly, given the humiliation you visited upon his son. But beware, Hawkwood, you're treading on very thin ice. I've allowed you a great deal of freedom in the past, but you would be wise not to try my leniency too far. For if there should come a time when I am required to choose between the good name of this office and the conceit of one of my officers, be assured that I will not shirk my responsibilities. Should you feel the need, therefore, to engage in any more personal vendettas, you'd be well advised to seek an alternative means of employment." The Chief Magistrate placed his hands behind his back and stood feet apart. "I'm placing you on notice, Hawkwood. Do I make myself clear?"

Hawkwood felt a wave of relief wash over him. Reprieve, of a kind, had been granted. "Yes, sir."

The magistrate threw him a long, piercing stare, followed finally by a sharp nod of acknowledgement. "So be it. We shall discuss the matter further when this case is concluded. You may go. Mr Twigg will furnish you with details of Runner Warlock's most recent assignments."

"Yes, sir."

"Oh, and Officer Hawkwood . . ."

Hawkwood glanced back. "Sir?"

The expression on the Chief Magistrate's face was one of wry cynicism.

"You look fatigued. In future, I suggest you keep your nocturnal exertions to a minimum."

"What the hell do you mean, there's no record?" Hawkwood stared at Ezra Twigg in disbelief.

The little clerk blinked behind his spectacles and shifted uncomfortably. "I'm sorry, Mr Hawkwood, but Officer Warlock never had a chance to make his preliminary

174

report. He never came back, you see." Twigg shrugged helplessly.

"Well, do you have *any* information? Who reported this damned clockmaker missing in the first place?"

"His manservant."

Hawkwood waited while Twigg, anxious to give the impression that all might not be lost, rifled through a stack of documents at his elbow. With a grunt of satisfaction, the clerk extricated a single sheet of paper and held it to the light. "Yes, here we are . . . Luther Hobb, manservant. It seems the staff became concerned when Master Woodburn failed to return home for his supper. The servant came to alert us. Officer Warlock was then dispatched to investigate."

"And that's the last time anyone from this office saw him alive?"

Ezra Twigg nodded unhappily.

The fact that Warlock had not been missed for a couple of days may have seemed incongruous to an outsider, but in reality it was not that unusual. Being few in number, Runners tended to spread themselves thinly, so it was not uncommon for an officer to delay his reporting back to Bow Street in order to pursue urgent and specific lines of enquiry. Thus Warlock's absence might have been frowned upon, but it had not given immediate grounds for concern; unlike the disappearance of clockmaster Josiah Woodburn.

Which didn't leave a vast amount to go on, Hawkwood reflected ruefully.

"All right, so what do we know about this clockmaker? Any skeletons in the cupboard, besides his being a strict Presbyterian?"

175

There was nothing. At least nothing that Ezra Twigg had been able to find. London clockmakers enjoyed a reputation second to none. And within that august fraternity the Woodburn name was held in the highest regard. The family had been making clocks for almost two hundred years. They had designed and crafted timepieces for kings and princes, merchants and maharajas. The Woodburn name was synonymous with the finest quality. Of Josiah Woodburn himself, there was little to relate. Sixty-eight years of age and a widower for ten years. The only item of note was the fact that he shared his house with his granddaughter, the child having been orphaned when her parents – Woodburn's daughter and son-in-law – had perished in a fire. Adversity being no barrier to good character, the man was looked upon by all as a veritable pillar of society.

All of which, though of moderate interest, added little to Hawkwood's store of knowledge. Which left only one option. To start from the beginning and retrace Warlock's steps; a time-consuming but necessary exercise.

"I assume we *do* have an address?" Hawkwood said. "Or is that too much to hope for?"

Ezra Twigg, feigning indignation, sighed resignedly. "They do say, Mr Hawkwood, that sarcasm is quite the lowest form of wit."

"Do they indeed?" Hawkwood said, unmoved by the clerk's put-upon expression. He waited in silence as Twigg scribbled.

The clerk passed the information across. "Oh, and there was a message left for you."

"A message?" He assumed it was from Jago. And about

176

bloody time, too. But his relief was short-lived for the message was not from Jago. It was from Lomax, the ex-cavalry captain in charge of the horse patrol, who wanted Hawkwood to meet him at the Four Swans in Bishopsgate between five and six that evening. Hawkwood frowned. He supposed it had something to do with the coach hold-up. Twigg, however, was unable to elaborate.

Hawkwood tucked the clockmaker's address into his waistcoat pocket and reached for his coat. A sound made him turn.

"You said something, Mr Twigg?"

The clerk's head was bowed. It was only as Hawkwood headed for the door, that Twigg deigned to look up. "I only said, Mr Hawkwood, that you should be careful how you go."

Hawkwood paused in the open doorway, and grinned. "Why, Ezra, you're concerned for my welfare. I'm touched."

Twigg dropped his chin and peered at Hawkwood over the rim of his spectacles. "In that case, Mr Hawkwood, might I offer a word of advice?"

"By all means, Mr Twigg."

There was a significant pause. The corners of Twigg's mouth twitched.

"Well, if I were you, Mr Hawkwood, I wouldn't go speaking to any strange women."

10

Josiah Woodburn's workshop was in Clerkenwell, which, along with St Luke's parish, housed a substantial proportion of the capital's clockmaking trade. It was there, within a cramped honeycomb of low-roofed attics and gloomy cellars, that the majority of jewellers, engravers, enamellers and case-makers plied their craft. The clockmaker's main residence, however, nestled behind a discreet façade at the eastern end of the Strand. The small, unobtrusive brass plate on the wall next to the front door bore the simple inscription: JOSIAH WOODBURN, CLOCKSMITH. Incorporated into the engraved plaque was the coat of arms of the Worshipful Company of Clockmakers. To this unassuming yet presti-gious location were drawn Josiah Woodburn's most discerning and wealthiest clients.

The marked lack of ostentation was confirmation of Woodburn's standing. A master craftsman at the pinnacle of his profession had no use for elaborate shop frontage or tawdry advertisements. The Woodburn name and reputation were all that was required to attract custom. The plain, unadorned entrance indicated that Josiah Woodburn's commissions, unlike those of his neighbours, were obtained strictly by appointment only.

Which no doubt accounted for the maid's hesitant look when she answered Hawkwood's summons on the door bell. Showing his warrant, which identified him as a police officer and thus not one of Master Woodburn's influential patrons, Hawkwood could tell the girl was debating whether or not to direct him to the tradesman's entrance. Hawkwood solved her dilemma by suggesting that she fetch Mr Woodburn's manservant. After another moment of indecision, she finally showed Hawkwood into the drawing room before making a grateful escape in search of reinforcements.

The manservant, Hobb, was trim and middle-aged with sparse salt-and-pepper hair above a square, honest face. Dressed in smart black livery, there was something about Hobb's bearing, the strong shoulders and upright posture, that suggested he had probably seen military service.

The thin woman by his side – Hobb had introduced her as his wife, the housekeeper – was of a similar age. She wore a plain grey dress, white mob-cap, matching apron and an apprehensive expression.

"I don't understand," the manservant said. "We told Officer Warlock all we know."

Hawkwood's response was blunt. "Officer Warlock's dead – murdered. His body was discovered this morning. I've taken over the investigation."

"God preserve us!" Hobb gripped his wife's shoulder

tightly. The housekeeper gasped, whether from the news or the strength of her husband's hand, it was impossible to tell.

The gravity of the moment was suddenly interrupted by a peal of laughter from the hallway. The door was flung open and a diminutive figure in a yellow cotton dress ran headlong into the room. Following close behind, ears flapping, bounded a tiny black-and-white dog of indeterminate breed.

"Grandpapa –" The child stopped in mid stride and stared around the room. Her gaze finally alighted on Hawkwood and he found himself looking into a pair of the widest blue eyes he had ever seen. The girl was about seven or eight years old and achingly pretty. A doll hung in the crook of her arm; a miniature version of herself, down to the identical coloured dress, lace petticoat and tiny white shoes. Hawkwood watched as the uncertainty stole across her face.

"Did I hear Grandpapa? Is he here?"

Mrs Hobb's anxiety at Hawkwood's news was momentarily eclipsed as she turned to address the look of disappointment in the child's eyes. The housekeeper stood and held out her arms and the little girl ran towards her. The dog, oblivious to the sombre mood in the room, lolloped around the furniture, nose to floor, tail wagging.

The maid appeared in the open doorway, flustered and out of breath. "Sorry, Mrs H. She was off before I could stop her."

Cocooned in Mrs Hobb's protective embrace, the child favoured Hawkwood with another penetrating stare before burying her face in the housekeeper's starched white apron, the doll crushed between them. The dog, spying a stranger, bounded across the carpet and began sniffing the heel of Hawkwood's boot.

Mrs Hobb petted the girl's hair. "Now then, my dear, no need to be shy. This gentleman's Mr Hawkwood, come to visit."

Slowly, the child turned. In a small voice that was full of expectation and renewed hope, she said, "When's Grandpapa coming home?"

The expression on the child's face transfixed Hawkwood. He had a brief vision of Pen, one of the urchins who had discovered Warlock's body. The two girls were near enough the same age, he supposed. Orphans both, yet living lives that were worlds apart. One born into privilege, the other into poverty. Ironic, then, that the expression on their faces, upon seeing him for the first time, had been disturbingly similar: suspicion tinged with fear.

Mrs Hobb squeezed the girl's shoulder. "Hush now, child. Your grandpapa will be home soon, just you wait and see. Isn't that right, Mr Hobb?"

"Certainly it is!" The manservant feigned cheerful agreement. "Just you wait and see!"

Hawkwood was aware that the couple were sending him an urgent message with their eyes, while at his feet the dog rolled submissively, legs splayed, waiting for its belly to be rubbed.

The little girl, as if sensing the unspoken signals, regarded Hawkwood unwaveringly. So intense was her study of him that Hawkwood felt as if her eyes were burning into his soul. Finally, after what seemed an eternity, her gaze broke and she looked questioningly up at the housekeeper.

Mrs Hobb smiled. "Now then, Elizabeth, off you go, there's a good girl. Jessie will take you to the kitchen for a glass of milk, and I do believe Mrs Willow's baked a cake."

The housekeeper shooed the dog which, having despaired of attracting Hawkwood's attention, was indulging in an energetic scratch. "And take Toby with you. Look at him – he's dropping hairs all over the carpet. Hetty will have a fit when she comes to clean."

Hearing its name, the dog emitted a shrill bark. The child's eyes brightened. Still clutching the doll, she tripped out of the room. Stopping on the threshold, she called the dog to her. As the animal scampered past her legs, she looked back at Hawkwood, as if about to speak. Then, evidently changing her mind, she was gone. The maid closed the door quietly behind her. Deprived of the child's presence, the room seemed a much duller place, as if a bright light had been extinguished.

"Bless her wee soul," Mrs Hobb said softly. She glanced towards Hawkwood. "Lost both her parents in a fire, poor mite. And now this." She gave a sorrowful shake of her head.

"When did it happen?" Hawkwood asked.

The housekeeper thought back. "Easter before last. Asleep in their beds, they were. It was the dog that sounded the alarm. Wasn't much more than a pup then, but if it hadn't been for Toby, the wee girl wouldn't be alive today. Inseparable they are now, as you can see."

"Why didn't her parents escape?"

"The father did," Luther Hobb said. "Carried Elizabeth right out of the house, but he went back for his wife and son. They were found in the ashes. All three of them together, the baby in its mother's arms. It wasn't the flames that killed them, you see. It was the smoke." The manservant shook his head sorrowfully.

"And she's lived here ever since?"

"Aye." The manservant's face softened further. "The master became her appointed guardian. Dotes on her, so he does. She has her mother's likeness. Everyone says so."

"How much does she know about her grandfather's disappearance?" Hawkwood asked.

The housekeeper shook her head. "We told her that he was called away on business. It seemed the best thing to do."

"And if he doesn't return home? What will you tell her then?"

The housekeeper took a handkerchief from her apron pocket and crumpled it in her hands. "I don't know, I truly don't." The housekeeper wiped her nose. "He's a good man, a gentle man. Never a harsh word in all the years we've worked for him. Mr Hobb and I can't bear to think of him not coming home. We've prayed for him every night, haven't we, Mr Hobb?"

"There, there, my dear." Hobb patted his wife's shoulder. "Officer Hawkwood will do his best to find him, never fear." The manservant frowned. "You think that Officer Warlock's murder had something to do with the master's disappearance?"

"I don't know," Hawkwood said. "But I intend to find out."

There was a pause, as if each of them was waiting for

one of the others to speak. Eventually, Hawkwood said, "Tell me about Master Woodburn. You were concerned when he failed to return home for supper. Is that right?"

The housekeeper shifted in her seat and nodded. "It was about half past six when Mr Hobb and I began to realize something might be wrong. The master's hardly ever late, you see. Almost always in the house by six, so's he can spend time with Elizabeth before she goes to bed. Regular as clock-work, he used to say. That was his little jest, on account of his working with clocks and the like." The housekeeper's face crumpled as she fought back the tears.

"If he was going to be late, he'd always send a message," Luther Hobb broke in.

"But not this time?" Hawkwood prompted.

The manservant shook his head. "Not a word. We waited. We thought he might only be delayed a short while, but by seven we began to fear the worst. I suggested to Mrs Hobb that perhaps I should go to his workshop to see if he was still there. I'd hoped I might meet him on the way but . . ." The manservant's voice trailed off.

"His workshop – where's that?"

"On Red Lion Street."

If Clerkenwell was the heart of the clockmaking trade, Red Lion Street was the main artery. Many of the premises, Hawkwood knew, had adjoining shops. Clerkenwell for the lower classes, the Strand for the swells.

"And you arrived there when?"

"I'm not certain of the exact time; perhaps half an hour later, or thereabouts."

"Was anyone there?"

"Only Mr Knibbs. Oh, and young Quigley."

"Who are they?"

"Mr Knibbs is journeyman to Master Woodburn. He's in charge when the master's absent. Work sometimes goes on after the master's left. When the work's over for the day, Mr Knibbs sees that everyone leaves before the workshop is locked up."

"And this Quigley? What does he do?"

"Odd jobs, mostly; running messages, sweeping up, that sort of thing. He also watches over the workshop at night. He has a mattress in a corner of one of the storerooms."

"He's an apprentice?

Hobb looked surprised at the question. "Lord, no, sir. He's Mr Knibbs' nephew."

Hawkwood was wondering why one qualification should preclude the other when the manservant gave an apologetic smile. "What I mean is that . . . well, the truth of it is the lad's a wee bit slow. 'Tis only due to the master's charity that he isn't out roaming the streets. Oh, don't get me wrong, Mr Hawkwood," Hobb amended hastily. "It's not that he's given to mischief or anything. In fact he's a gentle soul as a rule, but apprentice? Sadly, no."

Hawkwood digested the information. "I presume you asked Mr Knibbs if he knew of Master Woodburn's whereabouts?"

"Indeed I did, but he told me the master had left the workshop at his usual time. A little after half past five that would be."

"Alone?"

"I did enquire if he'd left with anyone, but Mr Knibbs assured me he had not."

185

"And how did Master Woodburn usually travel? By carriage?"

"No, it was his custom to walk, unless the weather was inclement. The master was – is – very fit for his age." The manservant coloured.

Hawkwood ignored the slip. "When he left here that morning, did Master Woodburn say anything to you about meeting anyone?"

The manservant stiffened. "The master's not in the habit of discussing his appointments with members of the household."

It was the first sign of irritation that Hawkwood had witnessed. It was a reminder that, for all their concern at their employer's absence and the obvious affection they held for his granddaughter, the Hobbs were, when all was said and done, not family but servants. And servants, more than anyone, knew their place.

"Nevertheless, it's possible you may have overheard something."

The look on the manservant's face told Hawkwood he had committed another unpardonable error. It was as if he'd asked a priest to reveal the secrets of the confessional. But servants, Hawkwood knew, were privy to all manner of conversation and gossip, and thus a prime source of information. On this occasion, however, no revelations were forthcoming. The Hobbs were, it seemed, genuinely bewildered by their employer's disappearance.

Following his visit to the workshop, the concerned manservant had retraced his steps, hoping his master had returned home in his absence. Finding that was not the case, Hobb had swiftly made his way to Bow Street where he had voiced his fears to Officer Warlock. The Runner had accompanied the manservant back to the Strand. By this time, two hours had passed since the Hobbs had felt the first flutters of apprehension and the household, understandably, was in some disarray.

Hawkwood eyed the servants speculatively. "And when Officer Warlock left you, did he reveal his intentions?"

"He told us he would be making his own enquiries at the workshop."

"But it was late. The place would have been closed by then, would it not?"

"I assumed it was his intention to go there the next morning."

"So that was the last you saw of him?"

The manservant nodded.

"Didn't you think it curious that you hadn't heard from Officer Warlock since then?"

The manservant looked embarrassed. "Well, to tell you the truth, Mr Hawkwood, we did wonder."

"But you didn't do anything?"

"We didn't think it was our place."

Hawkwood swore inwardly. But their reservations, he knew, were understandable. As servants, it was not the Hobbs' responsibility to question police procedure. It was their function to go about their duties, unburdened by conscience or responsibility. Convention dictated that domestic staff were a breed that was seen, not heard.

Hawkwood gnawed his inner lip. The trail was growing colder by the minute. He glanced at the clock on the mantelpiece. It was almost half past four. He remembered he still had to meet Lomax at the Four Swans.

187

Clerkenwell and Red Lion Street, however, were not far. It was just possible that he could kill two birds with one stone.

Hawkwood wondered how old Isadore Knibbs was. The old man had a face like parchment and yet, despite his age, his eyes were as bright as a jackdaw's. He was also very small. His hands were like the hands of a child, tiny and delicately formed. Only the web of veins visible under the semi-translucent skin betrayed their age. They also appeared remarkably supple for a person of his advancing years. Apart from failing eyesight, arthritis for a clockmaker, Hawkwood mused, must be the worst kind of infirmity.

Josiah Woodburn employed five journeymen, Isadore Knibbs being the most senior. He also employed two apprentices, the maximum allowed under the articles of the Clockmaker's Company. There were ways to bend the rules, Mr Knibbs whispered, as he led Hawkwood through the workshop, a five-roomed gallery overlooking a courtyard at the corner of Red Lion Street and George Court, but Josiah Woodburn, a master clockmaker of impeccable repute, was, in that regard, totally beyond reproach.

"Forty years I've worked for Master Woodburn," the journeyman volunteered proudly, "and a finer man I've yet to meet. Why, he even lets me sign my own work, and there's not many would allow that."

A rare honour indeed. Journeymen were generally not permitted to trade in their own right. Nor were they allowed to put their signatures on any kind of work, clocks or otherwise, even if their employer had never laid a hand on the finished instrument. Everything produced in a workshop was the property of the master. Which indicated Josiah Woodburn as an exceptional employer, albeit an absent one; a state of affairs for which Mr Knibbs could offer no rational explanation. The journeyman was as much in the dark as the Hobbs, and just as concerned. He confirmed that Master Woodburn had left the workshop at the usual time. No one had seen him since. But Mr Knibbs was perfectly willing for Hawkwood to look around the premises and talk to the other workers.

The premises were divided into separate workshops according to task, Mr Knibbs explained as he led Hawkwood through the cluttered carpentry shop. He gestured towards a row of hollow clock cases which lay against one wall like a line of upended coffins. Only the very best wood was used: pine and Honduran mahogany for the casing, oak for doors and bases, English walnut for the veneer. A solitary worker was bent over a saw-horse, ankle-deep in sawdust and wood shavings. The air was heavy with the smell of glue and freshly planed timber.

They walked through an archway and entered an adjoining work space containing several benches, each one strewn with clock innards, as if something mechanical had died and been disembowelled. The walls were hung with a bewildering array of charts and drawings showing cogs, wheels, rings, ratchets and pendulums in anatomical detail.

Not all the working parts were manufactured on the premises, Mr Knibbs confided. Some items were supplied ready-made. Springs, for example, along with spandrels, wheels and clock-plates. Although they possessed the knowledge, Mr Knibbs told Hawkwood, very few clock-makers cast their own brass. It was more convenient to obtain supplies from a brass founder. It was also possible, the journeyman muttered scornfully, to buy in ready-made movements but, thankfully, Master Woodburn belonged to the old school. Generally, he preferred the working parts to be assembled in his own workshops. This made it easier to control the quality of the finished product.

With the exception of the carpenter, the rest of the work-force laboured in silence, heads bowed, lips pursed in studious concentration. A couple of men looked up briefly at Hawkwood's entrance before returning to their work. The two apprentices were easy to identify by their age, probably no more than thirteen or fourteen and no more than a few months into their term of indenture.

In the far corner of the gallery a pimply-faced youth was sweeping metal filings into a wooden tray. The boy was painfully thin, with a tar-coloured bonnet of hair that looked as if it had been attacked by a pair of blunt pruning shears. Hawkwood noticed that the boy dragged his left foot as he walked. The boy looked up, as if conscious that he was being observed. He gazed vacantly in Hawkwood's direction before bowing his head to continue sweeping. Hawkwood saw that the lower part of the boy's face was lopsided, as if the jaw had been dislocated and incorrectly reset. Hawkwood presumed this was the nephew, Quigley.

A thought occurred to Hawkwood as he surveyed the row of hunched shoulders and he asked Isadore Knibbs if anyone had been dismissed recently. There was always the possibility that Woodburn's disappearance had to do with a disgruntled employee seeking revenge, but Isadore Knibbs discounted that idea without a second's thought. Every worker, with the exception of the apprentices, had been with the Woodburn firm for at least ten years. Their loyalty was beyond question.

As was their total inability to account for their employer's whereabouts.

Hawkwood asked Mr Knibbs if there had been anything in Master Woodburn's mood that might have explained his disappearance. The journeyman greeted the question with something approaching horror.

"Surely you're not suggesting the master might have . . . done away with himself?"

"I'm not suggesting anything, Mr Knibbs. I'm merely exploring every avenue."

The journeyman blinked and Hawkwood sighed. "Mr Knibbs, it's been my experience that people disappear for a variety of reasons: of their own free will, by misadventure, or foul play. As far as Master Woodburn is concerned, from what I've learned from the servants and yourself, I'm inclined to eliminate the first alternative. Nothing I've heard so far suggests that your master has disappeared voluntarily. On that basis, I doubt we'll find him dead by his own hand. No, don't look so shocked, Mr Knibbs, it's been known to happen. There's many a fine gentleman who's hung himself over a ten-pound debt or a two-guinea whore."

Isadore Knibbs looked like a man who'd just swallowed a gourd of sour milk.

"Which leaves us, Mr Knibbs, with a rather unpleasant prospect."

191

"But someone must have seen something!" the journeyman blurted. "The master can't have vanished into thin air!"

Hawkwood was on the verge of telling Isadore Knibbs that people vanished all the time, usually to reappear with a knife in the back in some dark alley or bludgeoned to death, face down in the mud on the river bank, but a nervous, stuttering voice at his shoulder gave him no chance.

"I s-seen the master."

Hawkwood and Isadore Knibbs turned together. The journeyman gave a sigh of exasperation. "Now then, Jacob, this is nothing that concerns you. Officer Hawkwood and I have business to discuss." The old man smiled apologetically. "He's my sister's boy. He means no harm." Mr Knibbs clapped his hands. "Come on now, lad, off with you! There's work to be done."

Hawkwood's guess had been proved correct. Up close, Quigley, with his angular body, unruly hair, misshapen face and deformed foot, resembled a stick insect. His bottom teeth were the reason for his uneven jawline. They protruded from his gums like crooked, yellowing tombstones. It was difficult to gauge Quigley's age. It could have been anything from fifteen to twenty. Either way, it indicated that Isadore Knibbs must have been at least a generation older than his sister.

Isadore Knibbs wagged a warning finger. "Come on, Jacob, I won't tell you again. Back to your sweeping, there's a good lad."

"But I s-seen him, Uncle Izzi. I s-seen Master Woodburn." The boy was gripping the broom tightly. His nails were bitten down to the quick.

Isadore Knibbs patted his nephew's arm. "That's right, Jacob. You saw the master. But there's no need to go bothering Mr Hawkwood now. Sorry, Mr Hawkwood, don't you pay him no heed. He's a good boy, but he gets confused. My sister had him late, you see," Knibbs added in an aside, as if the admission was sufficient explanation.

"I t-told the other gentleman and he gave me a p-penny!" For a moment, the dullness in the boy's eyes was replaced by a bright gleam of excitement.

It was Isadore Knibbs' turn to be confused. He stared at his nephew. "What other gentleman, Jacob?"

And Hawkwood felt the first faint glimmer of hope.

"Asked me if I'd seen Master Woodburn, he did. And I said I 'ad and he gave me a penny."

Hawkwood and Isadore Knibbs looked on as Jacob Quigley, tongue protruding, reached into his pocket. His hand emerged accompanied by a triumphant grin. He held the coin out. "S-see! I ain't even spent it yet. I've been saving it," he said in a conspiratorial whisper.

Hawkwood reached into his own pocket. "Tell you what, Jacob. I'll give you another penny if you can tell me who the gentleman was."

The boy eyed the coin with greedy speculation.

"Who was it, Jacob?" Hawkwood coaxed. "Who gave you the penny?"

Suddenly, the boy's expression changed again. His eyes lost their focus. He stared down at the ground, refusing to meet Hawkwood's gaze.

Isadore Knibbs spoke softly. "What is it, Jacob. What's the matter?"

Quigley shook his head, as if a fierce struggle was going on in his mind. "Ain't supposed to let no one inside."

He meant the workshop, Hawkwood realized. "When was this, Jacob?" he asked.

The boy shrank back.

"It's all right, lad," Isadore Knibbs said gently. "No one's going to punish you."

Jacob Quigley's lower lip trembled. "It were dark."

"When, Jacob? When was this?" Hawkwood tried to keep the urgency from his voice. The last thing he wanted was the boy clamming up with fear.

"It were when M-Mr Hobb came to see Uncle Izzi."

Hawkwood's pulse quickened. He looked at Isadore Knibbs. "What time did you leave here that night?"

Knibbs was staring at his nephew. He dragged his attention back to the question. "Quarter to nine. I remember it exactly because I recall comparing my pocket watch with a clock I had been repairing for a client. An arched dial lantern, it was, due for collection the next morning. I wanted to check it was keeping good time."

Hawkwood turned back to the boy. "This gentleman, Jacob. What did he look like?"

No immediate response. Hawkwood tried again. "Was he a tall man? A short man. Thin or stout?"

The boy chewed the inside of his cheek. "'E wanted me to let 'im in. I t-told 'im I wasn't to open up for anyone. M-Master Woodburn and Uncle Izzi's orders. Told 'im to go away, I did. But he said I 'ad to let him in, on account of 'e was a p-police officer."

A surge of excitement moved through Hawkwood.

194

"He showed me his stick." The boy's voice faltered. He stared haplessly at his uncle.

"Stick?" Isadore Knibbs echoed, obviously bewildered.

Hawkwood reached into his coat and pulled out his ebony tipstaff. "Is this what he showed you, Jacob?"

The boy's eyes widened in recognition. He nodded vigorously.

So, Warlock hadn't waited until the next morning. He'd left the Hobbs and gone to the workshops that same night.

"It's all right, Jacob," Isadore Knibbs said. "You did the right thing."

Plainly relieved that he wasn't going to be punished, the boy suddenly seemed eager to talk. "Wanted to know if I'd seen the master. Told me the master hadn't come home and that everyone was worried 'bout him. I s-said to him that I had seen the master and that they wasn't to worry none."

"Well, of course you saw him, Jacob. He was here with us, all day."

"I knows that, Uncle Izzi, but I s-seen him afterwards, as well."

Isadore Knibbs sighed. "I don't think he understands, Mr Hawkwood. It's as I told you. He gets confused."

Hawkwood stared hard at the boy. "Where did you see him, Jacob?" Hawkwood held up a hand to stop Knibbs from interrupting.

"Riding in a carriage, he was, like a real swell."

"A carriage?" Hawkwood frowned. The manservant, Hobb, had told him that the clockmaker did not generally travel by carriage, preferring to walk, unless the weather was bad. The weather on the evening in question had been dry and mild.

"Was the master on his own, Jacob, or was there someone with him?"

"Didn't see no one."

Which didn't necessarily mean the old man had been alone, just that the boy hadn't seen anybody else. "Tell me about the carriage, Jacob. What was it like?"

The boy's eyes lit up. "A fine carriage, it was. Pulled by two big black horses. Beautiful they were, with their coats all s-shiny an' all."

Not a hell of a lot of use, Hawkwood thought despairingly. The description would have fitted most of the chaises in London.

"There was a dragon, too," Jacob Quigley added, in a hushed, almost reverential tone.

Hawkwood thought he must have misheard. "Dragon?" He glanced at Isadore Knibbs, hoping for assistance, but it was clear from the blank response that the old man was equally in the dark.

"What dragon, Jacob?"

"It was like I showed the other gentleman."

Presumably he meant Warlock. "Showed him what, Jacob?"

"The dragon."

"What dragon, Jacob?" Repeating the question, Hawkwood tried to keep his voice calm while suppressing a growing urge to grab the boy by the shoulders and shake him violently.

"'T'were same as the other one."

"Other one?"

"The other dragon, o' course!"

Hawkwood bit back a scream of frustration. This was like pulling teeth.

196

He was unprepared for what happened next. Jacob Quigley threw his broom aside, lunged forward and grabbed Hawkwood's wrist.

"Jacob!" The alarm in the old man's voice caused several heads to lift. Around the workshop, mouths gaped at the spectacle.

Normally, Hawkwood's reaction to an unprovoked attack would have been to retaliate swiftly, but a sixth sense, allied to the obvious lack of malice in the boy's expression, told him that Jacob Quigley's intention was not to do him harm but to gain his attention. The boy, Hawkwood realized, had acted out of similar frustration to his own. Clearly, Jacob Quigley was trying to tell him something he thought was important, but what?

Hawkwood was astonished at the strength of the boy's grip. It would have taken no small effort for him to break free. Mystified, and with an agitated Isadore Knibbs following close behind, he allowed himself to be pulled across the room.

The boy was breathing hard, dragging his deformed foot across the floorboards. They passed through another archway and entered a storage area. Timepieces of every description lined the walls: lantern clocks, long-case clocks, tavern clocks, water clocks, bracket clocks and barometers occupied every inch of shelf and floor space.

Jacob Quigley halted suddenly, turned to Hawkwood, and pointed excitedly towards the wall. Hawkwood followed the end of the boy's gnawed fingernail and found himself confronted by a row of long-case clocks.

"I don't understand, Jacob," Hawkwood said. "What are you trying to tell me?" He stared at Isadore Knibbs in mute appeal, but the journeyman shook his head and spread his hands helplessly.

Jacob Quigley lurched towards the row of clocks, pulling Hawkwood with him. He pointed again.

The clock was tall, nearly eight feet in height. Cased in oak, with mahogany and shell inlays. A twelve-inch white dial, circled by Arabic numerals and bisected by a pair of ornate brass hands. It was a magnificent specimen.

"The time, Jacob? Is that what you're trying to tell me?"

The clock's hands were set at fifteen minutes to six.

"You saw Master Woodburn at a quarter to six?"

The boy shook his head and jabbed his finger once more. Hawkwood stared at the clock.

Jacob Quigley let go of Hawkwood's arm and limped forward. He reached up and jabbed urgently at the clock face. "Dragon! See the dragon!"

Hawkwood stared.

And then, at last, he saw it, and, cursing his stupidity, wondered why it had taken him so long. It wasn't the time the boy was attempting to draw his attention to, it was the engraving on the clock's cabinet. A shield, flanked on one side by a bear, on the other by what was, unmistakably, a dragon. Hawkwood stared at the design. A coat of arms. He looked closer. There was a ship, a pair of crossed swords and what looked like some kind of elaborate leaf motif. He continued to stare. It occurred to him that the design seemed familiar.

Jacob Quigley was grinning slackly, rocking himself from side to side as he watched the understanding dawn across Hawkwood's scarred face.

"All right, Jacob, I see it." Hawkwood traced his hand over the enamel. "And this is what you showed the other gentleman?"

The boy nodded. "'T'were on the door."

"The door of the carriage?" Hawkwood prompted.

Another vigorous nod of confirmation.

Alleluia! Hawkwood thought. "All right, Jacob, you've earned your penny." Hawkwood pressed the coin into the boy's hand. "Mr Knibbs, tell me about this clock."

"That one? Er . . . it's an eight-day –"

"I'm not interested in its damned workings! I want to know who it's for. It's a commissioned piece, is it not?"

"Why, yes."

"For whom?"

Isadore Knibbs blinked at the aggressive tone.

"Come on, man, hurry!"

But before the old man could respond, it came to him.

It had been the night of the ball. He'd seen the coat of arms on the doors, on the panelling, and on the uniforms of the footmen. How could he have forgotten?

It was the Mandrake family crest.

11

It was almost six o'clock by the time Hawkwood arrived at the Four Swans. The inn was a hive of noisy activity. The early evening coach had just pulled in. Passengers were being disgorged and baggage lay strewn around the yard. Hawkwood picked his way through the crowd, ducked through the open doorway, and entered the tap room.

He did not spot Lomax immediately and wondered if the former cavalryman had grown tired of waiting. Then he saw a darkened figure rise and beckon him from a dimly lit booth in the far corner.

"Good to see you," Lomax said, resuming his seat. A quarter-full mug of ale and a bowl containing the remains of a fatty stew sat on the table before him. Next to the bowl was a wooden platter bearing several chunks of bread and a wedge of butter.

Lomax looked beyond Hawkwood and signalled to a passing serving girl. "What'll it be?"

"I'll take a belch," Hawkwood said.

Lomax gave the order, ignoring the girl's stare. He picked up one of the bread chunks with his left hand and began to mop up the gravy from the bottom of the bowl. When the bread was well soaked, he popped it into his mouth, bit down hard and chewed with relish.

"If you're hungry, I can recommend the mutton," Lomax said, licking the grease from his fingers before wiping them on his breeches.

The girl returned with Hawkwood's beer. Hawkwood took a swallow and wondered how, with only one eye, Lomax could see what he was eating. The lighting in the booth was atrocious. The candle in the middle of the table was worn down to a stub. He realized that Lomax had positioned himself so that the injured side of his face was against the wall. It was only when Lomax turned his head that the ravaged side of his face became clear. Hawkwood suspected this was Lomax's usual ploy. The look on the serving girl's face had told its own story.

A thin dribble of gravy trickled down Lomax's chin. Hawkwood averted his gaze but not quickly enough. Lomax had seen the gesture for he lifted his arm unselfconsciously and wiped his mouth with the edge of his sleeve.

The ex-cavalryman grimaced. "Shaving's the real bugger. Can't feel a damned thing. Why, I could slit my own throat from ear to ear. Wouldn't know it 'til I nodded my bloody head."

Hawkwood laughed. He couldn't help it.

Lomax grinned crookedly and raised his mug. "Confusion to the enemy!"

201

"Amen to that," Hawkwood said. He was coming to like Lomax's sense of humour.

Lomax set his drink down and pushed his plate aside. "I left the message because I've some information for you."

Hawkwood sipped his beer.

"It concerns our highwaymen. I presume you're still hunting them?"

"What have you got?"

Lomax toyed with the handle of his mug. "To tell the truth, I'm not sure. Might be nothing. It came to me after our last meeting. Something one of the coach passengers said. Didn't think about it at the time, but now, looking back, the more it strikes me as odd."

"What was it?"

Lomax hesitated. "Got any urgent appointments to keep?"

Hawkwood thought about the need to make contact with Jago and the startling information he had picked up at the workshop, but if Lomax had a lead, his return journey into the rookery could wait. He shook his head. "No, why?"

In answer, Lomax stood and tossed a handful of coins on to the table. "Because I think you and I should pay a little visit."

"To where?"

Lomax reached for his hat while Hawkwood drained his beer.

"The horse's mouth."

The Reverend Septimus Fludde reminded Hawkwood of the vultures he had seen in Spain and South America. Ugly, mean-tempered creatures, with pronounced beaks and beady little eyes. Reverend Fludde even moved like a long-legged bird, in a sort of high-stepping, round-shouldered stalk, giving the bizarre impression that he was about to spread his arms and launch himself into the air. The reverend's sober plumage – his black clerical garb – added to the illusion.

"He's a cantankerous old bugger, but he's the nearest thing we've got to a reliable witness," Lomax had warned as he'd led the way along Bishopsgate to the dilapidated church of St Jude.

"What about the driver and the other passengers?" Hawkwood asked.

Lomax shook his head. "Waste of time. The driver ain't much more than a gibbering idiot. Took straight to his bed and hasn't stirred since. Mind you, the poor bastard did see two men killed in front of his eyes, so it's no small wonder he's come down with a touch of the vapours."

"And the rest?"

Lomax gave a snort of derision. "Ah, you mean Justice Coverley and his lady wife."

"A *judge?*" Hawkwood could not disguise his astonishment.

"Stipendiary magistrate, to be precise. Presides on a bench over Gloucester way. You didn't know?" Lomax looked equally surprised.

Hawkwood cast his mind back to his briefing with James Read. The latter had made no mention of the fact, though it did go a long way to explain why the Chief Magistrate's condemnation of the crime had been so vociferous. Presumably Justice Coverley had used his rank to harness the

203

resources of the Bow Street office to hunt down the thieves who had stolen his wife's jewellery. How fortunate it was to have influential friends, Hawkwood reflected cynically.

"A right bastard," Lomax said with feeling. "And his wife wasn't much better. Mostly wind and piss, of course, and a face on her that'd curdle milk." Lomax chuckled drily. "Not that I can talk, mind. Anyway, seems they were travelling home after attending some family festivity. A wedding, I believe it was. Told me they weren't prepared to tarry on account of his honour having to attend monthly assizes. Pity the next poor bloody wretch who comes up before him. The mood M'lud was in, he'll be after a hanging, and for tying the knot himself, I shouldn't wonder."

"Which leaves us with the Reverend Fludde . . ."

"Indeed," Lomax agreed. "Spitting fire and farting brimstone. Though, if you ask me, his bark's worse than his bite."

In the event, it had proved to be more of an indignant squawk than a bark, though of sufficient intensity to indicate the reverend's displeasure at having the preparation of his Sunday sermon disturbed by a pair of unwanted visitors. His disenchantment was made plain the moment the two men were shown into his gloomy study by the elderly housekeeper.

Seated at his paper-littered desk, Fludde had peered quizzically at the two peace officers. "Officer Lomax, isn't it? Well, sir, have you apprehended the scoundrels?"

"I regret not," Lomax said.

It was clear from his glare that this was not the answer the clergyman had been seeking. As if noticing Hawkwood for the first time, the reverend's head swivelled. Hawkwood could have sworn he heard joints creak.

"And who, pray, is this?"

"Allow me to present my colleague, Officer Hawkwood, special constable from Bow Street," Lomax said.

Fludde did not look very impressed. "Really? So, why are you here, instead of scouring the streets?"

Lomax cleared his throat. "I was wondering, Reverend, if I might take you back to the night of the robbery. It was when the passenger was killed. You told me that the man who shot him said something. I wonder if you recall what that was."

Reverend Fludde's chin came up sharply. "Of course I can recall! I may be advanced in years, Officer Lomax, but I'm not senile!" The churchman's Adam's apple bobbed alarmingly.

"Of course, Reverend. My apologies," Lomax amended hastily. "I meant no disrespect. But I'd be obliged if you'd repeat what you heard to Officer Hawkwood here."

"And will this assist you in catching the villains?"

"I've every confidence it will, sir, yes."

Reverend Fludde sighed impatiently. "Oh, very well. Let me think. As I recall . . ." he said, throwing the ex-cavalryman a withering glance, ". . . he had his pistol pointed at the fellow's head."

To Hawkwood's amazement, Reverend Fludde stood up, teetered momentarily on his spindly legs, extended his right arm and aimed his long, bony index finger at Lomax's face. In a thin, reedy voice, he said, "I remember the words exactly. He said, 'All right, Lieutenant. If you insist.'"

205

"And then he shot him?" Lomax said.

The vicar's face twisted in painful memory. He lowered his arm. "That is correct."

"And you are quite certain about the words the killer used. There's no doubt in your mind?"

"None whatsoever." Fludde shuddered, then, evidently overcome by his theatrical exertions, he reached for his chair and sat down.

Lomax threw a sideways glance at Hawkwood. Hawkwood stared back at him.

"Thank you, Reverend," Lomax said. "That's all I wanted to ask. You've been most helpful. Rest assured, we are doing everything in our power to see that the culprits are brought to justice and that your property is restored."

The reverend smiled sourly. "In that case, Officer Lomax," he wheezed, "don't let me detain you. My housekeeper will show you out. Good day."

And with that, Reverend Fludde returned to his sermon.

"Well?" Lomax said, when they were back on the street. "You do agree? It's curious, is it not?"

Hawkwood said nothing. He was too preoccupied.

"My thoughts exactly," Lomax said into the silence. "I don't know how many highwaymen and footpads I've come up against in my time, but it's a fair few. And I'll tell you this. There's not a single one of 'em'd know an admiral from a bloody midshipman! And yet our highwayman referred to the passenger as 'Lieutenant' . . ." Lomax paused for effect. His one eye glinted brightly. "So, the question we have to ask ourselves is this: how the devil did he know?"

*   *   *

206

How indeed? As he made his way through the quiet back streets towards the Blackbird, Hawkwood's brain struggled with the implications. His thoughts were also occupied with his visit to Josiah Woodburn's workshop, for there too, lurked a conundrum. If the boy Quigley had not been mistaken in seeing Master Woodburn in Lord Mandrake's carriage – and there was no reason why he should have lied – why had no one heard from the clockmaker since?

As far as the Woodburn case was concerned, the obvious course of action would be to pursue enquiries at Mandrake House. Had Warlock gone down that road? If so, and if the dead Runner had not been merely the victim of a robbery, what chain of events had led to his body ending up on the river bank?

Somewhere in the tangled mess of contradictions there lay solutions to both riddles, though, for the life of him, Hawkwood couldn't begin to see where those solutions might reside.

But he wasn't thinking straight. He was tired and he was hungry. He should, he thought, have taken up Lomax's recommendation and ordered a bowl of stew. No matter, he'd ask Maddie to provide something for him. Even a cold platter would suffice. A couple of hours sleep wouldn't come amiss either. But before he could lay head to pillow he would have to make his report to Magistrate Read. Food first, therefore, followed by a brief call into the Shop, and then bed. By which time, there might even be a message from Jago. Stirred by the possibility, he quickened his pace.

But when he walked through the tavern door he was barely given a chance to draw breath, let alone put in a request for supper. Maddie was on him before he could stop her.

"I want you to get rid of him! Right away! The little devil's been hanging around for hours. It's got so my customers daren't venture outside for fear of being relieved of their valuables! I told him you weren't here and that I didn't know when you'd be back, but he insisted on waiting, cheeky beggar! Wanted to wait inside, as well, but I warned him on no account was he to set foot through that doorway. Wouldn't be at all surprised if he had fleas, from the looks of him! I do declare, Matthew Hawkwood, for a police officer, you keep strange company and no mistake!"

It took Hawkwood a moment to realize that Maddie had ceased her remonstration. He smiled. "Go easy, Maddie, you've lost me. Who are you talking about?"

"Why, that boy, of course. Who else?"

"Er . . . what boy?"

"That one!" Maddie's eyes flashed green fire as she pointed an accusing finger.

Hawkwood looked around. A small, grubby face was peering round the edge of the doorframe. A hand beckoned urgently.

An ominous sigh sounded close by. Hawkwood realized it was emanating from between Maddie's tightly clenched teeth. He sensed the landlady was about to erupt, spectacularly.

"All right, Maddie," Hawkwood interposed quickly. "Leave it to me. I'll deal with it."

Hawkwood walked to the door and stepped out into the alleyway.

"Davey?"

"Over 'ere, Mr 'Awkwood!"

The urchin emerged from the shadow of a nearby archway. One hand was hidden inside his ragged jacket. He looked around nervously.

"What the hell's going on, Davey?" Hawkwood asked.

"Got a present for you, Mr 'Awkwood."

Slowly the boy took his hand from inside his coat. He was clutching something. Hawkwood couldn't quite make out what it was. "Reckon I should give you this."

The boy held out his hand. Hawkwood stared at the object. His heart went cold.

It was a Runner's baton.

Hawkwood found his voice. "Where'd you get it?"

The boy looked down, avoiding Hawkwood's eye.

"Davey?"

"Sorry, Mr 'Awkwood. It were Ned. I didn't know he 'ad it, honest."

Ned? Hawkwood had to think for a moment. Then he remembered it was the name of the boy who had discovered Warlock's corpse.

"Where did he find it?"

"Said it were next to the body. Half-buried, he told me. Didn't plan on tellin' no one on account of he thought he could clean it up and flog it. It were Pen who told me he 'ad it. I made 'im 'and it over."

Instinctively, Hawkwood reached into his pocket, but the boy shook his head. "Nah, that's all right, Mr 'Awkwood. Don't want nothing fer it. You been good to us. Treated us fair and square. That other geezer, too. Don't seem right, takin' money off you this time. My way of thinkin' is you

209

can 'ave this 'un with our compliments." The boy grinned. "On the 'ouse, you might say."

Hawkwood gripped the ebony baton tightly. "I'm obliged, Davey. I mean that."

The boy nodded solemnly. There followed a moment of awkward silence, eventually broken by the urchin. "Well, I'd best be gettin' back. Don't like leaving the rest of 'em on their own for too long. No knowin' what manner o' mischief they'll be gettin' up to without me to 'old their 'ands."

Hawkwood nodded. "Take care of yourself, Davey. You tell Ned I said thanks. I owe you."

The boy laughed. "Think I don't know that? Next time, we'll charge you double!"

Still laughing, the boy ran off. Hawkwood, assailed by a sudden and inexplicable feeling of melancholy, turned and walked back into the tavern.

Maddie Teague raised the coffeepot and arched an eyebrow suggestively. "Would the kind gentleman care for anything else?"

Hawkwood sat back as the beverage was poured. The landlady's free hand rested on Hawkwood's shoulder. Covertly, her fingers traced the nape of his neck. "Fancy some company later?"

Hawkwood knew he still had to find Billy Mipps to arrange another meeting with Jago. "Sorry, Maddie. Not tonight."

Framed by the neckline of her bodice, the shadow between Maddie's breasts darkened invitingly.

"You're sure?"

Hawkwood shook his head. "Can't, Maddie. Duty calls."

Maddie straightened abruptly and tossed her fiery mane in mock annoyance. "Well, there's a fine thing! It occurs to me, Matthew Hawkwood, that *some* men don't know when they're well off!"

Hawkwood watched Maddie pout and flounce away. Despite the sense of despondency that had gripped him earlier, he couldn't help but smile at the landlady's theatrics. Maddie Teague had that effect.

As he followed Maddie's departure, Hawkwood thought about Catherine de Varesne, her dark sensuality so different from Maddie's pale, Celtic beauty. Unaccountably, he felt a sharp stab of guilt at having made the comparison, for there had been many occasions when Maddie Teague had been a welcome visitor to Hawkwood's bed.

Maddie Teague was a widow. Her late husband had held a captaincy with the East India Company and had purchased the inn from profits made on the Far Eastern spice routes. The captain had perished, lost at sea along with the rest of his crew and a cargo of Chinese porcelain, when his ship had foundered on a reef during a storm off the Andaman Islands.

Maddie had inherited the Blackbird along with several outstanding debts and a small coterie of creditors. The accumulation of debt had meant that the tavern had been at risk. Salvation had come with the timely arrival of Hawkwood, newly returned from the Peninsula, with a letter of commendation from Colquhoun Grant to the Chief Magistrate at Bow Street, and a need for a roof over his head.

211

Maddie Teague had welcomed him with a cautious smile. The open arms had come later.

Hawkwood had enjoyed his fair share of women. During his years in the army his dark good looks and the uniform had ensured he had rarely been without female company. But military life and the hardship of campaigning were demanding mistresses and it was an understanding woman who was prepared to put up with the life of a soldier, whether it meant staying at home or following him into battle with the other regimental wives.

Becoming a Runner had brought little change in his circumstances. The job and the inherent dangers that accompanied it were all consuming and there had been scant opportunity to develop lasting friendships, let alone anything resembling romance. Male friends were hard enough to find, never mind women.

Not that Hawkwood had ever viewed himself as the marrying kind. Hearth and slippers? He didn't think so. It wasn't in his nature. It might have suited someone like Runner Warlock, but Hawkwood valued his independence too much. So he had taken his pleasure as and when it became available, mostly with molls. There were always willing participants to be found among the better Covent Garden establishments, but they were fleeting liaisons of little consequence. So, now and again, when the mood took them, Hawkwood and Maddie Teague would seek each other's company and, for a short while, perhaps a night or two, they would take comfort in each other's embrace and try to keep the loneliness at bay.

Hawkwood took a slow sip of coffee and surveyed the

scene and tried to put the thoughts of the two contrasting women out of his head. As if he didn't have enough to contend with.

A low hum of conversation filled the tavern. There was the usual mix. Several lawyers, a few of whom Hawkwood knew by name, a smattering of clergy, and a brace of well-dressed individuals who could have been either bankers or doctors. Candlelight created strange moving shadows in the oak-beamed room. The atmosphere was relaxed and cordial.

Warlock's baton lay on the table at Hawkwood's right elbow. It looked decidedly out of place. There had been a clumsy attempt to clean its pitted surface, but traces of dried mud could still be seen engrained in the grip and on the small brass crown at the tip. Hawkwood picked it up and hefted it in his hands. There was something about the baton, the weight and feel, that was strangely comforting. A Runner's baton was a measure of the man who carried it. It gave him great authority: the power to search, to seize, to interrogate and to arrest, a right granted to very few officers, less than the number that could be counted on the fingers of two hands. It was privilege hard earned, often feared, and much envied.

Thoughtfully, Hawkwood held the stem of the baton in his left hand. Then, clasping the tip in his right hand, he gripped hard and twisted.

At first nothing happened. He tried again, with the same result. It was only after he had smeared the join liberally with grease from his discarded plate that the two halves of the tipstaff came grudgingly apart.

To the uninitiated, a Runner's baton was a solid wooden club. In fact, it was hollow. It was here that a Runner carried his sealed warrant. Signed by the Chief Magistrate, the warrant was a further symbol of his authority as well as proof of identification.

Warlock's warrant, Hawkwood saw with some surprise, was still in place. Carefully, he drew it out. As he did so, he realized the warrant was not the only item concealed within the ebony shaft. Wrapped within the furled document were two wafer-thin pieces of onion-skin paper. Frowning and laying the warrant to one side, Hawkwood smoothed them out.

Drawings. Hawkwood peered closer. No, not drawings, something else. They looked like plans.

The first one appeared to show the workings of some kind of mechanical device. There was a four-sided casing, one corner of which was curved. Inside the casing, several long spindles were connected to a series of interlocking cogs of various sizes. There were also two objects that looked like cotton spools, and a flywheel at top and bottom, one large and one small.

Mystified, Hawkwood turned the sketch around until the curved corner was at the top left of the drawing. A thought struck him. He'd seen similar sketches before, on the walls of Josiah Woodburn's workshop.

The second sketch was even more intriguing, though less illuminating. It showed the outline of what looked to be another container, this one square in shape, divided into two halves. There was no mistaking the object contained in the top half of the square. It was the firing mechanism of a gun: hammer, jaws and flint, spring and firing pin. The bottom half of the square was also divided in half. In the left-hand compartment, directly under the hammer of the gun, was a cogwheel, connected to the hammer by a thin, curved, incisor-shaped object. The head of the incisor was hooked under the back of the hammer head. The point of the incisor rested in a space between two of the cogwheel's teeth. The right-hand compartment was empty.

Hawkwood sat back. If he were to hazard a guess, he'd have said the larger sketch showed the working parts of a clock while the smaller of the drawings looked to be some kind of timing device. He considered the possibilities. Could they be the plans for a new type of timepiece? Woodburn was an acknowledged master of his craft. Perhaps this was some sort of revolutionary winding mechanism, something he wanted to keep secret from rival clockmakers. If that was so, how did it fit in with his disappearance? And what about the other components, the hammer and flint? Hawkwood stared at the images before him. Whatever they represented, Warlock, at least, had considered them important enough to warrant concealment from prying eyes. But that begged another question: from whom had they been concealed?

A smudge at the bottom right-hand corner of one of the sketches caught Hawkwood's eye. He leaned forward, reached for the candle and held it over the paper, careful not to let any of the wax drip.

Writing, barely legible.

Hawkwood put the candle-holder on the table. Lifting the paper, he held it up and angled it towards the light. The letters remained obstinately faint, as if the ink had run. Two words. The penmanship left a lot to be desired. Possibly the words had been written under duress, or in a hurry. Hawkwood moved the paper closer to the flame.

There was a *T*, most definitely, followed by what could be an *h*. The *e* was more clearly defined: *The*.

Another *t*, followed by *i*, followed by an *s*.

The this

Two words, one of them incomplete, with no discernible meaning. Hawkwood sat back and frowned.

The striking of the tavern clock brought him out of his trance. It was half past seven. The Bow Street Public Office closed at eight. Hawkwood knew, however, that in one room at least the candles would continue to burn brightly. He rolled up the sketches and replaced them inside the baton. Yet again he would have to delay his attempt to contact Jago. It was time to report back to James Read. Two heads were supposed to be better than one. It seemed an ideal opportunity to put the theory to the test.

It occurred to Hawkwood that throughout his period of service at Bow Street he must have been privy to every permutation of mood change the Chief Magistrate had to offer. Anger, frustration, irascibility, sarcasm, amusement, and, on the odd occasion, even the depths of despair. The one thing he had never witnessed, however, had been James Read's inability to produce speech. Until now.

The look on the Chief Magistrate's face as he removed the sketches from Warlock's tipstaff would remain for ever etched in Hawkwood's brain. James Read sucked in his breath and paled as the full details of the drawings came to light.

Hawkwood could not recall seeing the man so profoundly shaken. After what seemed an age, the magistrate raised his head.

"I want you to describe exactly how you came by these. I urge you to leave nothing out – nothing."

As Hawkwood spoke, the Chief Magistrate listened in silence. Not once did Read's piercing blue eyes leave the Runner's face. When Hawkwood had given his account, James Read continued to stare down at the drawings.

Hawkwood, unable to curb his impatience, broke the silence. "What are they?"

Without looking up, Read said, "It is my belief they are the former contents of the dispatch pouch stolen from the navy courier murdered during the mail coach hold up on the Kent Road."

The room turned as cold and as quiet as a tomb. "I don't understand," Hawkwood said. "What the hell does a navy courier have to do with clocks?"

"Clocks?" The Chief Magistrate stared at Hawkwood aghast. "Clocks? Do you seriously think that's what this is about – the design for some newfangled timepiece? Good grief, man, if only it were that simple!" Without further explanation, the Chief Magistrate turned towards the door. "MR TWIGG!"

The door opened almost before the summons was out of the magistrate's mouth.

"Sir?" Ezra Twigg blinked and waited for his instructions.

Read reached for a pen and wrote quickly on a sheet of notepaper. Folding the paper and sealing it, he wrote an address and handed it to his clerk. "You are to deliver this posthaste, Mr Twigg. You'll note that Caleb is waiting outside. Be so good as to inform him there will be two passengers. We'll be down directly."

Spurred by the urgency in the magistrate's tone, Twigg nodded. "Yes, sir. Right away."

As the clerk scampered out of the office, the Chief Magistrate reached for his cane.

"Why wasn't I told?" Hawkwood tried to keep his voice calm.

The Chief Magistrate paused. "Told what?"

"What was in the pouch. You knew what the contents were when you assigned me to the case. Why didn't you tell me that's what they were after all along? The passenger's valuables were a diversion. You knew that."

"I thought it was a possibility. There was always the chance it was a simple highway robbery and, if that was the case, there was no point drawing unnecessary attention to the dispatch pouch or its contents. But enough of this, we're wasting time."

"You should have trusted me," Hawkwood said.

The magistrate's head came up swiftly. There was a flash of annoyance in his eyes. "For what it's worth, Hawkwood, I *do* trust you. Keeping you in ignorance was not my choice. My hands were tied. However, if you want to find out the true facts behind this case, I suggest you rein in your vexation and come with me." Without waiting for a response, the Chief Magistrate turned and hurried out of the room.

Hawkwood swore under his breath. If it wasn't about clocks, what the hell was it about? And, more to the point, how in God's name had the proceeds of the coach robbery ended up in Warlock's possession? None of it made any sense.

It wasn't until he heard Read give the waiting coachman his instructions that he learned their destination. Which made even less sense.

The Admiralty Building, Whitehall.

12

Hawkwood closed his eyes and wondered what the punishment was for throttling an Admiralty clerk. The continuous scratching of nib across paper had become a kind of torture, like the insistent buzzing of a wasp trapped against a window pane.

The cause of Hawkwood's irritation, a lieutenant who didn't look a day over sixteen, was not unaware of the effect his labours were having. During the last ten minutes, on each occasion the lieutenant had dared lift his head to take a surreptitious peek at the tall, grim-faced man seated on the bench against the opposite wall, his perusal had been met and returned with such brooding intensity that he had been forced to lower his eyes quickly lest he be turned to stone by the basilisk stare.

It was thus with considerable relief that the lieutenant responded to the jangling of the admiral's bell. He looked up briefly. "You may enter."

Hawkwood stood and eased cramped muscles. He had begun to wonder if the Chief Magistrate had forgotten him. Since their arrival at the Admiralty offices and Read's disappearance through the doors of the Board Room, with instructions to wait until sent for, Hawkwood had been left to cool his heels. Only the indistinct murmurings, barely audible beyond the closed doors, had persuaded him that his presence might still be required.

Composing himself, he opened the door.

Aside from the Chief Magistrate, there were three men in the room. Hawkwood did not recognize any of them. James Read beckoned him forward. "Come in, Hawkwood. These gentlemen are anxious to make your acquaintance. Allow me to present Sir Charles Yorke, First Lord of the Admiralty. His fellow board members, Admiral Dalryde and Inspector General Blomefield. Gentlemen, Officer Hawkwood."

Anxious, maybe, Hawkwood thought, but not overly happy at the prospect, if their expressions were anything to go by.

The First Sea Lord's face was as dark as a thundercloud, though it could have been the subdued lighting that had manufactured that effect. The admiral, seated behind the long table, was looking at Hawkwood the same way he might have regarded something he'd picked up on the sole of his boot. Of the three, only Inspector General Blomefield showed what might have been a hint of genuine interest. There was something else in the man's gaze, Hawkwood sensed. If he didn't know any better, he'd have sworn it was amusement.

Hawkwood's eyes were drawn to the table and the two sketches that lay upon it.

The First Sea Lord threw an accusatory glance at James Read. "Does he know?"

Read shook his head. "Not yet."

"Perhaps it's time I did," Hawkwood said. He'd had enough of being kept in the dark.

The admiral's head came up quickly. Charles Yorke grimaced. "By God, Read, you breed impudent pups!"

Before James Read could respond, Blomefield spoke. "Actually, I'd say the fellow has a point, under the circumstances. Wouldn't you, Sir Charles?"

There was an uneasy silence. Hawkwood felt the eye of the First Sea Lord upon him, sensed the displeasure at the apparent disrespect for authority.

After several moments, and somewhat grudgingly, the First Sea Lord finally nodded. "Very well, Read. I suppose you'd better tell him."

Before the Chief Magistrate could respond, however, there came a sharp tap on the Board Room door. The door opened. The admiral's clerk stood on the threshold. The lieutenant opened his mouth, but he was given no chance to speak as a uniformed figure bustled past him.

"Profound apologies, gentlemen. Came as speedily as I could."

Blomefield grinned. "Better late than never, Colonel. Bit like your bloody rockets, eh? Ha! ha!"

Colonel? Rockets?

To his consternation, Hawkwood found himself being scrutinized keenly.

"Officer Hawkwood, Colonel," James Read said. "Hawkwood, this is Colonel Congreve."

Hawkwood stared at the latecomer, taking in the uniform, the bearing, the restless energy. Then it came to him. Colonel William Congreve, eldest son of the Comptroller of the Royal Laboratory at Woolwich, officer of the Royal Artillery, and inventor of the naval rocket.

Congreve's rockets had first been used against the French at Basque Roads. They'd proved so erratic in behaviour they'd been as much a danger to the British vessels transporting them as they had to the enemy fleet. Three years later, however, the design had improved sufficiently for the army to form two rocket companies. Hawkwood had seen Congreve's rockets in action and he wasn't afraid to admit that they'd scared the hell out of him. Fortunately, the French had been even more terrified, but that still didn't answer the immediate question. What was he doing *here*?

"Hawkwood? Ah, yes, of course," Congreve said. Then, to Hawkwood's surprise, the colonel held out his hand. "An honour, Captain."

Captain? Behind his back, Hawkwood heard the First Sea Lord clear his throat disapprovingly.

The colonel ignored the slight. "Well, gentlemen, to what do I owe this hasty summons? Judging by the way your man hammered on my front door, Master Magistrate, I assume it's important?" The colonel moved towards the table and his eyes widened. "Good God Almighty!"

"Well?" Yorke demanded. "What say you, Congreve? Is it the same?"

The colonel bent low, moving his eye over the drawings, examining them closely. Finally, he straightened, his face grave. "Hard to tell from these damned sketches, but, no, I'd say

223

this is quite different. Oh, there are similarities, no doubt about that, but if I were to hazard a guess, I'd say this looks like a much more advanced design." The colonel turned to James Read. "How the devil did you come by them?"

The colonel listened as the Chief Magistrate explained.

"A dead Runner, you say? Damned curious business. How about you, Hawkwood? Any thoughts on how they came to be in your late colleague's possession?"

Hawkwood said wearily, "Colonel, I don't even know what the hell it is we're talking about."

Congreve stared at the Runner then at the Board members.

Admiral Dalryde sighed. "The Chief Magistrate was about to explain when you arrived, Colonel. However, perhaps you'd do the honours, seeing as you're our *scientific* expert."

Had there been a hint of sarcasm in the Admiral's voice? If so, the Colonel appeared not to have noticed, or else had chosen to disregard it. He looked thoughtfully at the two drawings before fixing Hawkwood with a steely eye. "Not one word of what I'm about to tell you leaves this room. Understood?"

Hawkwood nodded cautiously.

"What we have here," Congreve said, "is quite possibly the most fiendish weapon ever devised."

A weapon! So, the trigger device was significant after all!

"Some kind of bomb?" Hawkwood ventured.

Congreve smiled thinly. "No, though your guess is not so wide of the mark. Tell me, Captain Hawkwood, how's your French?"

"Sir?"

"*Le bateau poisson* is what the Frogs have christened

224

it. Well, some of them have. Others call it *le bateau plongeur*."

Fish boat? Plunging boat? "Sorry, Colonel, I'm not with you. Plunge where?"

Congreve looked at Hawkwood, his face a picture of incredulity. "Where the hell do you think, man? Underwater, of course! It's a bloody submersible!"

Hawkwood stared back at him helplessly. "A what?"

It was the Chief Magistrate who came to Hawkwood's rescue. "A boat that can travel under the sea."

Even as he heard the words, Hawkwood thought there had to be a mistake. He stared down at the drawings. A *boat*? The contraption didn't look like any boat he'd ever seen. And what the hell were plans for an undersea boat doing in Warlock's baton?

"Oh, I know what you're thinking," Congreve said, mis-interpreting Hawkwood's look of confusion. "But it's possible, believe me. I've seen it with my own eyes."

James Read said, "The inventor's an American. His name's Robert Fulton."

"And the bastard's working for Bonaparte," Charles Yorke growled.

Hawkwood felt as if he was wading thigh-deep through thick mud. Try as he might, he still could see no resemblance to a boat. If not a clock, his next best guess would have been the inside of a music box.

"Come," the colonel said, taking pity on Hawkwood's bewilderment. "I'll show you."

Hawkwood approached the table. The first thing he realized, as the colonel turned the first drawing on its side, was that he'd been viewing it from the wrong angle. He'd been looking at it as if the cylinder was standing vertically instead of lying horizontally.

The colonel took a pencil from a tray on the table. "Let's see if I can make it a bit clearer." The colonel traced the outline with the pencil point. "This is the hull. Here, the curve of the bow, the keel, deck, and stern. Now, if I add a mast and boom, you'll get the idea." The colonel drew quickly. "There, you see?"

Unbelievably, Hawkwood could. "And this?" Hawkwood pointed to what looked to be a raised section of deck, just forward of the drawn-in mast.

"A metal dome, It's from here that the vessel is controlled. Imagine an upturned barrel placed over a hole on the deck. It allows the commander to stand upright inside the boat. His head and shoulders would protrude into the barrel. Understand?"

"How can he see where he's going?" Hawkwood asked.

"The dome has windows. They're small and made of very thick glass. If you were to ask me, I'd say it's like looking through the bottom of a brandy decanter."

Hawkwood was sorely tempted to say that he'd known a number of army officers who'd spent their entire careers in similar straits, but discretion forbade him. He made do with what he hoped was a sage nod of comprehension. "What makes it go?"

"Muscle power. The crewman turns a crank, which operates a set of revolving blades at the stern. They serve to push the craft through the water. Here – see?" The colonel pointed to the drawing.

Hawkwood looked sceptical.

"Oh, it works very well, Captain. On the surface, with two men working the crank, it'll travel as fast as two men rowing. Submerged, it's about the same. You have to appreciate that the watchword is stealth, not speed."

"How's it constructed?"

"Copper skin over a wooden frame, iron ribs for supports."

Hawkwood watched and listened as the colonel explained and gradually, incredibly, it began to make a kind of sense. What at first sight had appeared to be a confusing jumble of cranks, cogs, spools and spindles had now acquired a totally new meaning. Hawkwood looked on in astonishment as the outer hull and interior of the submersible boat began to take shape before his eyes.

"How does it go up and down?"

"Pumps. They regulate the submergence of the boat underwater. There's a ballast compartment along the bottom of the hull. To sink, you pump water in. To rise, you pump water out. Ingenious!" The colonel shook his head at the wonder of it. "You steer it like an ordinary boat, by the rudder here. That's also controlled by a system of gears. There's a second, horizontal rudder, which turns on a pivot passing through the main rudder. You use that to maintain depth. The keel, by the way, is metal. The weight keeps the vessel level. It's detachable in an emergency, to allow for rapid ascent."

Hawkwood's brain was spinning. "How big is it?"

The colonel shrugged. "Hard to say for certain. The first one was twenty-one feet long, with a diameter of seven feet."

"The *first* one?" Hawkwood said.

"Oh, didn't I say?" The colonel raised an eyebrow. "The weapon's not new. It was offered to us seven years ago."

James Read said softly, "I think, perhaps, we should start at the beginning, don't you?"

"We've been following his career for some time," the colonel said. "A very industrious fellow is our Mr Fulton: artist, engineer, canal builder . . ."

"Canals?" Hawkwood echoed dully.

Congreve nodded. "Came to Europe from Philadelphia in '87, originally. For his health, if you can believe that. Worked with Bridgewater and Brindley for a time."

Hawkwood's face betrayed his lack of knowledge.

"Lord Bridgewater? Came up with a plan to link Manchester to the sea? You remember?"

Vague memory of a rumoured scheme stirred distantly in Hawkwood's brain.

Undeterred by Hawkwood's ignorance, Congreve continued. "It was Fulton who came up with the idea to use winches to haul canal barges over hills. Even wrote a book about canal navigation, versatile bugger. That's what took him to France in '97. Hoped to take out a patent, get the Frogs interested in the idea. Grew sympathetic to the revolution, stayed, and became an engineer for the Directory."

"And this . . . submersible?"

It was Blomefield who broke in. "Ah, that stemmed from a notion he had that the welfare of nations could only be achieved if liberty of the seas was maintained. In other words, destroy the world's navies, establish free trade, and everyone lives happily ever after. Total rot, of course. My apologies, Colonel. Didn't mean to butt in. You were saying?"

"I was going to say that the man's half Irish," Congreve said, without rancour. "So three guesses as to whose navy he planned to destroy first."

The First Sea Lord, a man clearly unused to someone else holding the floor for any length of time, snorted derisively. Unflustered, Congreve resumed his story.

"He took the idea from an American revolutionary, name of Bushnell. Bushnell built himself a diving boat. Called it the *Turtle*. The plan was to sail it under Earl Howe's flagship in New York harbour, attach an explosive device, then withdraw. Fortunately for the admiral, the plan failed. Not enough control of the vessel underwater, plus the flagship's hull was too tough. But Fulton thought the idea was sound enough to attempt improvements. Turns out Bonaparte thought so too. He financed the vessel's design and manufacture. Took the bugger three years, used the Seine as a test site. Even gave the thing a name: called it *Nautilus*."

"From the Greek," Blomefield cut in. "Some sort of mollusc, apparently."

"Indeed," the colonel observed patiently, before continuing. "Well, by this time we'd begun to pick up reports from our agents in France that Bonaparte's engineers were conducting experimental underwater explosions. Didn't think too much of it at the time, but a gradual increase in rumours led us to believe the Frogs were developing a secret weapon, and then Fulton's name kept cropping up.

"At first we thought it was some kind of sea mine. We'd heard reports of barges being blown up and so forth, but then we heard about something else. A submersible boat. Sounded fantastical, but the rumours persisted. Then we had a stroke of luck.

"We heard the vessel had been tested at sea, but we weren't able to confirm it until a month or so later, when the captain of a Revenue cutter got into conversation with the master of a brig that had been anchored off the Marcoufs around the same time as the trials were said to have taken place.

"The brig master had a curious tale to tell. Told the Revenue man he'd been chased by a whale! Now, how many whales do you suppose there are in the English Channel, eh?"

Hawkwood didn't respond. To his ears, the link seemed pretty flimsy, but there was more, as the colonel explained.

Two days previously, one of the brig's lookouts had observed a small sailboat in trouble; mast and canvas had all but collapsed and the vessel was taking in water. The brig altered course to assist, but by the time they reached the spot, the sailboat had disappeared completely. No wreckage, no bodies, nothing. After searching the area, the brig had resumed course.

"And then something strange happened." The colonel's voice was couched low, as if fearful of eavesdroppers. "The brig's stern lookout spotted what looked like another sailboat in distress! Only this time it was closer in to shore. It was only when the brig master took a look through the glass himself that he recognized it as the same boat! And here's the rub. He said this time the boat wasn't sinking, he swore it was *rising out of the water*!

"It was definitely the same vessel," Congreve continued. "It was the odd shape of the rig, you see. The master said he'd never seen the like of it before. Said it looked like a half-opened parasol."

"And the rest," Blomefield prompted eagerly. "Tell him the rest!"

"Yes, yes." The colonel waved a hand impatiently. "I'm coming to that. You see, Hawkwood, the brig master estimated the distance between each of the sailboat's positions to be at least one mile. A mile! It was proof, don't you see? The Frogs *did* have a vessel that could sail under-water!"

The colonel checked his excitement. "But what to do? How could we defend ourselves against such a weapon?"

The solution had at first seemed simple. The British government had dispatched an agent to Paris to try and entice Fulton to England.

Thomas Blomefield took up the story.

Fulton had run into trouble with his French allies. A change of administration at the Ministry of Marine had brought with it a sudden reversal of enthusiasm for the American's invention.

"Decres it was who took over. Looks as if he's changed his tune since, though, but at the time he thought Fulton's idea was barbaric, more suited to a pack of corsairs than the Imperial Navy. Put Fulton's back up, as you can imagine. Fortunately, it coincided with our plan to bring him over to us. Excellent timing on our part. Mind you, he was a greedy bugger!

"Had this agreement with the Frogs. They were to pay him a bounty for every ship destroyed. He demanded a similar contract from us. Also told us if we wanted him to provide details of his submersible and his submarine bombs, it would cost us a hundred thousand pounds for the privilege. Bloody nerve!"

For a moment Hawkwood thought his ears had deceived him. A Runner's salary was twenty-five shillings a week, plus an extra fourteen shillings for expenses; a little over one hundred pounds a year. A thousand times that was an unimaginable sum. What was it about the American's invention that made it worth a king's ransom?

"Anyway," Blomefield said, "we refused to agree any sort of price until his inventions had been examined and tested in England."

"In other words," Congreve put in, "far better to have him inside the tent, pissing out."

The First Sea Lord and the Admiral smiled weakly. James Read's expression remained neutral, though Hawkwood thought he detected a faint tremor at the corner of the magistrate's mouth.

A further inducement had been employed. Fulton had been experimenting with steam as a means of propulsion. While in Paris, he'd written to the Birmingham firm, Boulton & Watt, asking them to build an engine for use in a steamboat in the United States. The British Government, not surprisingly, had refused an export permit. However, should Mr Fulton choose to move to England . . . well, anything was possible.

"Have to confess, I was rather taken with the fellow," Congreve smiled. "I was on the commission, you see."

Fulton had travelled to England in April 1804. No sooner had he set foot ashore than Prime Minister Pitt had appointed a special commission to examine the American's inventions. Other appointees had included the distinguished scientist Henry Cavendish, Admiral Sir Hope Popham, and Sir Joseph Banks, President of the Royal Society. The initial findings, however, had not been well received by Fulton, as the colonel revealed.

"Oh, the design was feasible enough, no doubt about that, but totally impractical in combat." As he spoke, the colonel's hand strayed to the sketches on the table. "Or so we thought at the time." The colonel gave a wry smile. "The commission was more interested in his submarine bomb – his torpedo, as he called it."

"His what?" Hawkwood asked.

"Torpedo. Named after a breed of fish. The beast uses an electrical discharge to stun its enemies. Not sure how exactly, I'm no expert in aquatic fauna."

Despite the explanation, Hawkwood felt none the wiser. The colonel might as well have been conversing in Hindustani.

Prime Minister Pitt, however, had been sufficiently impressed to put his signature to a contract agreeing to pay Fulton £40,000 for demonstrating the principles of his submersible and the surrender of all rights to his invention. A very generous amount, even without the additional supplement of £200 a month salary, a credit limit of £7,000 and a further £40,000 for the first French ship destroyed. Admiralty dockyards and arsenals were ordered to furnish materials and equipment as required.

"We tried out his torpedoes at Boulogne later that year," Congreve said. "Without much success, frankly, but we saw the potential right away. And just the rumour was enough to put the fear of God into the Frogs. There was a lot of refining to do, more testing and so forth. Took another year before we were ready to try again. Remember the *Dorothea*, Blomefield?"

"By God, do I!"

The *Dorothea*, the colonel explained, had been an ancient Danish brig anchored in Walmer Roads, off the Dover coast. Fulton's submarine bombs had reduced the ship to matchwood.

"That was the result we needed. We were all set. We planned to use Fulton's torpedoes and my rockets against the French fleet at Cadiz. Would have been the grandest bloody firework display in Europe!" Colonel Congreve shook his head in regret.

"Only our one-eyed admiral got there first," Blomefield said.

They meant Trafalgar.

Blomefield sighed. "The brave bugger only went and annihilated the Frog fleet. No need for Fulton's newfangled bombs after that. Nothing left for us to blow up!"

"Didn't stop him demanding his bloody fee, though!" the First Sea Lord grumbled.

As a final settlement, Fulton had asked for £10,000 for switching allegiance, £100,000 for demonstrating that warships could be destroyed by his invention, a £2,400 annual pension for life, and £60,000 for agreeing not to use his inventions against the British fleet.

The Board of Arbitration consulted and decided Fulton hadn't done enough to warrant the extortionate payments he was requesting. The Board had eventually awarded him

234

£14,000 plus salary and incidentals already earned, which had amounted to the far from princely sum of £1,640.

"So the bugger dismantled all his equipment and packed off home," Blomefield said. "Lock, stock, and bloody barrel."

"Bearing a very aggressive bee in his bonnet," the colonel added.

"So," Hawkwood said, "the man has a grudge."

"A bloody big one, would be my guess." Congreve sucked at his lower lip reflectively.

"And you think he's back in France?"

Congreve shook his head. "No, not Fulton. The fellow's not in the best of health. An emissary, sent in his place."

"His name is William Lee," James Read said. "He's an old friend of Fulton, been working with him for the past five years. Our contacts informed us that he arrived in France at the beginning of the year."

"Why would the French still be interested after the last time?" Hawkwood asked, mystified. "Why have they changed their minds?"

"Because Bonaparte's losing the war." The voice was the Admiral's. It was the first time he had entered the conversation. "Our little corporal's on the run!"

Congreve nodded. "And it would give Fulton a chance to get back at us. It's no secret that relations between ourselves and the Americans have become somewhat strained." The colonel pursed his lips. "There've been several incidents between our ships at sea. The navy's been stopping American ships to search for deserters. The Americans have accused us of piracy. It would come as no surprise to me if the situation worsened."

"You mean war?" Hawkwood said, disbelievingly.

At this, the First Sea Lord gave a meaningful cough. It sounded suspiciously like a veiled warning. Congreve shrugged. "Who knows?"

While Hawkwood was contemplating the noncommittal answer, the colonel looked towards Dalryde. "Would you care to continue, Admiral?"

Dalryde cleared his throat. "We thought it might pay us to keep an eye on Lee. We suspected Fulton had made a number of improvements. He wrote a book last year: *Torpedo War and Submarine Explosions*. We managed to secure a copy. The contents were disturbing enough for us to dispatch an agent to France to investigate. Resourceful fellow, name of Ramillies, one of our very best men. We'd used him on several previous occasions."

The admiral looked back at the colonel, as if suggesting he might like to take up the story. The colonel duly obliged.

"Lieutenant Ramillies unearthed evidence suggesting that Lee had definitely constructed a more advanced submersible. Through contacts in the Bourbon resistance he was able to secure employment in the dockyard where the submersible was being built. From there, at great risk to himself, he managed to gain entry into Lee's workshop and made copies of the submersible's plans." The colonel indicated the drawings. "Not exactly draughtsman's quality, I'll grant you, but more than sufficient for our needs. A short time later, he learned that trials of the weapon were due to be conducted on the Seine and infiltrated the area to observe proceedings."

"But he was discovered," the admiral broke in, shifting

236

in his chair. "He managed to escape by the skin of his teeth, with the drawings of the submersible, but he was severely wounded. He was sheltered by Royalist sympathizers until he was well enough to travel. They then arranged passage for him back to England. He was landed at Dover and was on his way to London when his coach was held up on the Kent Road. He was murdered and his plans of the submersible were stolen . . ." The admiral paused. "The rest you know."

The colonel picked up one of the sketches and stared at it intently. "We believe the submersible boat is now operational and ready to be used against our convoys. We also believe that Bonaparte has contracted Lee to attack a specific target. What we do not know is the nature of that target."

Hawkwood was still having trouble with the logistics. "But how does the weapon work? How does it deliver the bombs?"

"What?" Congreve perked up. "The bombs, you say? Ah yes, of course, well, it's dashed simple, really." The colonel smiled suddenly. "But then they say the best inventions always are."

Hawkwood wondered if the colonel was alluding to his own experimental rockets. Recalling their erratic behaviour, they had looked anything but simple.

The colonel picked up the pencil once more. "Now, where are we?" The colonel reached for the sketch of the submersible and pointed. "You see the dome? There's a barbed spike attached to a rod that sticks out from the top of it. Fulton called it the horn. When the submersible is positioned beneath the target vessel, the bottom of the rod is struck from inside the dome, driving the spike up into the target's hull. You follow?"

Hawkwood nodded.

"When the spike is secure, the submersible detaches itself, leaving the spike embedded in the target's hull. At the bow of the submersible there's a windlass controlled from inside the craft. A line runs aft, from the windlass, through a ring in the spike to the submersible's stern . . ." the colonel moved the pencil point ". . . where it's attached to a copper barrel containing gunpowder and a primer. As the submersible moves off, the line on the windlass is released. When all the line is played out, the forward motion of the submersible is transferred to the barrel by means of the line passing through the hole in the spike. This detaches the barrel, drawing it against the side of the target. The contact causes the primer to spark and ignite the powder." The colonel grinned. "The rest I'll leave to your imagination."

Ingenious, Hawkwood thought, didn't begin to describe it. He peered past the pencil point, still hovering above the sketch. "How big would the charge have to be?"

The colonel shrugged. "Not that great. Twenty pounds, perhaps. That amount of powder will do more damage under water than it would on land. The force of a detonation doesn't disperse as easily in water as it does in compressible air."

Astonishing, Hawkwood thought. And you'd never hear a damned thing until it was too late. "And the hammer and trigger – some kind of timing device?"

The colonel nodded. "That would be my guess."

"And the writing?" Hawkwood asked.

"Writing?" the colonel said.

"There," Hawkwood said, indicating the faint lettering.

The colonel turned the paper in his hand and peered myopically.

"It doesn't make much sense," Hawkwood said. "The . . . t-i-s – the rest of the word's missing."

James Read moved to look over Hawkwood's shoulder.

The colonel shook his head. "Means nothing to me. What about you, gentlemen? Sir Charles? Admiral?"

The First Sea Lord frowned, looked down, and his eyes widened. "Good God!" Charles Yorke turned towards the Admiral. He looked to be a man on the verge of a seizure. *"Thetis!"*

Dalryde's face went white.

Not two words then, only one. Yet Hawkwood was still none the wiser. He threw a glance of mute appeal towards James Read but, to his consternation, the Chief Magistrate appeared equally perplexed, by both the word and the reaction it had provoked.

"Greek mythology, I believe. Thetis was one of the Nereids, a sea god." The magistrate's brow furrowed in doubt as he caught the exchange of looks between Dalryde and Charles Yorke. "Then again," he said softly, "perhaps it has another significance."

The First Sea Lord was the one who spoke. After a further glance at Dalryde he said, "She's a warship."

"Warship?" Read echoed.

Thetis, it transpired, was not only a Greek deity. HMS *Thetis* was a brand-new seventy-four-gun Surveyors' class two-decker currently moored at Deptford naval yard in preparation for upcoming sea trials. After which, the ship was destined to join the Royal Navy's Channel Fleet.

James Read looked sharply at the Admiral. "When?"

Dalryde blinked. "The twenty-seventh – two days' time. She's due to call in at Woolwich to be coppered and rigged, then Sheerness to take on armament and the rest of her crew. She'll be at sea for a week, then it's across to Portsmouth to join the squadron."

There followed a silence, during which the First Sea Lord continued to look pensive.

"Something else, my lord?" James Read enquired.

Charles Yorke hesitated, then nodded. "The Prince Regent."

The Chief Magistrate looked nonplussed. "Another ship?"

But that wasn't what the First Sea Lord meant. He shook his head unhappily. "No, I mean *the* Prince Regent. His Royal Highness, the Prince of Wales."

Read stared back at Charles Yorke. "What about him?"

"It's His Royal Highness's intention to visit the ship and accompany her on the first part of her journey."

"*To Sheerness?*" The Chief Magistrate's face was a picture of incredulity.

Charles Yorke shook his head again. "Woolwich."

Hardly an epic voyage of discovery, Hawkwood thought. It sounded as if the Prince was fulfilling one of his many and increasing fantasies. It was well known that His Royal Highness held several delusions above his already exalted station. It was not unheard of for the Prince to dress up as a famous warrior from history – a medieval monarch, even a Chinese mandarin – and relive scenes from a blood-soaked and glorious military career, usually to the acute embarrassment of friends and sycophants who were either too loyal

240

or too afraid to tell him the truth: that his prowess on the battlefield existed only in his own fertile imagination.

No doubt, Hawkwood reflected, the Prince's trip along the river would metamorphose at a later date into a second Battle of the Nile, with the prince a veritable hero of the quarterdeck.

The Chief Magistrate fixed the First Sea Lord with a gimlet eye. "And why was my office not informed of this?"

The First Sea Lord shrugged. "Perhaps his Royal Highness did not want to burden you with trivialities."

"Trivialities?" Read responded sharply. "I would hardly consider the protection of the Prince Regent a triviality."

Charles Yorke sighed. "This was not perceived to be a civilian matter, Read, and His Royal Highness will not want for protection. A contingent of marines has already been drafted in from the Woolwich yard. He'll be escorted for the entire journey. There's no cause for concern."

"There was no cause for concern," Read said venomously. "I would submit that circumstances have changed somewhat in light of this new development, wouldn't you?"

Charles Yorke straightened. "Good grief, man! His Highness will be perfectly safe. He's only going as far as Woolwich. It's not the bloody Baltic!"

"You still intend him to go through with the visit?" Read said.

The First Sea Lord gave a tight smile. "It'd take a braver man than me to tell his Royal Highness that his visit's been cancelled. Word is, he's already taken delivery of a new uniform from Schweitzer and Davidson. Let's pray it's something appropriate and that he doesn't turn up looking like the Sultan of Ranjipur." The First Sea Lord lifted a caustic eyebrow. "You know what he's like." Adding quickly, "No offence, Colonel. I know you count His Highness as a friend, but sometimes . . ."

Congreve gave an amused shake of his head and waved a hand. "None taken, my lord."

Charles Yorke was being surprisingly indiscreet, Hawkwood thought, though he could well understand the First Sea Lord's apprehension. The Prince was renowned for his flamboyant costumes, often of his own design, incorporating everything from leopard-skin sabretaches to gold epaulettes, all of which bore little resemblance to any recognizable regimental attire.

"Besides," the First Sea Lord continued, "he's in no danger, not in the middle of London." He turned to Dalryde. "However, once the ship reaches the estuary, that is a different matter. I want her captain summoned. And send a signal to the senior officer, Sheerness Dockyard. No, better still, issue a dispatch to *all* commanders on station in the Thames Estuary. 'Utmost vigilance to be employed in the defence of *all* vessels.' Best to be on the safe side."

As he gave the order, the First Sea Lord moved briskly to the wall above the fireplace. Affixed to the wall were a dozen rolled charts. He chose one and lifted it down. A space was cleared on the table and the chart was unfurled. Hawkwood saw that it covered the mouth of the Thames from Tilbury eastwards to Harwich, then south to Margate. To Hawkwood, it looked to be a vast area. How could you protect a vessel from something you couldn't see?

"We can increase patrols," Yorke said, as if reading

Hawkwood's thoughts. "Lower netting, deploy boats to form a defensive ring, post extra lookouts."

"Why not warn vessels to head for port?" Hawkwood suggested.

"Certainly not!" The First Sea Lord bristled. "You can't have the ships of His Majesty's Navy scurrying for cover like frightened rabbits! No, by God, we'll face this threat with grit and determination. We'll show Bonaparte it's still Britain who rules the waves, not some colonial upstart in an upturned bloody rum cask!"

As the Board Members continued to examine the charts, the Chief Magistrate drew Hawkwood aside. "You see now," Read murmured, "why it is imperative we track down our highwaymen? We must find out who they were working for."

"You think French agents?" Hawkwood said.

"Quite possibly. We know full well Bonaparte has spies in England. It's likely Ramillies' pursuers in France got word to them. It's probably how they knew Ramillies was on the coach. It's vital, therefore, that we run our villains to ground. Likewise, we need to know Runner Warlock's role in all this. How did the plans come into his possession? The Mandrake connection certainly concerns me. I suggest you make enquiries in that direction, especially as we've not yet heard from your underworld friends."

"There is someone who may be able to help," Hawkwood said.

"Good," Read said. The Chief Magistrate glanced towards Yorke's broad back. His face was neutral. When he turned back to Hawkwood, he kept his voice low. "Do what you have to do. Whatever it takes."

13

"Why, Captain Hawkwood! You swore to me you were no longer a soldier, I remember distinctly!" Catherine de Varesne arched an eyebrow in mock reproach before smiling and dropping her gaze suggestively. "Yet, here you are, standing to attention like a grenadier!"

Her hand reached down and Hawkwood winced.

She paused in her caress. Her eyes widened in concern. "Your wound still pains you?"

"You took me by surprise, ma'am," Hawkwood said, grinning.

The frown lifted and she returned his smile. "In that case, my love," she murmured softly, "I will be very gentle." She bent forward and kissed him. While her hand continued with its tender manipulation, her tongue flickered teasingly between his lips. Her dark, cat-like eyes glowed.

They were seated on her bed, close together, hip to thigh.

Lit by candlelight, their bodies projected bold silhouettes on to the canopy above.

She moved in closer, her lips soft against his cheek. "Tell me what you would like to do with me, Matthew," she whispered, still stroking him. "Anything you desire . . . anything."

Hawkwood stroked her slender waist and heard her breath catch. She raised her hips, eased herself on to him and lowered herself slowly. She leaned away, pelvis pressed down, head thrown back. Her full breasts lifted provocatively. Hawkwood placed a hand on the base of her spine and pulled her to him. Her arms enfolded him and they began to move as one.

Afterwards, cross-legged among the tangled sheets, they sipped wine. A plate of pear quarters lay on the bed beside them. She had selected the fruit and used the engraved stiletto to core and split the ripe white flesh. Dipping one of the pear segments in the wine, she offered it up to him. Hawkwood bit down, severing the slice in two. She raised the remaining half to her own lips. As she did so, a drop of juice splashed on to her breast. Stemming the watery trickle with the end of her finger, she traced it around her nipple, raised it to her mouth and, in lascivious display, slowly sucked the juice from her skin. At no time did her eyes leave his face.

Hawkwood had arrived at the house an hour before midnight, unsure of his welcome. In the event, she had greeted him with a glowing smile and invited him in. And, as before, had offered herself with a hunger that had left him breathless.

She rose sinuously from the covers and reached for her robe.

Hawkwood sipped wine, admiring her smooth naked body. "Tell me about Lord Mandrake."

Catherine frowned. "Lord Mandrake?"

"What do you know about him?"

She smiled brightly. "I know he is rich."

"That much *I* know," Hawkwood said. "What else?"

Mandrake's wealth emanated from many sources, chiefly trade. In their capacity as merchant adventurers, the Mandrakes had, over successive generations, established a lucrative import business, involving tobacco from America, silks and spices from the east, and other luxury goods, including Indian tea, and fine wines.

She slipped the robe around her shoulders. "Why all these questions, my love?"

Hawkwood shrugged. "Idle curiosity."

"You're a little jealous, perhaps?" Amusement danced in her dark eyes. She returned to the bed, laughing at his expression. "There's no need to be." She climbed up beside him, making no attempt to secure the robe. The material parted. Her dark-tipped breasts moved tantalizingly beneath the silken sheath.

She took the glass from him, took a slow sip of wine and shrugged. "He's been a friend to my uncle's family for many years. They've shared several business ventures. Most of the wines imported by Lord Mandrake come from grapes grown in the family's vineyards in Portugal. When my uncle saw that I intended to remain in Europe, he asked Lord Mandrake for his help. He has been a very loyal friend. He

246

has even given me the use of this house while I am in London. I think he's one of the kindest men I have known, and he has been most generous in his support for the Comte d'Artois."

He could afford to be, Hawkwood reflected, recalling the opulence of the ball.

"What about his friends?"

"I know he has a great many. I do believe he even dines with your Prime Minister." She looked at him quizzically. "Why, Matthew, you sound as if you suspect him of something. Why is that?"

Hawkwood allowed himself a grin. "I'm a police officer. I suspect everyone."

"Even me?"

Her expression was beguiling, but her words jolted him. She was looking at him over the rim of the glass.

"No." Hawkwood smiled. "Should I?"

She gazed at him perceptively. "Everyone has something to hide, Matthew." She lifted her palm to his neck and traced the area of bruising. "Isn't that so?"

The footman stared at Hawkwood with a mixture of confusion and distrust. Hawkwood, presuming the man had misunderstood his announcement, repeated it.

"Special Constable Hawkwood, here to see Lord Mandrake." Hawkwood held out his warrant. He wondered if the servant could even read, but he knew the document's official seal would probably be enough to gain him access to the house.

His evening with the insatiable Catherine having yielded

no useful information, other than the fact that Lord Mandrake was on nodding if not intimate terms with most of the government of the day, Hawkwood had decided that his only recourse was to take the more direct approach, and revisit Mandrake House.

The footman's eyes scanned the warrant. "His lordship's not at home."

"When do you expect him back?"

The footman hesitated, his caution suddenly heightened by Hawkwood's sharpened tone.

"Well?" Hawkwood said, returning the warrant to his tipstaff.

"I'm not certain. His lordship's gone, you see."

"I know he's gone," Hawkwood said, with rising exasperation. "You've just told me that. Gone where?"

"His estate at Northwich. I believe it was the Comte's wish to visit the country."

"Comte?"

"His lordship's house guest, the Comte de Rochefort."

The Frenchman, the student of Montaigne, who had displayed an unusual degree of interest in Hawkwood the night of the ball. Hawkwood wondered what de Rochefort would think of the north. Northwich was in Cheshire, a long way from the capital's fashionable salons and enticements. There was always fox hunting, of course, though, from Hawkwood's recollection, the Comte had not looked the type to engage in strenuous activity of any sort, unless it involved pitching dice or fanning a hand of cards.

The door began to close slowly.

"Not so fast, culley," Hawkwood said. Jamming his boot

through the gap in the door, he pushed past the servant, and was immediately aware, even as he entered the vast entrance hall, of how quiet the mansion was. It was in complete contrast to his previous visit when the house had been filled with bright lights, music and laughter.

"Sir, I protest!" But the footman's objections went unheeded. With the servant trotting abjectly in his wake, Hawkwood checked the ground floor. Their footsteps echoed hollowly in the lofty passages. No doubt about it, the cupboard was bare. Hawkwood heard voices, but when he investigated the source, he found only servants performing last-minute chores, cleaning fireplaces and placing dust covers over the furniture.

"When did they leave?" Hawkwood asked.

Lord Mandrake, accompanied by his wife and guest and a not inconsiderable amount of luggage, had vacated the house early that morning. Very early, it transpired, not much past first light.

Was it usual, Hawkwood asked pointedly, for Lord Mandrake to depart for his northern estates at this time of year? And if so, was it also his lordship's custom to depart at the crack of dawn?

The servant's reply wasn't much help. Lord Mandrake visited his estates whenever the mood took him. As for setting off early, it was a long journey, therefore, the earlier the family left, the earlier the family arrived.

Hawkwood bit down on his frustration. A thought struck him.

"Tell me, has his lordship been having any trouble with his clocks?"

The footman blinked uncomprehendingly. "Clocks?"

"Yes, his bloody clocks, damn it! Were any of the household clocks in need of repair?"

"Er, no, sir, not as I recall." It was apparent from his expression that the footman had begun to harbour serious doubts about Hawkwood's sanity.

Well, it had been a random shot, anyway. They returned to the front door, where the servant could not hide his relief at showing Hawkwood out. The Runner stood on the steps and reflected. There was little doubt that Lord Mandrake had left in unseemly haste.

But for what reason?

Coincidence or conspiracy?

"And so we commit his body to the ground. Earth to earth, ashes to ashes, dust to dust. In sure and certain hope . . ."

The parson's voice droned on, flat and unemotional, giving the impression that the burial service was a task to be endured. Hawkwood found himself wishing for what would probably be the Reverend Fludde's more strident style of oratory. He stared into the open grave at the rough wooden coffin, and wondered if his own funeral would be so sparsely attended. Probably, he concluded ruefully.

It was late afternoon. The corner of the tiny churchyard was dappled in fading sunlight. Next to Hawkwood, James Read leaned on his stick, his face sombre. Aside from Hawkwood and the Chief Magistrate, there were only three other mourners. There was Ezra Twigg, looking suitably solemn. At the clerk's shoulder, a heavy, thick-set man: Runner Jeremiah Lightfoot, currently on assignment with the Bank of England. Standing several paces away, shaded beneath the branches of an apple tree, a slight black-shawled woman, face drawn with grief, sobbed into a handkerchief. Warlock's sister, whose husband, Hawkwood had learned, had been killed at Almeida. Henry Warlock had been her last surviving kin. Over by the railings, a pair of gravediggers squatted against a moss-encrusted tombstone, smoking clay pipes as they waited patiently for the parson's signal.

The cost of the burial had been borne by the Public Office; a small courtesy, but it had meant the Runner's remains could be buried in the same plot as his wife and infant son. Without it, Warlock's body would have been consigned to an unmarked poor hole. James Read, Hawkwood knew, would never have countenanced such an indignity for one of his officers. The Chief Magistrate looked after his own.

There was no eulogy. The parson, his duty done, clasped his hands devoutly, and nodded to the waiting gravediggers.

While the Chief Magistrate, accompanied by his clerk and Runner Lightfoot, went to offer condolences to Warlock's grieving sister, Hawkwood watched as the gravediggers replaced the soil. It took time. Read had ensured that Warlock's body was buried deep. The resurrection men tended to work during the winter months when the anatomy schools were open, but it wasn't unheard of for the body snatchers to operate out of season. So the precaution had been taken and Henry Warlock would sleep soundlessly in his grave, free from disturbance. Hawkwood stared down at the low mound of earth and the modest headstone bearing the names of Warlock's wife and son. The Runner's own name had yet to be inscribed. Small compensation,

251

Hawkwood reflected, for fifteen years' loyal service and a fractured skull.

He sensed he was being watched and looked up. The child's presence came as a shock and he wondered how long she had been there. Jenny, the waif who had escorted him to his meeting with Jago. She approached him slowly, picking her way between the gravestones. Her bare feet made no noise on the soft grass.

"Told ter bring you this –" she said, and held out her hand.

Hawkwood took the scrap of paper and opened it. The scrawled message was succinct.

Rats Nest. Ten o'clock.

It was signed *J*.

14

Bound with brass, dark and pitted with age, the oak chest had survived a score of bloody campaigns. It had belonged to a major in the Guards before falling into Hawkwood's possession. The major had died from wounds on the retreat to Corunna, and Hawkwood had acquired the chest at auction, the proceeds having gone to the major's widow.

It contained the mementos of war.

Hawkwood opened the lid. The sheathed sword rested on top. A heavy, curved sword, with a blade designed to cleave bone and muscle. With great care, Hawkwood removed the weapon and laid it to one side.

Beneath the sword, carefully folded, lay the dark green, black-braided officer's tunic. The tunic had been patched many times, most noticeably around elbow and shoulder. The stitching, though worn ragged by time, had been neatly executed. The mending had been done by the wife of a Chosen Man. A seamstress by trade, she had been one of the many camp followers who'd accompanied their husbands to the war.

Next to the tunic, also folded, lay a pair of grey cavalry breeches, reinforced with leather inserts down the inside of the leg. Like the tunic, they showed numerous signs of wear and tear. Alongside the breeches, the sash; once bright crimson, now tattered and torn and the colour of dried oxblood.

The officer's greatcoat lay underneath. Weighty and warm, it had protected Hawkwood during the harsh Spanish winters; wind and rain, sleet and snow, nights so cold a man's piss froze before it hit the ground.

Secured at both ends by ribboned ties, the long, grey oilcloth-wrapped bundle lay diagonally beneath the coat. Hawkwood reached in and lifted the bundle out. He hesitated before untying the ribbons.

The rifle barrel gleamed brightly in the candlelight. Etched on to a brass plate on the polished stock was the inscription: *Ezekiel Baker & Son, gunmakers to His Majesty, London.*

A hundred memories were stirred as Hawkwood re-wrapped the gun and laid it on the bed. With this rifle he had shot and killed the Spanish general atop the ramparts at Montevideo. It had accompanied him into Portugal and Spain and it had served him well. In return, he had cared for it as if it had been a child. He had even slept with it at night. It had been as close to him as any woman.

There was more clothing and equipment. Shirts, hats, belts and boots, a case of duelling pistols, tools and moulds for making bullets, ammunition pouches, a powder horn, a bayonet, a brass telescope; the accoutrements of a lifetime's soldiering, and more besides.

Hawkwood made his selection, returning the unwanted articles, including the rifle and sword, to the chest. Then he dressed.

The Rat's Nest was in Shadwell and not the first place Hawkwood would have chosen for a meeting – not even in daytime, let alone the dead of night. He supposed Jago had his reasons for choosing it. To go there in normal attire would be to invite trouble. Remembering his welcome at Noah's Ark, a degree of subterfuge was therefore required.

The person reflected in the mirror bore little resemblance to the austere, well-cut figure of a Bow Street Runner. Gone were the shirt and cravat, the tailored coat, the smart waistcoat and the dark breeches. In their place a threadbare brown shirt, a shabby woollen jacket, a pair of frayed and shiny-bottomed trousers bearing the scarlet seam of the 3rd King's Own, and on his feet a well-scuffed pair of boots. Hawkwood had liberated the boots from the body of a dead French officer. French boots were good quality. This pair looked to have seen better days, but they were sound and comfortable and that's what mattered.

Hawkwood knelt by the fire grate. Scooping up a handful of ash, he rubbed it into his clothes. Untying the ribbon at the back of his neck, he smeared the rest of the ash into his hair. He returned to the mirror and studied the result. Not a bad transformation. Cursory, but it would have to do. No one would take him for a law officer. A labourer, perhaps, or a discharged soldier down on his luck.

Satisfied with his disguise, Hawkwood tucked his baton into his belt and left the room. Using the back stairs, he descended into the passageway at the rear of the tavern and slipped silently into the night.

Hawkwood proceeded with caution. Shadwell lay at the eastern end of the Ratcliffe Highway. The streets were becoming narrower and increasingly claustrophobic. There were no lamps here, no link-men to guide the way. It was as if the cobblestones had absorbed all the light. It might just as well have been the dark side of the moon. No honest men walked here at night, not if they valued their souls.

The sound of a bottle shattering against stone halted Hawkwood in his tracks. He melted into a patch of shadow, face half-turned to the wall, and waited. Across the street, two figures struggled in a drunken embrace. A bottle was raised and swung. One of the brawlers went down. The victor leaned over his fallen companion and booted him viciously in the side of the head. Then, after conducting a hurried search of the victim's pockets, he rose and staggered away, the remains of the bottle trailing loosely in his hand.

Hawkwood stepped out, past the body sprawled in the gutter. He did not bother to check for signs of life. He knew, as soon as he was out of sight, the scavengers would move in, jackals drawn to a rotting carcass. The remains would be picked clean in minutes.

The houses were crude affairs, some wood-built, most of them brick, all packed tightly together; a breeding ground for disease. There had been an outbreak of typhus here not so long ago. It was unlikely the contagion had died out completely. Most likely, it was only lying dormant, biding its time, like an enemy in the undergrowth.

Hawkwood was no stranger to the area, though he didn't know it well. Like the inhabitants of the rookeries, the people here kept themselves to themselves. Strangers weren't welcome. He would have to tread carefully. Turning into a narrow lane, he headed towards the river.

He saw it as soon as he emerged from the alleyway: a dark, monstrous shape tethered to the far end of the wharf. Beyond its black hulk, a forest of mastheads reared towards a full moon, a bright pearl suspended against a curtain of black velvet. A thin veil of mist hovered over the water, as eerie as dragon's breath. In the darkness every sound seemed unnaturally loud; the grating of a ship's hull against a wharf stone, the groan of an anchor chain as a vessel moved against the tide, the slap of rigging against a masthead. Somewhere across the river, a ship's bell tolled mournfully.

There were rumours that she'd started life as a merchantman for the East India Company transporting ivory and muslin, but had later been judged too small to turn a profit. Others hinted that she had plied a more odious trade, ending her days as a slaver on the notorious Middle Passage.

Whatever the truth, she had probably been beautiful in her prime, bows thrusting proudly into the wind and spray, sails spread against an azure sky. But that had been a previous incarnation. Now, left to her fate, she sat embedded in the Thames mud, a rotting derelict.

No one could remember her name. The letters that had adorned her once graceful stern had long since faded away. She'd gained her sobriquet by what she had become.

Countless strays had sought sanctuary within her reeking hull. Homeless seafarers originally, many of them foreigners;

257

former East India men, abandoned by John Company and left to fend for themselves in a hostile land. Destitute, with no knowledge of the language and no means of finding a passage home. Strangers on a strange shore who had gravitated towards this dreadful place to be among their own kind. Wharf rats.

Hawkwood approached the vessel with caution. Away in the murk, something whimpered, as if in pain. A woman, or a child, it was impossible to tell.

There was a dampness in the air and a smell he could not place, sickly and cloying. It wasn't coming from the river, he realized, it was seeping out of the hulk. As he drew closer, the smell grew stronger. When he stepped off the gangway on to the deck, the full stench hit him. He knew then what it was: the foul foetor of human misery.

Looking around, Hawkwood could see that almost every inch of deck space had been utilized. Every broken spar, every last strip of canvas, rigging and ratline had been pressed into service to form makeshift shelters. The result was a coagulation of tents, shacks and driftwood lean-tos that would have made a tinkers' encampment a palace by comparison.

The forward deck grating had been removed, revealing the top rung of a steep companionway. Next to the open hatch, silhouetted by the faint lantern glow issuing from inside the hull, a shrunken figure squatted on its haunches. A pair of half-closed, slanted eyes, set in a wizened, jaundice-yellow face, peered up at him. A thin clay pipe jutted from the creature's lips. A bony hand, with claw-like nails, reached out, palm uppermost. Hawkwood dropped the coin into the outstretched fingers. The hand withdrew and Hawkwood descended into the pit.

Hawkwood was no stranger to life on board ship. The voyage across the Atlantic to retake Buenos Aires had not been the most pleasurable of experiences. Life below deck had been hard. Hawkwood remembered with loathing the closely packed bodies, the sickness and the appalling food, not to mention the inability to walk upright. The voyage home had been even worse. Violent storms had tossed the vessel around like a cork. There had been times during the passage when, spewing his guts over the lee rail, he would have welcomed death with open arms. But not even those weeks of purgatory could have prepared him for this.

The smell was overpowering, as if something had died and been left to decompose. There was illumination, of sorts, from oil lamps and candles, but if ever a place could be truly called a hell-hole, Hawkwood decided, this was it.

He was standing on what looked to be the remains of the mess deck. There were several crudely built benches and tables, some of them occupied. Whether by the living or the dead, it was hard to tell. Dressed in rags and slumped like corpses, they could have been either, or both. Rats slithered past his feet and darted across the table tops. The air was as rank as a sewer.

Hawkwood picked out the corner of an empty pew and sat down. He felt something slither over his boot. He kicked out and was rewarded with a faint squeal.

"You want grog, culley?"

Hawkwood looked up. The man's surly expression indicated that he didn't care one way or the other. Hawkwood nodded, though he had no intention of allowing anything to pass his lips in a sty such as this. A dirty tin mug was placed in front of him and the noxious brew was poured. Hawkwood wiped a sleeve across his face and handed over a coin. The pot man shuffled away. Nothing else to do now except wait, and wonder what had possessed Jago to choose such an unsavoury place for a rendezvous.

Half a dozen benches away, close by the port bulkhead and out of Hawkwood's line of sight, the pot man answered the summons of a crooked finger.

"Well?"

The pot man nodded sullenly. "It's 'im."

"You're sure?"

"I'm sure. 'E's dressed rough, but I saw the scar, didn't I? Under 'is eye, right where you said it'd be. Looks an 'ard bastard, if you ask me."

A coin was placed on the table. "No one's asking you, Cooter. On your way."

The disgruntled pot man pocketed his earnings and slunk off. The receiver of the information stood up.

Hawkwood was staring into his mug and wondering how much harm a single sip would do when he sensed a presence.

"You lookin' fer Jago?"

The whispered enquiry came from Hawkwood's elbow, literally. The speaker was the height of a small boy, but that was where the similarity ended. The seamed forehead was high and broad, the nose flat, while the eyes were large and set wide apart under a heavy brow. The speaker's lack of stature was matched by the incongruity of his dress: a brocade frock coat over a filthy ruffled shirt and striped pantaloons, the latter held up by a wide leather belt. On his feet, a pair of knee boots. The vision was topped off by a blue turbaned bandana. The costume would not have looked out of place on the deck of a Caribbean privateer.

Hawkwood eyed the creature with caution. "Who's asking?"

"The name's Weazle."

Hawkwood hesitated. "Where's Jago?" The little man, Hawkwood saw, even sported a large hooped earring.

"Last-minute spot o' business to take care of. Sent me to fetch you, on account of 'e didn't want you blunderin' around in the dark. Now, you comin', or what?"

The stunted figure was already waddling away. Hawkwood cursed and rose to his feet.

In the outside world, Weazle's size would undoubtedly have placed him at a disadvantage, making him the target for prejudice and intimidation. On board ship, it was a different matter. In the country of the blind, the one-eyed man is king. In the confined, claustrophobic space between decks, the little man was in his element. While his guide trotted confidently ahead of him, Hawkwood was forced to assume an awkward, neck-straining stoop. More than once he had to duck even lower to avoid striking his head on a protruding beam.

The deeper inside the hull they penetrated, the darker it became, and they were not alone. It would have been impossible to count the number of persons on board. In the disciplined world of a ship of the line, all hammocks would have been slung neatly in rows and aligned stem to stern to conserve space. In the Rat's Nest no such regime existed. There were bodies everywhere. Sleeping sacks were suspended from the deck beams like seed pods, and judging from the number of limbs sticking out from beneath blankets, many of the hammocks were double occupied. The moans and groans and movements of the occupants confirmed the fact.

Hammocks were not the only form of sleeping accommodation. There were bunks, too, though that might have been too fine a description for what were, in effect, little more than coffin-sized niches. The place was a catacomb. If the rumours of her former trade were true, Hawkwood thought, it was doubtful if any slave had endured more privation than these pitiful souls. The only difference was that her current residents weren't wearing shackles. At least, none that he could see.

It was as he followed the dwarf through the racks of suffering that his nose had begun to detect another strange aroma, sweet and syrupy. When he saw the weak glow coming from inside the cramped cubbyholes and the pipes, he understood.

He'd seen it before, in the cellars of St Giles and the worst of the Wapping doss houses, and it had always intrigued him. It had begun with the Orientals – Chinese and Lascars mainly – but the habit had started to spread among the Europeans. Forced to exist in the most primitive living conditions, without furniture, bedding, warmth or comfort, it was small wonder that so many of these forgotten folk had turned to crime or begging. While others had resorted to a less arduous means of escape.

262

It had been the ships of the Elizabethan Levant Company that had first brought the black mud into the country. During that time the dealing had been controlled by Turkish merchants. Now, the opium was shipped in by the East India Company, and it was an expanding business. Controlled by legitimate concerns like the Apothecaries' Company, the main brokers operated out of Mincing Lane. Auctions were held at Garraway's Coffee House, close to the Royal Exchange. Over druggists' counters it could be purchased as Kendal Black Drop or the Elixir. In the more disreputable districts of the East End, it was the pipe. The main dens were run by the Chinese, in Stepney, Poplar, the Limehouse Causeway, and Shadwell. In those areas, the Chinese also ran strings of lodging houses. It was a captive market.

What struck Hawkwood most as he ducked past the lolling smokers were the blank stares and the emaciated state of their bodies. He watched one of the addicts prepare his smoke. The tiny ball of opiate was placed on the point of the needle with great care, before being turned in the lamp flame. The bamboo pipe was placed over the lamp and the sticky knobule was inserted into a hole in the pigeon egg-shaped bowl. The smoker drew carefully on the pipe, his effort rewarded by a low gurgling sound. The look on the man's face transfixed Hawkwood. He had expected hope-lessness, yet what he saw was a kind of serenity, something completely at odds with the foetid surroundings.

"Don't mind them," Weazle said. "They won't bother you none." The dwarf chuckled throatily. The sound was not dissimilar to that made by the gurgling pipes.

A few paces further on, the little man halted outside a

heavy wooden door. "Here we are – Captain's cabin." Weazle winked broadly. "Let's see if he's at 'ome."

Weazle opened the door and Hawkwood followed him in.

The cabin was low-ceilinged. Large stern windows indicated it had probably been the master's quarters. A lantern hung from the underside of a deck beam. There were a few items of furniture: table and chairs, a battered dresser, a wooden bunk bearing a stained mattress and several grubby blankets.

"Well, it's about bleedin' time. We'd just about given you up!" The gravelled voice came from behind, while a dark form detached itself from the shadows by the window and moved into view. A handsome face, grey hair cut short, the features quite recognizable.

Instinctively, Hawkwood spun, his hand clawing for the baton beneath his jacket. But he was too late. He felt the cold kiss of steel against his throat, and watched the grin spread wide across Weazle's face.

"Move an inch, culley, and I'll split you like a hog. They'll be scooping your innards up with a spoon."

The speaker moved into view. Bull-necked, shaven-headed, and a twisted smile of triumph on his lips. The bruiser from the dog pit.

Scully.

And the thought that flashed through Hawkwood's mind was as painful as someone plunging a blade between his ribs.

For the last person he would have expected to betray him was Nathaniel Jago.

15

"Sorry about the restraints, Officer Hawkwood." The grey-haired man smiled pleasantly. "Barbaric, of course, but useful when the need arises."

They had relieved Hawkwood of his baton. A still grinning Weazle had produced a set of manacles and secured his wrists and ankles, looping the wrist chain through the arms of the chair. Job done, the dwarf touched his forelock in mock salute and left the cabin.

"I was told you'd gone north with Lord Mandrake," Hawkwood said. Unobtrusively, he tried twisting his wrists inside the manacles, but there was no give at all. He was held fast.

Another smile. "You were misinformed."

"I was also told you didn't speak much English," Hawkwood said.

"Wrong again."

"And I suppose you're going to tell me that your name isn't de Rochefort, either."

"What do you think?"

"It's a wild guess," Hawkwood said, "but I think your name's William Lee."

"Well now, aren't you the clever one. And how did you figure that?"

"There was an American officer fought with Sherbrooke at Talavera. You sound just like him."

"Do I now? That's interesting. And how come an American was fighting for an English king?"

"I don't remember," Hawkwood said. "How come you're fighting for Bonaparte?"

And why was Jago working for the enemy?

Lee folded his arms. "I have my reasons."

"Money." Hawkwood spat out the word as if it were an obscenity.

Lee's face hardened. "You think that's what this is about?" The American smiled thinly. "Oh, they're paying me well, friend. I'll not deny that. But the money ain't the main incentive, Captain Hawkwood. It never was."

The American fell silent.

Hawkwood waited, but Lee seemed wrapped in thought.

"So, what was Mandrake's price?" Hawkwood asked.

And Jago's.

"Ah, now, that's more straightforward. We made him an offer. Advised him, quietly of course, that if he didn't help us, the United States Government would no longer guarantee the integrity of his . . . how shall I put it? . . . overseas investments? As you know, Lord Mandrake still enjoys a

266

substantial income from the tobacco trade – plantations in Virginia, and so forth."

As if to add emphasis to the explanation, Lee reached into his pocket and extracted a half-smoked cheroot. The American opened the lantern and lit the cigar from the flame. Taking a long, luxuriant draw, Lee held the smoke in his lungs for several seconds before exhaling.

"As you may have deduced, not only is my Lord Mandrake a remarkably astute businessman, he's also a pragmatist." William Lee smiled once more and examined the end of his cheroot.

"You mean he's a bloody turncoat!"

"That kind of depends which side you're on, doesn't it?" Lee took another appreciative pull on his cigar.

"Are we going to top the bastard, or not?"

Hawkwood had forgotten Scully. The voice in his ear and the hand on his shoulder reminded him.

Lee flicked ash. "Easy, Scully. Me and the captain here are having a conversation."

Hawkwood said, "How did you know I was a captain?"
Fool! Because Jago would have told him.

Lee rested his haunches on the table and rolled the cheroot between fingers and thumb. "Oh, you know, friends in high places. Word gets around. I know quite a lot about you. Question is, how much do you know about me?"

"We know everything," Hawkwood said. Even as he said it, he knew it didn't sound very convincing.

"Oh, I doubt that," Lee said drily, picking a shred of tobacco from his lip. "I really do."

"We know about the plunging boat." Immediately, Hawkwood wondered if that had been a wise admission.

"Well, of course you do," Lee said. "I'd be mightily surprised if you didn't."

The American's nonchalance was disconcerting. Hawkwood was gaining the distinct impression that he was missing an important part of the picture. How come Lee was so damned cocky? Notwithstanding he wasn't the one tied to a chair.

"If you kill me," Hawkwood said, "they'll only send someone else."

"Oh, I believe you," Lee said jovially. "I surely do. But by then it'll be too late."

"Can I do 'im now?" Scully, pleading.

"Patience, Scully. You'll get your chance. My apologies again, Captain, but Scully here don't take kindly to police officers, or any kind of officer, come to that. Ain't that right, Scully?"

"They're all sons of bitches, every man jack of 'em. Alive or dead, makes no difference."

"See what I mean?" Lee said.

"The bastard belongs in Bedlam," Hawkwood said. "How come he's working for you?"

"What's he say?" Scully demanded.

"He doesn't like you," Lee said. "He thinks you should be in an asylum."

"Does he now?" Scully said.

Scully's fist thudded against the side of Hawkwood's skull. For several seconds the world went dark. Hawkwood wondered if his jaw was broken. He probed the inside of his mouth with his tongue. A couple of teeth felt loose.

"Looks like the feeling's mutual," Lee observed.

The American took another lingering pull on his cheroot. "Actually, Scully here was recommended. Came across a shipmate of his in Le Havre. Said he'd sailed with Scully in the old days. Told me that he knew the river like the back of his hand and that he didn't take much to authority. Told me he didn't care much for your King George either. Sounded like a perfect combination to me. A man I could use."

Scully grinned then. Hawkwood was reminded of a dog wagging its tail at the mention of its name.

"Funny," Scully said, "but you 'as to laugh. Don't see a bloody officer for months, then three of 'em come by all at once. Am I lucky, or what?"

It took a moment for the words to sink in.

"You killed Warlock," Hawkwood said hollowly.

"Warlock?" Scully frowned. "You mean your Runner pal? Aye, s'pose I did, when you think about it. Enjoyed every minute of it, too."

Only the manacles prevented Hawkwood from going for Scully's throat. He stared at Lee. "On your orders?"

Lee was coming to the end of his cheroot. He blew out smoke and shook his head. "Your colleague's death was regrettable and it wasn't my choosing. His lordship over-reacted, I'm afraid. Though once your friend had blundered in, we couldn't just let him walk away."

So, like the good bloodhound that he was, Warlock had followed the clockmaker's trail to Mandrake House. Somehow, he'd discovered a connection between the clockmaker's disappearance and Lee's plan for the submersible, and made a run for it with the drawings. But then he'd been found out, and they'd killed him. Or rather Scully had.

"Does that mean the old man's dead too?"

"The clockmaker?" Lee shook his head again. "He's more use to us alive."

But Scully had said something about three coming by all at once. What did he mean . . . ?

And suddenly, things became infinitely clearer.

"It was *you*," Hawkwood said. "*You* held up the mail coach."

Who better to have recognized a lieutenant's uniform than an ex-seaman?

Hawkwood said, "You shot the courier. You cut his hand off."

Scully's knowing grin said it all.

Lee grimaced. "A mite excessive, I'll grant you, but we had to retrieve the plans. Couldn't risk your Admiralty boys getting their hands on them. Oh, I know they'll have had access to Fulton's earlier designs, but there've been a few improvements since then. No sense in making it easier for them. Mind you, full marks to that agent of yours. Led Bonaparte's men a right merry dance. Why, they lost him so many times, they didn't know whether they were coming or going. Sheer luck we were able to pick up his trail. Found out he'd taken passage on a smuggler's ketch out of St Valery. Turns out the contrabandist was another of Scully's old cronies. Been worth his weight in gold, has Scully. Ain't that so?"

Hawkwood said, "So, who was your partner on that job, Scully? Who was it killed the driver? One of your mutineer

270

friends?" Hawkwood's gaze shifted to William Lee. "Or maybe it was you."

Scully laughed. "It were neither, squire. An' if I told you, you'd never believe me. If you only knew . . ."

Jago? Surely to God, not Nathaniel!

But, even as that thought entered his mind Hawkwood knew it couldn't have been either Lee or Jago. From the witnesses' descriptions, the robbers were like master and apprentice. Both Lee and Jago were too old.

"That's enough!" Lee said, the warning implicit.

The grip on Hawkwood's shoulder tightened perceptibly. Hawkwood tasted a coppery wetness on his lip. Blood, he guessed; Scully's blow having split the skin.

Lee clicked his tongue. "Y'see, Captain, there's the rub. You ask too many damned questions. And right now, I ain't inclined to provide any more answers. Which means you'll just have to die in ignorance." The American shrugged apologetically. "Sorry, Captain, but I don't have a choice. You've become a nuisance. You might not know every last detail, but you're still a risk we can do without."

We?

"Come on now," Lee said reassuringly. "Don't look so aggrieved. You did damned well to get this far."

This far? Hawkwood thought. As far as he could see, he hadn't got anywhere. He'd managed to follow a half-cold trail which had led him precisely nowhere. A dead end. Literally, as it was turning out.

Lee pushed himself away from the table. "All right, Scully, I guess his time's up. I'll leave you to it."

Hawkwood said desperately, "We know about *Thetis*."

271

Lee smiled and shook his head. "No you don't. You think you do, but you don't."

"I'm going to enjoy this," Scully hissed. "My oath, I am."

The big seaman reached into his belt. Hawkwood was expecting him to draw the sword. Instead it was a length of blue metal. Hawkwood felt his stomach turn over. It was a marlinespike.

"And this time," Lee said, his hand on the door latch, "make sure and hide the body. We don't want him found like the other one."

"Don't you worry." Scully gave a dry chuckle. "I've got just the place."

Hawkwood said, "Whatever you're planning, Lee, you won't get away with it."

The American smiled, unperturbed.

"The Devil will come for your soul, Lee," Hawkwood said. "You'll burn in hell for this."

The American raised an eyebrow in surprise. "The Devil? Why, Officer Hawkwood, don't tell me you're a student of Marlowe? And here was I thinking you were just a simple peace officer. You continue to amaze me, you really do. But it's a tad late I'm afraid." Lee smiled disarmingly. "What was it the good doctor said? '*My heart's so hardened. I cannot repent*'?"

"They'll hunt you down," Hawkwood said. "They'll find you and they'll hang you."

"They can try," Lee said, "but they'll be too damned late." He pulled the door open. "Your servant, Captain." The American paused. "By the way, did you know that Kit

Marlowe died in Deptford? Curious that, don't you think? A brawl over an unpaid bill, I believe. Well, I'll warrant it won't be a playwright's death that Deptford'll be remembered for. Not after I've done." Lee winked, jammed the stub of the cheroot between his lips and bowed mockingly. The door closed behind him.

"Just you and me now, squire," Scully said, breaking into Hawkwood's confused thoughts. He tapped the marlinespike suggestively against the palm of his hand. His eyes were as black as stone.

An image of Henry Warlock's shattered skull leapt uninvited into Hawkwood's mind. Pierced, Dr McGregor had said, possibly by a chisel. Staring at the pointed shaft of metal in Scully's meaty fist, it looked such an obvious murder weapon it was hard to believe they could have considered anything else.

"You'll swing for this, Scully. You'll be crow bait, too."

"Funny," Scully said. "That's what your mate said, and look what 'appened to 'im."

Hawkwood tugged at the chains, knowing it was futile. "Christ Almighty, Scully! The bastard's working for the French!"

"So?"

"So, they're the enemy, in case you've forgotten!"

"I ain't forgotten nothing, squire. I ain't forgotten the stinkin' pay nor the stinkin' food. I ain't forgotten the bleedin' arse-wipes who called themselves officers, neither, nor the floggings. You ever been flogged, *Captain* Hawkwood? Nah, don't suppose you 'ave. Christ, you sound like you expect me to be grateful! Why d'you think I went

273

over to the bleedin' Frogs in the first place? You can't be that bloody stupid?" Scully hefted the spike. "Come on, I've 'ad enough of this. Time to die!"

Surprise, Hawkwood knew, was his only weapon. Scully would be expecting him to draw back, to shrink away. Hawkwood decided that attack was the best policy. He knew he'd only get the one chance. He had already braced himself. When Scully stepped forward, Hawkwood clamped his manacled hands around the arms of the chair and heaved himself to his feet. Scully grunted and jerked back. Hawkwood twisted his body, driving the side of the chair into Scully's hip. If he could tip him off balance . . .

But Scully was ready for him and it had always been an unequal contest. Sidestepping with ease, Scully kicked Hawkwood across the thigh. Hawkwood's legs folded. Unable to put his hands out to break his fall and encumbered by the chair, he crashed on to the deck. He landed on his side, his elbow striking the wooden boards with a sharp crack. The pain was excruciating. Scully, spitting profanities, moved in. His free hand moved to his belt. This time it was the sword, the blade short and broad: a navy cutlass.

"Nice try, cully, but you're dead. I'm going to break your skull, then I'm going to chop you up. The night soil men can take the pieces downriver. They'll be burying your bones with the rest of the shit, come morning."

Hawkwood couldn't move. His right arm was paralysed. He was as helpless as a turtle on its back. He tried aiming a double-footed kick at Scully's ankles, but it was a futile gesture. The chair hampered all movement.

Scully laughed contemptuously. "Thought you'd put up

a fight, did you? Won't do you no good." Scully juggled the marlinespike in his hand. "Y'know, your mate was tougher than he looked. I spiked 'im hard. Thought 'e was dead when we put 'im in the boat. We were goin' to take 'im upriver and dump 'is body, too. Couldn't believe it when 'e went over the side. Figured 'e'd gone under for good when we couldn't find him. I 'eard 'e actually made it to shore. Game sod!"

There was nowhere to run, nowhere to crawl.

"Rot in hell, Scully!"

Scully raised the marlinespike. Hawkwood turned his head away and waited for the blow.

The door crashed open. "SPIKERRRR!"

Scully whirled, the grin dying on his lips as the body hurtled towards him. The cutlass swept down. The sound of the blade carving into flesh was sickeningly loud.

Hawkwood looked on in horror as Weazle's body hit the floor beside him. Blood was pumping from the gaping wound in the little man's throat. The dwarf's eyes were wide open, but Hawkwood doubted Weazle had even seen the blow that had struck him. A gag had been tied round Weazle's mouth to prevent him from crying out a warning. As he watched, Hawkwood saw the light in the dwarf's eyes flicker and die.

The speed and force of Jago's shoulder-charge lifted Scully off his feet and pitched the seaman across the table. As the two men tumbled backward, the cutlass point struck the overhead lantern, sending it smashing against the bulkhead. Burning oil splashed over the unmade bunk, igniting mattress and blanket. Small flames began to lick the deck.

275

Jago got to his feet. His right hand was clamped around a heavy wooden cudgel.

"Cap'n!" He bent down and saw the chains. "Christ!"

"Nathaniel!" Hawkwood yelled the warning as Scully rose into view from behind the table, eyes blazing.

Jago stood up and turned. "I warned you, Scully! Harm him and you'd answer to me!"

Scully was still holding the sword. His left hand gripped the marlinespike like a dagger. "Jago, I'm going to rip your heart out!"

Scully came round the table and lunged forward. Jago leapt backwards, the sword blade missing his ribs by a hair's breadth. Scully cursed and tried again. Recovering his balance, Jago countered quickly, scything the cudgel towards Scully's head. Scully ducked. The club caught him on the shoulder. The big seaman bellowed in anger and retreated.

The fire from the broken lantern had begun to spread. The oil-soaked bedding was now well alight. The wooden bunk was also burning. The flames had traversed the deck and were lapping the bottom of the bulkhead and the underside of the door. The hem of Weazle's coat had begun to smoulder.

Hawkwood struggled to get himself upright. Feeling was returning to his arm. Placing his boots against Weazle's corpse for purchase, his first intention was to try and push himself clear of the expanding flames.

In the confined space, Scully and Jago circled each other warily. Scully slashed the cutlass towards Jago's arm. Firelight danced along the blade. Jago swapped the cudgel to his other hand. Parrying the steel, he smashed the cudgel against Scully's exposed wrist. Scully roared as the bone snapped.

The sword fell from his nerveless fingers. Desperately, he jabbed the marlinespike towards Jago's throat. Jago swatted the spike aside and followed through, ramming the end of the cudgel into Scully's stomach. Air exploded from the mutineer's lungs.

Jago didn't hesitate. Kicking the marlinespike out of Scully's hand, Jago drove the cudgel head hard against the seaman's bald skull. Scully toppled sideways. His heel caught the table leg and he went down. Jago moved in. The seaman was on all fours, trying groggily to push himself off the deck. He had retrieved the marlinespike. Blood was streaming down Scully's face. Jago stood over the kneeling mutineer, his face dispassionate. He raised the cudgel and brought it down for a second time. There was a noise like an axe splitting a melon in two. Scully's carcass pitched forward and lay still. The marlinespike clattered across the deck.

Jago viewed the body with disgust. "Gutless piece of shit!"

Weazle's hair and clothing were ablaze. Hawkwood could smell burning flesh. The pool of blood from Weazle's throat was sizzling like bacon fat in the heat. Smoke filled the cabin. Shouts of alarm could be heard outside.

Hawkwood found his voice and nodded towards the dwarf's pockets. "The key! Look for the bloody key!"

The search seemed to take for ever, until, with a grunt of satisfaction, Jago held the key aloft. Quickly, he knelt down, unlocked the manacles and hauled Hawkwood to his feet.

Hawkwood rubbed circulation into his wrists. The cabin was now well and truly alight. The fire had taken full control and the heat was ferocious. Hawkwood looked frantically for an escape route. "The window!"

He had his foot halfway over the sill when Jago said firmly, "Not on your bleedin' life!"

"What?" Hawkwood gasped as he saw the big man draw back.

"I ain't jumpin'," Jago said.

"Christ, Nathaniel! The bloody ship's on fire!"

Jago shook his head. "Take a look. It's as black as a witch's crotch down there. Can *you* see what you're jumping into?"

The roar and crackle of the flames were getting louder. Hawkwood could hardly see the door for smoke. He stared at Jago in disbelief. "You jumped ship to avoid the provost, for God's sake! What's the difference?"

"Difference is I could see what I was doin'! It's the middle of the bleeding night f'r Chris'sakes!"

"I don't believe this!" Hawkwood swore, pulling his foot in. "All right, we'll use the bloody door!"

He was halfway across the cabin when he paused. It was Jago's turn to swear as Hawkwood stepped over Scully's body and ran back to the table. The sergeant watched as Hawkwood appeared to thrust his hands into the fire. Then Hawkwood had the ebony baton in his fist and he was following Jago out of the door.

Entering the passage, Hawkwood was unprepared for the astonishing speed with which the fire had taken hold. Already the flames had travelled beyond the stern of the ship and into the sleeping areas. Hammocks and bunks were being abandoned in haste, though a number of the addicts, Hawkwood saw with amazement, were still stretched out, clutching their pipes, oblivious to the danger. Among the rest, blind panic had taken over. People were scrambling for safety. Pockets of fire, caused by upturned lamps and candles, had broken out all over the deck. No effort was being made to douse them. Everyone was too intent in finding an escape route and saving his or her own skin.

Hawkwood couldn't see a damned thing. The back of his throat was raw. His eyes were streaming. It felt as if his lungs were being grilled. He sensed Jago moving ahead of him, pushing bodies aside, many of them half naked. A man howled in pain as he tripped and fell. His cry for help was cut off by the trampling feet of those coming up behind him.

The blaze was not only spreading upwards, it was moving down, into the bowels of the ship, destroying everything in its path. Burning hammocks were disintegrating and dropping through open hatchways, igniting material on the lower decks. A rising tide of humanity was fleeing for its life, climbing over everything in its path, like a rat pack in a drain. The Rat's Nest was being devoured.

Smoke had fast become the main enemy. In the inky darkness below decks it was insinuating its deadly coils into every nook and cranny. The air was heavy with the pungent smell of burning hemp, tar and opium.

Hawkwood was thinking that he should have pushed Jago out of the stern window when he'd had the chance. They might have suffered a broken arm or leg, but it would have been better than burning to death. Hawkwood knew they didn't have much time. The air was being sucked from his lungs.

And then, mercifully, he felt Jago's massive hand on his collar and he was being pulled upwards. They were at the bottom of the companionway and Jago's strong arm was around his shoulder, guiding him up the stairs. Smoke was billowing out of the hatchway as Hawkwood clambered on to the deck and the night air, which before had seemed the foulest concoction, had never tasted so pure.

If the establishment had a name, Hawkwood could not recall it. He assumed it was just one of the many two-penny houses that existed within the river districts, where a sailor with money in his pocket could find himself a bed and a bottle, and a whore for the night.

They had been admitted to the house by a hard-faced woman, who had greeted Jago not with annoyance or surprise at the late visit, but with warmth and affection. After a murmured conversation, during which no introductions were made, the woman led them through to the small kitchen at the back of the building. Bidding them goodnight, she left, the sound of her footsteps fading as she made her way upstairs, candle held aloft.

Jago pointed to a chair. "Sit yourself down."

Hawkwood watched as Jago raided the pantry, returning with a jug and two tin mugs. "Get some of this down you."

"This from Boney's cellars too?" Hawkwood asked, pouring from the jug and taking a sip. He winced as the brandy rinsed the split in his gum.

Jago grinned and raised his own mug. "Just like old times. You in the wars, and me lookin' after you."

Jago's words, spoken with a grin, were like nails being driven into his heart.

The ex-sergeant frowned. "What?"

"I thought it was you, Nathaniel. I thought you'd fed me to Scully."

"You talkin' about the note?"

Hawkwood nodded. "I should have known. I'm sorry, Nathaniel. I was a bloody idiot."

"Is that all? Bloody hell, Cap'n. If I'd been in your shoes, I'd have thought that too. Don't go tearing yourself up. We been through too much together for me to hold that against you."

"Which is why I should have known better," Hawkwood said, shaking his head. "I was a damned fool." Then the thought struck him. "So, how the hell *did* you know where I was? How did you know about the note?"

Jago shook his head. "Blind luck. I finally had a tickle from Lippy Adams over in Bell Lane, regardin' the goods 'oisted from your coach 'old-up. Lippy owes me a favour or two. Couldn't believe my luck when he told me it was Spiker who'd dropped the stuff off. Figured I'd get a message to you, using young Jenny. Would you credit it, she told me she'd passed one message on already. From bloody Spiker, no less! Which was when alarm bells started ringing. Mind you, Jen weren't much use. Can't read, can she? She couldn't tell me what the bleedin' note said!"

Hawkwood waited patiently. He knew Jago would get to the point eventually.

"Well, Spiker's nowhere to be found – no big surprise. But then I gets to thinking that likely as not he can't read nor write neither. Which means he must 'ave 'ad someone write 'is note for him. And in our neck o' the woods there's only one scribe who'd do that for 'im. Solly Linnett."

281

"So, you had words with Solly."

"That I did. In fact we 'ad an entire conversation. Very obligin', is old Solly, given the right inducements. Told me everything I needed to know, and not a moment too soon, from what I could see." Jago's face split into another disarming grin. "Swear to God, I don't know what you'd do without me. You're not safe to be let out on your own." The ex-sergeant's expression turned suddenly serious. "Now, would you mind tellin' me just what the bleedin' 'ell's goin' on?"

"I'm not sure you'd believe me," Hawkwood said wearily.

"Try me," Jago offered. "We ain't goin' nowhere."

So Hawkwood told him. Beginning with the coach robbery, through to the missing clockmaker, Warlock's murder and William Lee and his submersible boat. By the time he'd finished, Hawkwood's throat, though well lubricated with brandy, felt as if it had been stuffed with nettles. He suspected it had as much to do with the amount of smoke he had inhaled as with his telling of the tale.

"Bloody hell!" Jago said, after a lengthy silence. "You weren't kiddin', were you? So, what happens now?"

"We find Lee and stop him."

"Whoa!" Jago said. "What do you mean, *we?* Jesus, you've got a bloody nerve!" The big man fell silent, then he sighed. "Christ, all right, I'm in. But how are we goin' to stop the bugger if we don't know where he is?"

"I don't know," Hawkwood said. "I've a feeling I'm missing something, something important."

Both men stared into their drinks.

"Bleedin' generals," Jago said.

Hawkwood looked at him. "What?"

Jago sighed. "Bleedin' generals – remember? What was it we used to say? They never tell you anything. They keep you in the dark and feed you on shit, like bloody mushrooms. Well, if you ask me, I reckon that's what's been happening here. I think someone up there ain't tellin' you the full story. I reckon once you find out what it is they ain't been tellin' you, you'll be able to figure it out."

"They should have made you a bloody general," Hawkwood said.

16

Hawkwood grinned at the big man's discomfort. "No need to look so worried, Nathaniel. You're safe. You're with me."

"If you say so." Despite the reassurance, Nathaniel Jago did not look like a man convinced.

But then at two o'clock in the morning, in the Chief Magistrate's chambers at Bow Street, Hawkwood thought with amusement, who could blame him?

A bleary-eyed Ezra Twigg had answered the door. The little clerk, clad incongruously in a calf-length nightshirt and tasselled cap, had taken one look at Hawkwood's smoke-blackened clothes and bruised face and the big man standing beside him, and let them into the house without uttering a single word.

"I need to speak with him, Ezra," Hawkwood said. "Is he up?"

"Course he's up," the clerk grumbled. "Still dressed, too.

284

Doesn't need any sleep, that one. Not like some of us," he added tartly.

As Twigg padded off, muttering dire threats of retribution, Hawkwood led the way upstairs.

Did the Chief Magistrate ever go to bed? Hawkwood wondered. When James Read appeared, shadowed by the now hastily attired Ezra Twigg, he looked as well turned out and as urbane as ever, and not at all put out by the lateness of the hour.

"Good morning, Hawkwood." James Read paused as his eyes took in both men. "Ah, the redoubtable Sergeant Jago, I presume?"

Jago shot Hawkwood a startled glance.

"Come now, Sergeant," Read said. "No need to be alarmed. Your description and reputation precedes you." Read looked Hawkwood up and down. "I suspect I'm going to regret asking this, but why do you look like something that has been trampled by a squad of dragoons?"

"I've been having words with one of our highwaymen."

The Chief Magistrate brightened instantly. "Have you indeed? Capital!"

"Not really," Hawkwood said. "He's dead. Nathaniel killed him."

James Read's face fell. "*That* is most unfortunate." The magistrate peered questioningly towards Jago. "His death *was* unavoidable, I take it?"

"He'd have killed *me*, if he'd had his way," Hawkwood said. "Nathaniel saved my life."

"In that case, Sergeant, we're much obliged to you." Read moved towards his desk. "So, who was he?"

"His name was Scully. Ex-navy, which explains his lack of horse sense. He was the one who shot agent Ramillies. He and his partner were working for William Lee." Hawkwood paused. "We met him, too."

It was almost comical the way the Chief Magistrate froze in mid stride. "You *met* Lee? He's *here*?" Suddenly Read checked, looking first at Jago then at Hawkwood. His eyes darted a warning.

"Sergeant Jago knows, sir. I told him everything."

The Chief Magistrate cocked an eyebrow. "Did you indeed? That was rather presumptuous of you."

"Nathaniel did save my life."

James Read's severe expression did not waver. "Yes, so you said."

"I thought he should know what he's got himself into."

"Quite." The Chief Magistrate did not speak for several moments. Finally, he broke the uncomfortable silence. "As you may have gathered, er . . . Sergeant, I'm well aware of your – how shall I put it? – current activities. I'm equally familiar with your background and your connection with Officer Hawkwood. It's for that reason, and due to your actions this night, I'm prepared to abide by his commendation. You've become privy to highly sensitive information, however. Do I have your word of honour you'll not speak of these matters to anyone outside these walls?"

Jago looked at Hawkwood then back at the Chief Magistrate. The ex-sergeant drew himself erect. "You have my word, sir."

Read met the promise with a curt nod. "Very well." The

Chief Magistrate took his seat. "All right, tell me about William Lee. You're certain it was he?"

Hawkwood nodded. "Turns out I'd already met him, though I didn't know it at the time. He was passing himself off as Lord Mandrake's house guest, probably as a means of taking a sly look at me, the cocky bastard. Anyway, the message from the girl was a ruse. Nathaniel didn't send it. Lee did. He wants me dead. It seems I've become a nuisance. They used the girl because Scully knew I'd recognize her." Hawkwood hesitated. "Scully killed Warlock, too."

A shadow passed over James Read's face. He listened in silence as Hawkwood recounted the details. When the Runner had finished, the magistrate sighed heavily. "I see. Then it appears we're doubly indebted to you, Sergeant. You've saved us the expense of a hanging." To Hawkwood, he added, "You say you still don't know the identity of his accomplice?"

"Not yet, but I'll find out."

James Read nodded. "Let's hope it's sooner rather than later. As for Lee, is there any way he could have perished in the fire?"

Hawkwood shook his head. "I doubt it."

"A pity. It would have saved us a deal of bother." James Read turned to his clerk. "Make a note, Mr Twigg. When we're done here, you're to summon Officer Lightfoot. His duties at the Bank of England are now complete. On my orders, he is to proceed north with all dispatch, to Lord Mandrake's estate at Northwich. He is to arrest Lord Mandrake on sight and return with him to this office. He is to use force if necessary."

287

"Very good, sir." The clerk's face betrayed no emotion. Ezra Twigg's lengthy tenure at Bow Street had prepared him for every eventuality. The apprehension of a peer of the realm was all in a day's work, no different to the arrest of a pickpocket or the protection of a bullion consignment.

"And what of the clockmaker?" Read asked. "Is Master Woodburn dead or alive?"

"Alive. They still need him, apparently. Lee didn't say why. My guess is it's for some sort of repair work to the submersible boat. Whatever it is, it must be something delicate, that only someone with a clockmaker's skill could attempt."

James Read looked thoughtful. "So, there's still some hope for him, at least. I suppose we should be thankful for small mercies."

Hawkwood said cautiously, "There's one thing that's been troubling me."

James Read nodded. "You're wondering how Lee knows so much. I confess it's been causing me some concern also."

"He has friends in high places."

"And upon what do you base that assumption?"

"It's no assumption. It's fact. He told me. I asked him how he knew I'd been a captain, and that was the answer he gave me."

Read frowned. "He'll have got that from Lord Mandrake surely, or this Scully fellow."

"Perhaps," Hawkwood conceded. "But I'm not so sure. It's just a feeling I've had. It wasn't so much what he said, it was the way he said it. *Friends in high places.* He was boasting. He wouldn't boast about Mandrake, certainly not about Scully. In any case, how did Mandrake know we were on to him? We *suspected* he might be a turncoat, but Mandrake *knew* we suspected him. That's why he left in such a hurry. But how did he know?

"And there's something else . . ." Hawkwood paused. "When I told Lee we knew about *Thetis*, he seemed to find that amusing. Said we only thought we knew. How does he know what we're thinking? Maybe somebody told him."

James Read closed his eyes and massaged the bridge of his nose. Suddenly, he looked tired, as though sleep had finally begun to catch up with him. He opened his eyes. "You realize what you're suggesting?"

"I could be wrong," Hawkwood said.

"And then again, you could be right." The Chief Magistrate's expression was grim.

"There's another thing," Hawkwood said.

The Chief Magistrate blinked. "What?"

"Christopher Marlowe."

"Who the bleedin' 'ell is Christopher Marlowe?" Jago asked. "Not another mate of Scully's?"

James Read frowned. "Not is, Sergeant, *was*. He was a writer of plays. He died over two hundred years ago. Forgive me, Hawkwood, but I fail to see the relevance."

"You ain't the only one," Jago said. "What the hell has this got to do with anything?"

Pointedly, James Read had not echoed William Lee's surprise at Hawkwood's familiarity with the playwright. A Bow Street Runner's duties were many and varied, including personal protection. Among Hawkwood's more notable and notorious clients had been the actor Edmund Kean. Kean, a small, unattractive man with a sour disposition, had appeared a year before at Covent Garden in a short season of Marlowe's works. Hawkwood had spent a good part of his time in the theatre wings. Whereas offstage Kean had been a rude and arrogant monster, onstage he was a genius, scorning theatrical convention and enthralling audiences with an ease that was a wonder to behold. When Hawkwood had returned to his regular police work he had taken with him a fascination and grudging respect for the actor's skills and a lingering appreciation for Marlowe's work.

"Lee quoted Faustus at me," Hawkwood said.

Nathanial Jago continued to look blank. The Chief Magistrate rode to his rescue. "Faustus is a character in one of Marlowe's plays; a doctor who promises his soul to the Devil in exchange for wealth and power." The magistrate grimaced. "Lee obviously sees a similarity with his current allegiance."

"Lee also told me where Marlowe died," Hawkwood said.

The Chief Magistrate's head turned slowly.

"He told me it wouldn't only be Marlowe's death that Deptford would be remembered for."

There was a pause. "Oh, dear God," Read said.

"Would somebody please tell me what the hell's goin' on!" Jago demanded.

James Read shook his head. "It means, Sergeant, that we have severely underestimated our American friend. By God, Hawkwood, I pray we're mistaken. If not, then not only is our William Lee an arrogant rogue, he is also possessed of a particularly callous sense of humour."

Jago looked helplessly from one to the other.

"The ship, Nathaniel," Hawkwood said, "he was talking about the ship."

Read turned to Jago. "The ship, Sergeant, remember? We believed Lee's mission was to destroy HMS *Thetis*. She's lying currently at the Deptford yard. We made the mistake of assuming Lee would be making his attack in open water, or at least that he'd wait until *Thetis* was in the estuary. We were wrong. Lee's presence in London and his remarks to Hawkwood confirm our misunderstanding. He's not going to wait. He means to launch his attack now, here! The enemy is not abroad, Sergeant. He is among us!"

The penny dropped. "Sufferin' Jesus!" Jago breathed.

"The admiral told us she sails on the twenty-seventh." Hawkwood said.

James Read nodded. "Today, Hawkwood. She sails today! With the Prince of Wales on board!"

Hawkwood's first reaction was to contradict and say it wasn't possible, but the more he thought about it, the more sense it made. Lee's devil-may-care attitude, his off-hand response to Hawkwood's revelation that his plan had been found out, his farewell remark; they all added up to one thing. They had thought they were one step ahead of the American. In reality, they were two steps behind.

"Which means the submersible's here," Hawkwood said.

Silence filled the room.

"So, where the hell is it?"

The Chief Magistrate placed his palms on the desk and pushed himself to his feet. "That, Hawkwood, is what we must find out. There's no time to lose."

"But it could be anywhere!"

"Then we must think carefully. We must apply logic."

"Logic?"

"We must narrow the field of search." James Read swung towards his clerk. "Mr Twigg, we're going to need maps. If you'd be so kind as to fetch Master Horwood's plans of London; the sheets covering the immediate vicinity of the river will suffice. Sharply now!"

"He must be mad if he thinks he can get away with it," Jago said, as the clerk hurried away.

James Read shook his head. "Not mad, Sergeant. Imagine if the situation was reversed and it was one of our own captains who'd managed to infiltrate a fireship filled with explosives up the Seine. We wouldn't call him mad. We'd call him brave, audacious, a hero!"

Not me, Hawkwood thought. I'd call him a bloody idiot. Unless, of course, he got away with it.

Hawkwood thought about the consequences if Lee's daredevil plan succeeded. Frankly, they didn't bear thinking about. If, or when, the public learned that a French secret weapon had destroyed a British warship a stone's throw from the seat of government, there'd be panic in the streets. And the terror wouldn't end there. No vessel would dare leave harbour for fear of being similarly attacked. And how could Britain command the seas if she couldn't even protect her own ports or rivers? The effect on trade would be catastrophic. And if the French built a fleet of submersibles, what then? How would the country combat such a deadly threat? How could it re-equip its armies abroad?

Bonaparte had tried to choke Britain into submission

before, through decrees issued in Berlin and Milan, forbidding countries under his rule to trade with his mortal enemy. Britain had retaliated by blockading foreign ports and the nations that had implemented the decrees. Admiral Gambier had even destroyed the Danish fleet at Copenhagen. As long as Britain retained mastery over the oceans, Bonaparte's plan would fail; but if the actions of just one submersible managed to bottle up the entire British Navy, the Emperor could start to breathe again. The balance of power would shift dramatically. The fabric of the nation was at stake.

Ezra Twigg returned, bearing maps. There wasn't room on the desk so they had to spread them out on the floor. By the time they had been laid out, there wasn't much carpet visible, but what they had amounted to a bird's-eye view of the Thames, stretching from Cheyne Walk to the River Lea.

Hawkwood looked despairingly at the distances involved. Nearly eleven miles of waterway, not to mention tributaries, canals and docks. How could they be expected to find one small boat, twenty feet in length?

"By elimination," James Read said. "For example, a hiding place upriver beyond the London dock is unlikely, otherwise he'd be giving himself too much water and too many vessels to negotiate."

"If I were Lee," Hawkwood said, pointing, "I wouldn't attack from downstream either. It would make more sense to run with the current. Once I'd destroyed the ship, I'd want to get out as quickly as possible."

The Chief Magistrate stared at the mosaic on the floor. "I agree. But where does that leave us? The area between Bermondsey and the Isle of Dogs, perhaps? A little over three miles, I fancy. So, where would be the best place to conceal a submersible?"

Hawkwood was trying to remember Colonel Congreve's estimate of the submersible's speed. Lee probably wouldn't want to expend too much energy or time manoeuvring the craft into position, and three miles still seemed an awful long way. But then, what else was it the colonel had said? Stealth was more important than speed.

Hawkwood looked down at the remaining map sheets. "The vessel was damaged. That's why they needed the clock-maker. They couldn't carry out repairs in the open, it would attract too much attention, too many prying eyes. Which means the thing has to be under cover somewhere. So we're looking for a shelter, a building, something opening on to the river – a warehouse, for instance. Lee isn't acting on his own. We know that. He has contacts. Which of them is most likely to have access to a warehouse? Someone who deals with cargoes and such? Some sort of trader? A merchant type, perhaps?" Hawkwood looked pointedly at the Chief Magistrate.

The Chief Magistrate slammed his palm on to the desk. "Of course! It's been staring us in the face!"

"It 'as?" Jago said.

The Chief Magistrate grabbed his clerk's arm. "Fetch the file on Lord Mandrake, Mr Twigg. We are looking for property owned or rented by his lordship, with river access."

"Very good, sir."

Jago caught Hawkwood's eye and grinned. "I can see why they made you an officer,"

Twigg left the office once more. He was gone less than two

minutes. When he returned he was clutching a bundle of documents bound in black ribbon. Even Hawkwood, familiar with Ezra Twigg's uncanny knack for accumulating and evaluating intelligence, was impressed. The Chief Magistrate, on the other hand, clearly took his clerk's abilities for granted.

"Very good, Mr Twigg. Locations, if you please."

As Twigg read out the details, Hawkwood's hope's began to fade. All the warehouses used by Lord Mandrake's trading companies were situated inside the new docklands.

London was the busiest port in the world. Because of their size, large cargo ships were unable to sail upriver beyond London Bridge, so unloading had been restricted to the north and south banks below the bridge, which meant, as trade increased, the buildings and wharves had extended downriver. As the size of vessels grew larger, so did the congestion in the port area. The wharves became crowded and confused. Ships sometimes had to wait weeks for their cargoes to be checked and for customs dues to be paid. Added to which was the problem of river pirates and all the other criminals who preyed on shipping. The profits from crime were huge. It was to ease the overcrowding and protect vulnerable and valuable cargoes that the first commercial docks had been built.

Ships could now come up the river at high tide and enter the dock basins. Cargoes could be unloaded and either stored in warehouses or transferred to smaller, shallower draughted vessels for immediate distribution.

Mandrake's warehouses were spread evenly between the London Dock in Wapping, the West India Docks, north of the Isle of Dogs, and the Grand Surrey Docks in Rotherhithe.

"Looks as if we were wrong," Hawkwood said, unable to

hide his disappointment. "There's no way Lee would risk taking his submersible inside the dock area. Too impractical, too damned public."

James Read nodded glumly. "I fear you're right. Even our Mr Lee wouldn't be that presumptuous. Though, perhaps we should have the buildings investigated anyway. I'll contact the River Police and have them make searches – discreetly, of course." Still despondent, Read turned to his clerk. "Thank you, Mr Twigg. As always your files have proved most illuminating. However, it appears we must look elsewhere for our information."

The Chief Magistrate frowned. His clerk was not paying attention. Ezra Twigg was staring intently at one of the documents. Suddenly aware that he was being observed, he looked up. "Forgive me, sir."

"Mr Twigg?" The Chief Magistrate regarded his clerk with concern.

The clerk blinked owlishly. "Er . . . I believe I may have found something, sir."

"And what might that be, Mr Twigg?"

The clerk gathered himself. He held up the document. "There's another warehouse, sir."

The Chief Magistrate gripped his clerk's arm. Twigg winced.

"It's entirely my fault, sir. It's just that when I was looking at the list of his lordship's premises, it occurred to me there was no mention of the timber yard."

"Timber yard?"

"Yes, sir. You see, when his lordship moved his businesses to the new docks, he sold his existing properties to raise the finance. They consisted of . . ." Twigg consulted the document ". . . warehouses at Griffin's Wharf, Battle Bridge, Brewers Quay and New Bear Quay. Also two properties at Phoenix Wharf, Wapping, and storage houses at Trinity Street in Rotherhithe. All sold, sir, all accounted for, except one. His lordship used to import timber from the east, sir. His company had a separate warehouse and timber yard for the purpose. I can find no record of the sale."

"And where is this warehouse, Mr Twigg?"

A pause.

"In Limehouse, sir."

Less than a mile and a half upriver from Deptford.

The Chief Magistrate read Hawkwood's mind. "Take Sergeant Jago with you."

"What about warning the ship?" Hawkwood asked.

The Chief Magistrate looked thoughtful. "That might be a problem. If Lee does indeed have other friends in high places, warning the ship will surely alert Lee that we're on to him. Neither would we want to start unnecessary panic. And don't forget, for all we know, Lee believes you're dead. That may work to our advantage. No, gentlemen, until we know for certain who is friend or foe, I fear we're on our own. Which means, Hawkwood, you have to find Lee and his submersible and stop him. By any means possible. There must be no quarter given. You understand what I'm saying, Hawkwood? I'm giving you carte blanche."

"Then we'd best get started," Hawkwood said. "Come on, Nathaniel, there's work to be done." He turned to the Chief Magistrate. "Where will we find you, sir?"

James Read considered the question. "I will proceed to Deptford. You may contact me there."

"You'll warn the Prince?"

"I'll speak to his advisors, suggest to them that it would be better if His Royal Highness postponed his visit to the yard until the next launching. Now, off with you both."

As Hawkwood and Jago left the office, the Chief Magistrate and his clerk exchanged pensive looks.

"I fear, Mr Twigg," James Read murmured softly, "that desperate times are upon us."

Twigg nodded. Behind his spectacles, his eyes gleamed. The game was afoot and the little clerk scented blood.

"Which means," Read continued, "that we must now deploy *all* our resources. Return to your files, Mr Twigg. I want everything you have on Sir Charles Yorke, Admiral Bartholomew Dalryde, Inspector General Thomas Blomefield and Colonel William Congreve. There is treason afoot, Mr Twigg. Treason is a canker and it is my intention to find it and cut it out!"

William Lee lowered his head towards the tin basin, closed his eyes, cupped his palms in the water and doused his face. He did it several times, gasping as the coldness stung his eyes. Finally he raised his head and ran his hands over his close-cropped hair. Water trickled down his cheeks and dripped from his chin. He reached for the drying cloth.

Lee stared intently at himself in the mirror. He searched his face, studied the familiar lines, the grey at his temples, the stubble on his cheeks. Dabbing his face with the cloth, his eyes moved to the window and he stared out at the wide grey river.

A recollection of childhood arose, unbidden, in his mind. His boyhood years had been spent on the family farm, close to the bank of another great river, the Delaware, and the small, pleasant town of Fort Penn, less than a day's ride from the city of Wilmington. There, in the company of his friends, he had explored the local creeks, levees and inlets on foot and in birch-bark canoe.

Until the horror.

It had been early morning when the squad of redcoats had come calling, rousting the family from their beds, giving them barely enough time to dress before dragging his father, Samuel, and his elder brother, Robert, out through the smashed and splintered door and across the yard to the low stone wall that ringed the house.

There had been no trial, no preliminaries, only a short proclamation read by a grim-faced lieutenant. The charge was sedition: providing food and shelter to officers of the rebel army. Sentence to be carried out forthwith. There had been barely time to grasp the true terror of the unfolding events before the morning was split by the sharp bark of command from the sergeant in charge of the firing squad, followed less than a heartbeat later by the ragged rattle of musket shots that rolled across the surrounding meadows like a volley of hail against a window pane.

They had left the bodies where they had fallen, crumpled in the dust at the base of the wall, leaving two sounds forever ingrained in Lee's memory: the tramp of marching feet from the departing soldiers, and the shrill, keening cries of his mother as she had cradled the head of her son, the blood of the slaughtered boy soaking into the white of her apron.

In the beginning, unsurprisingly, Lee's hunger for vengeance had been all consuming. His hatred of the British Crown had burned like a furnace in his breast and his desire for revenge had never diminished. Over the intervening years, however, as he had grown older and wiser, the heat of his anger had gradually given way to a low simmer and he had been content to wait, to bide his time until the opportunity presented itself. Thus there had been no strategy in Lee's vow to his dead sibling, no deadline, just a silent oath that somebody, somewhere, would eventually pay the price.

And then, into his life had stepped Robert Fulton, artist, inventor, showman, philosopher and revolutionary. And only then, bonded by a mutual desire for justice and freedom, and fired by Fulton's imagination and genius, had the awesome nature, scale and means by which he could exact his revenge revealed itself.

The distant clang of a ship's bell jolted Lee from his uneasy reminiscence. He looked down at his hand, recalling the tremor as he had taken the tiny cylinder from the carrier pigeon's leg and extracted the message telling him the waiting was over. A message from an emperor.

Although four weeks had passed since his meeting with Napoleon Bonaparte, it seemed like only yesterday.

It had been another early-morning rendezvous.

Touched by the pale light of dawn, with remnants of sea mist hanging low over the still water, the Seine estuary was a desolate place, inhabited only by mosquitoes and waterfowl. It was a perfect proving ground: hot and humid in high summer, windswept and icebound in winter, and cut off from the surrounding countryside by a latticework of muddy ditches and foetid marshland, the only means of passage through the region a spider's web of decaying wooden causeways.

They had moored the gribane in the middle of the estuary. Sitting heavily on the water like some scaly weed-encrusted sea monster newly arisen from the deep, the squat Seine barge had certainly seen better days.

In a black, unmarked coach, bracketed by his chausseur escort, the Emperor had arrived accompanied only by his swarthy Mameluke bodyguard, Rustam, and his Minister of Marine, the short, stoop-shouldered admiral, Denis Decres. It had been Decres who had persuaded the Emperor to give Fulton's device one more chance. It was well known that Emperor Bonaparte had small interest in matters nautical, but Decres was the man in charge of all invasion operations against Britain, so when the little admiral spoke, the Emperor listened.

The testing area had been guarded by a detachment of the imperial guard under the command of a one-eyed veteran of Bonaparte's Italian and Egyptian campaigns, Major Jean Daubert. The major, Lee learned, had lost his eye during the siege of Acre, in a hard fought, bloody skirmish with Turkish irregulars. He was one of the most arrogant men Lee had ever met.

While the major had fussed and fretted over the Emperor and his entourage, Lee and his two crewmen had boarded the submersible and taken her three hundred yards upstream.

From the shelter of a ruined barn close by the water's edge, with the stocky greatcoat-clad Emperor waiting impatiently at his side, Admiral Decres had given Lee the signal and the vessel had submerged to launch its attack.

The destruction of the gribane had been sudden, spectacular and total, to the delight of Lee and his crew, the amazement of the Emperor and the alarm of every bird within a half-mile radius. The sound of the explosion had reverberated across the marshland with the force of a thunderclap.

Back on shore, with the barge split in two, driftwood scattered across the grey water, and wooden splinters piercing the surface of the mud flats like arrows, the Emperor had invited Lee to walk with him. There were important matters to discuss.

But that had been after the discovery of the interloper.

It had been in the aftermath of the attack on the barge when – unbeknownst to Lee and his crewman who were still aboard the submersible – all hell had broken loose.

Ironically, it had been the one-eyed Major Daubert who'd spotted the flash of sunlight glancing across the spyglass lens, spearing a warning into the major's brain, igniting the realization that they were being observed. The major's response, born of instinct, had been immediate.

Daubert had led the chase, sword drawn, barking orders at his men, galvanized by the sight of a man's shape breaking from cover and disappearing around the far side of a high sand dune. At which point the chasseurs had joined the hunt, spurring their mounts forward, using their superior speed to cut off the fleeing figure's line of retreat. It had been a foregone conclusion that the grenadiers and the mounted escort would run their quarry to ground. There was nowhere for him to go. Escape was impossible.

And so it had proved, but not before the bodies of two grenadiers lay dead in the sand, slaughtered by pistol ball and sword blade respectively.

That one man on foot should have wreaked such havoc should have given the major a degree of warning that this was not some local peasant out poaching for game and that it might have been wiser to apprehend the felon alive in order to question him about his origins and intentions.

The sharp crack of a chasseur's carbine, however, had put paid to that possibility. The fleeing man had reached the water when the ball struck low on his left side, propelling him into the shallows. The major, seeing the quarry stagger towards the middle of the stream, had shouted at his men not to fire again. As the body disappeared beneath the surface, the major had spurred his men forward, but it had been too late. Dragged under by the current, the corpse had been swept away.

Or so it had been assumed.

They had found the discarded pistol close to the body of one of the dead grenadiers and had shown it to Lee upon his return to shore. Lee had immediately put paid to the major's speculation that the man had been nothing more than an inquisitive local and the admiral's suggestion that he may have been a would-be assassin sent by Bourbon exiles.

The pistol, Lee had revealed, was English-made; "York", the city of manufacture, engraved on to the stock had been

303

the giveaway. Probably naval issue, Lee had surmised, an officer's sidearm.

Which meant what?

The British knew of the device, Lee had told the Emperor. It had been offered to them seven years before. They'd turned it down. However, it wasn't outside the realms of possibility that they'd received fresh intelligence relating to the improvements in design. It would have been only natural for them to dispatch agents to investigate.

It's what I would have done, Lee had admitted.

Which was when the Emperor had suggested they take a walk, and the mission had been born.

Lee had been surprised by the Emperor's candour.

The war in Spain was going badly, the Emperor had admitted. Wellington was proving a formidable opponent. His victories were undermining the will of France's allies. Allegiances were changing. It was not only the southern borders that were under threat. It had been hoped that Tsar Alexander's support would remain steadfast, but doubts had been expressed. Severe measures might have to be taken.

It had been Lee who had voiced the unthinkable.

"Your Majesty would attack *Russia*?"

The Emperor, to Lee's astonishment, had merely shrugged. "Perhaps."

Which would have meant the Emperor's armies would be split, and thus considerably weakened.

"We are very much in need of a miracle," the Emperor had told him with a grim smile. "A small one would suffice."

It was possible that Fulton's device was the key, the means by which Britain's supply lines to Spain could be disrupted, giving the French time to regroup and push Wellington back into the sea. Which in turn would undoubtedly force Tsar Alexander to reconsider his responsibilities.

"All things are possible, Your Majesty," had been Lee's tactful response.

The Emperor had given Lee one month. Whatever was required would be made available. He was to report directly to Admiral Decres.

And remain vigilant.

But they had not allowed for Lieutenant Harry St John Ramillies' return from the dead.

It had been Bonaparte's agents who, following the interrogation and execution of suspected Bourbon sympathizers, had passed word that, miraculously, the British spy was still alive, recovering from his wounds, and on the run, aided by the Royalist underground. Moreover, it was believed he carried copies of the submersible's design.

A brave run that had been brought to an abrupt and bloody end on a lonely, rain-lashed stretch of heathland. But the death of Ramillies, allied to the recovery of the drawings, meant that the mission could at last proceed as planned.

Until, like a pair of inquisitive, meddlesome magpies, Runners Warlock and Hawkwood had come calling. Not that it hadn't been inevitable, Lee supposed, that the disappearance of Master Woodburn, a craftsman of some repute, would attract the attention of the authorities.

What hadn't been expected was the competence displayed by the men assigned to track down the missing clockmaker. These were not your usual run-of-the-mill constables, ineffective, corrupt Charlies, but professional thief-takers.

But now, they too, had been dealt with. The seaman, Scully, had seen to that. Scully might be a bruiser, short on brains and heavy on brawn, but he had nevertheless proved exceedingly useful. He had removed both Warlock and Hawkwood, and in removing those two, he had provided Lee with a clear run to his objective. The destruction of which was now only a matter of hours away.

Lee's eyes moved to the window once more. The Thames was the city's life force. The femoral artery. But an artery that was about to be severed in spectacular fashion. The wound might not be fatal, but it had the potential to paralyse the nation and set back the British war effort for some considerable time, allowing Emperor Bonaparte the opportunity to marshal his forces and launch an offensive.

So now a ship would burn, a prince would die, and the British would quake in their beds.

And a father and brother would be avenged.

Revenge, Lee thought, as he began to dress, was indeed a repast best served cold.

Hawkwood, seated in the bow of the rowing boat, rested his elbows on the oar and tried to ignore the sticky rivulets of sweat trickling uncomfortably down his back and beneath his armpits. His discarded jacket lay on the seat beside him. Jago, resting on his own oar, chuckled at Hawkwood's discomfort.

Suspecting that the river would be the most practical means of access, Hawkwood had used his warrant to commandeer the boat from a wherryman at the Ratcliff Cross stairs. The canny boat owner had tried to extract the exorbitant sum of one shilling for the inconvenience and temporary disruption to his livelihood, until a glare from Jago warned him not to push his luck. In the end, Hawkwood had compromised and paid sixpence, four times the normal crossing charge. Better to keep the man quiet, he reasoned, than have him blab to every Tom, Dick and Harry that a Runner was on the prowl.

They were drifting fifty yards off the Limehouse shore. Looking over his left shoulder, Hawkwood could see the bend in the river and the western entrance to the canals and lagoons that formed the huge West India Docks. Beyond the dock entrance, the river widened out to almost a quarter of a mile as it ran southwards towards Deptford and the Isle of Dogs.

With the sun barely over the rooftops, the river was already bustling with activity. Lighters, barges, bumboats, cutters and colliers vied for wharf space and an opportunity to discharge their loads and take on new cargoes, while further down-stream the tall, slender masts of the larger vessels, East Indiamen and Royal Navy warships, could be seen outlined against the rapidly brightening sky.

Onshore, it was just as congested. Jetties groaned under the weight of coal sacks, tobacco bales, baulks of timber, liquor casks, and crates of bleating livestock. The smells emanating from the river bank reflected the myriad trades plied within the borough, from the sharp, acrid stench of the lime kilns to the throat-souring odour of the tar yards.

Suddenly, Jago sat up and nodded towards the river bank. "Land ho, Cap'n."

Hawkwood twisted in his seat, and followed Jago's gaze.

There was little to distinguish the warehouse from the rest of the waterfront buildings, save for the faded name board nailed on to the wall above the jetty. Located adjacent to the entrance to Limekiln Dock and abutted by a densely packed collection of granaries and storehouses, the warehouse, with its adjoining yard, was not much different from a thousand other commercial properties lining the river from the Tower to Tilbury, albeit in slightly better repair than most.

Both men picked up their oars. "Well, now," Jago murmured softly, as they sculled closer to the bank. "Take a lookee there."

Hawkwood followed the big man's gaze.

A narrow channel and loading dock separated the two-storeyed building from its nearest neighbour, effectively isolating the property from the rest of the waterfront. At the end of the channel, in the shadow of a low stone archway, directly beneath the warehouse at river level, was a pair of heavy wooden doors.

Jago grinned. "Mighty convenient, ain't they. You thinking what I'm thinking?"

Wordlessly, Hawkwood continued to stroke them towards the main shore, to where a weathered stone stairway reached down into the murky water. As the bow of the rowboat nudged the bottom step, Hawkwood shipped his oar and picked up his coat. Jago got to his feet.

"Not you, Nathaniel," Hawkwood said.

Jago blinked. "Say again?"

Hawkwood turned, foot balanced on the gunwale. "I'm going in alone."

"The hell you are!" Jago rasped.

Hawkwood stepped ashore. Relieved of his weight, the boat rocked alarmingly. Jago staggered as he searched for balance. "Christ!"

"I need you to keep watch," Hawkwood said.

"An' if you run into trouble?" Jago glared. "Bearin' in mind what 'appened the last time you went gallivantin' around on your own."

"Give me an hour. If I'm not back by then, contact Magistrate Read."

"And then what?"

"He'll know what to do."

"Bleedin' 'ell!" Jago said. "An' that's your grand strategy, is it?"

"Unless you've a better one."

Jago stared at Hawkwood. Finally, he shook his head in exasperation. "Can't say as I do, off 'and."

Hawkwood reached inside his jacket and took out his baton. He held it out. "Take this."

"What the bleedin' 'ell do you expect me to do with *that*?"

"You may need it. If anything happens to me and you need to get to Magistrate Read, it'll help open a few doors."

Reluctantly, Jago accepted the offering.

"Don't lose it," Hawkwood said. "It's the only one I've got."

"I'll stick it up my arse. No one'll find it there."

Hawkwood grinned.

As Hawkwood climbed the steps to the quayside, the burly ex-sergeant shook his head and stared glumly at the Runner's retreating back. "I bloody 'ope you knows what you're doin', you mad bugger," he grunted.

As Hawkwood made his way along the quay, he wondered if it had been such a good idea to leave Jago behind. The ex-sergeant was a good man to have at your back, but it didn't make sense both of them walking into what might be the lion's den. So Hawkwood, against his better judgement, and to Nathaniel Jago's understandable dismay, was on his own.

At least he was having no trouble blending into his surroundings. He'd had no time to return to his lodgings since reporting back to James Read. His long hair remained unbound and he was still wearing the remnants of his old uniform. To anyone on the dockside, he was just another ex-soldier turned river worker. No one spared him a second glance. Hawkwood picked his way along the busy waterfront, senses alert.

Very few people had permanent jobs on the river. Most were casual workers, or lumpers, who lived in the crowded alleys and lanes that ran down to the water, their livelihood dependent solely on the movement of vessels. Most lumpers were either holders, who worked inside the ship's hold, or deckers. Deckers lifted the cargo to and from the vessel, either on to the dockside or via a lighter. It was hard, backbreaking work, requiring brawn rather than brain. But no man complained if it put a roof over his head or food on the table.

The waterfront was piled high with produce. A heap of sugar sacks sat on the quay in front of him. Without breaking stride, Hawkwood swung the top sack on to his shoulder and carried on walking. He waited for the angry cry but none came. Using the sack to partially conceal his features, he continued along the jetty.

Hawkwood had no clear idea of how he was going to gain access to the warehouse and yard, other than by stealth or deception. He was still considering his options when his attention was caught by a group of men lounging in the doorway of a grog shop. One in five buildings along the riverfront sold liquor in one form or another. Most innkeepers acted as agents, supplying men to ships. Needless to say, they also supplied liquor to the men, deducting the cost from their earnings. It was a lucrative business and there was no shortage of labourers looking for work, so there was nothing untoward about the scene itself. It was the face of a man leaving the grog shop, a knapsack slung over his shoulder, that had caught Hawkwood's eye. It was a face he recognized, though he couldn't put a name to it. Then he remembered. It belonged to one of the group who had shared a table with Scully, in Noah's Ark.

Coincidence? It couldn't be that simple, surely? But there wasn't time to dwell on the matter, the man was on the move, heading towards the timber yard. Hawkwood, increasingly conscious of the dead weight he was carrying on his own shoulder, considered his lack of options and set off in cautious pursuit.

For one nerve-shredding moment, Hawkwood wondered

if his quarry knew he was being followed. At the end of the gangway spanning the loading dock, the man paused suddenly and looked behind him. Hawkwood turned away quickly. When he looked back the man had resumed his journey. He's being careful, Hawkwood thought. He doesn't know he's being followed, but he's checking to make sure, and that in itself was cause for thought.

They were approaching the end of the quay. The warehouse and yard lay directly ahead, and the crowd was beginning to thin. Suddenly, twenty paces in front of Hawkwood, the man turned away from the river and ducked into an alleyway. Hawkwood paused, adjusted the sugar sack on his shoulder, then followed around the corner. He found himself un-expectedly at the top of a short wooden stairway. At the bottom of the stairway was a door. Hawkwood's quarry was there, knapsack at his feet, fumbling with a key. As Hawkwood's boot hit the top step, the man looked up. Hawkwood was given no time to turn aside. Startled, the man's eyes widened in shock, then recognition. His hand snatched towards his waist.

Hawkwood hurled the sugar down the stairs. The heavy sack struck his target full in the chest, knocking him off balance. The knife he'd drawn from his belt rattled to the ground. Hawkwood went down fast. His boot thudded into the man's crotch. As his victim collapsed in a gargling heap, hand clutching his genitals, Hawkwood picked up the knife and jabbed the point of the blade under the unshaven chin.

"Now then, culley, that's no way to greet an officer of the law."

No response, other than a low whimper.

Hawkwood bent low. "Sorry? What's that? Can't hear you."

Another groan of pain.

Hawkwood sighed. "All right, let's start with your name."

"S-Sparrow." The reply came in a whisper. "W-Will Sparrow."

"You're Spiker's mate," Hawkwood said.

Sparrow stared at him. "S-Spiker's dead."

"I know that," Hawkwood grated. "I watched him die."

Fear drove the last of the colour from Sparrow's face.

"So," Hawkwood said, "I'm wondering what brings you to this neck of the woods. Running errands for William Lee? Rushing to tell him the news about Spiker, maybe? That it, Sparrow? Is Lee inside?" Hawkwood reached out and pulled the knapsack towards him. He put a hand inside. Some bottles, a loaf of bread and what felt like a slab of cheese. "What's this then, breakfast for the troops?" Hawkwood pressed the point of the knife under the skin of Sparrow's throat. A tiny bubble of blood appeared beneath the tip of the blade. "I think you and me should have a little talk, culley. In private, where no one can hear us. What do you say?"

Sparrow blinked fearfully. Then his eyes moved and Hawkwood heard the faint hiss of breath. Sparrow wasn't looking at him, he realized. He was looking at something behind him, in the doorway. Hawkwood started to turn, but he was about a thousand years too late. He sensed the shadow above him, heard the soft footfall, followed by a massive explosion of pain as he was struck hard behind the right ear.

The thought that passed through his mind as he went down was, curiously, not how much the blow had hurt, but that this was the second time he'd been taken by surprise in nearly as many hours. It was getting to be a nasty habit. Or maybe it was a sign that he was growing too old for this sort of game. The second thing that struck him as he began to slip away was that the attack had clearly affected his sense of smell. He could have sworn that the impact upon his skull had been accompanied by the faint yet unmistakable scent of lemons.

17

Hawkwood saw the rat as soon as he opened his eyes. It was impossible to miss. It was huge, at least a foot and a half long from nose to tail. There were rich pickings to be had along the waterfront and the rodent looked well fed and healthy, its pelt as shiny as velvet. Unafraid, the rat sat back on its hind legs, front paws raised, and sniffed the air, whiskers twitching. Finally, curiosity overcoming caution, it dropped back to all fours and scampered fluidly across the floor. Six feet away, it paused and stared at Hawkwood with bright, beady-eyed expectation.

Hawkwood raised his head. A big mistake. Pain lanced through his skull. He groaned and closed his eyes, willing the hurt to subside. He opened his eyes again, cautiously, his cheek against the cold stone. The view hadn't changed. The rat was still there, watching him.

Something touched his shoulder. Instinctively, Hawkwood

jerked away and regretted it instantly as another bolt of lightning seared along his optic nerve.

"Easy, my boy, easy." The voice was gentle and soothing. "Here, let me help you up."

Hawkwood felt guiding arms around his shoulders as he was assisted into a seated position against the wall. He put a hand to the back of his skull and winced as his fingers explored broken skin and what felt like dried blood. Slowly, he raised his aching head.

"Master Woodburn, I presume?"

The elderly man who was looking down at him with anxious eyes frowned then smiled. "You've the advantage of me, sir. I don't believe we've met."

"My name's Hawkwood."

"So, Mr Hawkwood, what brings you to *my* humble abode?"

"I've been looking for you," Hawkwood said.

The old man's eyebrows lifted. "Have you, indeed?"

"I'm a special constable. A Runner."

What might have been a flicker of hope flared briefly in the old man's eyes, to be replaced almost immediately by a weary resignation. The clockmaker regarded Hawkwood's unshaven face, lank hair and smoke-blackened clothing and nodded sagely. "Well, I'm delighted to make your acquaintance, my boy. I only wish it could have been in more propitious circumstances." The old man waved a hand expansively, then beckoned. "Come, let's get you on the bed so that I can examine your wound. I assume, from the manner of your arrival, that you were set upon by the same ruffians who are holding me here?"

As the old man helped him up, Hawkwood took note of their surroundings. A low trestle bed sat in the corner. The only other items of furniture were a table and chair. On the table sat a bowl and jug, a tin cup, and a plate containing bread and cheese; the groceries collected by Sparrow. High on the opposite wall, a small, square, barred window admitted a solitary shaft of sunlight. Had Hawkwood not known otherwise, he might well have thought himself inside one of the cells at Newgate.

Josiah Woodburn patted the bed. "Sit, my boy, sit."

As his scalp was examined, Hawkwood made his own diagnosis. He could see that the clockmaker's face was pale and that his clothing, dark coat and breeches, which at first glance had appeared without blemish, was in places soiled and stained. Hawkwood was no physician but, even to his untrained eye, Josiah Woodburn looked like a man who, faced with unaccustomed adversity, was trying bravely to hold on to both his dignity and his sanity.

The old man clicked his tongue in sympathy. " 'Pon my word, you look as though you've been in the wars. You'll live, though, have no fear. The skin's broken, nothing more." He patted Hawkwood's knee paternally. "So, how did you find me?"

Hawkwood was about to answer, when the old man held up a hand. "Let me attend to Archimedes first. If he doesn't get his breakfast, he'll only make a nuisance of himself."

Archimedes? It took Hawkwood a second to realize the old man was talking about the rat. Intriguingly, the animal was still there, staring up at them, whiskers twitching, still without a trace of fear. Hawkwood watched as the old man took a small wedge of cheese from the plate on the table and tossed it on to the floor. As soon as the morsel had stopped rolling, the rat darted forward, picked up the cheese in its mouth and scampered back the way it had come, disappearing through a dark crevice in the corner of the room.

"There," the clockmaker said with affection. "He won't bother us again. So, tell me, what clue guided you here? Was it Officer Warlock? Did he manage to evade their clutches?"

Hawkwood felt as if he had just been struck by one of Reuben Benbow's uppercuts. He stared at the old man in amazement. "Warlock was *here?*"

To Hawkwood's consternation, the clockmaker appeared to find the question surprising.

"But, of course, before his escape, we –"

The old man broke off, struck by the expression on Hawkwood's face.

Hawkwood found his voice. "What do you mean '*before his escape*'?"

Josiah Woodburn gasped. Hawkwood looked down and found he was gripping the clockmaker so tightly that the old man's wrist had turned white. He let go quickly.

The clockmaker looked at Hawkwood in confusion. "But I thought that was how you came to be here. Did Officer Warlock not get word to the authorities?"

"Officer Warlock's dead," Hawkwood said. "They killed him."

The clockmaker's face fell. "Then how . . . ?"

"I think it should be *me* asking *you* that question," Hawkwood said, and waited expectantly.

It took some time before the clockmaker had composed

318

himself sufficiently to explain, but once started, the tale did not take long in the telling. It transpired that Warlock had followed the old man's trail by the simple expedient of questioning Lord Mandrake's coachman. This had been as a consequence of his visiting Josiah Woodburn's home and workshop and his meeting with the boy Quigley, who had told him, as he had told Hawkwood, that he'd seen Master Woodburn in Lord Mandrake's carriage. Warlock had subsequently made his way to Limehouse, where he'd managed to gain entry to the warehouse, only to fall into the clutches of Lee and his fellow conspirators. Which answered a number of questions; all but the most important ones. How had Warlock managed to effect an escape and why hadn't he taken the clockmaker with him?

"Effecting your colleague's escape was no problem, Officer Hawkwood," Josiah Woodburn said matter-of-factly. "I simply opened the door for him."

Hawkwood thought he must have misheard. Either that or the blow to his head had done more damage than had first been supposed.

"You forget, my boy, I'm a clockmaker. I've been crafting delicate timepieces for more than fifty years." The old man smiled and held up his hands. "These are my tools. Simple locks hold no secrets from me."

As Hawkwood continued to stare in astonishment, the clockmaker reached under the bed. His hand emerged holding a bent iron nail. "You see?"

Hawkwood looked at the nail then at the old man. "Why didn't you go with him?"

The old man twisted the nail in his hand and sighed.

"Because I couldn't risk my granddaughter's life. She's everything to me, my dear, darling Elizabeth. When my daughter Catherine died, I almost lost my faith. But now, when I look at my granddaughter, I know Catherine's still with me. She lives in her, you see?" The old man clenched his fists. In a voice that was close to breaking, he added, "They threatened to kill Elizabeth if I didn't do what they asked. They said she would be taken from me and I'd never see her again. She's only a child, an innocent child! I couldn't bear the thought of what they might do to her, so I didn't dare try to escape. You do see that? I had no choice. That is why I did what he asked of me."

"William Lee?"

The old man nodded and laid a hand on Hawkwood's arm. "A duplicitous rogue. He is plotting something terrible."

"We know about the undersea boat," Hawkwood said.

Josiah Woodburn nodded again. "His submersible; ah, yes, a remarkable device." Gathering himself, the old man said, "I knew of Fulton's invention, of course. In fact, I actually met the fellow once. We've a mutual acquaintance, Sir Joseph Banks. Sir Joseph was on the committee convened by Prime Minister Pitt to evaluate the submersible's potential six years ago, just before Trafalgar."

Hawkwood recalled his conversation with Colonel Congreve. This would have been the same committee that had deemed the submersible technically feasible, but likely to be impracticable in combat.

"Tell me about Lord Mandrake," Hawkwood said.

The old man sighed. "He told me he had a close friend who wanted to commission a timepiece. Said his friend was

320

confined to his bed and unable to call personally. He offered me the use of his carriage to take me to the client. Alas, it was but a ruse to deliver me into the hands of our captor."

Josiah Woodburn looked up. "Has his lordship been detained?"

Hawkwood shook his head. "Not yet, but he will be. And then he'll hang."

Josiah Woodburn gave a dry smile. "I suspect Lord Mandrake will be made to answer to a much higher authority for *his* brand of treachery."

"But why *you*?" Hawkwood asked. "What did Lee need *you* for?"

"They were sailing the submersible here when they were hit by a storm in mid Channel. The timing device was damaged. It's clockwork, you see, and very delicate. They needed someone with special skills to repair it; a clockmaker such as myself."

"A timing device for what?" Hawkwood cut in.

Josiah Woodburn looked puzzled, as if the question had been superfluous. "Why, for his submarine bomb, of course. His torpedo."

So the madman really was going to go through with it, Hawkwood thought.

"I discovered copies of Lee's drawings of the submersible," Josiah Woodburn said, "and gave them to Officer Warlock so that he could pass them to the authorities." The old man shook his head. "But, given what you've told me, I don't suppose he was successful."

"We found them," Hawkwood said. "The Admiralty has them."

321

So the Chief Magistrate had been correct in his surmise. They were indeed the drawings taken from Lieutenant Ramillies' corpse during the coach robbery. Serendipity had delivered them into the hands of the clockmaker and the unfortunate Warlock.

The old man let go a long breath. "We had so little time. I had but a moment to write the name of the ship. All I could do was hope that the authorities would make sense of it."

Which explained the hurried calligraphy, Hawkwood thought.

"We know about *Thetis*."

A light flared in the clockmaker's eyes. "Thank God!"

Suddenly, Hawkwood felt his arm gripped. The clockmaker placed his mouth next to Hawkwood's ear. "There's something else, Officer Hawkwood, another reason why I didn't go with Officer Warlock. I must tell you. I —"

But before the clockmaker could elaborate, there came the rattle of a key in the lock and the door swung open. Hastily, the clockmaker thrust the nail back in its hiding place. Hawkwood had a moment to notice that the hinges had been oiled, like those of the outside door, which had been opened so quietly he hadn't heard the approach of the person who had knocked him out.

William Lee, grinning broadly, stepped into the room. He held a lantern aloft. "Well, now, I see you two gentlemen have gotten acquainted. I trust you slept well, Master Woodburn?" Lee stared at Hawkwood. "Sparrow tells me Scully's dead. I was wondering why I hadn't heard from him." The American clicked his tongue in mock annoyance.

"I do declare, Officer Hawkwood, you are one persistent son of a bitch! With the devil's own luck, too."

Hawkwood said nothing.

The American frowned. "Was it you that killed him?"

"No," Hawkwood said. He saw no point in embellishment.

Lee held Hawkwood's gaze for what seemed like several minutes before he shrugged and said, "No matter. He was a liability and no loss as far as brains are concerned. It means I'm a man short, though, and that's an irritation I could do without. I swear, Officer Hawkwood, you try a man's patience, you really do."

"You can't win, Lee," Hawkwood said. "I have men outside."

Lee shook his head and laughed. "No you don't. If you did, we wouldn't be having this conversation. They'd have come running when we carried you in here. We'd be knee-deep in constables. No, sir, you're on your own. Which means you're all mine."

I have one man, Hawkwood thought. I have Jago. Maybe.

A movement behind Lee caught Hawkwood's eye. Sparrow, he assumed, but then the figure stepped into view – a slim figure, dressed in a dark, tight-fitting coat, matching breeches, and black, calf-length leather riding boots. And suddenly it all began to make perfect sense.

"Good morning, Matthew," Catherine de Varesne said. The pistol in her right hand was cocked and pointing directly at his heart.

Hawkwood smiled. "Hello, Catherine."

She frowned. "You don't seem surprised."

Hawkwood touched the wound on his head. "It was your perfume. It's very distinctive."

Catherine de Varesne's dark eyes shone with amusement. The pistol barrel did not waver.

Lee grinned. "Well, now, isn't this something?"

Hawkwood looked at him.

"She's Bonaparte's best agent, my friend, and she's been playing you like a trout on a line."

Friends in high places, Hawkwood thought.

He closed his eyes and wondered how he could have been so bloody stupid and why it had taken him so long. When he opened his eyes, he saw that she was still smiling.

"We knew you'd been assigned to the coach murders," Catherine said. "We knew of your reputation, Matthew, your tenacity. What we didn't know was how to deal with you, how to get you out of the way. The ball presented us with our opportunity."

Hawkwood recalled his briefing with James Read. It was now clear why Lord Mandrake had asked for him specifically. It had been a heaven-sent opportunity for Mandrake and Lee to observe and take the measure of the man who had been put on their trail.

It was also now clear why Lord Mandrake hadn't been home when he'd called. It had been Catherine who had alerted him, sending word, probably via her maid, that Hawkwood had begun asking awkward questions.

A thought struck him. "Was Rutherford part of it, too?"

Catherine snorted scornfully. Her eyes flashed. "Rutherford's an arrogant fool. I merely made use of him."

"You led Rutherford on," Hawkwood said, understanding.

"He and his friends were drunk. You made them think they could have you, then you acted the innocent, and you waited for me to come to your rescue."

"My knight in shining armour." Her dark eyes mocked him. "It was simply a matter of setting the scene. We knew you couldn't resist helping a lady in distress."

The servant must have been in on it as well, Hawkwood realized. Which accounted for the man's less than co-operative attitude when Hawkwood had revisited Mandrake House.

"You knew Rutherford wouldn't take no for an answer," Hawkwood said. "You knew that he wouldn't back down in front of his cronies, that he'd call me out! What were you hoping? That he'd kill me?"

As he spoke, he wondered about Lawrence's contribution, but knew instinctively that the major could only have been an unwitting and convenient ingredient in the broth.

She smiled. "More likely you'd kill him, Matthew. Either way, we would be rid of you."

"But you confounded us, Hawkwood," Lee interposed. "Damn it, man, you let the bugger live!"

Did you kill him?

Hawkwood remembered her question in the carriage, following the duel. That indecipherable expression on her face had been, he now realized, one of half-concealed expectation. He recalled what had happened at the house; how, after she had tended his wound, she had initiated their energetic coupling, leaving him breathless and drained. It had been the knowledge that they had fought over her, that blood had been drawn, that had excited her, igniting the passion.

"Well now," Lee said, "much as I hate to interrupt this happy reunion, we've work to do. So, gentlemen, if you'd be so kind as to follow me. Time and tide, they say, wait for no man, especially today. Oh, and a warning, Captain Hawkwood; if you're thinking of attempting something heroic, don't. It won't be you the mademoiselle'll shoot first, it'll be the old man."

Lee turned and led the way out of the cell, along a stone-flagged passageway. Their shadows, trapped in the lantern light, accompanied them in a flickering procession. Hawkwood had the distinct impression that the passageway sloped downwards and he suspected they were nearing the river. Certainly, the putrid smell of the water seemed to be getting stronger. His suspicions were confirmed when, after turning several corners and descending a narrow flight of stairs, they emerged into the warehouse's main gallery.

The gallery was long and narrow and must have stretched the full width of the warehouse. The walls were of wood but the stonework at the base of the walls indicated that this was probably the oldest part of the building, resting upon the original foundations. Half the gallery was taken up with the interior loading dock. It was here that cargoes would have been transferred from barrow to barge, and vice versa. The stout wooden doors that Jago had drawn to Hawkwood's attention earlier were located at the end of the dock. They were still closed, but there was sufficient space between them for daylight to penetrate. Further illumination came courtesy of two narrow, high-set windows and several lanterns hanging from hooks. The place reminded Hawkwood of a flooded church vault.

"Well, then," Lee said. "What do you think of her?"

Hawkwood stood and stared.

The submersible was tethered to the dock by lines fore and aft. She looked bigger than he had expected; about twenty-five feet long. At first glance, with her wooden deck and tapering bow and stern, the vessel looked like any other small river craft. On closer inspection, however, a number of differences were discernible. Below the shortened bowsprit, protruding vertically from an extended prow, was a thin metal rod from which radiated four elliptical blades, each about two feet in length. Aft, below the stern rail, a similar device, horizontally set, could be seen. There was no mast, Hawkwood noticed; then he looked closer and saw that the mast, with boom and furled sail attached, was in fact lying along the deck. It was hinged, he realized, thus enabling it to be raised and lowered into its socket at will. On deck, immediately forward of the mast socket, was positioned an upturned, barrel-shaped, metallic protuberance; the tower, as Congreve had called it, from where the commander of the craft controlled operations. The rear of the tower was hinged open, forming a hatchway which gave access to the craft's interior. Hawkwood's attention moved to the stern of the vessel. Attached to a raised wooden frame was a copper cylinder the size of a small rum keg. A lanyard ran from the cylinder to the tower where it passed through what looked like the eye of a large needle embedded in the tower's roof before disappearing through a small hole in the forward deck. Hawkwood remembered Colonel Congreve's description of the submersible and realized with a shock of understanding that he was looking at the submarine bomb, Fulton's torpedo.

327

"Beautiful, isn't she?" Lee could not keep the pride from his voice.

Hawkwood was silent. There was movement on deck as Sparrow emerged from the hatchway. He now had a pistol stuck in his belt. His fingers brushed against the pistol butt and he stroked the cut on his throat, favouring Hawkwood with a stare of undiluted hatred before stepping nimbly on to the dock.

Lee stepped forward. "All in order, Mr Sparrow?"

The seaman nodded.

"Capital! In that case, please be so kind as to see to the doors and prepare the vessel for departure."

Hawkwood stared at the woman, at her slim figure, her mannish dress, at her hair held in a tight chignon, at the pistol in her hand and her smile. And in a moment of startling clarity it came to him. Scully's taunting when he'd been asked if another mutineer or Lee had been his partner in the coach hold up.

It were neither, squire. An' if I told you, you'd never believe me. If you only knew . . .

Not a mute boy and certainly not Jago, as he had ludicrously supposed, but a woman whose accent would have betrayed her the moment she'd opened her mouth. She had shot the guard in cold blood and, judging by her present disposition, Hawkwood suspected that she hadn't lost a moment's sleep since.

Lee's voice cut into his tumbling thoughts. "What's the matter, Officer Hawkwood? Cat got your tongue?"

Before he could answer, the rattle of a chain sounded from the end of the dock. Sparrow was opening the doors.

As the gap between the doors slowly widened, light began to infiltrate the interior of the warehouse. Beyond the low archway, Hawkwood could see out to where the channel joined the river, flowing broad and smooth past the end of the outer quay. He wondered if Jago was still out there, still waiting.

Sparrow, his task complete, rejoined them. The seaman took the pistol from his belt and cocked it.

"Well, Captain Hawkwood, it's time to go. What can I say? It's been a pleasure. Truly." The American grinned roguishly and stepped nimbly on to the submersible's deck.

"Make it quick, Mr Sparrow. We haven't got all morning."

Sparrow grinned. He lifted the pistol and motioned Hawkwood to the edge of the dock.

"Kneel down."

Hawkwood didn't move.

He felt the muzzle of the pistol pressing against the nape of his neck. Heard the hiss of Sparrow's voice in his ear.

"On your knees, you bastard! Do it!"

Hawkwood heard a groan of anguish. The clockmaker, about to witness his death. The pressure of the gun barrel prevented him from turning his head.

Hawkwood knelt.

The muzzle moved upwards, against the back of his skull, forcing his head down. Hawkwood found himself staring into the dark water.

"Dear God, no!" The clockmaker cried, beseechingly.

Sparrow chuckled. The sound was like small bones rattling in a tin cup.

"Good bye, *Captain*," Sparrow said.

*   *   *

329

"Piss and damnation!"

Nathaniel Jago swore violently and checked his pocket watch for what felt like the hundredth time. Where the hell was Hawkwood? The hour had come and gone, but Jago had continued to wait, stubbornly pacing to and fro on the dockside like a caged bear, trying to ignore the crawling feeling in the pit of his stomach that was telling him something had gone badly wrong.

Jago was angry. He was angry with Hawkwood, he was angry with the world, but mostly he was angry with himself for letting Hawkwood go off on his own. Experience had taught him that if trouble were to be found then, sure as sunrise, Hawkwood would find it – as illustrated by the incident aboard the Rat's Nest. It had been sheer good fortune that had seen Jago arrive in the nick of time on that occasion. Jago had not pulled Hawkwood out of the fire, almost literally as it happened, in order for him to go wandering off again, sticking his nose into places it wasn't wanted. All right, so the man *was* a police officer, but for Christ's sake, didn't he *ever* bloody learn?

"Bugger it!" Jago knew he couldn't wait any longer. What had Hawkwood told him to do in the event of his non-appearance? Contact Magistrate Read? Jago shook his head in exasperation. Well, if the captain was expecting him to go running off to Magistrate Read, then the captain had another bloody think coming. Bending down, Jago secured the dinghy's painter to the ring by the side of the jetty steps. Then, with another muttered curse, he set off along the busy waterfront.

*　　*　　*

"No! Wait!"

Sparrow's finger whitened on the trigger.

"I said hold your fire, damn it!"

The pressure on Hawkwood's skull eased fractionally, enough that he was able to lift his head. He heard Lee's voice.

"Y'know, Sparrow, we've only Officer Hawkwood's word that the authorities suspect Lord Mandrake's involvement in our little enterprise, but they've no positive proof. It could be sheer coincidence that his lordship's headed north. Likewise, we could be using his warehouse without his knowledge. Lord Mandrake's a valuable ally with powerful friends at the heart of the government. Be a damned shame if we couldn't continue to make use of him. If we leave Hawkwood's body here, there's a connection. But if Officer Hawkwood disappears, what then? They'd have nothing. If his Bow Street brothers come looking for him, they'll find themselves up a blind alley with no trail to follow, and his lordship will live to serve another day. No, I say we dispose of Officer Hawkwood's body somewhere else."

"And how the hell do we do that?" Sparrow said. Light dawned in the seaman's eyes. "Christ, you mean we take him with us? You can't be serious?"

Lee shrugged. "Can't say I like it any more than you do, but it makes more sense. We'll transport him downriver, drop his corpse off later."

Sparrow thought about it. "So I shoot him now and we take his body on board? All right, I can live with that." Sparrow aimed the pistol.

Lee sighed. "I've no desire to try and lift his dead weight through the damned hatchway. It's constricted enough as it is. Besides, I don't want his blood all over my breeches. No, he can climb below by himself. And don't look like that, Sparrow. My decision, and there's an end to it. Don't worry, you'll get your chance later. Now, tie his wrists. The mademoiselle there'll keep her eye on him."

With a look that could have flayed skin from bone, Sparrow did as he was instructed.

"And Master Woodburn?" Hawkwood asked, when Sparrow had performed his task and retrieved his pistol.

Lee smiled. "Don't worry, he's in safe hands – providing you do as you're told. Bring him aboard, Mr Sparrow. Lively now."

With Sparrow's pistol at his back, Hawkwood stepped off the dock on to the submersible's deck. The vessel moved gently beneath him.

Lee turned towards the woman. "You know what to do?"

She nodded. "Of course."

"Then we'll rendezvous later, as arranged."

Lee brandished his own pistol and nodded towards the mooring lines. "I have him, Mr Sparrow. Cast off, if you please."

Hawkwood looked back in the direction of the dockside and the old man. There was a strange, almost haunted look on the clockmaker's face. Hawkwood suddenly felt as if he was missing something. He couldn't put his finger on it. Was the old man trying to pass him a message? If that was so, Hawkwood was unable to decipher it, though he had the uncomfortable feeling that the expression on Josiah

Woodburn's face would remain etched in his memory for ever. He glanced at the woman.

Catherine de Varesne smiled. "Goodbye, Matthew."

"I'll see you in hell," Hawkwood said.

A tiny inclination of her head, as if acknowledging the possibility. "I'll look forward to it."

She turned away. Sparrow used an oar to push the vessel off from the landing stage. With smooth precision, the submersible slipped through the doors and out into the river.

Jago let himself into the warehouse using a set of lock picks he'd confiscated from Irish Willie Lonegan. The picks were steel and of superior quality. Jago had confiscated them because Irish Willie was, as his name implied, from across the water, County Donegal, and thus not wise to the ways of the local fraternity of cracksmen. Willie had come a cropper the night he broke into an Eaton Square mansion and relieved the lady of the house of a jewellery box containing a fine selection of family heirlooms, including a ruby pendant, three sets of pearl earrings and a diamond necklace. His downfall came when he had paid a celebratory visit to Mistress Lovejoy's Finishing School for Young Ladies on Bedford Street, and bragged drunkenly to his pliant companion of the evening about his exploits. Irish Willie barely had time to tuck himself back into his breeches before he was hauled unceremoniously before a glowering Jago, who had explained the rules very carefully. London was his patch and no itinerant bog-trotter was going to encroach on his territory without permission. Punishment was swift and severe. Irish Willie was relieved of his tools, the remains of his takings, and both thumbs. On reflection, the Irishman had considered himself lucky. As for the picks, as Jago had remarked at the time, waste not, want not.

Maybe, Jago thought, as he stepped over the threshold, this wasn't such a good idea after all. He wished he was carrying something more substantial than a cudgel and a Runner's baton. A pistol would have been much more reassuring. A rat skittered past his feet. Jago ignored it. The warehouse seemed unnaturally quiet and permeated by an air of neglect and abandonment. He turned a corner and found himself facing a dark passageway. The hairs along the back of his neck prickled. Jago was no stranger to fear. He had faced many dangers, on the battlefield and among the pitch-black alleyways of the Rookery, but the sense of dread that accompanied him along that corridor was as heavy as if the Devil was sitting on his shoulder. There was something terrible here, Jago knew. Something wicked.

"Damn fine morning, Officer Hawkwood. Wouldn't you agree?" William Lee grinned, stuck the cheroot between his lips and puffed expansively.

Hawkwood didn't answer. He was sitting on the deck, back against the gunwale, hands bound in front of him, eyeing the pistol in the American's hand and wondering if it might be possible to overpower Lee without getting his head blown off. The odds, he decided, were not favourable, certainly not trussed as he was. And there was still Sparrow, now manning the tiller, to contend with. The mast had been raised and they were under sail, heading downstream, hugging the eastern shore, close hauled into a light south-easterly breeze. Mill Wall lay to port. Wells's Yard lay off the starboard beam on the opposite side of the river.

Emerging from the warehouse and into the main river, Hawkwood's eyes had moved instinctively to the steps where he'd left Jago. The boat was still there. Jago wasn't. Had the boat been absent, it might have suggested that Jago had done as he was told and was now en route to alert Chief Magistrate Read. The fact that the boat was still in place meant it was more than likely that Jago had disobeyed Hawkwood's instructions. Knowing Jago, the sergeant, restless at Hawkwood's failure to return, had probably gone looking for him. No surprise there, Hawkwood thought, feeling a sudden rush of affection for the big man. Jago riding to the rescue, again. Only this time he'd be too damned late.

"Master Woodburn told me the vessel suffered damage," Hawkwood said. He had the strong urge to keep Lee talking. As a means of delaying the inevitable, he didn't think it would be that effective, but at this juncture, he was prepared to try anything.

Lee took a leisurely draw on his cheroot and flicked ash over the gunwale. "Nothing that couldn't be fixed." He looked at Hawkwood with amusement. "Storm in the Channel it was. Lost a man, too. Which is how I ended up with Sparrow there. Scully brought him in." Lee took the cheroot out of his mouth and jabbed the stub towards Hawkwood's face. "Now I've lost Scully, too. You, sir, have a great deal to answer for."

"So, why here?" Hawkwood voiced the question that had

335

been gnawing at him since he and Jago had left James Read's office. "It's bloody madness. You could have waited until the ship was in the estuary, given yourself room to manoeuvre, given yourself an escape route. Christ, man, this is a bloody death trap!"

Lee drew on his cheroot and spread an arm. "You know why they built the yards here, Officer Hawkwood? It's so they'd be close to London and protected from foreign invasion. Deptford ain't the largest, it ain't the most strategic, and it ain't Chatham or Portsmouth, but by Christ it's the one that's going to make 'em sit up and take notice! Can you imagine the effect when I sink your newest goddamned ship in the middle of your goddamned capital city, and with the Prince of Wales on board? Your Admiralty boys'll be soiling their breeches for a month! It'll set back your war effort so far, you might as well go ahead and scuttle your whole damned navy! That's why we're *here*, Officer Hawkwood."

The door to the cell stood ajar. Jago used the cudgel to push the door open and the smell of death hit him. The body lay across the bed, face up. The artery in the neck had been punctured and there was a great deal of blood. The room stank of it.

Jago was not, by nature, a religious man, but he crossed himself nonetheless, and as he stared down at the corpse he felt himself torn by twin emotions: intense rage at the manner of death, and the absolute gut-wrenching certainty that he was unlikely to see Hawkwood alive again.

*   *   *

336

Lee stared out over the bow. They had been making good headway. To port lay the Isle of Dogs, a low-lying stretch of sparsely inhabited meadow and marshland. Only two roads served the Isle. The Deptford and Greenwich Road followed the shore, granting land access to the few isolated wharves and industries that occupied the east bank. The Chapel House Road bisected the Isle, connecting the Ferry House, on the southern bend of the river, with the Blackwall entrance to the West India Docks. Lee turned his eyes to the opposite bank, which was far more congested. Thickets of tall mastheads had begun to clutter the skyline as the heavily laden merchantmen awaited their turn for admission into the big dockyards. The entrance to the No. 1 Commercial Dock was visible over the starboard beam. Next to it, the smaller East Country Dock marked the Surrey-Kent border. Immediately south of the border was Dudman's Yard, with its mooring docks catering for the transports carrying convicts to the other side of the world. Beyond that, less than a mile distant, lay the Royal Dockyard, and his prey.

At a nod from the American, Sparrow, with quiet assurance, eased back on the tiller, taking them off the wind. The bow dipped. Without the advantage of the breeze, the sail began to flap listlessly.

Lee narrowed his eyes, and flicked the remnant of his cheroot over the side. "I'd say it's time, Mr Sparrow."

Sparrow lashed the tiller and moved to the mast. It took only seconds to lower the sail, lift the mast out of its socket and secure it to the deck.

The American touched his temple in salute and indicated

337

the open hatch. "This way, *Captain* Hawkwood, if you please."

Hawkwood hesitated. He was conscious that behind him Sparrow's pistol was now drawn and cocked, and pointed at the back of his skull. Hawkwood rose to his feet and watched as the American backed down the hatchway. Lee had been right. The hatch was very small. It looked like a tight fit. Hawkwood stepped across the deck. He knew he had no choice. He couldn't take on two armed men. The sensible thing, therefore, was to follow orders in the hope that an opportunity for retaliation would present itself in the not too distant future. Heart thumping, he followed Lee down the ladder and into the boat.

At the bottom of the ladder, Lee stepped aside. "Officer Hawkwood, welcome to the *Narwhale.*"

Emerging from the warehouse, Jago hawked and spat on to the cobbles. So much for *that* idea. He had searched the building from top to bottom. No Hawkwood, and no mysterious undersea boat either. But there had been a dead body, and given what he had been told by Hawkwood, it hadn't been difficult to guess the identity of the corpse. It had to be the clockmaker. Which meant it was likely the conspirators *had* been using the warehouse as a rendezvous. And the old man's death could only mean one thing: he had outlived his usefulness. The American, William Lee, was covering his tracks. Which meant Jago had to get word to James Read, and fast.

But where the hell was Hawkwood?

Back at the jetty, Jago stared down at the river. At least the bloody dinghy was still there. He knew he was missing something, but what? Then it hit him. When he'd searched the warehouse, the doors to the underground loading dock had been open. When he had arrived at the jetty with Hawkwood the doors had been closed. The thought occurred to Jago that instead of watching the warehouse and the comings and goings on the wharf, he should have been paying more attention to the bloody water. And there was something else.

The old man's blood was still wet.

Jago looked around quickly, his eyes lifting. Then he was running.

They were known as widow walks: balconies that ran around the top floors of the warehouses and riverside storage buildings. It was here that sailors' wives kept watch for the ships carrying their menfolk home. Years ago, from the highest platform on a fine day, an observer with a keen eye and a good spyglass could see clear across the flat expanse of the Isle of Dogs to the East India Docks, Bugsbys Marsh and the stretch of river beyond. On some of the older buildings a spyglass was a permanent fixture, enabling merchants and ship owners first sight of returning vessels. In nature the early bird catches the worm. And so it was in commerce. News that a ship had been sighted would radiate through the city like ripples in a pond. Tea, tobacco, spices and silks; the earliest arrivals always commanded the best prices. For want of a spyglass a healthy profit could be won or lost.

From the high balcony of Maggot & Sons, Wool Merchants, Jago, with a borrowed telescope jammed against his right eye, quartered the river. Part of his brain told him that looking on top of the water for a vessel that could travel beneath the surface was an exercise in futility, but he didn't know what else to do and he had to do *something*.

Jago recalled the words of James Read: *We must apply logic.*

If the open doors meant that the submersible had been in the warehouse and departed, possibly with Hawkwood on board, how far could it have travelled? Jago, ignoring the vessels traversing the river, turned the lens on to the traffic heading downstream. How long was the submersible? Twenty feet? He began to concentrate on the smaller craft, increasing the distance from the jetty with each sweep.

Jago didn't believe in miracles. Not until the glass settled on a small triangular patch of dun-coloured sail receding slowly down the left-hand side of the river. He blinked the sweat out of his eye and moved the glass down the mast. Just another wherry was his first thought. No cargo save what looked like a small cask at the stern and another upturned one forward of the mast. Flour, probably, or molasses. One man at the tiller, two more further down the boat, one seated at the gunwale, his back to the stern. Jago cursed and went to move the glass away, when, as if conscious of being spied upon, the man at the tiller turned. A sharp, familiar face floated into view. Jago stiffened, and swore.

Will Sparrow!

Jago tried quickly to bring the features of the other men into focus, but the boat heeled suddenly and the sail obscured his view. Jago cursed, tried to steady the glass once more, but the faces of the anonymous duo remained obstinately out of view. Jago knew a decision was required.

For the second time that morning, he began to run.

340

18

"*Narwhale?*" Hawkwood said.

Lee stroked the bulkhead affectionately. "*Monodon monoceros.* A small whale, native of the northern oceans. With one unique feature: a single horn in the centre of its forehead. Tulpius named it *unicornus marinum*, the unicorn of the sea. You know of the unicorn, Captain? A mythical beast, small, fast, elusive, it attacks the powerful, braves all dangers, seeks out carnage and has no equal in battle." Lee smiled. "A small indulgence of mine. Much more romantic than naming her after a shellfish, wouldn't you agree?"

Hawkwood said nothing. *Who the hell was Tulpius?* he wondered.

He looked around. The interior of the vessel was like nothing he'd encountered before. They were in the space below the tower, the only part of the boat where a crew member could stand fully upright.

The deck was flat, but the hull, supported by a frame of

metal stays not unlike the ribcage of a large fish, curved around them, enclosing them inside a bewildering array of levers, cranks and cogwheels, the solid manifestation of the drawing he had found in Warlock's baton. He was immediately aware that the inside of the boat was smaller than its outer measurements suggested.

"She's double-hulled," Lee explained, patting the bulkhead. "Keeps us watertight and we use the space between for storage and ballast." Lee tapped his foot on the deck. "Main ballast is down below. We don't need much. Ten pounds or thereabouts." Lee pointed to a small lever. "Pump water in, we sink. Pump water out, we float. The same way a fish moves through the ocean. They have a swim bladder. It's by the bladder's dilations and contractions that the volume of the fish is increased or diminished, enabling it to rise to the surface or sink to the bottom."

Lee was like a child with a new toy, pointing to and explaining the function of the controls; from the handles that turned the blades at bow and stern – Lee called them wings – to the cranks that controlled the horizontal and vertical rudders. Depth was measured by a crude barometer, direction by a small compass. Lee nodded through the tangle of ratchets and gears, towards what looked like a large copper globe tucked against the aft bulkhead. "And that's our air reservoir; two hundred and fifty cubic feet; enough to sustain four men and two candles for five hours. We used to precipitate carbonic acid with lime or carry bottles of oxygen, but they took up too much damned room. With this system, I can release air into the vessel when I require it."

Four men! Hawkwood tried to imagine what that would be like in such a confined space. Even with just the two of them below and Sparrow still on deck, the sense of claustrophobia was stifling, as was the smell; it carried with it the slight redolence that lingered in a ship's bilges; breathable but not exactly pleasant.

Lee grinned at Hawkwood's expression. "Snug, ain't she? But don't worry, We won't be down as long as that. Maybe an hour or two. Spent six hours in her once, bottom of Le Havre basin. That was a day to remember! Mind you, that's nothing compared to the *Mute*."

"*Mute?*" Hawkwood said.

"Fulton's new design. He tells me she'll be nearly four times as long as this boat. Probably be able to stay down ten, twelve hours at a time."

As Hawkwood's brain tried to grasp the awesome implications of that statement, a boot heel on metal announced Sparrow's arrival.

"She's ready," Sparrow said.

Lee nodded. "Very well. Officer Hawkwood, you take a seat on the deck over there. Secure his hands to that rib, Mr Sparrow. Don't want him running around loose, do we?" Lee grinned. "And when you've finished making our guest comfortable, I'd be obliged if you'd close the hatch and stand by the pumps."

Hawkwood, held fast to the bulkhead, watched as they prepared the boat for submergence.

The hatch clanged shut. There was a finality to the sound that made Hawkwood's mouth go dry. A spasm of panic moved through him and he had a fleeting thought that this

343

was what it must be like to be buried alive. And then he saw, unexpectedly, that he was not sitting in total darkness. There was light inside the boat. Half a dozen thin shafts of pale luminescence pierced the submersible's interior. He saw that Lee was watching him with an amused expression.

"Did you think Sparrow and I had supernatural powers, Captain? That we could see in the dark?" The American smiled. "Candles consume air, my friend, and air is valuable. I've constructed several small windows in the deck. Not large – two inches in circumference and an inch in depth. Each window, as you can see, is guarded by a valve. In the unlikely event of the glass breaking, the valve will close and keep out the water. They're quite sufficient for our needs. Even under the surface, I'll be able to consult my watch and compass, and in the event of an unexpected solar eclipse, we do carry a lantern on board." Lee grinned. In the semi-darkness, the American's teeth looked as if they'd been carved from ivory.

Hawkwood did not smile back.

Lee, suddenly brisk, stood inside the tower and pulled down a small hinged seat. Perching himself on the rest, the American pressed his eye to a small rectangular bubble of glass set in the forward-facing curve of the tower. Three more identical windows gave views to port, aft, and starboard. They did not provide a complete 360-degree panorama, but the restricted view from each was sufficient for him to judge the boat's position and its relation to other vessels that might be in the vicinity.

"Stand by, Mr Sparrow."

"You're mad, Lee," Hawkwood said. "You think people aren't going to notice the bloody boat going down?"

Lee took his eye from the window and shrugged. "Oh, they might notice, but what are they going to do? By the time the nearest vessel gets within boarding distance, we'll be beneath the surface, invisible. They'll think they imagined it, that their eyes deceived them."

Sparrow's hands rested ready on the pump handle.

Lee turned his back and watched the river. Despite his response to Hawkwood's taunt, the submersible was not entirely immune to danger. The time between lowering the sail, clearing the deck and closing the hatch was when the *Narwhale* was at its most vulnerable. With no one on deck, the boat *would* look as if it was drifting and therefore, to those of an unscrupulous disposition, available for the taking. Lee was relying on surprise and his own ability. Fulton had been able to submerge the *Nautilus* in two minutes. Lee, by redesigning the efficiency of the pumping system, had cut down the *Narwhale*'s diving time to a fraction over ninety seconds. For those on board, however, it would still seem like a lifetime.

Lee discovered, as he always did at this critical juncture, that he was holding his breath. He let it out slowly, keeping his eye to the glass. The nearest vessel, as far as he could see, was a collier, one hundred yards over the bow, heading downriver. It didn't appear to be making much headway, indicating that the breeze had dropped considerably. From his low angle of vision, the river looked vast, with only a slight swell disturbing the sullen surface.

Timing was crucial.

"Now, Mr Sparrow!"

Sparrow gripped the lever with both hands and pushed down. Immediately, a low gurgling sound filled the hull. The vessel trembled. Using both hands, Sparrow began to pump, his movements steady and unhurried. Hawkwood felt the deck shift beneath him and braced himself against the hull. Slowly, the submersible's bow began to tilt. Sparrow's hands continued to depress and raise the pump lever. Each motion was accompanied by what sounded like bellows inflating and deflating. Hawkwood discovered that his fists were clenched so tightly his nails were digging into his palms.

The gurgling continued, but the vessel's movements were becoming less pronounced. Gradually, the deck began to level off. Suddenly the light dimmed. Hawkwood looked up. One by one, the thin shafts of illumination from the windows were fading. Hawkwood felt the cold bubbles of sweat break out beneath his armpits. He looked towards Lee. There was a translucent sheen to Lee's skin. The tiny windows set into the deck were acting like prisms, absorbing the light filtering down from the surface, inscribing the American's features with a curious reptilian caste.

"Stop pumping, Mr Sparrow." The American's voice was very calm.

Sparrow ceased his exertions. Five feet beneath the surface of the Thames, the *Narwhale* hovered, like a fly trapped in amber. The sense of stillness was uncanny, as if the submersible was suspended in time. Hawkwood was relieved to discover that the American had been right and that there was still enough light to see. A low rasping sound, like fingernails being drawn across a slate, broke the spell and Hawkwood started violently.

"Just our movement with the current. No need to be alarmed." Lee left his seat and began to peer closely into the darker recesses of the compartment. Hawkwood assumed the American was checking for leaks. Evidently satisfied that the integrity of the hull was secure, Lee caught Hawkwood's eye and smiled. "Tell me you're not impressed."

Hawkwood didn't answer. He was too preoccupied with his own heartbeat, waiting for it to stop pounding like a tinker's drum.

Lee appeared unperturbed by the lack of response. "And this is only the beginning. Imagine a fleet of these vessels at your command. War would become obsolete, a fairy tale told only in story books."

"How so?" Hawkwood finally found his voice.

"They say a country's only as strong as its navy. Destroy a nation's warships and you take away its backbone." The American paused and shrugged. "At least, that's what Fulton and Bonaparte reckon. You want to know Bonaparte's plan?"

"I've a feeling you're going to tell me anyway," Hawkwood said.

"Bonaparte thinks my blowing up *Thetis* will frighten the British Navy into submission. Confidence in your seamen will vanish, your fleet will be rendered useless. The Emperor believes that'll be the signal for British republicans to rise up. With Britain a republic, the seas will be free, and liberty of the seas will mean a guarantee of peace for all nations."

"Then Bonaparte's mad," Hawkwood said, and wondered, even as he spoke, if there was such a creature as a British republican. It was a possibility, he supposed, but it was doubtful there'd be enough of them to ferment and organize revolution.

Lee appeared to give the possibility the same degree of consideration. "Maybe, but he's the one with the money, so who am I to disagree?"

"How much is he paying you?"

Lee smiled. "For *Thetis*? 250,000 francs. After that, it'll depend on the size of the vessel. Up to twenty guns, 150,000 francs; twenty to thirty guns, 200,000 francs; and 400,000 francs for anything over thirty guns. Sufficient for my modest needs."

Hawkwood recalled his conversation at the Admiralty Office and the huge sums demanded by Lee's predecessor, Fulton. It appeared Bonaparte was paying the American the going rate. In other words, a small fortune.

"How do you plan to get out? Even if you do manage to destroy the ship, you'll never make it back to the sea."

"Oh, we'll make it, never you fear."

"How?"

Lee smiled knowingly. "Same way we came in. Under tow. There's a Dutch brig moored off High Bridge. Her captain's a sympathizer. Well, no, that's not strictly true. The Frogs are holding his wife and family hostage so he doesn't get any fancy ideas. I'm listed as first mate, Sparrow's down as cook. She'll be the swan to the *Narwhale*'s cygnet." Lee jerked his thumb. "The tower's detachable. We'll stow it inside a wine cask, lash it to the deck with a few others, tie up to the brig's stern rail, and it's homeward bound. Couldn't be easier. We'll drop you off downriver. You'll be dead, of course, but sacrifices have to be made, I'm sure you understand."

You certainly couldn't fault the man's confidence, Hawkwood thought. The taste of bile rose sour in his throat. "So, what happens now?"

Lee angled his pocket watch towards one of the small ports and squinted at the dial.

"Now we wait."

Hauling back on the oars, Jago cursed his creaking bones and reflected that he hadn't done this much hard labour since he'd left the army. His palms were raw from the scrape of the oar handles. In the Rifles, he had always prided himself on his fitness and stamina, but he was a civilian now, damn it. He should be taking it easy, enjoying the fruits of his labours, not running around like a bloody lunatic. It was all Hawkwood's fault, of course. Give the man an inch and he took a bloody mile. But Hawkwood, all things considered, was probably the closest thing Jago had to a friend. And if there was one thing the army taught you, it was that you stood by your friends. And Hawkwood had stood by Jago more times than the ex-sergeant could count. Now, Hawkwood was in trouble. It was time to repay his debts.

Jago paused, twisted in his seat, wiped sweat from his brow, and looked downriver. Without the advantage of height, his view was restricted by the ever-changing flow of traffic. He could no longer see the sailboat with Sparrow at the helm, and he was beginning to wonder if he'd imagined it. He swore viciously. No, it *had* been Sparrow he'd seen, he was certain of it. But so what? He didn't know for sure that Sparrow even had a connection with Lee and his undersea boat. On the other hand, Sparrow had been a mate of Spiker's and, though the link was tenuous, it was all he had to go on. Nathaniel Jago was running on instinct. He tried not to think about the consequences if he was wrong. They were worrying enough if he was right.

I know you're out there, Sparrow. I can bloody smell you! So come on, you bastard, show yourself!

Without warning, a gap suddenly widened between the vessels ahead of him, giving a clear view of the open stretch of water beyond, and it was then that he saw it. The sailboat was some five hundred yards over the port bow. The vessel didn't appear to have made much headway since his last sighting. It was still hugging the eastern side of the river, close-hauled against the oncoming breeze. But then, even as Jago watched, the stern of the sailboat began to come around.

An angry bellow erupted from Jago's starboard side. A heavily laden bumboat was on a collision course. Jago dug in his oars as the vessel cut across his bow, heading for the Dog and Duck Stairs.

"Move your bloody arse!" Jago bellowed. The bumboat wallowed past with infuriating slowness. The tiller-man raised an angry fist. The gesture was accompanied by a torrent of oaths. With his way eventually clear, Jago, echoing the tiller-man's curse, plunged the oars back into the water and began searching urgently for his quarry.

Where the hell was it?

Jago blinked. The sailboat could hardly have been out of his sight for more than a couple of minutes at the most. There was no way it could have made it to shore in that time. It had to be out there somewhere. He should have purloined the spyglass, he thought, brought the damned thing with him. But Jago's eyesight was good. He had been a rifleman, and riflemen needed the eyes of a hawk to target enemy officers. So Jago narrowed his eyes and scoured the river. Plenty of similar vessels about, but not the one he was looking for. No sailboat with a brandy keg at the stern. Shit and piss!

Then he saw the arm, pointing.

The arm was attached to a crewman on a dirt boat. The dirt boat was cutting across the river, probably en route to the Deptford yard with a hold full of ballast. Something had caught the crewman's eye. Jago followed the direction of the outstretched arm, squinted hard. There was something in the water.

A barrel, bobbing incongruously with the current, probably lost overboard by some passing lighter or merchantman; nothing to get excited about. And yet . . . Jago looked back at the dirt boat. The crewman had been joined by one of his mates. Both of them were pointing now. It seemed an undue amount of attention for a discarded wine cask.

Wine cask?

Jago stood up, stared harder, and watched as the cask sank slowly beneath the water. Not a single ripple marked its passing.

Christ on a bloody cross!

Showing remarkable speed for such a big man, Jago

dropped down into the boat and scrambled for the oars. Nathanial Jago had walked the cold stone passage of Mandrake's warehouse as if the Devil had been on his shoulder. Now he began to row as if the Devil was at his heels.

"What happens if it sinks?" Hawkwood asked.

Lee glanced up from his pocket watch and frowned. "It's a goddamned submersible. It's supposed to sink."

"I don't mean on purpose," Hawkwood said. "I mean if something happens. How do you get out?"

Lee appeared unperturbed by the likelihood. "You detach the keel, and float up."

"And if that doesn't happen?"

"Then you hold your breath, and pray."

Hawkwood stared at him.

Lee sighed. "If you can't detach the weight of the keel, the only way out is through the hatch. But you can't simply open it and swim out. The incoming water pressure would be too great. The only way would be to open the valves and allow the hull to flood. Once the hull's flooded, there's equal pressure inside and out. Only then could you open the hatch and swim to the surface." Lee chuckled darkly. "I commend you, Officer Hawkwood. Your desire for self-preservation is quite admirable. Futile, but admirable."

Lee snapped his watch shut. "But enough. The tide's reached its height. Time we were making a move, Mr Sparrow. Stand by to take her up."

Lee relayed crisp instructions and the submersible began

to rise. Lee pressed his eye to the forward window. "Hold!"

Hawkwood sensed that the top of the submersible's tower had breached the surface. He watched Lee. The American was concentrating on the river and studying his watch and compass, taking bearings.

Sparrow took the opportunity to remove his shirt. Clothed, Sparrow's physique had seemed insubstantial. Now, Hawkwood could see the man was wiry rather than thin. As a deckhand, Sparrow would have been no stranger to ropes and rigging and manual graft, and the muscles in his upper body and his flat stomach hinted at both strength and stamina. Sweat glazed his chest and forearms. Hawkwood found himself staring at the seaman's back. Sparrow's flesh was a mosaic of crisscrossing scar tissue. The scars were old, Hawkwood saw, but there was no disguising what they were: the legacy of a severe flogging, possibly more than one. It probably explained why, like Scully, he was working for the American. Another abused, disaffected seaman – in all likelihood a former mutineer – looking for vengeance.

Eye pressed against the tiny window, Lee's hands moved to the rudder controls. "Now, Mr Sparrow. Steady as she goes."

Sparrow began to turn the crank. His effort was accompanied by the sound of cogs meshing, as if a clock was being tightly wound. The *Narwhale* vibrated. Hawkwood felt the vessel shift on its axis. Slowly, the submersible began to come about. At first, the movement was uneven, but as Sparrow eased into his rhythm, progress through the water became smoother. Only the hypnotic click of the gearing mechanism and Sparrow's breathing as he turned the propeller crank gave any indication that the vessel was in motion.

Lee's eye was glued to the tiny window. Occasionally his gaze would shift to the compass dial and his hands would alter the angle of the rudder to maintain the vessel's course. He knew this would be the last time they could raise the *Narwhale* without attracting attention. After this it would be too risky exposing the tower so close to unfriendly eyes on ship and shore.

Lee did not have a lot of room to play with. Even at the height of a spring tide, the river bottomed out at a little over three fathoms, which didn't leave a great deal of leeway either above or beneath the hull. And over the years, the river had been gradually silting up. There'd probably come a time, not too far distant, when the dockyard would no longer be able to handle ships of large tonnage. As it was, Deptford was too far upriver, with insufficient depth of water, to allow ships to sail down to the mouth fully armed and victualled. Current practice, once a ship had been launched, was to rig a jury mast and float her down to Woolwich, where she would be docked, coppered and rigged in preparation for sea trials.

And HMS *Thetis* was about to make that first auspicious journey.

The warship looked mightily impressive, Lee conceded, as he peered through the glass. As bright as a new pin in the morning sunshine. He could see that the jury mast had been raised. Cut from a single Norfolk Island pine, it rose tall and slender, as straight as an arrow from her midsection, A temporary boom had also been attached. Bunting and flags fluttered gaily from every rail. It was going to be a grand occasion.

He could see movement at her bow and stern as the crew made final preparations for departure. A tremor of excitement moved through him.

Hawkwood looked over his bound wrists, saw the American stiffen and sensed they were close and that Lee probably had the target in his sights. Which meant that he was fast running out of time. Lee was about to commence his attack and there wasn't a thing he could do to stop him.

"She's a beautiful sight, my friend." Lee grinned. "But you'll have to take my word for that." Lee turned. "Pity she's going to end the day as kindling. Steady, Mr Sparrow. We don't want any mishaps this close to home."

The submersible moved ahead cautiously and Lee pressed his eye to the glass once more. He was looking for defences, festoons of netting, fenders, a ring of decoys – anything that would indicate that they were anticipating an attack. But, astonishingly, the ship appeared to be unprotected. Lee recalled Hawkwood's attempted bluff, when the Runner had told him he had men outside the warehouse. There had been no men, no support, no reinforcements. Hawkwood had been on his own. Which indicated that Hawkwood's assertion that the authorities knew about the attack on *Thetis* had also been an exaggeration. They undoubtedly thought the attack was going to take place further downriver, in the estuary, not in the middle of London. Lee grinned to himself. Damned fools! He was about to deliver a blow that would shake the British out of their complacency.

Lee gave the order to submerge. As silently as a ghost,

the *Narwhale* sank beneath the waters of the Thames. Less than two hundred yards separated the submarine from its unsuspecting prey.

19

"You've got a choice, Corporal," Jago growled. "Either you find Chief Magistrate Read and bring 'im here, or else you take me to 'im. Either way, you'd better be quick, or else I'm going to tear your bleedin' head off, piss down your neck, an' go and look for 'im myself. What's it to be?"

The marine gripped his musket and swallowed nervously. An angry Jago was an awesome sight, and the corporal who had stopped Jago at the top of the dockyard jetty stairs was beginning to regret his dedication to duty. Not that he'd had much say in the matter; his orders had been clear. Halt and prevent all unauthorized personnel from entering the dockyard area. The directive had been handed down by Sergeant of Marines Burnside, and where Corporal Elias Watkins was concerned, Sergeant Burnside's word was law. So the corporal stood his ground.

"Can't do that. You ain't got authorization." The corporal stumbled over the last word.

Jago reached under his jacket. "This here's all the authorization I need, laddie." He held out Hawkwood's baton. "So, why don't you stick your neck back in, and you and me can take a little walk. What about it?"

The corporal looked Jago up and down.

"Right now would be a good time," Jago hinted ominously.

The corporal regarded the baton, its royal crest, and the fearsome expression on Jago's face, then took a cautious look over his shoulder. Indecision furrowed his brow. Finally, after what seemed like an age, he shouldered his musket.

"You'd best come with me."

The big warship lay at anchor, paintwork gleaming. Her two-decked hull was mustard yellow, her upper wales and gunports jet black. She dwarfed the flotilla of smaller dockyard support vessels that hustled and bustled feverishly around her high chequered sides like worker ants around a queen.

Cutters, buoy boats, hoys, pinnaces, skiffs and lighters scurried between ship and shore, loaded to the gunwales with equipment and victuals, while yachts, yawls and gigs transported officers and men with all the dexterity of waterborne sedan chairs.

Her name was inscribed boldly for all to see on the counter of her stern: *Thetis*.

The dockyard rang with the sounds of industry. Enclosed within the yard's stout protective walls were all the workshops and raw materials vital to maintaining the British Navy's command of the high seas. From launching and building slips, wet and dry docks, mast houses, boat ponds, saw pits and timber berths to tar and oakum stores, sail lofts, rigging-houses, rope-walks, smithies and copper mills, and accommodation for a score of other trades besides.

Adjacent to the dockyard lay the huge victualling yard. Had the capital, by some cruel circumstance, found itself in the grip of a deadly epidemic, the chairman and commissioners in charge of the navy's Victualling Board could rest easy, secure in the knowledge that the Royal dockyard and its workforce would emerge from the plague unscathed. All they'd have to do was bar the gates. The yard was as self-sufficient as a small town. Aside from dry-storage facilities, the Deptford yard boasted its own bakery, brewery, cooperage and slaughter-house. This was evidenced not only in the sounds that carried across the water but also in the smells that accompanied them. Some pleasant, like the warm aroma of freshly baked bread and biscuits and fermenting hops, some not so agreeable: the pungent odour of boiling tar and the sweet, sickly whiff of cow shit, untreated hide, fresh blood, and offal.

James Read stood by the side of the launching slip and surveyed the activity before him. His right hand toyed idly with the handle of his cane.

"You think she'll pass muster?" The voice came from the man at his side.

Commissioner Ezekiel Dryden was tall and loose-limbed. His heavy-lidded eyes and languid exterior gave the impression of a lifetime spent in idle pursuits. Dryden, however, was a former naval captain, as were the majority of dock-yard commissioners. He had commanded ships in action. Now he was in charge of both the Deptford and Woolwich dockyards. He had full authority over all dockyard personnel, both military and civilian, and movement of all vessels therein. He reported directly to the Navy Board.

James Read looked pensive. "She'll have to. I fear time's against us."

A movement on the dockside diverted the Chief Magistrate's attention. Two men were approaching, a marine and a civilian. Read's heart quickened.

The marine drew to a halt and saluted. "Beggin' your pardon, your honour . . ." But he was given no chance to expand as James Read held up a hand.

"Thank you, Corporal. You may go."

The corporal blinked at the curt dismissal. He looked towards Dryden, as if seeking some kind of moral support. When none was forthcoming, he glanced at Jago with renewed respect and not a little confusion.

"Don't let us detain you, Corporal." Commissioner Dryden's dry voice broke into the marine's thoughts.

"Yes, sir. Very good, sir." Discipline finally overcoming curiosity, the corporal gave a flustered salute, shouldered his musket, and turned on his heel, no wiser than he had been before the big man had arrived.

Read wasted no time. "You have news, Sergeant?"

Jago nodded. "Aye, an' none of it's good."

"Explain."

Read and Dryden listened in silence as Jago described his own entry and investigation of the Mandrake warehouse. Read's expression grew even more severe as Jago described his discovery of the clockmaker's corpse.

"God in heaven!" Dryden, though a seasoned officer,

experienced in the harsh reality of war at sea, was plainly shaken by the cold-blooded murder of Josiah Woodburn.

"And Officer Hawkwood?" the magistrate prompted. "You say there was no sign of him?"

Jago shook his head. "It's my guess they took 'im."

Read frowned. "Took him where?"

"On board with 'em."

The magistrate looked taken aback. "On board? You mean the submersible?"

"I reckon."

"God almighty!" Dryden said. The commissioner turned and stared balefully out at the river.

From the other side of the wall, separating the dockyard from the victualling yard, there came a sudden mournful lowing followed by a succession of ear-piercing grunts and squeals; the cacophony heralding a fresh intake of stock, newly arrived from Smithfield. Somewhere nearby, a hammer clanged against an anvil. The reverberation was followed by a wail of invective. While in a distant corner another, more strident voice, could be heard berating some hapless unfortunate for botched workmanship. Life in the yard went on.

"And you definitely saw the craft submerge?" Read pressed.

Jago hesitated. "You're askin' if I'm positive I saw the bloody thing. Can't say as I am. All I can tell you is that the boat was there one minute and gone the next, Sparrow along with it. Could've been the top of a bloody barrel that I saw go under, could be the two shit-shovellers were lookin' at something else, but if it *was* this submersible you told us about, then it's still out there –" Jago nodded towards the water. "Somewhere."

All three men gazed out at the river. The water looked suddenly deeper and darker and infinitely more menacing than it had a few moments before.

"So what do we do now?" Jago asked.

The Chief Magistrate remained silent. Dryden looked down at his shoes. Jago didn't like the way they were avoiding his eye. "We've got to stop the bloody thing! What about the captain? What are we goin' to do about him?"

James Read continued to gaze at the river. "Officer Hawkwood, I fear, is on his own. If he is on board the submersible, then we must pray that he finds a way to disable the vessel and gain the upper hand. If not, then there's nothing any of us can do to assist him."

Jago swore under his breath. They were not the words he had wanted to hear, even though he knew the magistrate was right, "But what about the ship? You've got nets out, right? And patrol boats?"

James Read turned slowly. There was a stillness about the magistrate's face which Jago had not expected.

"No, Sergeant, we do not have nets out. Neither have we employed extra patrol vessels."

Jago stared at the magistrate in horror. "But she's a sittin' duck!"

"Indeed she is, Sergeant."

Jago looked at the ship, at the boats bobbing around her, at the men on her deck. "Oh, Jesus! What the hell have you done?"

James Read followed Jago's gaze. The magistrate's mouth

was set in a grim line. "We have a contingency plan. Should Officer Hawkwood fail in his mission, we intend to let William Lee continue with his attack."

Jago's face distorted with shock. "You're not bleedin' serious?"

"Perfectly serious," Read said.

Jago stared first at the magistrate then at the commissioner. "You can't do that. You've got to stop the bastard!"

James Read raised his cane to shoulder height and swung the tip in an encompassing arc. "Take a look around, Sergeant. Tell me what you see."

"What?" Jago blinked, temporarily thrown by the magistrate's cool manner.

"Tell me what you see," Read repeated calmly.

Jago shook his head in frustration. What the hell was going on? A ship was about to be destroyed by a madman and innocent men were going to die. And he was being asked to admire the view?

Which consisted of what?

Ashore, as far as he could see, there was nothing untoward. Plenty of activity, as might have been expected of a working yard. There were possibly more marines in evidence than usual, but that was about all. There were no marines stationed at Deptford, Jago knew. Those on current duty, like the vigilant corporal, would have been sent up from the Woolwich yard. But other than that, Jago couldn't see anything that merited special attention.

His gaze moved to the water. There was the new warship, conspicuous in its gaudy paintwork, with several dozen small support craft flitting back and forth. Lying close by was the sheer hulk, the yard's largest support vessel. The hulk was traditionally an old warship, cut down, with a mast fixed amidships. Fitted with extra capstans, sheer frames and tackles, the vessel was used to heave out or lower masts into newly fitted ships of the line. The hulk was the dockyard workhorse. The Deptford hulk was a particularly decrepit-looking craft, obviously long since fallen from grace, with its scabby hull more reminiscent of a coal barge than a retired man-of-war.

Further downstream, just beyond the dockyard limits, he could make out the prison ship. All the dockyards had them. Like the sheer hulk, they were usually former ships of the line or else captured vessels too old and too far beyond repair for further sea duties. At permanent moorings, they'd been used initially as temporary accommodation for transportees, but now the navy used them largely as holding pens for prisoners of war. There was a fleet of them on the Thames, lying off the mudflats in a scattered convoy stretching all the way down to the estuary. With their cut-down masts and decks and rigging often hung with drying laundry and mildewed bedding, they had become an ugly and all too common sight along the shoreline, though many a canny boatman continued to turn a handsome profit by running sightseeing trips to see the convicts at work digging and dredging the foreshore in preparation for some new riverside construction.

Jago's eyes moved back to the warship and the movement of craft around her. There were a number of men onboard, he saw: a skeleton crew ready to take her downriver. Jago looked along her deck. A group of sailors stood clustered at her stern rail. By their dark blue coats and bicorne hats, Jago could see that most of them were officers. Nothing remiss, as far as he could tell. Other than the flags and bunting, there was not the sense of jubilation among the onlookers he might have expected, given the launch of a new ship, but this was a working dockyard and the experience was probably old hat to the local workforce. Jago dismissed the thought and was about to turn his attention elsewhere when the group at the ship's rail broke apart to reveal the figure in its midst. Stouter and taller than his companions, he cut an imposing, colourful vision due, not only to his size, but to the wide sash around his waist, the ceremonial sword at his hip, the ribbons, medals and tassels adorning his broad chest, and the tuft of feathery white plumes in his hat.

Jago gaped. The reason why there were more marines around than usual was suddenly made clear. He swung towards James Read. "God Almighty! It's Prinnie! What the hell's he doin' here? You were supposed to stop 'im!"

The Chief Magistrate did not reply. The corners of his mouth twitched. Commissioner Dryden studied his toes.

Before he could remonstrate further, a splash and a cry from one of the support boats reached Jago's ear. He turned towards the sound.

A seaman had missed his footing transferring from bumboat to warship and fallen into the water, much to the amusement of his shipmates. Their laughter as he was hauled back aboard the bumboat in an undignified heap floated over to the quayside. It was what happened next that caused Jago to gasp. As the luckless seaman lay floundering in the well of the bumboat, the marine seated in the stern of the craft slammed the butt of his musket across the seaman's shoulders. He was further amazed when the seaman's companions rounded on the marine and let loose a broadside of abuse.

It had not been the spectacle of the blow from the musket or the seamen turning on the marine that had stunned Jago so much as the language that had been used. His first thought was that he must have misheard, but as he looked on the insults continued to be traded back and forth until a sharply issued command from the stern of a nearby officer's gig stung the seamen into an uneasy silence.

Jago searched for the source of the order. There were half a dozen or so officers in the gig, and another armed marine. Jago looked closer. Something about the officers' appearance didn't sit quite right. He wasn't sure what it was, but there was definitely something odd about them.

The commotion had drawn the attention of the men on the warship's deck. A group of them had gathered by the starboard rail to see what the fuss was about. Another cry went up as a dark object tumbled from the rail. A feather bedecked hat. It spiralled down, bounced off the side of the ship and splashed into the water like a wounded seagull. Before it had time to sink, however, it was rescued by a member of the bumboat's crew. Another derisive cheer marked the hat's expeditious retrieval. The seaman who had performed the rescue waved the hat above his head. The hat had not survived the fall undamaged. The feathers lay flat and sodden. What was more noticeable, however, was that one side of the hat had been newly branded by a broad yellow streak.

Jago's stomach turned over. He looked quickly from the

366

hat back up to the warship's deck. Deprived of the sheltering brim, the features of the hat's owner were now clearly defined. It was a disclosure that rocked Nathaniel Jago to the core.

"Bloody hell!"

Jago swung round to discover that Chief Magistrate Read and Commissioner Dryden were regarding him closely.

Senses reeling, Jago took another, longer look at the occupants of the officer's gig. What was it about the uniforms that had caught his eye? True, they weren't the smartest he'd ever seen; decidedly scruffy, in fact, considering the occasion. If Jago didn't know any better, he'd have said the state of the uniforms was more reminiscent of a slop chest's contents than of a newly commissioned crew set to join a brand-new man-of-war.

And then it hit him like a bolt of lightning. He spun, taking it all in: the ship, the men on board her, the activity on the dockside, the presence of the marines, and the words that had been bandied in jest by the men in the boats.

"Mother of God!" Jago said in awe. He looked at James Read with horror on his face. "You're mad! It'll never bloody work!"

William Lee stroked his jaw tenderly, feeling the bristly beginnings of his new stubble, and a welcome sense of pleasure moved through him. He had missed the feel of a beard. He had worn one for the last ten years or so and felt naked without it. Now that his mission was coming to an end, with the necessity for disguise no longer paramount – it would have been unusual for a French aristocrat to have been so hirsute, Lord Mandrake had advised him – he was looking forward to the beard's return. It would be like greeting the appearance of a long-lost friend.

Lee took his hand from his chin and prepared to deploy the *Narwhale*'s eye.

It was an invention of his own, independent of Fulton's design, and necessitated by a fundamental flaw in the operation of the submersible. In order to keep its target under constant observation, the vessel had to keep breaking the surface, which inevitably increased the risk of the dome being spotted. The obvious key to the problem, Lee had reasoned, lay in providing a means by which the commander could keep the target in sight while remaining submerged. The solution, after much trial and error, had been simple and ingenious: a two-inch diameter sealed metal tube with a reflecting mirror set into each end. The surface of the mirrors ran parallel to each other at a 45-degree angle to the axis of the tube. Opposite each mirror, set into the side of the tube, was a small inlay of glass. Looking through either glass into the adjacent mirror one could see a reflection from the mirror at the other end of the tube.

Lee had sunk the device into the roof of the tower. Seated beneath the dome, the commander of the vessel could raise or lower the tube at will. With the vessel submerged and the tube raised, the commander, by looking into the bottom mirror, could see what was reflected in the top mirror, above the surface of the water.

Through experimentation, he had settled on twenty-six inches as the optimum length of the eye tube. Any longer and the image relayed back from the surface was severely distorted and too small to be of any use. Taking further inspiration from a spyglass, Lee had attempted to incorporate a series of lenses between the mirrors in an effort to magnify the image, but so far he had not been successful.

Lee raised the eye and wiped a tear of moisture from the rim. The device, though effective, had its drawbacks. The sealant – a concoction of pig grease and wax – had a tendency to leak over prolonged periods. Once water had seeped inside the tube, the mirrors would mist over with condensation. Lee hadn't yet managed to solve that problem. He'd tried various methods of prevention and, although each successive attempt had been an improvement, he was still some way from devising a foolproof, not to say waterproof, solution. But for the time being it would suffice. At a distance of eighty yards from the target, the eye enabled him to observe the ship in close proximity. He could even see the name board at her stern. Lines were being hauled on board and made fast. The fleet of support craft was dispersing. Through the glass he could see the bunting and the flags in fine detail. He searched and picked out the one that marked his target: the standard of the Prince of Wales. It meant the Regent was on board, probably among that group of men at the stern, he reasoned.

"Closer, Mr Sparrow, if you please."

The hull of the ship rose broad and sheer out of the water like the side of a cliff.

Lee lowered the eye. He discovered that his mouth was as dry as sand.

He looked at his watch. It was time.

"Take her down easy, Mr Sparrow. Gently does it."

Lee adjusted the rudders. *Narwhale* crept forward.

Hawkwood pulled impotently at the bonds securing his wrists. There was some give in the rope, but not nearly enough. He glanced towards Sparrow. The seaman's scarred back was towards him. Carefully, Hawkwood eased himself into a sitting position and drew his knees towards his chest.

"Rest easy, Mr Sparrow. We're almost there." Lee's voice was a hoarse whisper.

Sparrow stopped turning the crank. Lee's hands continued to move gently on the rudder controls, relying on the submersible's momentum to carry them forward. Slowly, a dark shape moved across one of the windows. One by one, the tiny slivers of light illuminating the interior of the hull were extinguished as the *Narwhale* slid beneath the warship's great hull.

A chill ran down Hawkwood's spine. Was it his imagination, or had it become colder inside the darkened compartment? He heard the strike of a flint. A pale, spluttering orange glow told him that Lee had lit the lantern.

There was a bump, followed by a scraping sound. Hawkwood realized what it was. The top of the submersible's tower had made contact with the bottom of the warship's hull.

It was Lee's signal.

Suspending the lantern from a rib in the roof, Lee worked quickly. He didn't have much time. *Thetis* would be underway within minutes. It would be impossible to drive the spike into the warship's hull while the vessel was in motion. Lee lifted two items from hooks on the bulkhead. One was a small iron maul. The other was a thin, rounded

T-shaped piece of metal. The stem of the T was threaded and resembled an auger. Lee lifted his head and probed the roof of the tower with his fingertips for the hollowed base of the *Narwhale*'s horn. Using his left hand for support he screwed the auger into the end of the horn. Ensuring that the join was tight, he reached for the maul.

It took four firm strikes with the maul to drive the barbed tip of the horn into the ship's hull. Satisfied that the horn was firmly embedded, Lee reached up and unscrewed the auger from the shaft. From his pocket he removed a small wax plug and, using the maul, tapped it into the end of the shaft to seal it. Satisfied that there was no seepage, he resumed his seat.

Hawkwood was astonished at the ease and speed of the operation. It had taken less than a minute to attach the horn to the belly of the ship.

"Stand by, Mr Sparrow." Lee leaned forward and released the lock on the forward windlass. "Now, take us down and out, if you please."

Sparrow began to crank. Slowly, painfully, inch by cautious inch, the *Narwhale* began to nose forward. The click of the windlass could be clearly heard as the line running from the winch through the cleft in the horn to the torpedo at the stern of the submersible was reeled out. As the vessel emerged from beneath the shadow of the warship's hull, light from the surface began to filter into the compartment once more and Lee extinguished the lantern.

It was in those few seconds, between the snuffing out of the lantern and the ingress of natural light, that Hawkwood was finally able to reach down, tendons stretched to breaking point, and remove the knife from the inside of his right boot.

Hawkwood had no idea how much time he had before the torpedo was set to explode. The count down to detonation was dependent on the length of the trigger line, and that, he suspected, given the diameter of the windlass, wouldn't be long. And while he was sitting there thinking about it, vital seconds were ticking away. With Lee and Sparrow preoccupied with making good the *Narwhale*'s escape, he knew it was the only chance he had left. Reversing the knife and gripping the shaft precariously in his left hand, Hawkwood began to saw at his bonds.

Sparrow was cranking hard. The muscles in his shoulders and forearms bulged as he powered the submersible through the dark water. His back and chest looked as if they had been smeared in oil. The sweat dripped off him as the submersible began to pull away.

Counting steadily under his breath, Lee took out his pocket watch once more and squinted at the dial.

The *Narwhale* was travelling at two knots. Two hundred feet from the warship, the submersible checked. The movement was barely noticeable, but it was the moment Lee had been waiting for. It meant the line on the windlass had reached its full length and the submersible's forward motion had been transferred to the keg at the stern. The torpedo had been released. It was heading unerringly for its target.

Ten seconds later, there was a second tug as the torpedo made contact with the warship's keel, severing the line and its last connection with the *Narwhale*.

Lee gripped the bulkhead. "Brace, Mr Sparrow!"

The last strand of rope parted. Hawkwood reversed the knife and came off the deck with the blade angled towards Sparrow's throat.

And the torpedo detonated.

20

Hawkwood knew he had failed. He knew it the moment he launched himself off the floor. He heard Lee's cry of warning, saw that Sparrow was already turning. The sound of the blast enveloped the boat, but it was the shock-wave, nudging the *Narwhale* off its axis as it moved out from the centre of the explosion, that tipped the balance, sending Hawkwood slithering across the deck as his feet shot out from under him.

Sparrow, accustomed to the pitch and roll of a ship at sea, was first to recover. With a bellow of rage he reached down, twisted the knife from Hawkwood's grip, tossed it aside, hauled the Runner to his knees by his hair, and took the pistol from his belt. The ratchet sound of the weapon being cocked was unnaturally loud. Helpless, Hawkwood watched Sparrow raise the pistol.

"Bastard!" Sparrow hissed. For the second time that morning, his finger whitened on the trigger.

The sound of the second detonation was ear shattering.

Sparrow's eyes widened in shock as a sliver of copper from the ruptured air cylinder sliced through his jugular, releasing a fountain of blood across Hawkwood's face and shoulders. Hawkwood looked up, awe-struck, as Sparrow, teeth bared in a silent, choking scream, buckled at the knees, the pistol dropping from his hand. There followed a second of blinding pain as the hair was ripped from his scalp by Sparrow's involuntary death spasm. There was barely enough time for the hurt to register before the incoming torrent of water slammed into him, driving the air from his lungs and hurling him against the starboard hull with the force of a mule kick.

The *Narwhale*'s bow dipped sharply and the submersible heeled violently to port. It was as if the vessel had been picked up by a giant hand and hurled against a wall. Hawkwood made a desperate grab for one of the iron ribs. As he did so, Sparrow's body, still pumping blood, fell forward, trapping him against the bulkhead. Hawkwood drew in his knees and kicked out. Only one boot made contact, but it was just enough to shift the seaman's dead weight. Hawkwood sucked in air, used the rib for support, and dragged himself upright. His eardrums felt as if they were on fire.

The submersible gave another massive lurch, this time to starboard. The motion was accompanied by what sounded like a heavy wooden door straining on a rusted hinge. Hawkwood felt the short hairs on the back of his neck stand on end. He managed to hang on by his fingertips and stared at the horror around him. Whatever the cause of the second explosion, the effect had been catastrophic. With her stern section severely holed, the boat was flooding at a phenomenal rate. Hawkwood looked forward and saw Lee working feverishly to regain control. But the lack of response from the vertical and horizontal rudders and the angle of the bow told their own story. With all power lost, the *Narwhale* was dropping like a stone.

The ship was ablaze.

The explosion had echoed around the dockyard like the voice of God, sending every man – labourer, seaman, marine and magistrate – diving for cover. Voices rose sharply in panic. Shrieking gulls wheeled across the sky in massed confusion. Somewhere an alarm bell began to clang loudly.

The *Thetis*'s midsection was a smoking ruin and she had lost her mast. It lay like a fallen tree across her foredeck, boom and temporary sail still attached, canvas draped over the gunwales like a huge grey funeral shroud. The standards that had flown so proudly above her now hung in tattered and scorched disarray. Flames licked hungrily from her gun ports and open hatchways. Slowly she began to list.

Several men had gone over the side, either catapulted there by the force of the blast or having leapt over the rails to escape the terrible conflagration. Thrashing limbs, splashes and urgent cries for help showed where they had landed. The water was tinged with blood. Many of the survivors were screaming.

Jago, ears ringing like Bow Bells, almost missed it.

What made him glance out over the river at that precise moment he would never know. Even then, he wasn't sure what he had seen: a commotion in the water, a hundred yards or so beyond the stricken warship. What looked like a small waterspout, or a splash, as if something had risen to the surface and dropped back down, causing a series of widening concentric ripples. A disturbance of some kind below the surface.

A marine hurried past, musket at the ready. Jago recognized him as the corporal who had stopped him earlier. "You, lad! Come with me!"

The look in Jago's eyes told the corporal that dissent was not an option. Without a word he followed Jago to the dockyard stairs, watched as the big man climbed into the row boat and picked up an oar.

"Come on, son, we ain't got all bleedin' day!"

The corporal shouldered his musket and stepped gingerly into the boat.

Jago untied the painter, pushed them away from the quay-side, and thrust the oar into the corporal's hands. "Now, boy, you row!" Jago picked up the second oar. "You bloody row until I tell you to stop!"

Below the surface of the Thames, as the pitch of the vessel altered, the angle of illumination penetrating the submersible from above was changing. It was growing darker by the second.

The underside of the bow hit first. In the gloom of the compartment, the sound of the submersible's keel scraping along the river bed was like a forty-two-pounder sliding across a storm-lashed deck, amplified a thousand-fold. It seemed as if a lifetime had passed before the noise began to diminish. Finally the tumult died. There followed a moment of eerie silence. Slowly the stern began to settle. Then, with a final protest from its creaking timbers, the *Narwhale* came to rest, canted at an angle like a broken barrel in a snowdrift.

Chest heaving, Hawkwood let go of the rib and checked himself for injuries. Miraculously he appeared to be unscathed. Self-preservation foremost in his mind, he groped frantically for the knife. The water was already hip-deep and icy cold. Sparrow's corpse lay face down and wedged against the pump handle. Hawkwood clambered over the inert body, feeling urgently with his fingers. His hand brushed what might have been the knife blade, but even as he knelt to retrieve the object, with the incoming water surging around his legs like a whirlpool, the blade slid from his grip and Lee was upon him.

The American had lost his own pistol in the confusion, but his hand held another weapon. Instinct had Hawkwood twisting aside, arm rising to ward off the blow as the iron maul curved towards his skull.

The maul-head missed Hawkwood's ear by less than a finger width. He felt the breath of its passing on his cheek. His hand encircled Lee's wrist and he used Lee's own impetus to over-balance the American and ram him against the bulkhead. He heard Lee grunt as his shoulder made contact with the metal rib. Hawkwood drove a fist into the American's belly and was rewarded with another gasp of pain. But Lee, recovering fast, lashed out once more. This time the attempt was successful. The strike took Hawkwood under the ribcage, slamming him back against the propeller crank. Lee, eyes suddenly bright with the expectation of victory, moved in. Through tears of pain Hawkwood watched the approach of death.

The submersible tilted violently and Sparrow's body rolled. In the water-filled darkness of the hull, Lee failed to see the obstacle in his path. His foot turned on Sparrow's thigh and, hampered by the water, he lurched off balance, the maul falling from his hand.

Hawkwood threw himself against the American. The two men went down. Hawkwood had but a second to draw air into his lungs before the water closed over them.

In the swirling darkness, Hawkwood clawed for a killing hold. Lee was the older man but he was strong, and he was fighting for his life. Lee's hands found Hawkwood's throat. A red mist descended behind Hawkwood's eyes as he fought for breath. The blood began to pound in his ears. The weight on his chest was colossal. His lungs felt as if they were about to explode. He gripped Lee's wrists in a frantic attempt to break the American's hold, but his energy was ebbing fast. He let go with his right hand, reached down, clamped his fingers around the American's balls, twisted and pulled hard. Immediately, Lee's hold slackened. Hawkwood released his grip and heaved himself upwards. His head broke from the water and inhaled greedily. He sensed Lee surface next to him, turned to meet the danger and took the full force of the knife thrust as Lee drove the blade deep into the muscle of his left shoulder.

Curiously, Hawkwood felt no pain until, with a ragged scrape of steel against bone, the blade was withdrawn. He felt it then. As if someone had poured fire into the wound. He fell back, his sound arm lifting in pathetic defence as the American stabbed down once more. The strike missed. Hawkwood went under, limbs flailing, fumbling in the inky blackness, scrabbling blindly for a weapon of his own – any object with which to defend himself. His fingers touched something, moved on, came back. Lee's hand was on his sleeve. Hawkwood sensed the shift in the American's weight, knew it would be over soon. The knife blade was coming around again. Summoning his last reserve of strength, he hurled himself out of the water and swung his arm.

The tip of the auger entered Lee's right eyeball, piercing the front of the American's skull with devastating force.

The scream that erupted from Lee's lips was inhuman.

Hawkwood tightened his grip, thrusting deeper, increasing pressure. The scream died away, fading to a low whimper. The knife fell. Lee's hands rose in mute supplication. A long, bubbling sigh emerged from the American's lips. His body jerked violently and then went limp.

For what seemed an age, Lee's body remained upright, suspended as if by an invisible hook, until Hawkwood finally relinquished his hold. He watched without emotion as the American's corpse fell away and sank from view beneath him.

Another deep shudder moved through the boat as the *Narwhale* settled further into the silt. Hawkwood was suddenly conscious of how high the water had risen. It was up to his chest. Before long it would be lapping his shoulders, then his throat. After that . . .

It struck him that he was going to die down here, alone in the blackness, with only the bodies of Lee and Sparrow for company. *Thetis* had been destroyed. He would die, having failed in his assignment; an ignominious end to a short-lived career. In the heat of battle, Hawkwood had faced death many times. On those occasions, he'd viewed the prospect without self-pity or recrimination. Facing an enemy with rifle and sword in hand, knowing you were going to die, was almost acceptable. But this . . . ?

The water was suddenly up to his chin. Christ, but it was cold! Shivering, he pushed himself towards the last place of refuge, the standing space in the tower. He was moving blindly now, all light having been extinguished. His left shoulder and arm were completely numb, partly from the pain, mostly from the chill. He had no idea how much damage had been inflicted by the knife blade. Not that it mattered, anyway. It wasn't the knife wound that was going to kill him. The lack of air and the water in his lungs would see to that. Already his body had begun to shut down. He wondered vaguely if drowning was a painful death. He'd heard men say that it was a peaceful way to go. He'd have preferred not to be finding out first hand.

He inched his way painfully along the deck. Every movement had become a supreme effort of will. The water was up to his nostrils. He was shivering harder now, uncontrollably. It was becoming increasingly difficult to breathe. There couldn't be much air left. He was amazed it had lasted this long.

He wondered about Jago. Had Nathaniel gone looking for him? Had he reached Magistrate Read? His last thought, as the water took him into its cold, eternal embrace, was that there was something important he had forgotten to do. He hadn't even had the opportunity to say his farewells.

*   *   *

Jago and the corporal stroked their way through the debris. Several bodies floated face down. Burnt and blistered flesh showed through scorched clothing. Here and there gobbets of burning pitch glowed like molten lava. The corporal's face was white as he surveyed the carnage.

Around them, the support boats were moving in on the men in the water. A bumboat had arrived alongside the warship's hull and an officer was leading half a dozen firefighters up the side ladder to the smoke-obscured deck.

A cry came from the water to their right. A seaman, treading water, his face bleeding and blackened, raised an arm in supplication.

The corporal looked at Jago. Jago shook his head. "Keep rowing, Corporal. Someone else'll pick him up. He ain't the one we've come for."

Jago ignored the questions in the marine's eyes. He was too intent on trying to gauge the spot where he'd seen the disturbance in the water. Not that he knew what he was looking for, exactly, only that he had the feeling he'd know it when he saw it.

Like pieces of driftwood, for example. Maybe they were from the warship, Jago thought, as he reached down and scooped one up. He examined the shard of planking, turning it in his hands. The section of wood was curved, not unlike a barrel stave. The ends were badly splintered. Jago bit his lip and stared out over the gunwale. The wind had freshened, the water was turning choppy. Jago tossed the stave over the side. Maybe his eyes had deceived him and it had only been wave movement after all. He looked towards the shore. There were others in the water, gravely injured men who needed their help.

The big man's shoulders slumped in defeat. "All right, lad, there's nothing here. Let's go back."

But the marine wasn't listening. He was pointing. "Wait. There's something there."

Jago looked. He couldn't see anything. He shook his head. "There's nothing, lad."

"No," the corporal said. "Look."

And Jago stared.

A patch of shadow, that was all, cast by the row-boat and themselves.

But there was something strange about the way it was moving. As if . . .

The surface erupted. From the centre of the maelstrom, a hand clawed skywards, followed by a head and shoulders, and the sound of a man gasping for air that had the corporal leaping backwards in terror, the hairs on the back of his neck as rigid as corn stalks.

Jago was the first to react. "Come on, lad! Help me!"

The corporal came out of his trance, but Jago was already there, reaching down, grasping the dead weight, hauling the body into the boat, hand over hand.

It had to be some kind of miracle.

The marine rowed them towards the shore. Seated in the scuppers, Jago cradled Hawkwood in his arms. He was holding his padded neckerchief against the wound in Hawkwood's shoulder. "It's all right, don't you worry, Cap'n. Jago's got you now."

Chest heaving, Hawkwood looked up at the big man. When he spoke, his voice was a faltering whisper.

Jago bent low. "Sorry, Cap'n. Didn't catch that."

Hawkwood took a deep breath, succumbed to a brief wracking cough, and tried again.

"Nathaniel?" His voice now a rasping croak.

"That's me."

"You were right."

"I was?" Jago frowned. "What about?"

A grin rearranged Hawkwood's face.

"It wasn't much of a plan."

And Jago started to laugh.

21

The surgeon, a burly man with a reassuring smile, stowed his instruments in his bag and turned to the Chief Magistrate. "The stomach wound is superficial; a scratch, nothing more. As far as the knife wound is concerned, I've cleaned it as best I can. He's strong. I see no reason why he shouldn't make a full recovery."

James Read received the news with a nod. "Thank you, Doctor."

As the surgeon stood, Commissioner Dryden, standing behind him, coughed discreetly. "If you'll excuse me, gentlemen, I too have duties to attend to. And I've no doubt there are matters you wish to discuss in ah . . . private." Dryden smiled, almost shyly, at Hawkwood. "Honoured to make your acquaintance, sir." A nod to James Read and to Jago, who was standing at the bedside, and he, too, was gone.

They'd taken Hawkwood to the commissioner's house.

Commissioner Dryden had summoned his own doctor to examine Hawkwood's injuries.

"He's an excellent man," Dryden had assured Read. "Served with Collingwood on the *Dreadnought.*"

James Read waited until the two men had left the room before turning to the patient. A rare smile hovered on the magistrate's lips. "Welcome back."

Sunlight flooded the room. A servant had arrived earlier to close the curtains, but Hawkwood had stopped her. His entombment in the submersible was still fresh in his memory. He craved light and warmth, lots of it. Those last moments in the *Narwhale* had been the most terrifying ordeal of his life. Trapped in the flooded tower, the water over his head, the will to fight slipping away until, in a moment of startling lucidity, he recalled Lee's words. *You hold your breath and pray.*

So, in the pitch darkness, Hawkwood had held his breath and prayed that he could open the submersible's hatch before the air in his lungs finally gave out. It had been a frantic few seconds, searching for the catch, one arm useless, the freezing cold invading his body with a crippling intensity. Eventually, the catch had yielded, and he was pulling himself through and clawing his way towards the light.

He did not respond to the magistrate's greeting.

James Read frowned. "Your wounds pain you?"

"I was thinking about Lee," Hawkwood said. "I wasn't able to stop him. He still blew up the ship."

A muscle twitched in the magistrate's cheek. He looked at Jago. Jago returned the look and raised an eyebrow.

"What?" Hawkwood said.

"No he didn't," Jago said.

"Didn't what?"

"He didn't blow up the ship," James Read said.

"Of course he did," Hawkwood said. "I heard it. I *saw* it, when Nathaniel brought me ashore."

The Chief Magistrate shook his head. "No. He blew up *a* ship, not *the* ship."

Hawkwood thought he might be going mad. Except Jago was grinning like a loon. He stared at them both.

Jago said, "They switched them, Cap'n. The sly buggers switched 'em."

Hawkwood closed his eyes, waited, opened them again. Jago was still there, still grinning.

Jago glanced at the magistrate. "Well? Are you goin' to tell 'im, or am I?"

James Read smiled. "I'd hate to deprive you of the pleasure, Sergeant."

"Well, *someone* tell me," Hawkwood said.

"All right," Jago said. "First off, it wasn't *Thetis* that blew up. It were the sheer hulk."

"The what?"

"It's what you might call the yard's work 'orse, used for fetchin' and liftin'. Dunno what 'er name was originally. Probably last saw action before we were born – well *you* at any rate. Now, where was I? Oh, aye . . . anyway, that's how they did it."

"The art of deception, Hawkwood. To hide in plain sight – isn't that what they say?" The Chief Magistrate walked to the window and looked out on to the dockyard, where work was returning to normality after the morning's excitement.

"It seemed a logical solution to our dilemma. What to do if you failed in your assignment. We decided to employ a decoy. The sheer hulk was the only vessel close enough and large enough for our purposes. Our main problem was her appearance. Fortunately, we were able to employ both the yard's workforce and the contents of her stores. We used two teams of men; one to paint the hulk, one to tarnish *Thetis*. Don't forget, *Thetis* only had a jury mast. Neither was she rigged or coppered. It was not that difficult: some muddy canvas strategically placed, a web of old netting here and there, black paint to cover the ochre. The hulk was a bigger challenge, but we had the paint and the men. The carpenter's shop provided us with a false name-board which we adhered to the hulk's stern. Add banners, the Regent's standard, crewmen . . . The disguise would not deceive a close observer, but we thought it might fool someone with a limited view, someone like William Lee on board his undersea boat."

"God Almighty," Hawkwood said.

"Our greatest enemy was time." The magistrate turned from the window. "We could only guess, if you were unable to stop him, that Lee would wait until the morning tide to make his attack. We barely had time to board her crew. It was a close-run thing."

"Paint was still wet," Jago said. "That's what finally tipped me the wink." Then he saw the expression on Hawkwood's face.

"You put a *crew* on board as well?" Hawkwood said. His voice was cold.

"We had to," Read said. "To complete the deception."

"Men died," Hawkwood said.

Read nodded solemnly. "Four dead, seven injured."

"An' not an Englishman among 'em," Jago said, then paused. "Well, save for one."

Hawkwood looked at him.

"They used Frog prisoners of war. Togged 'em up in cast-offs from the yard's slop chests. That's another thing that caught my eye: state of the officers' uniforms. Bloody disgrace, they were. No self-respectin' English officer'd be joining his ship lookin' like he'd just walked out of the poor 'ouse. Thought it a bit strange. That, and the fact that everyone started yellin' at each other in Frog. Weren't natural."

"I know what you're thinking," James Read said quietly, interpreting Hawkwood's expression. "That there are conventions covering the treatment of prisoners of war. Quite true, though I would urge you not to grieve for the prisoners who perished on *Thetis*. Their fate had already been sealed. Had they not been killed in the explosion, they would have met their death on the gallows."

Hawkwood continued to stare at the Chief Magistrate.

"The men who died were the ringleaders of a plot to gain control of the prison ship *Gryphon*. Four days ago, two dozen prisoners, under the leadership of a Lieutenant Duvert, led a revolt. Two marines were murdered. Their bodies were hung, naked, from the hulk's gun ports. It was only through the bravery of the hulk's commanding officer, Captain Childers, who led his marines into the bowels of the ship to apprehend the culprits, that the revolt was quashed and disaster averted.

"Some of the scoundrels attempted to conceal themselves among the *rafales* in the hulk's lower decks to avoid detection. They even shed their clothes to blend in. Fortunately, the ruse

389

failed. They were given up by their fellow prisoners who were sickened by the violence. It also helped that there was no love lost between Duvert and his cronies and the *rafales*."

Hawkwood had heard of the *rafales* from a former marine who'd served as a prison guard on the hulks at Chatham. The *rafales* occupied the bottom rung of the prison ladder, literally. They lived in a state of perpetual darkness in the lowest parts of the prison hulks. Naked as moles, or with only a blanket for warmth, their miserable existence was due to their mania for gambling, which led them, upon the loss of their money, to part with their clothes, bedding and rations. The stronger-willed prisoners – such as Duvert and his followers – preyed upon them with the cold-blooded detachment of sharks. Which accounted for the *rafales*' willingness to betray Duvert and his henchmen, Hawkwood supposed.

"Duvert and his men had already received their sentence before we learned of Lee's plans for his submersible. I'll lose no sleep in having consigned them to an earlier grave. I agree, Hawkwood, that the rules of war carry with them obligations, as do the regulations covering military prisoners. I shed no tears for cold-blooded murderers, however. Duvert and his men forfeited their rights as prisoners of war when they displayed the bodies of those two marines like plucked fowl on a butcher's block." The Chief Magistrate frowned. "We did make some allowances, endeavouring to reduce unnecessary carnage by positioning them all at the bow and stern, deducing that those would be the areas least likely to suffer damage. Though, in that regard, it would appear we made a severe miscalculation."

"You said there was an Englishman."

Jago nodded. "Aye. A mate of yours, as it happens." The big man threw a glance at the magistrate.

James Read pursed his lips. "Proof of the pudding, Hawkwood. We had the ship, the flags, the Royal standard. We weren't sure how good Lee's intelligence was, how close he might get, so we needed the one thing that would convince William Lee that he had the correct target in his sights. We needed the Prince of Wales."

Hawkwood rose from the pillows. Pain lanced through his shoulder. He sank back with a grimace, which changed to an expression of disbelief. "The Prince was on board?"

Read shook his head. "A substitute. A flesh-and-blood decoy who could pass for the Prince at a distance. Someone with the right girth and stature."

"And he was a friend of mine?"

Read smiled. "Not exactly. The sergeant was being facetious, though you are acquainted with the individual." The magistrate paused. "Certainly with his mother."

Jago said, "They used Eli Gant."

"Gant!" Hawkwood winced as pain flared again. These revelations were doing nothing for his chances of a speedy recovery.

"I recalled that he and the widow were occupying berths on one of the transportation ships at Dudman's Yard, awaiting passage to the colonies. We did not inform the widow of the reason we were borrowing her son. Young Eli seemed quite taken with the notion. He liked the clothes." The magistrate's tone darkened. "I'll see he's buried in them. It seems only fitting."

There was a silence in the room.

"Why the deception?" Hawkwood asked. "Why didn't you put out nets? Why not just stop Lee? Why did you want him to carry out the attack?"

The Chief Magistrate remained silent. Hawkwood sensed a deep disquiet. Finally James Read spoke.

"Because we needed to see if the submersible worked."

Despite the sunlight slanting through the windows, a chill moved through Hawkwood.

James Read, sensing the change of mood, threw a meaningful look at Jago. "Come now, you need rest and time to gather your strength. We'll talk again soon. Everything will be made clear. You'll join me, Sergeant?"

Jago nodded, but before he left he moved to the bed. He bent low and spoke low so that only Hawkwood could hear. "Remember what we talked about, Cap'n? Bleedin' generals. They tell you nothing. You and me, that's all that matters." He touched Hawkwood lightly on the arm and followed the Chief Magistrate out of the room.

Ezra Twigg looked up and smiled as Hawkwood entered the ante-room. "Why, Mr Hawkwood! A pleasure to see you back, sir. And looking very fit, if I may say so."

"Good to see you, too, Ezra. He's in, I take it?"

The clerk nodded towards the inner door. "He is, and he's waiting for you."

Hawkwood entered the office. There were three men present: James Read, Colonel William Congreve and a stranger. They were in conversation but fell silent and looked up as Hawkwood entered.

"Ah, Hawkwood, there you are." The Chief Magistrate stepped out from behind his desk.

The Colonel smiled. "Captain! Good to see you! Fully recovered from your adventures, I trust? Excellent! Capital!"

"Colonel," Hawkwood said, shaking the proffered hand.

The stranger was regarding Hawkwood with interest. Hawkwood returned the examination. The man was tall, with a strong, sun-browned face and penetrating blue eyes.

"Officer Hawkwood, Captain Thomas Johnstone."

Johnstone nodded but did not offer his hand.

Captain? Hawkwood thought.

The magistrate moved towards the door. "Thank you, Captain Johnstone. That will be all for now. The Colonel will contact you in due course. My clerk will see you out." Read opened the door. "Mr Twigg?"

Johnstone did not seem in the least put out by the abruptness of his departure. He left without a backward glance.

The Colonel's expression was benign, but Hawkwood had the distinct feeling that the colonel did not set much store in Johnstone's character.

Read returned to his desk. The Colonel moved to one of the chairs and sat down. The magistrate did not offer Hawkwood a seat. He seemed preoccupied with his thoughts. Finally he spoke: "We discovered what Lee meant by friends in high places."

Hawkwood waited. The Colonel shifted in his chair.

"It was Admiral Dalryde."

Dalryde! An Admiralty Board member. No wonder Congreve looked uncomfortable, Hawkwood thought.

"It appears the Admiral had amassed rather heavy

gambling debts," Congreve continued. "His main creditor was White's. It was his gambling losses that brought him to the attention of a fellow club member."

"Mandrake?" Hawkwood ventured.

Read nodded. "Indeed, and it was Mandrake who introduced him to the woman. The Admiral told Mandrake you were the officer I'd assigned to the case. He was at Mandrake House the night of the ball."

The shadow in the bushes, Hawkwood thought. His jaw tightened at the memory.

"Do not reproach yourself, Hawkwood. There was no way you could have known. The woman's a skilled courtesan. She has considerable charms and knows how to use them. In Admiral Dalryde's case, she used her wiles to manipulate him into providing her with information. In exchange for her favours and the promise that his debts would be covered, the Admiral gave her details of the naval courier's travel arrangements, the date of *Thetis*'s departure from the Deptford yard, and the progress of our enquiries into both the coach robbery and Officer Warlock's murder. The latter investigation, of course, held special interest because of its connection to the deployment of the submersible."

"The bastard was right under our noses!" The colonel slammed a fist against his knee and stood up. Restlessly, he began to pace the room.

"I take it we arrested him?" Hawkwood said.

Read nodded.

"So he'll be charged with treason," Hawkwood said.

Read shook his head.

"Why the hell not?"

"Because the bugger beat us to it," the colonel snapped.

Hawkwood looked to the magistrate for an explanation.

"The admiral hanged himself in his cell this morning."

"God's teeth! What about Mandrake? Don't tell me he's cheated the hangman, too."

James Read placed his palms flat on the desk. He pushed himself to his feet. "My Lord Mandrake boarded a ship at Liverpool and took passage to the Americas. I'm afraid Runner Lightfoot returned empty-handed."

Hawkwood didn't believe what he was hearing. And he knew he still had to ask the obvious question. It wasn't something he could put aside. "And the woman?"

"Ah, she is being held, I'm happy to say. And she's under constant watch. Before he killed himself, Dalryde was questioned. He was kind enough to reveal Lee's escape plans. We were able to board the Dutchman and impound her. The crew has been transferred to the hulks."

"So," Hawkwood said, "who the hell is she?"

Read frowned.

"I'm assuming," Hawkwood said, "that she's not really the Marquise de Varesne."

"Ah," Read nodded in understanding. "Well, you assume correctly. The lady's name is Gabrielle Marceau, and she's certainly no aristo – though there's no doubt she played the part to perfection. She is, or rather was, a house servant."

"*House servant?*"

"To the real marquise. Which is how she was able to wear the mantle with such aplomb. It seems her family was employed on the Varesne estates for several generations. She became a companion to the marquis's daughter. They were of a similar age and I understand she did bear an uncanny resemblance to the real Catherine. A resemblance which the Directory and latterly Bonaparte's intelligence service used to full advantage."

"And the real Catherine?"

James Read's expression hardened. "Dead, I fear, along with her mother and father and, I gather, a younger brother. Madame Guillotine is no respecter of youth. The entire family was erased in the Terror. Which made it easier for Mademoiselle to assume the role. A part she's been playing for some time with considerable success. My sources tell me she is highly regarded by her employers."

"It's a pity your sources didn't tell you that a lot earlier," Hawkwood said. "It would have saved us a deal of trouble."

The Chief Magistrate nodded. "I'll not disagree with you."

"And no one was aware of the deception?"

"Anyone who might have known the family or discovered her secret is dead, killed during the purges. Either that or eliminated in the event a suspicion was raised. She was well protected. She was . . . is . . . one of their best agents. Her speciality was infiltrating the Royalist underground. She was able to provide Bonaparte's intelligence service with names of Bourbon sympathizers, prior warnings of assassination attempts, invasion plans and so forth. She was ideally placed to co-ordinate Lee's attack on *Thetis*."

"And now *we've* got her."

"Indeed," Read said.

"So they'll hang *her*, at least."

But again, to Hawkwood's astonishment, the magistrate shook his head.

"But it's not just Lee she was involved with! The bitch killed two people! She shot the coachman and she stabbed Master Woodburn to death!"

The cold-blooded manner of the old man's death had shaken Hawkwood more than he cared to admit. Lee had said he had not wanted to leave Hawkwood's body at the warehouse as evidence. It had been his reason for taking Hawkwood on to the submersible. The woman, clearly, had not harboured the same degree of reservation. She had killed the clockmaker and left his corpse displayed for all to see.

It had been James Read who had suggested the motive behind her actions.

"I suspect the lady knew that Mandrake's premises would be compromised anyway and that your presence there was not a random event. She probably felt that, with you in Lee's hands, her mission was, to all intents and purposes, complete. Having Master Woodburn under her feet would hamper her movements, possibly hinder an escape. No, by her reasoning, Master Woodburn had become an inconvenience, something to be discarded at the earliest opportunity."

The Chief Magistrate's words made sense, terrible though they were. It came to Hawkwood then, the awful truth. The message that had been in the clockmaker's eyes when he had boarded the submersible. It had been the moment when Josiah Woodburn had known that he, too, was under sentence of death. With Hawkwood dead, the old man was the only other witness to Mandrake's treachery.

In an uncharacteristic gesture, James Read placed his hand on Hawkwood's arm. "Do not reproach yourself. There was little you could have done."

"I left him to die," Hawkwood said.

"I suspect Master Woodburn knew you had no choice." The Chief Magistrate sighed. "Our clockmaker was a very courageous gentleman."

Hawkwood's shock at the murder and the ease with which he had been duped had fuelled a rage and a grim determination to bring all those responsible to account, especially the woman.

It was with a leaden sense of guilt that he had raised himself from his sick bed and retraced his path to the house on the Strand. There had been no requirement for him to make the journey. James Read had already taken it upon himself to relay the news of Josiah Woodburn's murder to the staff. The Chief Magistrate had not wanted to entrust the onerous responsibility to a subordinate. Hawkwood, however, had felt he owed it to the old man to pay his own respects. The knowledge that he had been unable to protect the clockmaker from a senseless act of brutality lay like a heavy weight upon his conscience and it wasn't the Hobbs he dreaded facing, it was the old man's granddaughter. He wondered if he would be able to look her in the eye without flinching.

The Hobbs had admitted Hawkwood to the house with the loss etched deeply into their worn faces, and he knew the moment he stepped over the threshold that the little girl was not there. The silence told him so, and he wasn't sure if he was relieved or not.

"She's with her aunt's family in Sussex," Mrs Hobbs told him. "Her uncle is a vicar. He has a small parish outside Rottingdean. They have a daughter of their own, the same

398

age as Elizabeth. It was thought the right thing to do, while the family puts the master's affairs in order." The housekeeper's face was as grey and drawn as her husband's. "A terrible business, Officer Hawkwood, a terrible business. The people who did this will be punished, won't they?"

"Yes," Hawkwood had promised them. "If I have anything to do with it."

At least that's what he had assumed.

"She's to be exchanged," James Read said.

"*What?*"

"She's Bonaparte's most valued agent in Britain. We can use that to our advantage. It's our intention to exchange her for British agents held in France. Overtures have been made. The French will release five of our men in exchange for her safe passage back to Calais. It's an excellent trade."

The Chief Magistrate's face softened. "I know what you're thinking, Hawkwood. We're at war and many good men have died: the coachman, Officer Warlock, Master Woodburn . . . But there is a higher agenda at stake here. If this conflict is to be resolved, accommodations must be made, diplomatic channels must remain open. That agenda was severely compromised when Bonaparte commissioned Lee to attack *Thetis*. A line was crossed. A precedent set. That was why we had no compunction in placing French prisoners on board the ship. An eye for an eye, if you will. But I believe it was an aberration and the arrest of the woman has given us an opportunity to step back from the abyss. The situation is recoverable. With an exchange such as this, each side can be assured that dialogue is still an option. It is sensible, Hawkwood. Above all, it is civilized."

399

Hawkwood tried to find words, but none were forth-coming. He wondered about the Chief Magistrate's use of the word *civilized*. Had it been civilized, he wondered, to sacrifice the French prisoners or the imbecile Eli Gant? This was a side to James Read that was new to him. Beneath the Chief Magistrate's cultured exterior, there existed a ruthlessness that would have done justice to some of the *guerrilleros* that Hawkwood had fought with in the Spanish mountains.

In the defence of the realm, it was now clear that any rule could be broken. All methods could be justified in the pursuit of a goal. Then Hawkwood remembered the unfinished conversation in the bedroom at the commissioner's house and knew instinctively there was more to follow.

"We knew from Lieutenant Ramillies' reports that improvements had been made to the submersible boat." It was Colonel Congreve who spoke. The colonel had stopped pacing and was standing next to the fireplace. "We needed to find out what they were and whether they had made the device a more viable proposition. William Lee's mission to attack *Thetis* gave us that opportunity. It meant we could observe the efficiency of the vessel first hand."

"What if I'd been able to destroy it?" Hawkwood asked.

"We still had the drawings the clockmaker gave to Officer Warlock. Those and the intelligence gleaned by Lieutenant Ramillies in France would have provided us with a basis for our own plans."

"Own plans for what?" Hawkwood said. Though he had begun to suspect what they might be.

"To build our own submersible boat, of course."

Hawkwood felt a swirl of nausea.

"And I have to confess," the colonel beamed, "we were damned impressed with the result. Tell me, is it true Lee had constructed a means by which you can see above the water when the vessel's submerged?"

"He called it the eye," Hawkwood said woodenly, wondering what madness was about to be unleashed.

"Splendid!" the colonel beamed. "I look forward to examining it in detail."

Hawkwood stared at him.

"Well, you didn't think we were going to leave the damned thing on the bottom of the river, did you?"

"That *thing*," Hawkwood said, "is a bloody death-trap. It blew up."

"That's right." Congreve nodded. There was a pause. "It was supposed to."

James Read ignored the look of bewilderment on Hawkwood's face. "Master Woodburn made it happen. When we retrieved his body from the warehouse, we also discovered his journal. He had been composing it in secret, using scraps of paper he managed to secrete during his incarceration. He describes the repairs he was forced to make to the submarine bomb's timing device. He also describes his own sabotage attempt. It seems he used to let himself out of his cell at night. His guard, Seaman Sparrow, had a habit of leaving the premises to frequent the local gin shop. He obviously thought the old man was securely locked up. Master Woodburn took advantage of his jailer's absence to make his own modifications to the submersible. Apparently, he was able to conceal a small amount of explosive and equipment to fashion a bomb of his own. Triggered by a clockwork mechanism, it seems, set in motion and timed to detonate once the torpedo had been released from the submersible's stern."

Hawkwood recalled the old man's manner in the cell. Josiah Woodburn had been about to tell him something when Lee had walked in with the woman. Presumably it was the other reason why he hadn't escaped with Warlock. It hadn't only been fear for his granddaughter's safety that had held the clockmaker back, but also his plan to turn the tables on William Lee's assassination plot. Again, there had been the expression on the old man's face as Hawkwood had boarded the submersible. Not only the knowledge that his own life had become forfeit but that Hawkwood was being forced on to what was, in effect, a doomed vessel.

"You're planning to salvage the submersible?" Hawkwood said, still not believing it.

Congreve nodded. "That's right. And we've got our own man to operate it."

And it all began to fall into place. "Captain Johnstone."

"Correct. The man's an indisputable rogue, of course. Talented, I grant you, but a rogue nonetheless. He worked with Fulton when he brought the *Nautilus* to England. A jack of all trades, you might call him. Been a Channel pilot, privateer, smuggler, even spent a time or two in a debtors' prison. Not the sort of fellow you'd invite to a soiree, but he's the best man for the job. No doubt about that."

Hence the colonel's less than benevolent expression earlier, Hawkwood thought.

"So, now it's our turn," Hawkwood said, unable to keep his anger in check. "What's it to be? Boney's barge on the

402

Seine? We're no bloody better than they are! What the hell's it all been for?"

James Read looked at him. "Why, victory, Hawkwood – what else?"

Runner Jeremiah Lightfoot was thinking of his bed. He was also thinking about his plump wife, Ettie, and how much he'd like her to be in the bed with him. They had not seen much of each other of late, what with his duties at the bank and his journey north in pursuit of Lord Mandrake; a wasted journey, as he kept reminding himself. He had been looking forward to spending an evening at home, with his loving wife cuddled at his side. But it was not to be. Instead, here he was, loitering on a dark quayside with nothing to keep him company save for the ship's cat and a small flask of brandy.

The cat was a friendly enough creature, rubbing up against his legs, purring whenever he reached down to stroke it, but he suspected the animal was more interested in the prospect of food than the force of his personality. Sadly, Lightfoot did not have any food, and if he had he sure as hell wouldn't have shared it with any flea-ridden moggy.

Apart from a watchman dozing in a hammock on the foredeck, Lightfoot was the only man on board. The rest of the crew were ashore, spending their last night enjoying the delights of the local taverns. The ship – a Portuguese-owned vessel called the *Madrilena* – was due to sail with the morning tide, and Runner Lightfoot's duty was to see that the woman sailed with her. The woman had been escorted to the ship late that afternoon by a brace of constables. She was currently occupying the main cabin.

The woman was beautiful and it had been no hardship watching her as she walked around the deck, taking the air, prior to going below. He knew she was aware of his attention. She had smiled at him several times with her dark eyes and Lightfoot had wondered what it would be like to be with someone like her. But Jeremiah Lightfoot loved his wife, so all he did was wonder.

Dusk was falling as the small, fleet-footed figure made his way along the quayside. Lightfoot watched the boy approach and drew himself up straight.

At the top of the gangplank the boy reached into his pocket and held up a folded piece of paper. "Got a message for the lady."

"Is that right? And what might your name be?"

"They call me Tooler."

Lightfoot stiffened and looked around. The watchman was still asleep in his hammock, dead to the world, and taking no notice of the visitor. "Wait here."

Lightfoot made his way down the companionway. There was a light burning behind the cabin door. He knocked softly.

"Enter."

She was seated at the small table, reading a book. Lightfoot glanced at the leather binding. Something in French; he could not make out the title.

She looked up. "Yes?"

Her hair was unfastened and hung to her shoulders. She was wearing a low bodice. Lightfoot could see the tops of her breasts. Her skin glowed in the lantern light. Lightfoot swallowed. "There's a boy. He says he has a message for you."

"A message?" She frowned. It didn't make her any less beautiful.

"A note. Says he didn't want to come below, but he has to give it to you personally. Says it's important."

A small lie wouldn't hurt, Lightfoot thought. Not in the long run.

"Here," Lightfoot said, "let me get your shawl." He found his hands were shaking.

The woman rose, accepted the shawl with a nod, and preceded Lightfoot out of the cabin.

The boy was waiting for her under the mast lantern. He watched her, thinking to himself that she was a looker all right.

"You have a message?" she said, drawing the shawl around her.

The boy held up the note, but did not move. "Told ter give you this –"

She stepped forward, held out her hand and the boy placed the note in it and moved away.

She unfolded the paper and held it up to the lantern glass. There was a single sentence.

Welcome to hell.

The rifle ball took Gabrielle Marceau through the right eye, snapping her head back and exiting her skull in a spray of blood and brain matter. As her body collapsed, the note slid from her hand and fluttered like a butterfly to the deck.

Lightfoot and the boy stood over her and watched as she died. Bending down, Lightfoot retrieved the note and placed it unhurriedly in his pocket. He turned to the boy. "Leave now. Forget what you have seen."

405

Wordlessly, Tooler turned and hurried back down the gang-plank to the dock. Lightfoot stared dispassionately at the woman. The blood was spreading out beneath her, staining the planking. In the lantern light it looked as black as tar.

Lightfoot straightened and ran towards the foredeck. The watchman was still slumbering, undisturbed by the crack of the gunshot which was already fading into the night.

Lightfoot took a deep breath, went forward, shook the man awake, and began to yell.

"Murder! Murder!"

The cry rose over the moon-flecked quayside.

Two hundred yards away, on the second floor of a disused warehouse, Nathaniel Jago, kneeling in front of an open window, the Baker rifle barrel resting on his shoulder, clicked his tongue in admiration. Smoke from the rifle's discharge drifted around his head like dissipating tobacco fumes.

"Nice shot."

Hawkwood lowered the rifle. His shoulder was still tender. The muscles had not recovered their full strength so he had used Jago as a rest. He laid the rifle on the oilcloth and began to wrap it up.

"The boy did well," Jago murmured.

"So did Jeremiah," Hawkwood said.

The rifle concealed inside the oilcloth bundle, the two men made their way downstairs and out of the building. The sound of running feet could be heard. Backing into the shadows, they watched as a figure ran past: the crewman, off to fetch the constables. Only when he had disappeared did they step out on to the dockside.

"They'll know it was you," Jago said, as they fell into step.

"They'll suspect it was me," Hawkwood said. "But it won't matter. The bitch is dead, that's the main thing. Besides, I'll have an alibi."

"That's right: you were with me, enjoyin' a wet over at the Dog and Goat. You think they'll believe it, me being a notorious villain an' all?"

"What do you mean, villain? Magistrate Read's spoken with his contacts at Horse Guards. You've been granted a full pardon. You're no longer a deserter, you're a pillar of society. It's official."

"Right," Jago said, grinning. "And you're the Emperor of China."

Hawkwood smiled at his friend. "It's true, Nathaniel, No more worrying about the provost, no more hiding."

"Sounds boring," Jago said. "Not sure I could 'andle that."

"You could always join me," Hawkwood said. "With Henry Warlock's death, there's an opening for a special constable."

Jago stopped in his tracks. "Bloody hell! Me a Runner? You ain't serious? Is this 'is honour's idea?"

"He suggested I ask you."

"Did 'e indeed? Suffered a crack on the 'ead recently, has 'e? Been struck by lightning, maybe?"

"It's a genuine offer."

Jago shook his head in disbelief, then looked up. "What's it pay?"

Hawkwood told him, and Jago started to laugh. Hawkwood grinned and began to laugh too.

They were still laughing as they reached the end of the quayside. The sound carried in the darkness as the night closed over them like a cloak.

HISTORICAL NOTE

On 9th December 1799, following Bonaparte's coup d'état, the American inventor and scientist Robert Fulton submitted a proposal to the French government advocating the construction of an undersea boat to be used to annihilate the British Navy. The response was favourable. The vessel, which Fulton called *Nautilus*, was built at the Perrier workshop, and was successfully tested on the Seine in June 1800.

The French, however, ceased their funding of the project on the grounds that it was too terrible a device to be used against an unsuspecting enemy. Meanwhile, word of a weapon capable of destroying entire fleets at a stroke began to reach the British government and agents were dispatched to entice Fulton to England. Fulton, frustrated and angered by the French rejection, arrived in England in April 1804. A special commission was appointed to examine the feasibility of his submersible and his submarine bombs, which he called torpedoes. Tests were successful, culminating in the destruction of the brig *Dorothea* off the coast at Walmer Roads, near Dover.

Following Nelson's victory at Trafalgar, however, the British lost interest in the idea and Fulton, in high dudgeon, returned to the United States.

In 1811, Fulton sent his own agent to France in a second attempt to interest Emperor Bonaparte in to using his weapon against the British.

* * *

408

Many of the individuals in the story did exist. The members of the Admiralty Board were as stated – with the exception of the fictional Admiral Dalryde – along with the individuals who made up the Commission convened to examine Fulton's invention. James Read did hold the post of Chief Magistrate, though I confess to having taken some liberties with his description.

The mysterious Captain Johnstone was also a real character and did work with Fulton. He went on to design his own undersea boats and was rumoured to have completed a working model powered by clockwork. The then British government, however, had second thoughts and withdrew support for the design, whereupon Johnstone was approached by both French and American agents who expressed interest in his work.

The final victory over Napoleon, at Waterloo in 1815, ended serious British interest in submarine warfare, though a rumour did begin to circulate that Bonapartists had contacted Captain Johnstone with a view to rescuing the Emperor from exile on St Helena using a submersible. History informs us no such rescue took place.

However, several of the minor events depicted in the novel did happen. British riflemen did shoot the Spanish general on the ramparts at Montevideo and Captain Renny was killed leading the forlorn hope through the gap in the wall at Montevideo, thus gaining Lieutenant Lawrence his captaincy.

The bounty that William Lee was to be paid for the destruction of each British ship is also accurate, reflecting the reward the French were prepared to offer Fulton for the use of his submersible. Even at the time this was an astronomical amount, the equivalent of several million pounds in today's money. Hawkwood's astonishment at the fee is, therefore, perfectly understandable. Documents detailing the monies that Fulton commanded upon his arrival in England, such as the £40,000 contract signed by Prime Minister William Pitt, are available for perusal at the Royal Navy Submarine Museum, Gosport.

HMS *Thetis* was a British warship, though she is not the one portrayed in the story. I merely took advantage of her name.

Fulton's place in history and his importance to submarine warfare cannot be over estimated, neither, inevitably, can his contribution to classic literature. Jules Verne clearly took inspiration from Fulton's *Nautilus* – as well as Fulton's own views on liberty of the seas and free trade – for his great adventure story, *Twenty Thousand Leagues Under the Sea*.

Bonaparte's liaison with William Lee and their failure to frighten the British Navy into submission and thus disrupt Wellington's supply routes was just one reason why France suffered defeat in the Peninsula. A hostile population, heavy military losses and the need to withdraw troops to fight on other fronts all contributed to a disastrous campaign. The Emperor's fear that the Tsar's resolve was weakening came to a head when Alexander reopened trade with Great Britain, in direct opposition to Bonaparte's "Continental System". It was the final straw. On 24th June 1812, Bonaparte's invasion force crossed the River Nieman into Russia. It was Bonaparte's greatest military enterprise, and it ended in catastrophic failure.

As for Matthew Hawkwood, London at the beginning of the 19th century was a very dangerous city. Crime had reached epidemic proportions and police officers like Hawkwood had to be tough in order to survive in their chosen profession. The Bow Street Runners were an elite force. They were few in number, between seven and ten officers in total, and their work took them all over the country. There is evidence to suggest that officers carried out assignments as far afield as Russia and the United States.

The war with France brought added intrigue and, given Hawkwood's links with Colquhoun Grant, who was acknowledged to be Wellington's most effective exploring officer, it would not be beyond the bounds of credibility that an officer of Hawkwood's capabilities would be called upon to perform intelligence duties abroad.

Whether that proves to be the case, or not, remains to be seen . . .